THE RYAN SHORTS AND NOVELLAS

THE COMPLETE COLLECTION

NEW YORK RUTHLESS

SADIE KINCAID

To all of my wonderful readers who have followed and loved Jessie and the Ryan brothers as much as I have.

This is their ultimate HEA and it's just for you.

All my love, Sadie xxx

NEW YORK RUTHLESS

These are short stories and novellas connected to the New York Ruthless series, set after the end of Ryan Renewed. It is a dark Mafia, reverse harem romance which deals with adult themes including scenes of a graphic sexual nature.

If you haven't read the series yet, you can find them on Amazon and Kindle Unlimited

Ryan Rule
Ryan Redemption
Ryan Retribution
Ryan Reign
Ryan Renewed

A RYAN RECKONING

A NEW YORK RUTHLESS SHORT STORY

JESSIE

I stand beside the elevator in between Liam and Mikey as Conor walks toward us.

He whistles as he approaches and when he reaches me, he pulls me to him, sliding his hands over my hips and onto my ass. "You look incredible, angel," he says as he gives me a squeeze.

"Thank you," I whisper as he stares into my eyes. "I know what you're doing, Conor Ryan."

He grins as his hands skim over my ass. He's checking I'm wearing panties, which I am. It was one of the conditions he agreed to the twins taking me to The Peacock Club tonight without him. It's an exclusive private members club that caters for every kink imaginable and we own a string of them across the US and Europe.

Given that I'm married to four men, it kind of feels like the perfect place for our date nights, but it has taken some convincing Conor – who, despite sharing me with his three brothers, takes possessiveness to a whole new level.

He presses his lips against my ear. "Good girl," he murmurs and my thighs tremble.

When he presses a soft kiss beneath my ear, I melt into him, wrapping my arms around his neck before I pull his face to mine and seal my lips over his. He kisses me back fiercely, grabbing my ass harder as he drags my body over his hardening cock.

When he finally pulls back, I'm left breathless and wanting. He keeps his arms around me while he looks over my head at his brothers. "You better fucking behave tonight," he warns.

"We will, Con," Liam replies.

"No public fucking. Nothing that gives anyone a glimpse of what is mine," Conor snarls.

"We know," Mikey sighs.

"You better know, Mikey, because if anyone sees my wife's pussy, I will fucking kill them. You got that?"

I press my lips together to stop myself from giggling because Conor Ryan in ultra possessive mode is super hot.

"Nobody will see anything," Liam assures him.

"But we might do something publicly in the dark, Con, just so you know," Mikey adds.

Conor's body stiffens as he hugs me tighter. "Just don't let anyone see her," he grinds out the words.

"You just take care of our babies and we'll take care of our girl," Mikey says with a chuckle and I feel Conor's hands fist in the fabric of my dress.

I rest my hand on his cheek and he presses his face into my palm. "We know the rules. We'll be good," I say, bringing his attention back to me.

"You gonna let her go any time soon, bro?" a voice calls from behind him as their oldest brother, Shane, walks down the hallway.

I turn my head and smile at him. He's just been checking on our seven month old twins.

"They okay?" I ask.

"Sleeping like babies," he replies with a wink. Then a second later he is standing right beside me and Conor. He arches an eyebrow at his younger brother. "May I?"

"I'm gonna fuck you into oblivion as soon as you get home, angel," Conor growls, but then he gives me a final kiss on the lips before he releases me.

"You look hot, Hacker," Shane says, then he wastes no time fisting his hands in my hair and pulling me to him for a kiss.

He tongue fucks my mouth while his brothers watch and wait for us to be done. I wrap my hands around his neck, pulling him deeper as warm heat pools in my center. Damn, these boys make me so horny.

When he finally lets me up for air, he grins at me. "Has Conor made you promise to be good tonight?"

"Yes," I purr. "And he made me wear panties."

"Oh that's damn shame, boys," Shane laughs as he looks at Liam and Mikey.

"Tell me about it, bro," Mikey says but he grins wickedly at his older brother.

"Are you wearing those goddamn crotchless panties?" Conor growls.

"They are panties," I reply with a shrug.

Conor leans over his brother and kisses my forehead. "You're going to fucking kill me, Jessie."

"Can we go?" Liam asks as he checks his watch. "Date night started five minutes ago."

"Don't be back too late," Shane says as he lets me go. "And don't wear our girl out."

As I turn to face the twins, he slaps my ass hard and I suck in a breath. I'm on the edge already and we haven't even left the apartment. I love The Peacock Club. We have been there once before as a group of five, but this is my first time with just Liam and Mikey and I'm so excited.

Wetness and warmth pools between my thighs as I watch the group at the table directly in front of us. One of the guys lifts one of the women onto the table and spreads her thighs wide open until her bare pussy is on full display. Liam coughs quietly beside me making me giggle. When I look at him, he is averting his eyes from the show before us.

I lean close to him and press my lips against his ear. "It's okay if you want to watch, handsome. I am."

"It feels weird sitting here with you and looking at another woman's pussy," he says with a shudder.

"Are you going to do anything other than look at it?"

He frowns at me. "No."

I press my lips against his ear again, tracing my tongue over the shell. "Whose is the only pussy you will ever touch for the rest of your life?" I whisper as I slide my hand up his muscular thigh.

"Yours, baby," he growls.

"Then there is nothing weird about you watching," I wink at him and turn my head back so I can rejoin Mikey, who is watching openly in fascination.

The other woman in the group sits directly in front of the one at the table, obscuring our view slightly before she bends her head and starts to eat.

"Fuck!" Mikey hisses as he rearranges his cock in his pants. "That's hot right, Red?"

"Uh-huh," I whisper as I stare too. It is so freaking hot to watch these two beautiful women with each other. The guys place a hand on each thigh of the woman on the table, holding her wide open to allow their companion better access to her pussy.

"She's really going for it," Liam adds as his hand slides between my thighs.

"This making you wet, Red?" Mikey groans as his hand joins his twin's.

I look at the bulges in their suit pants and smile. "About as wet as it's making you two hard."

"Seeing you so fucking turned on by all this is what's making me hard," Liam says before he buries his head in my neck and starts to pepper kisses along my throat.

I moan softly and Mikey's hand slides further up my dress until his fingertips can brush my damp panties.

"You think public finger-fucking is okay?" Mikey asks Liam.

"Not here like this," Liam chuckles against my skin. "Conor will kill you if someone sees Jessie's pussy, bro."

"He will, and you did promise," I breathe even as I want Mikey's hand to go further. But we did swear we wouldn't.

"Fuck!" Mikey hisses as he pulls his hand back and gives me a kiss on the forehead instead. "Back to watching for now then?" He winks at me.

I fix my eyes on the table in front again as Liam goes on nuzzling my neck. I squeeze my thighs together to try and get some relief from the throbbing between them but I find none. "We are going to have to find a dark corner somewhere soon or our girl is going to implode," Mikey chuckles as he takes my hand and laces his fingers through mine.

"I'm not," I lie as I blow a strand of hair from my face. "I'm happy right here just watching."

"Liar," Liam mumbles.

I watch in fascination as the woman on the table throws her head back. Her thighs tremble as she tries to press them together but the guys continue holding her wide open.

"I bet that women are really good at eating pussy," I say, entirely innocently, or so I thought.

Liam stops kissing me and Mikey turns his face from the show in front of us and stares at me.

"What?" they both say at the same time, their eyes burning into me.

I squirm in my seat. "Well, their mouths are so soft. And I mean... because they would know exactly what to do... having the same equipment, right?"

Mikey looks at his twin. "Did our wife just say that women can eat pussy better than we can?" he asks.

"I think she did." Liam nods his agreement.

"I did not!" I protest.

"Kinda sounded like you did, baby," Liam says.

I look between the two of them as my stomach starts to churn. Oh, hell! Have I offended them, because I really didn't mean to? All four of my husbands eat pussy like they enjoy it as much as I do and if it was an Olympic sport they'd all have to share gold. I am one very lucky lady and I know it.

"I didn't mean..." I start to say but the two of them have a devious look in their eyes that I know all too well.

"Sounded like both an insult and a challenge?" Mikey says to Liam, ignoring my protestations.

"It sure did." Liam winks at him and my heart starts to race. What are these two deviants up to?

"I think we owe it to ourselves and our older brothers to punish her for that, do you, bro?" Mikey asks.

"Sure do," Liam agrees and then the two of them stand.

"You coming, Red?" Mikey grins at me and Liam holds out his hand.

"Where are we going?" I whisper as I allow Liam to pull me up.

Liam laughs softly. "You think we'd bring you here and not reserve a room?"

I follow them through the crowd and to the stairs that lead to the corridor of rooms in the basement.

"Good evening, Mr. Ryan. Number one is ready for you," the bouncer says to Mikey as he moves the thick black velvet rope to allow us through.

The rooms are only for VIP guests and they have to be booked in advance here. They're always full and I wonder who had their plans canceled tonight when Mikey and Liam demanded a room for us at short notice.

I follow Mikey along the hallway with Liam close behind me as we make our way to the room at the end with a silver number one fixed on the door. The three of us step inside and Liam closes the door behind us.

I've been in this room before with all four of my husbands the first night we came to the club together. Each room is decorated and furnished slightly differently to cater for different tastes, but this one is my favorite. There is a huge four poster bed in the center and a large mirror on one wall. There is a two way mirror on the opposite wall too, but tonight it's covered by a curtain. So even if someone were allowed in the small room behind, they wouldn't be able to see what we were doing in here.

"Get naked, Red," Mikey orders as he stares as me with his hands in his trouser pockets, stretching the material taut over his thick thighs and impressive erection.

I bite on my lip as I stare back at him, aware of Liam standing directly behind me.

"Now, Jessie!" Liam hisses in my ear making a shudder run the length of my spine.

So my bossy twins are out to play?

"Fine," I purr as I pull my dress off over my head and toss it onto the chair nearby.

I look at Mikey again as Liam's hands skim over my backside. "This is so fucking beautiful," he groans before he gives me a slap that makes me squeal in surprise.

"I said naked," Mikey growls as he goes on staring at me. His eyes are dark and dangerous and I swallow hard as I unhook my bra and let it fall from my arms before peeling off my panties. As I pull them off my feet, Mikey holds out his hand to me and I press the damp material into his palm. He holds it to his nose and takes a huge sniff that makes my cheeks flush pink. "You smell so fucking good."

"Go lie down, baby," Liam whispers in my ear, his warm breath dusting over my skin and making me shiver.

I do as they ask, lying on the bed until I'm staring up at my two gorgeous husbands who look even hotter than usual when they're playing at being angry with me. At least I think they're playing.

"So what is my punishment?" I ask as they move to either side of the bed. They work entirely in sync with each other as they take my wrists and wrap them in leather cuffs before fastening them to the chains that hang from the bedposts.

"You'll see," Mikey says with a devilish grin before he runs his hand down my arm and to my breast before squeezing.

"Hmm," Liam mumbles as he glides his hand over my body, over my thigh and calf until he reaches my ankle and pulls it to the corner of the bed before securing it in place with another cuff. A few seconds later, Mikey does the same to my other ankle until I am bound and spread open for the two of them.

"Fuck! You ever seen anything so damn beautiful?" Liam asks his twin as he stares at me with such intensity that my skin feels hot from his gaze alone.

"Nope," Mikey agrees as he starts to pull off his clothes and I watch the two of them strip.

My pussy floods with wet heat at the sight. Mikey isn't wearing any underwear so he stands completely naked, his cock standing thick and tall. Liam is wearing boxer briefs and he leaves them on, but the tip of his cock sticks out of the waistband and it glistens with precum.

"This doesn't feel like much of a punishment," I giggle, earning me a stern look from each of them.

"Because we haven't started yet," Liam says with a wink.

"Hmm," I bite my lip as I pull on my restraints. "I can't imagine anything that you two are going to do to me that I'm not going to love."

"You not so keen on a woman eating your pussy now then, Red?" Mikey asks with a flash of his eyebrows. "You decided you'd prefer us after all?"

"I never said that I would prefer a woman to eat my *pussy*," I whisper the last word and heat creeps over my neck.

"I love the way you blush when you say filthy words, baby," Liam laughs and Mikey joins in.

"She's so fucking sweet," he agrees as he crawls onto the bottom of the bed.

"You got to finger her pussy in the car, bro," Mikey says to Liam, reminding me of Liam making me come on his lap in the car on the way here. "That means I get to go first, yeah?"

"Be my guest." Liam grins at his twin as he lies beside me.

I look down at Mikey as he lies on the bed in front of me, his head dropping between my thighs as he edges closer to my pussy.

"What are you two planning?" I gasp as he starts to trail feather light kisses up my thighs, because this sure as hell doesn't feel like any kind of punishment at all.

Liam grabs my chin in his powerful hand and turns my head. "Look right here," he says before he seals his lips over mine and slides his tongue into my mouth.

At the same time, Mikey swirls the tip of his tongue delicately over my clit and I moan into Liam's mouth. I was already on the edge before they got me in this room and now I'm about to ready to melt into a puddle.

Liam keeps on kissing me, but he lets go of my chin and he doesn't touch me anywhere else. I try to shift my body closer to his and press myself against his hands but I can't move far enough in my restraints. I concentrate on his mouth instead, his tongue gently dancing against mine, but I miss his touch.

I notice that Mikey doesn't have his hands on me either. Usually he'd have them around the back of my thighs or he'd be pressing down on the inside of them while he eats me out, but all I feel is the soft flicking of his tongue.

I wrench my lips away from Liam's. "Why aren't you touching me?" I pant, almost on the verge of tears because I hate this. I hate them not having their hands on me.

Mikey looks up at me, his eyes locking with mine. "You don't want our big manly hands on you, do you, Red?"

So this is the punishment? Assholes!

"I never said that," I protest but Liam turns my face and silences me with another soft kiss.

Mikey takes a little pity on me and moves lower, his tongue swirling over my entrance. I buck my hips against him, but he pulls back, chuckling as he does.

I break mine and Liam's kiss again. If this is the game they want to play, then I'll play.

I look down at Mikey and he is still watching me. "You know women have fingers and hands too, right?"

"She's got a point, bro," Liam says.

Mikey holds himself up on one powerful forearm. "She does," he says with a nod and then he holds up one of his huge hands. "Not as big as ours though, right?"

"Nope," Liam laughs and shakes his head and I groan in frustration.

"Like one of mine would be two of Jessie's right?" He holds his index finger in the air.

"Yeah, but not as long," Liam replies and I glare at him.

"Hmm." Mikey examines his finger closely. "So just like half way in, you think?"

"No!" I protest.

Liam nods. "Yep. I'd say that was about the equivalent of two of Jessie's."

Mikey takes his finger and presses the tip into me and I whimper shamelessly. "You want this, Red?" he taunts me as he edges in a little more.

"Yes!" I pant. I'm over this game now. I want him and his brother inside me right now. "Please, Mikey?"

"I got you," he mumbles as he goes back to softly sucking my clit while he works the tip of his finger in an out of me. Waves of warm pleasure roll through my body but they never quite reach the peak that I need to get off. I groan into Liam's mouth as he goes on kissing me softly and even his kisses, which are usually so fierce and full of passion, leave me wanting. My boys are holding back their bodies from me and I don't like it at all.

"This not doing it for you, Red?" Mikey asks as he pushes himself up and wipes his mouth with the back of his hand. "I mean you're soaking wet here, but you're not moaning my name."

Liam laughs softly as he pulls back from me.

"You know it's not. You've proven your point," I snap in frustration.

"And that is?" He arches an eyebrow at me.

I should say what he wants to hear. The truth. That I can't imagine anyone eating my pussy better than he and his brothers do, but to my horror those are not the words that leave my mouth.

"That you're an asshole," I say instead and my frustrated inner horny demon groans loudly while the feminist in me cheers me on.

Liam laughs loudly as Mikey blinks at me before he starts laughing too. "Oh, Red," he says with a shake of his head.

I close my eyes and curse inwardly, but when I open them again I decide to front it out. "I thought the idea was to prove you could eat pussy better than a woman?" I arch an eyebrow at him.

He narrows his eyes at me. "That wasn't good for you?"

"I've had better."

Liam presses his lips together, no doubt to stop himself from laughing.

Mikey looks at his twin. "I do love our little firecracker," he says with a raise of his eyebrows. "You think we need to step this up a little, bro?"

"I'm all in," Liam replies as he pushes himself up from the bed.

I look between the two of them, wondering what they have in store next. My whole body is desperate for some release now and I don't know how much more of their teasing I can take.

"Let's untie her then." Mikey jumps up and a few seconds later my cuffs are unfastened and my limbs are completely free. I rub at my wrists and stretch my legs. Mikey climbs onto the bed again, sitting back against the pillows.

"Come here, Red." He opens his legs wide and pats the space on the bed between his thighs.

I shuffle back until I'm sitting between them and he pulls me until my back is flush with his chest and his cock is pressing against me. Then he hooks his feet inside my calves and spreads my thighs apart as he places his forearms over my arms, holding me in place.

"Fuck, she looks so good like that," Liam growls as he crawls onto the bed in front of us. "I love you holding our girl down for me, Mikey."

"I love holding her down," Mikey groans as his cock twitches against the seam of my ass.

I have to admit I kind of love it too, but I stay silent as I wait, my breath held in anticipation.

Mikey presses his lips against my ear. "The idea, Jessie, is that we show you how much you crave what only we can give you."

I'm about to ask what he means but I'm distracted by Liam's hot tongue licking the length of my pussy. My hips jolt upward but Mikey holds me still and I groan.

"Please, Liam?" I beg him because he'll take pity on me, won't he?

"Tell me what you want, baby," he mumbles as his tongue dances softly over my folds.

"I want you to touch me," I plead.

"I am touching you," he growls against my skin making my legs tremble.

Then he edges a finger inside me and my walls squeeze around him, trying to pull him in deeper but he refuses to let me.

"Just wait until we tell Shane and Conor what you said about women being better at eating pussy," Mikey whispers in my ear and it sends pleasure and fear skittering along my spine.

"Mikey," I groan. "You know I never said that."

His responding chuckle vibrates through his chest and I feel it in my bones. I close my eyes as Liam goes on sucking me softly, bringing me tantalizingly close to the edge but never giving me enough to get me there.

"Tell us what you want, Red," Mikey says, his lips brushing the skin of my neck and making me whimper. "Tell us and we'll give it to you."

I don't want to give in. I don't want them to be able to play me the way they do, but the truth is that they can, and I wouldn't have it any other way.

"I want both of you inside me," I pant.

Liam edges his finger slightly deeper and I hiss out a breath.

"Like that, baby?" he groans.

"More," I whimper.

"Our girl wants more," Mikey groans. "Shall we give her what she really wants, bro?"

"Fuck, yeah, because I'm gonna fucking blow my load if I keep eating her pussy," Liam says as he lifts his head and stares at me. "You taste so fucking good, Jessie. You're fucking soaking down here, you know that?"

"Yes," I breathe.

Mikey releases my arms and legs. "Turn around," he orders and I scoot up and do as I'm told. He pulls his legs closer together so I'm straddling him and his hard length is twitching against my throbbing pussy.

"Is this what you really want?" he growls as he rocks his hips upward and I bite on my lip as I stare into his eyes.

"Uh-huh," I groan.

"Hmm." He burrows his hand between my thighs and starts to circle my clit until the warm waves of pleasure start rolling through my body again. "Because you love having your pussy eaten don't you, Red?"

"Yes."

"And who eats your pussy good?"

"You and your brothers do," I admit, my body weak from their constant teasing.

The bed dips behind us and Liam is at my back, pressing soft kisses over my shoulder blades. "And you love being finger fucked too, don't you, baby?" he whispers as he slides his hand between me and his twin and pushes one of his thick fingers deep inside me causing me to release a rush of wet heat.

"Fuck! Yes," I moan loudly and they both groan appreciatively.

"But what do you love most, Jessie?" Mikey chuckles as he lifts my hips slightly, so that his cock is nudging at my entrance.

"You inside me," I whimper as they work their fingers on my clit and in my pussy until I'm grinding myself on their fingers and Mikey's cock.

Then Liam pulls his hand back and I whimper shamelessly. "It's okay. I got you," he chuckles in my ear and grabs hold of my waist. "Lean forward for me."

I bend my hips until I'm leaning on Mikey's chest and that's when I feel the tip of Liam's cock nudging at my ass. It's already wet and sticky with lube.

"What do you love the most?" Mikey asks again as drags his teeth along the sensitive skin of my throat. "Say the word because I want to see you blush."

"Mikey," I plead with him as I try to push myself down onto his cock but he and his twin hold me in place.

"Say the word, baby, and we'll give it to you," Liam adds.

Damn them! "I love your cocks," I gasp and they both drive into me at exactly the same time and the rush of relief at being full of them and the euphoria that charges through my body almost makes me pass out.

"Good girl," Mikey growls and a rush of wet heat slicks his cock as my first orgasm washes over me. My head rolls back until it's resting on Liam's shoulder and he snakes one arm around me, squeezing my breast in his large hand and tugging on my nipple. I press my body into his hand, desperate for his touch after he withheld it for so long.

"You like my hands on you, Jessie?" he growls in my ear as he drives his cock in and out of me.

"Yeah," I gasp. "Don't ever keep them away from me again."

"But where would be the fun in that?" Mikey asks, driving his hips upward and hitting the spot deep inside me that makes me tremble and shakes a guttural moan from my body.

"You already on the edge again?" Liam asks.

"Yeah," I say as I grip Mikey's shoulders tightly, trying to gain some leverage and a little control as they rail into me because if they carry on like this, I will pass out – or they might just fuck my soul from my body. They know me so well that they both ease up a little, allowing me to set a new pace as I roll my hips slowly over Mikey's cock.

"You okay, Red?" he asks as he brushes my hair back from my face and stares into my eyes.

"Yeah, I just need a breath is all," I reply as I smile at him.

He grins back at me. "You're so fucking incredible, you know that, right?"

"You both make me feel incredible," I whisper, snaking one arm behind me so that I can wrap it around Liam's neck. I pull him closer to me until I am tightly pressed between their two hard bodies. "I love you both so much."

"We love you too, baby," Liam says as he nuzzles my neck.

Mikey glances at the curtain covering the two way mirror.

"Don't even fucking think about it," Liam chuckles. "Conor will fucking kill you."

"I know," Mikey laughs too. "But one day, Red, I'm gonna eat your pussy in this room while people watch us."

The thought of that makes my walls contract around him and he flashes his eyebrows at me. "Oh, you like the sound of that?"

"Maybe," I whisper.

"Why are you and Shane so into the public fucking thing?" Liam asks and I can't help but smile.

Liam isn't keen on anyone watching us either, but for

different reasons than Conor. Liam is just a little shy and prefers to keep those things between me and his brothers, but he doesn't mind if Shane, Mikey and I want to do stuff a little more publicly. Conor, however, hates the thought of anyone other than him or his brothers seeing my body. I understand why and actually I find his possessiveness kind of hot.

"I love the idea of people seeing my girl and knowing that she's mine," Mikey says with a shrug. "Watching her come undone for me and knowing that they will never even get to touch her hair, because if they did I would cut off their fucking hands," he says that last part so matter of factly that it should send chills down my spine. He means every word of it, but it only makes me want him more.

"Can you imagine if people were watching us through that mirror now, Red?" He growls as he wraps his arms around me possessively. "You'd be making their dicks hard and their pussies wet."

My cheeks flush pink at his words and he smiles. "I'm pretty sure they'd be looking at you and Liam more than me," I whisper.

"Are you fucking kidding?" Liam says against my ear. "You are hotter than fucking hell fire."

"You fucking are. They'd all be jacking off watching your perfect body coming all over our cocks."

A breath gets caught in my throat as their praise washes over me. I cannot believe how lucky I am to have these amazing men worship me the way they do.

"Can you both fuck me again now?" I whisper when I can breathe again.

"Anything you want, baby," Liam groans as he starts to thrust deeper into my ass.

"We gonna make you squirt your sweet cum all over us,

Red?" Mikey asks as he pulls my hips down, impaling me on his length.

"Yeah," I nod.

"Good girl."

They go on fucking me, their hands and mouths roaming over my body as they give me exactly what I need while taking what they want from me. Every nerve in my body sizzles with electricity and fire as my climax builds to a precipice before finally bursting out of me in a torrent of wet heat.

"Damn, Jessie," Mikey groans.

"You've soaked us," Liam adds as he pushes me flat against Mikey's chest so they can fuck me harder until they each find their own release.

When they are done, they gently ease out of me and I lie between them, melting into their bodies as though I'm made entirely of Jell-O.

"That was..." I trail off because I don't have the words.

"Fucking epic, Red," Mikey finishes for me as he plants a soft kiss on the top of my head.

"I hope you know we're coming back here every damn week?" Liam says before he kisses my shoulder blade.

"I'm gonna hold you to that, Liam Ryan," I giggle. Then I close my eyes and bask in the warm fuzzy feelings that being adored by these two give me.

A RYAN REWIND

A NEW YORK RUTHLESS SHORT STORY

CHAPTER 1

JESSIE

As usual, Shane is busy working in his office after I put our seven month old twins down for their afternoon nap. He looks up when I walk into the room.

"Hey, sweetheart," he says with a smile. "Everything okay?"

"Ella and Finn and sleeping," I reply as I walk toward him.

He narrows his eyes at me and the wicked glint in his eye makes me shiver. "And my brothers?"

"Mikey is out for a run. Liam and Conor are at the club going over some stuff. They'll all be back for dinner. Mikey is making chili."

I'm the very lucky lady who gets to be married to all four Ryan brothers, and I thank my lucky stars every damn day that I share my life with the four sexiest and most incredible men in the entire universe, not to mention our two adorable babies.

"So we're alone?" he asks.

"Yep."

He holds out a hand to me. "Come here."

I take his hand and allow him to pull me onto his lap until I'm straddling him.

"Actually," I whisper as I run my hands over his chest and onto his shoulders. "I wanted to talk to you about something."

He plants a soft kiss on my neck, making goosebumps prickle over my skin. "What is it?" he murmurs as he goes on kissing my throat.

I lean into him, so easily distracted by his expert mouth. When his hands slide beneath my dress and onto my ass, I suck in a breath. "You have a one track mind, Shane Ryan."

He chuckles softly. "Says my wife who needs four husbands to keep her satisfied." He lifts his head from my neck and grins at me. "So, what is it?" he asks again.

I run my fingers through his hair and stare into his beautiful green eyes. "I love you."

He slips a hand between my thighs, brushing his fingertips over my panties and arching an eyebrow at me in amusement when he finds them already damp. "I know that, but tell me what you want to talk about, so that I can bend you over and fuck you on my desk before the twins wake up."

"Okay," I take another deep breath. "I – I feel like you treat me differently since the twins were born."

He frowns at me and the hurt that flashes in his eyes makes me want to take back what I just said. But it's too late. It's already out there. "Do I?"

"Kind of. Don't you think that you do?"

"No," he says, pulling his hand from between my legs and running it over his jaw. "How do I treat you differently?"

"Like..." I chew on my lip as I think of an example. "You never get really pissed at me anymore."

He stares at me. "What?"

"I still try to push your buttons but you never really get mad," I whisper, realizing how foolish I sound.

"Fuck, sweetheart. I thought you were being serious," he says as his brow furrows in annoyance.

24

"I am. Don't you notice it too? You hardly ever punish me anymore. Take the other night for instance. You specifically told me to wear those pink panties for our date and I purposely didn't, but you didn't even get a little mad."

He blinks at me. "I asked you to wear crotchless panties, sweetheart, and instead you chose to wear none at all. How the fuck was I supposed to be mad about that?"

"But you would have been. Once. You would have punished me for it. I miss your punishments, Shane."

"I spanked your ass with my belt last night," he reminds me.

The memory of him doing that makes warmth spread through my core. "I know," I shuffle forward on his lap, my pussy rubbing over his semi-hard cock. "That wasn't real punishment though. We were just playing."

"I don't know what the fuck to say." He shakes his head in bewilderment again.

"I've noticed it's been since the babies were born. You're almost always sweet to me."

"I can't believe you're complaining about this," he laughs.

"I'm not. I mean, I love your sweet, gooey side. But I also miss the asshole I fell in love with."

"You want me to be an asshole to you?"

"No. Not all the time. It's just..." I shrug. I'm finding it hard to put into words without offending him. I place my hands on the back of his neck and chew on my lip as I stare into his eyes.

"Okay. I admit that things that would have made me pissed before don't now, but that's because you..."

"I'm your baby momma?" I arch an eyebrow at him.

"Maybe," he admits. "I just can't be pissed with you because whenever I look at you, I remember that you made me the happiest man in the world when you made me a dad."

"Oh, Shane," I breathe as the emotion wells in the throat.

"But I didn't realize me being nice to you was such a problem."

"It's not. I just want to be able to make you mad sometimes, is all."

He narrows his eyes at me. "Well consider that goal accomplished, sweetheart."

Before I can respond, the sound of Ella crying fills his office. The baby monitors are wired to every room in the house.

"I'll go," he says, lifting me from his lap. He presses a soft kiss against my temple before walking out of his office and making me regret initiating that entire conversation.

CLOSING the door to the nursery, I turn around to creep down the hallway toward the den, only to come face to face with Shane. I've hardly seen him since our little chat yesterday afternoon and I was starting to worry I might have offended him. The look on his face tells me I probably did.

He stands with his hands in the pockets of his suit pants. He wears a crisp white shirt, open at the collar. The tattoo of my name at the base of his neck is partially visible and it makes me smile despite the way he's glaring at me.

"Come with me, Hacker," he barks and I flinch at his tone.

Hacker? He hasn't called me that for a long time. It was his pet name for me when he used to pretend that he didn't like me.

"Where are we going?" I whisper as I look behind him, wondering if any of his brothers are in on whatever this is.

"You'll see," he snaps and then he turns and heads toward the elevator.

"What about the twins?" I ask as I fall into step behind him.

"You think I'd leave our babies up here alone?" he snarls without even looking at me.

"No, I just wondered if anyone else was joining us?"

"They're not."

He presses the button to call the private elevator to our apartment and we wait in silence. I glance sideways at him but he remains staring straight ahead — his jaw set and the vein in his neck bulging.

Oh, fuck me! I have really ticked him off.

We take the elevator to the basement without speaking and I resist the urge to ask where we're going again. I'm barefoot so I guess we're not leaving the building and my suspicion is confirmed when Shane walks toward one of the small concrete, windowless rooms down here. He walks inside and I follow him. Up until now, I'd been mostly curious about his plans, but at the sight of this room, my heart stars to beat wildly in my chest.

He closes the door behind us and the steel bangs against the frame, sending a shudder down my spine.

"You remember this place?" he growls.

I narrow my eyes at him. "Of course I do. It's the place where you called me a whore..." I wait for a response from him. I know how guilty he feels about that, but the expression on his face doesn't change at all. His jaw is clenched tightly shut as he glares at me with such intensity that my skin burns with heat. "And then you hate fucked me against that wall." I nod to the far side of the room as the memory of that day makes wet heat sear between my thighs. He was the king of assholes back then, but the way he took what he wanted from me was so freaking hot.

"Angry fucked," he corrects me.

"Oh yes, of course. You didn't hate me at all, did you? You just pretended to," I purr as I take a step toward him.

27

He stands still. His hands stuffed into his trouser pockets stretching the expensive material taut over his muscular thighs. God, he makes me want to lick him from head to toe.

I lick my lips instead, waiting in breathless anticipation, but then he moves so fast I gasp for breath. He pounces on me, wrapping one of his huge hands around my neck as he pushes me back against the wall.

I swallow hard, my throat constricting in his grip as his green eyes burn into mine. He presses his body against me until I feel his hard cock against my abdomen. I groan shamelessly as heat floods my body and my legs tremble in anticipation.

"I have never hated you, Hacker," he whispers before he runs his nose from the base of my neck, along the column of my throat, inhaling deeply before he goes on. "Even when you drove me crazy, even when you left me and my brothers after promising that you never would, even when you ripped out my fucking heart with your bare hands, I never hated you."

"Shane, don't," I breathe as tears prick at my eyes. I hate being reminded of how much I hurt them.

He tightens his grip on my throat slightly and presses me closer to the wall until I'm struggling for breath. "I might play nice with you now that you're my wife and the mother of my children, Hacker," he snarls, his face so full of anger that it sends a shiver of fear skittering along my spine. "But make no mistake that I am the same man I always was. If you ever leave me again... if you ever betray me, I would think nothing of keeping you here in this room for the rest of your life. Do you understand me?"

I blink at him and he squeezes tighter. "Do you?" he barks.

"Yes," I whisper. *What the hell have I done?*

He slides his free hand under my dress and between my thighs and my cheeks flush with heat as I remember I'm not wearing panties. When his fingers brush over my bare pussy, he presses his lips against my ear. "Where the fuck are your panties?"

"Mikey took them."

"Why?"

My cheeks redden further as I recall his younger brother finger fucking me in the den before he left for work. I had to put the twins down after that, and then I was intending to put some on when Shane accosted me in the hallway.

"Why?" Shane snaps again.

"He made me come and then he wanted to take them with him to work for the night."

"So he's gone to meet some of our biggest competitors with a pair of your cum-drenched panties in his pocket?"

"I guess."

"Deviant little fucker," he mumbles, rubbing his stubble over the delicate skin of my neck and making me squirm as his fingertips glide through my folds.

Then without any further warning, he drives two of his thick fingers deep inside me, making me suck in a shaky breath as his hand still grips my throat. "So fucking wet," he hisses. "Your cunt is so greedy for us, Hacker. Our fingers. Our tongues. Our cocks."

My walls squeeze around him and I moan softly, completely proving his point as he drives in and out of me. But then he stops just as suddenly as he started and I groan in frustration.

"But you have to earn all of those things, Hacker, and I don't think you have," he chuckles darkly as he lets go of my throat and pushes himself back until our bodies are no longer touching. I lean forward instinctively, needing his touch, but he takes a slight step backward so he remains out of reach.

Then he looks down at his groin. "Get on your knees and suck my cock."

I obviously don't acquiesce to his request quickly enough because he scowls at me.

"Now!" he snarls and I drop to my knees, hitting the concrete floor a little harder than I'd intended.

My fingers tremble as I reach for his belt and zipper, opening them as quickly as I can. I pull his cock free from his boxers and wrap my hand around his thick shaft, pulling it close to my lips. Precum glistens on the tip and I dart out my tongue and lick it clean, biting back a smile as it makes him groan softly.

I wrap my lips around him as his hands fist in my hair. Then I take him all the way to the back of my throat, savoring the taste of him. When I look up, he's looking down at me, his eyes narrowed as he watches me suck his cock. He rocks his hips against me and my eyes water as he hits the back of my throat.

"Who taught you to suck cock so good, little hacker?" he growls as he palms the back of my head, holding me in place as he fucks my mouth.

I suck greedily — desperate to please him. His hands fist in my hair, pulling it at the roots and sending tiny sparks of pain and pleasure tingling through my head. When I glance up at him again, the look of pure desire on his face makes me suck him harder and deeper.

"Fuck, you feel so good," he mumbles almost incoherently as his eyes roll back in his head. I feel the warm glow of victory at my ability to make him lose control even when he works so hard to maintain it.

As I bring him closer to the edge, his fingers dig into my scalp and he pushes deeper, fucking my throat so hard that I have to hold onto his thighs to keep myself steady. But I take everything he can give me, reveling in his dominance over me, and with a few final flicks of my tongue against his shaft, he comes hot and heavy. It hits the back of my throat and he pulls back slightly, allowing me to swallow every drop.

He stares down at me and even though his eyes burn with fire and anger, there is so much love in them too. He can't hide it, no matter how hard he tries and the realization makes my heart swell in my chest.

"Up!" he pants as he pulls his cock free from my mouth.

I wipe the saliva from my chin and stand quickly, waiting for my next instruction.

He begins unbuttoning his shirt and my pussy gently throbs in expectation. "Bend over the end of the bed and grab the rail," he says as he continues undressing.

I swallow hard and do as he asks, leaning forward and holding onto the metal rail on the end of the bed until I'm at a forty-five degree angle, with my ass in the air and my head hanging down.

He moves behind me. "Spread them, Hacker. I want to see my pussy."

I shuffle my feet along the concrete floor, peering between my thighs so I can watch him. The sight of his muscular, tattooed body and the things he does to me with it makes the slight throb in my pussy turn into the thrum of a Harley engine.

When he's removed his shirt, socks and shoes, he pulls his belt from his suit pants. Palming the buckle, he wraps some of it around his fist, leaving half of it swinging free. Wet heat surges between my thighs making my legs tremble. To my shame and annoyance, I moan softly.

"This isn't going to be about your pleasure, Hacker," he growls. "I'm going to make this hurt."

"I know," I pant, but he's wrong. No matter how much he makes it hurt, it will still be pleasurable. Nothing this man does to my body isn't.

He trails the soft leather between my thighs and it runs

softly over my skin, making me shiver. Then with a quick flick of his wrist, he spanks my pussy, grazing my clit as he does. It's light, but it stings and the pain and pleasure course through me. I bite on my cheek to stop myself from begging for more.

"Your cunt is dripping onto my belt," he snarls before he draws his hand back and brings the belt smacking down over my ass cheeks with a loud crack. It stings like a bitch.

"Jesus, Shane!" I hiss as the heat sears across my skin.

"I told you I was going to make this hurt," he says as he trails the leather over my pussy again and I squirm beneath its teasing touch. "Stop moving!" he barks and my body stills at his command.

He flicks the tip of the belt against my clit again, hitting the perfect spot and I moan loudly as I release a rush of wet heat.

"Do not fucking come," he snarls before he smacks the belt over my ass again.

Then he goes on spanking me with his belt, on my ass and my pussy until my entire body is screaming with both pain and the need for some release. This is the hardest spanking he has given me for as long as I can remember.

My ass burns.

My pussy throbs.

I am desperate for him to fuck me.

He slides two fingers inside me instead and the loud moan that erupts from my body makes him laugh. "So fucking needy for me, Hacker. Aren't you?"

"Yes," I whimper as I push my hips back, trying to take more of him inside me but he slaps my ass with his hand.

"Did I give you permission to move?"

"No," I groan.

"Who does this belong to?" he growls as he pushes in deeper and I have to hold tighter onto the bed rail to stop myself from falling flat onto the bed.

"You," I breathe.

"You'd better fucking believe it, Hacker. Who. Do. You. Belong. To?" He punctuates each word with a thrust of his fingers and I am teetering on the edge of oblivion — so much so that I can barely form the word.

"Y-you," I stammer.

"Mine to fuck. Mine to use. Mine to do whatever the hell I want with. Isn't that right?"

"Y-y-yes!" I scream as he curls the tips of his fingers inside me and presses on my G-spot, making the orgasm that has been threatening, spill out of me in a torrent of heat.

"Did you just come, Hacker?" he growls as he pulls his fingers out of me, leaving me feeling empty as the last tremors of my climax ripple through my body.

"I'm sorry," I pant. "I t-tried n-not to."

"Then you didn't try hard enough," he snarls. "Now, lie on the fucking bed."

I take a deep breath and push myself up, then I crawl onto the bed on shaky knees and roll onto my back. When I look up at him, he's glaring at me with such fire in his eyes that I swear my skin burns from his gaze alone.

He walks to the head of the bed. "Hands on here. Now," he orders as he taps the metal frame above my head, the belt still wrapped around his palm.

I do as he asks and in a few swift movements he has my wrists bound and shackled tightly with the soft leather.

"Do I have to remind you again to spread those legs so I can see my pussy?" he snaps.

I obey quickly, wanting to please him.

"You're dripping wet, Hacker. And you taste so fucking sweet when you've been spanked hard, but I don't think you've earned my mouth yet, have you?"

I glare at him, my eyes locking with his. "Yes I have."

"Not even close." He shakes his head as he kneels on the bed between my legs.

Sliding his hands up the backs of my thighs, my skin shivers at his expert touch as he lifts me slightly, shuffling his body forward so that my thighs are resting on his. He wraps my legs around his waist so that my hips and ass are off the bed. He pushes his thighs wider apart, taking mine with them before he unzips his fly and pulls out his stiff cock.

I look up at him. Molten heat pooling in my center as I wait for him to give me what I need. My pussy practically quivers in anticipation, desperate for him to fill me and give me the relief my body is craving.

Then he reaches into his pocket and pulls out a condom and I swear my racing heart stops beating in my chest. "W-what is that for?" I stammer.

He tears open the foil packet with his teeth, edging his cock against the seam of my ass and I realize he is at the perfect height to fuck my ass rather than my pussy. But we have never used a condom before — not even once. I swallow hard as a wave of confused emotion washes over me. Is this part of the punishment?

He doesn't answer me, instead he stares into my eyes as he rolls the rubber over his thick shaft.

"Shane? Are you planning on...? With no lube? Because I'm kind of sore..." I murmur.

He fucks my ass after spanking me all the time, but not usually when he's doled out the kind of punishment he just has. My poor backside is throbbing and kind of tender and I'm not sure I can take the hammering that he seems intent on.

"And why would I give a fuck if you're sore, Hacker?" He arches one eyebrow at me. "I mean if we were upstairs in my bed, where you're my wife, then I'd care, wouldn't I? But down here, you're not my wife, you're just the woman who walked out on me and ripped my fucking heart out."

I drag in a shaky breath. What the hell have I done? I want my sweet husband Shane back. Why did I ever miss this asshole?

But even as I ask myself the questions, nervous excitement skitters along my spine. I have no idea of the logic behind it, but I have missed him. I've missed this.

"You're an asshole," I hiss.

"This is who you wanted though, right? No more nice guy, Shane, who would do anything for you. No more making you come over and over again just because I can, or just because you beg me. No, you're gonna work for your pleasure now, Hacker, and you already took one that I didn't give permission for."

"I-I," I stammer but I don't know how to finish the sentence because this is what I asked for, right? And I love him like this. I love the angst and the tension and the angry fucking, but not as much as I love the man who worships the ground I walk on.

"I don't want to hear your excuses, Hacker," he says dismissively.

He reaches into his other pocket and takes out something that I can't see because it's hidden in his huge hand. Then he's squeezing something into his palm before coating his thick shaft and I almost sigh with relief when I realize he is using lube after all. But I still don't understand the condom and it hurts me that he's using one with me.

When he's finished with the lube, he tosses the small plastic tube onto the floor and grabs my hips before shifting position so that his cock is pressing against my asshole.

"Shane?" I whimper as he glares at me.

He's never taken me like this before — fucked my ass while staring deep into my eyes and it makes the skin from my chest to my face burn with heat.

SADIE KINCAID

Without any further warning, he pushes deep inside me. He's not gentle by any means, but he's not rough either and I gasp as he fills me with his cock. When he starts to circle my clit with the pad of his thumb, I moan louder and pull at my restraints. I want to touch him so badly.

"You seem to be enjoying this punishment a little too much, Hacker," he says as he pushes two thick fingers deep into my pussy and if my hips weren't held in place through being impaled on his cock, I swear they would have jolted six feet up into the air.

"Shane!" I hiss as the pleasure rockets around my body.

My eyelids flutter closed for a second and he drives deeper into me.

"Look at me!" he barks until I open my eyes again and they lock on his.

He fucks my ass and finger fucks my pussy, and he watches every expression on my face while he does it. Watching me as I completely fall apart for him.

He hasn't given me permission to come, but I'm going to have to take it anyway because there is no way that I can stop the huge orgasm that is about to crash over me. I feel it cresting a wave and he slows his movements slightly, keeping me on the very edge of the precipice for what feels like an eternity before he allows my body the release it so desperately needs.

When I finally climax, I scream his name so loudly that it fills the small room completely and I wonder if the people in the nightclub next door heard me.

When my eyes are able to focus, I see him still glaring down at me while his cock twitches in my ass. He pulls out of me slowly and pulls off the condom before throwing it onto the floor. Then he unhooks my legs from around his waist and moves back until I'm flat on the bed again and no longer resting on him. He leans over me, his forearms beside my head and his warm breath on my neck.

I gasp for breath as I wait.

As much as I love him fucking my ass, my pussy is throbbing with a dull aching emptiness. At least now I understand why he used the condom, but what the hell is he waiting for?

"I want you inside me, Shane," I pant. "Please?"

He presses the tip of his cock into me and I suck in a breath.

"Of course you do, because this is always what you really want, isn't it?" he says as he edges deeper inside. "I'm going to fuck you so hard, you'll still feel me inside you for the rest of the week."

"Then do it," I pant as I try to move my hips to meet his but he holds me in place.

"Soon. I want to hear you beg some more. I want you desperate for my cock inside you."

"I already am, Shane. Please?"

He closes his eyes and takes a breath and then he drives into me so hard, the small metal bed-frame rattles against the wall.

"Oh, fuck," I hiss as my walls squeeze him, trying to pull him deeper even as he fills me completely. "You feel so good."

"Because your cunt was made for my cock," he growls. "You were made for me, Hacker."

"I know," I groan as he nails me to the bed, his face buried in my neck.

I want his lips on mine so I turn my head to try and kiss him and that's when I see his watch.

It's the Breitling I bought for his fortieth birthday — the one I got engraved with a quote that reminds me of him and suddenly I don't want asshole Shane at all.

I want my Shane back. "I love you," I whisper as the emotion wells in my throat.

"I know," he grunts as he drives harder and deeper, hitting

that sweet spot over and over again until every cell in my body is trembling.

Only when I'm on the edge again does he lift his head and look at me. He dusts his lips lightly over mine, taunting me with the promise of a kiss, which he then denies me.

I groan loudly, pulling at my wrists to free them from the belt until the leather bites against my skin. "Shane? Please?" I beg.

"You gonna come for me again, Hacker?" he chuckles.

"Yes," I gasp.

"You're so fucking easy."

"Assho-" I start to say, but before I finish the word, he seals his lips over mine, sliding his tongue inside and making me whimper shamelessly as he claims my mouth like he just did my ass and pussy.

He is so right though. I am easy when it comes to him. I would let him do anything he wanted to my body because I trust him implicitly.

As he goes on kissing me, he reaches up and frees my wrists and as soon as I can move, I wrap my arms around his neck and my legs around his waist, pulling him closer and making a soft growl rumble in his throat.

He slides his hands beneath my body until his arms are wrapped around me and we are no longer two people at all but one tangled bundle of arms and legs. My walls squeeze him too as I try to take everything from him, and when my next orgasm hits I wrench my lips from his so that I can suck in a breath before I pass out.

"You squeeze my cock so fucking tight when you come, sweetheart," he groans as he drives into me a few more times before he finds his own release.

He buries his head into my neck again, biting down on the soft skin there as he grinds out every last drop of his cum inside me. When he's done, he lies on top of me, his forehead pressed against mine as we both pant for breath.

"You fuck like a demon," I gasp.

"Because you turn me into one, sweetheart," he says as he rubs his nose over my throat and I squirm as his stubble tickles me.

"You realize you could never actually keep me down here, right?" I breathe. "Theoretically speaking, obviously. I mean this bed isn't very comfortable."

Shane frowns at me and then he shifts me onto my side as he rolls onto his, until we're lying face to face on the small bed.

"Theoretically speaking, why would I care about your comfort if I'm keeping you prisoner here?" he asks with a frown.

"Not my comfort." I flash my eyebrows at him. "I'm talking about yours."

His frown deepens. "Mine?"

"Well, we both know there isn't a chance in hell you could stay away from me. You'd be sleeping down here with me almost every night, so I think we'd need a bigger bed. Not to mention your brothers would want in on the action too." I flash my eyebrows at him.

"You're pretty sure of yourself, Hacker."

I brush my fingertips over his cheek and smile. "No. Just sure of you."

He cups my chin in his hand and pulls my face to his before pressing his lips over mine and kissing me softly. I lean into him, my body melting into his as his tongue slides into my mouth. Then he glides his hand down my body, over my hip and onto my ass, pulling my groin against his until I start moaning softly.

That makes him pull back and smile. "You're so fucking needy, sweetheart."

I snake my arm around his neck. "For you, I am," I whisper.

"Hmm," he rubs his nose over my hair. "You smell so fucking good, Hacker. I could fucking eat you all day every day."

"And yet you didn't," I say with a soft sigh.

"Yeah, well, you'd have enjoyed that way too much, wouldn't you?" He winks at me and my heart flutters in my chest.

"Yes, but I enjoyed all of it," I remind him. "But the condom?"

He brushes my hair back from my face. "I knew I was fucking all of your holes, and I wanted to save my favorite for last." He gives me a wicked grin.

"So you fucked me in order of preference?" I feign my indignation.

"I suppose so," he laughs. "You should have seen Conor's face when I asked him to pick me a pack up from the store this morning. I thought he was going to punch me in the face."

"Did you tell him what you had planned?"

"Yes."

"And what did he say?"

"He said I should *change my running order,* and that I was crazy to even consider wearing a rubber with you. And I gotta say, sweetheart, now that I have, I think he was right. So we're never doing that again."

"Fine by me. I didn't like it anyway."

"It felt different to you too?" he asks as he brushes his fingertips over my cheek.

"Not much but I just didn't like you using one," I whisper. "I thought it was part of the punishment."

"No," he says before he kisses me softly and sure enough I am pressing my groin against him and trying to dry hump him.

He chuckles again as he breaks our kiss.

"Thank you for tonight," I whisper.

"You're welcome, sweetheart. It's not over yet though. There is a huge tub full of bubbles upstairs with our name on. I even bought some of those candles you love that smell like cotton candy."

"A bubble bath? For both of us? So we're not sleeping down here then?" I giggle. A soak in a bubble filled tub with Shane is my idea of heaven.

"No." He cups my chin in his hand and stares into my eyes. "I can be that guy I just was for you, Jessie, but you gotta let me take care of you after too. Okay?"

"Okay," I whisper.

"No running to my brothers to make you feel better."

"I don't do that," I protest and he arches one eyebrow at me. "I mean, I know I used to, but I don't now," I say softly.

He rubs his fingertips over the belt marks on my skin, making me shudder against him. His eyes narrow as he stares at me. "You regretting asking me to be that asshole who locked you in this room, sweetheart?"

"No," I say with a soft shake of my head. "Because when you had me bent over this bed earlier, I realized something."

"What's that?"

"That you can never be that guy for me. Not anymore."

"Oh? Why not?"

"Because I used to be a little bit scared of him," I admit, my voice barely a whisper. "But no matter what you do, Shane, I could never be afraid of you."

"Isn't that a good thing?"

"It's a very good thing." I smile at him. "I do like the role playing though."

He arches an eyebrow at me. "You knew I was faking the whole time?"

"Yes, but you really got into it. It was so hot."

"Hmm. If I ever did keep you prisoner, little hacker," he

growls as he rolls on top of me and starts to pepper soft kisses over my throat. "It would be in my bed."

"Well, by all means keep me prisoner any time you like." I grin at him.

He brushes my hair back from my face. "After I scrub you clean in the tub..." he whispers before he trails soft kisses over my neck that make me squirm.

"You're going to what?" I pant.

He lifts his head and looks at me again. "I'm going to spread you wide open on my bed and eat your pussy until you squirt all over my face."

Wet heat sears between my thighs.

"And then I'm going to hold you down and fuck you real slow, sweetheart. I'm going to bury my cock so deep inside your sweet pussy."

"You are?" I whimper as his hand slides between us and he starts to circle my clit.

"Yeah. I'm going to fuck you like that for hours. Making you come over and over again until you won't even know what day it is." He goes on rubbing my clit as he talks.

"Shane!" I moan as he brings me to the edge again. Warm waves of pleasure roll through my core, converging at the sweet point where he has his fingers on me. My thighs tremble as he starts to kiss my neck again.

"Where's my good girl?" he whispers and I'm gone.

Completely undone.

My orgasm goes off like a firework display on the Fourth of July. He goes on rubbing my clit until every last spark has fizzled from my body and I lie in a complete boneless heap beneath him.

"I love your filthy mouth, Shane Ryan," I whisper.

"I love you, sweetheart."

"I know."

A Ryan Restraint

A NEW YORK RUTHLESS SHORT STORY

CHAPTER 1

JESSIE

It's late afternoon when I walk into the gym expecting to see two of my four husbands, (yes four, I'm a lucky gal) Mikey and Conor, for my regular workout, but only Conor is in here. He's standing in the center of the boxing ring — dressed in only a pair of shorts. His huge arms folded over his broad, tattooed chest as he stares at me.

"Where's Mikey?" I ask with a frown.

"No Mikey today, angel. It's just me and you. Climb in," he says, walking to the edge of the ring and lifting the middle rope.

I walk over, admiring his bare chest as I do. "We're boxing today?"

"We are."

"I thought it was leg day." I pull a face and he chuckles softly.

"I'll make your legs tremble, don't worry."

I catch my bottom lip between my teeth and pop one eyebrow at him.

"Not that kind of trembling, angel," he says, his deep voice dropping another octave. "Not today. You're here to work."

"You're no fun." I pout as I climb inside the ring.

He narrows his eyes at me. "Me? I'm so much fun. Pretty sure you were enjoying yourself riding my cock a few hours ago."

"Yeah, well," I say with a dramatic sigh. "That was then."

"You always complain about working out, but you secretly love it," he laughs as he smacks my ass. "Now get your gloves on."

I pick up the pair of powder blue and gray fingerless mitts on the floor and slide them onto my hands. He stands, hands on his hips as he waits for me and I take a moment to appreciate his incredible body — all muscles, tattoos and abs. He must have been warming up before I arrived and a thin film of sweat covers his entire body, making him look even more delicious — if that were humanly possible.

Conor used to be a bare knuckle boxing champion back in Ireland and boxing remains one of his passions in life. He was undefeated as a fighter and whilst he spars with his three brothers all the time, only Shane and Liam have ever knocked him on his ass — and that only happens when he's having an off day.

"You know it's rude to stare at your trainer like that, right?" he chuckles darkly.

"You're not just my trainer though, are you? You're my husband, and I'm pretty sure gawking at your hotness whenever the hell I want to was one of our marriage vows."

He arches one eyebrow at me. "It was?"

"Well, I definitely meant to say it, even if I didn't," I purr, stepping close to him and running a gloved hand over his pecs.

He takes a step back, leaving my hand suspended in mid-air and I groan in frustration. "But right now in this gym, I'm your personal trainer, and this could be construed as sexual harassment. I mean I could sue your ass."

"Well, if my trainer was dressed more appropriately,

perhaps I would be better behaved?" I offer with a shrug of my shoulders.

He looks down at his one item of clothing. "I'm wearing boxing shorts. This is literally what fighters wear in the ring."

"Hmm," I chew on my lip. "I suppose I should just wear my bottoms then?" I ask as I reach for my sports bra and go to pull it off over my head.

"No," he growls, gripping my wrist in one of his huge hands. "We're here to work out. Besides, your ass in those skin tight pants is enough to drive me to distraction as it is."

"You really are no fun this morning."

He picks up the pads at his feet, slipping them on before raising his hands. "No, I'm not. Now let's warm up."

MY HEART IS BEATING WILDLY in my chest and beads of sweat trickle down my back as I blow out a long breath. I swear Conor's boxing workouts are enough to bring an Olympian to their knees. You think he'd go easier on me because I'm his wife, right? But nope. In fact, he makes me work harder than I've worked in my life. He pushes me like no-one else. Wanting me to be faster and stronger. Although I grumble about it, usually I love my workouts with him and Mikey. They make me feel accomplished and strong.

But today, he is looking way too fine and I am feeling far too horny to concentrate.

"Come on, Jessie," he barks. "You got two more minutes before you can rest. Now move."

He jabs his arm out and I dodge it. Then he switches his stance, bouncing on his toes and my eyes are drawn to the outline of his very impressive semi-hard cock in his shorts — so much so that I forget to dodge the next jab and he grazes the side of my head with the pad, causing me to wobble.

Fortunately, he catches me. Wrapping me in his huge biceps, he spins me around until my back is pressed up against his chest. "You okay, angel?" he asks.

"Yes," I pant, feeling like an idiot.

He presses his mouth against the shell of my ear, sending a shiver of pleasure up my spine, not to mention all manner of unholy thoughts into my brain. "You shouldn't allow yourself to be so easily distracted," he whispers before he trails his lips over my neck, pressing his body closer to mine.

"You shouldn't be so damn distracting then," I groan as I wiggle my ass against him.

He gives me a soft kiss on the back of my neck before stepping back again. "That's all the break you're getting, angel. Let's go," he laughs softly.

Groaning in frustration, I spin around and raise my guard again.

"That's my girl," he says with a wink.

Holy fuck! He knows those words do something to me. Jackass!

I start punching again as he resumes his coaching. He's actually an amazing trainer, but I am way too focused on making him squirm now. But how?

I don't do dirty talk very often, unless I'm completely lost in the moment. It makes me feel kind of embarrassed. My four husbands on the other hand, take dirty talk to a whole new level. The filth that comes out of their mouths would be enough to make a porn star blush. I'm pretty sure some of that must have sunk in, right? I mean it's worth a try.

"Focus, Jessie," Conor interrupts my musing.

Here goes nothing. "Kind of hard to, big guy, when all I can think about is sucking on your beautiful cock until you come down my throat."

He blinks at me, caught completely off guard and I aim a right hook at the pad on his left hand. But he doesn't hold it up in time and I catch him square on the jaw. He was also in the unfortunate position of shifting his weight from one foot to the other and so when I strike him, he's balanced on one leg. The result of those two things happening at the same time, causes him to fall flat on his ass — his head smacking back against the canvas with a thud.

"Fuck!" he hisses, his tongue darting out and licking the small cut I've just given him on his lip.

"Conor!" I drop to my knees, straddling him as I run my fingertips lightly over his lip where he's bleeding. "I'm so sorry."

He winces as he shrugs off one of the pads and rubs the back of his head. "Don't be. I should have been paying more attention."

"Have I hurt you?"

"Only my pride, angel," he says with a grin.

"Well, you really shouldn't allow yourself to get so easily distracted," I purr as I roll my hips over him and feel his cock hardening against my pussy.

He pulls off the other pad and rests his hands on my hips. "Stop it!" he orders but there is a devious twinkle in his eye.

"I'm just enjoying the moment. I mean I just knocked *the* Conor Ryan on his ass."

He rolls his lips together and narrows his eyes at me.

"I did," I smile wickedly. "I knocked you on your ass."

"Jessie Ryan, you have been knocking me on my ass every damn day since I met you."

Heat flushes over my cheeks and my heart swells with love

for him. "That is very sweet. But I actually did it for real today though."

"You did."

I pop one eyebrow at him. "So, I guess this means our workout is over?"

"No," he says with a frown. "I'm fine."

"Yeah, but if you don't stop this grueling session and take me to bed instead, I'm going to tell everyone I just knocked you on your ass."

"Everyone?" he smirks at me.

"Well, your brothers at least."

He laughs loudly and the sound rumbles through his body and into my thighs as they stay pressed against his waist. "You think they don't already know that I'm a simp for you, angel. I'm pretty sure they think I let you get the better of me on purpose when we spar anyway."

"They do not," I insist, but a tiny sliver of doubt creeps into my mind. "You never let me off that easily. Do you?"

"Never," he says with a smile. "But they don't know that."

"They don't, huh?"

"No, because they know that I would kneel at your fucking feet every second of every day if you wanted me to, angel," he growls and that deep rumble travels straight to my pussy now.

Dear God, this man drives me to constant distraction. "Is that so?" I purr as I push myself up to a standing position.

"You know it is."

I put one hand on my hip and stare down at him. His chest rising and falling and his abs tightening as he glares back up at me. "So prove it, big guy. On your knees."

Without any pause, he sits up and in one swift and agile movement presses his knuckles onto the mat and springs onto his knees before me.

I bite down on my lip as he looks up at me, his beautiful

brown eyes smoldering and I wonder what the hell I have ever done to deserve him. I must have been a goddamn saint in my former life.

"Now what?" he growls.

Now what? A thrill of pleasure shoots right through me as I contemplate just how far my possessive, control freak husband is willing to let me push him. Placing my hand under his chin, I smile at him. Then I give him a quick kiss on his busted lip before taking a step backward. "Now crawl," I command as I keep walking back until I'm leaning against the ropes.

He remains in place as his eyes roam over my body. The muscles in his neck twitch and his jaw ticks as he clenches it shut while he considers my request. I narrow my eyes at him — daring him to do it.

I smile as he slowly begins to edge forward. He doesn't crawl, so much as walk on his knees and the closer he gets, the more every cell in my body begins to tremble with need, anticipation, and just a little trepidation for good measure.

He stops when he's directly in front of me — his body just a few inches from my own. I can't deny that the sight of one of the most powerful men in the country on his knees for me makes me feel weak in mine.

He looks up at me, his eyes so full of fire I feel them burn into my skin.

"Now I want you to-"

"I don't think so, angel," he interrupts me, and the deep timbre of his voice vibrates through my bones, making me shiver.

Oh fuck!

His warm hands grip my hips and he pushes me back until I'm sitting on the middle rope. "Just because I'm willing to worship you on my knees..." Taking my left hand, he starts to weave my arm through the top rope as he goes on talking in

SADIE KINCAID

that low, gravelly growl that turns my insides to molten lava. "Don't go thinking that means that you're in control here."

Once my left arm is secure, he does the same to my right until I'm held securely by the thick, tight ropes. My heart starts racing even faster than it was when he was pushing me to my limits a few minutes earlier. Meanwhile my entire body is flushed with heat and desire.

"What are you doing?" I whisper.

"Worshipping you, angel," he chuckles darkly as he runs his hands down my legs to my feet before pulling off my sneakers and tossing them onto the gym floor.

They bounce with a thud but I can't take my eyes off his as his hands slide back up my thighs, making pleasure roll through my core. He hooks his thick fingers into the waistband of my pants before pulling them off over my hips and ass. A second later, he tugs them off completely, along with my socks, before throwing them over his shoulder. I never wear panties with my workout gear so now I'm naked except for my sports bra. The cool air of the gym dances over my damp skin, making me shiver.

"Conor," I whisper as he grabs hold of my right ankle and begins to secure my leg to the bottom rope in a similar way he did with my arms. Holy fuck, in about five seconds time I'm not going to be able to move.

"Yeah?" he asks with a wicked grin.

"I'm sorry," I breathe as goosebumps prickle out all over my skin at the thought of what he's about to do to me.

"Sorry you made me crawl on my knees to you?" he chuckles darkly.

Yes. Say yes, Jessie! "No, for the cut on your lip," I snigger and he narrows his eyes at me. "Because having you crawl on your knees to me was kinda hot."

He runs his tongue over the cut on his lip again which has

52

now stopped bleeding. "You know you're about to pay for it though, right?"

"But I thought we were working out?"

"Oh, I'm gonna work you out, angel. By the time I'm done with you, you will ache in every single part of your body."

My cheeks burn with heat and my pussy contracts in expectation as Conor rocks back on his heels. "I wish you could see how fucking beautiful you look right now, angel. All spread open for me. Your pussy is fucking dripping already. Do you feel that?"

"Y-yes," I pant as my breathing grows ragged.

"My horny little angel's gonna drip all over this canvas for me, right?" It's a statement and not a question and we both know he is more than capable of making that happen. "But there's still one thing that's not quite right." He winks at me as he leans forward and grabs hold of the front of my sports bra in his huge hands.

"This is new, Conor," I protest.

"Too late," he says as he tears it down the middle, leaving it dangling from my shoulders.

I suck in a deep breath as my breasts spring free from the confines of the fabric. My nipples are stiff peaks and we both know it's not from the AC.

"That's much better," he chuckles. "Look at you, angel. All tied up and waiting for me to fuck you. Just how I like you."

I stare at him, watching his eyes roam over my body before they settle on my exposed pussy. I am so screwed — or at least I'm about to be. How did we go so quickly from him kneeling at my feet to me being tied up and literally spread open for his pleasure?

"You just can't help yourself, can you? You always have to be in control," I purr.

He runs his hand up the inside of my thigh. His touch is

warm and soothing — both rough and soft at the same time. It sends shivers of pleasure and excitement skittering up my spine. "You like it though, don't you? Me being in control?"

My breath stutters in my throat as his fingers lightly brush my pussy.

"When I'm fucking you anyway?" he adds as he slips the tip of his pointer finger into my opening and wet heat surges between my thighs.

"Y-yes," I whimper.

"Such a good fucking girl for me," he groans as he pushes his finger all the way inside. Then he bends his head low, trailing his tongue from my knee, all the way up my inner thigh before he reaches my pussy. He presses delicate, butterfly kisses on my wet folds as he adds a second finger. Then his tongue trails higher, dancing softly over my flesh as he teases me.

"So fucking sweet too," he mumbles against my skin.

"Stop tormenting me," I whimper.

He looks up at me, face still so close to my pussy that his beard tickles me when he growls, "You deserve to be fucking edged all day long for that crawling stunt, angel. But lucky for you, I'm in a good mood."

Then he starts to feast on my pussy like he's a man starved. He sucks and licks my sensitive flesh while he finger fucks me.

"Oh, fuck, Conor!" I gasp as his tongue swirls over my clit and my orgasm rushes to the surface, heating my skin and making my thighs tremble.

He responds by pushing his fingers deeper, curling the tips against my G spot. "Come hard for me, angel. I want you dripping on my tongue while you're bound in my ropes."

Instinctively I pull on my bindings, trying to draw my arms and legs toward my body as my climax starts to rip through me. I buck and shudder while I'm held in place by both Conor and the thick cord around my limbs, and the whole time he keeps sucking on my clit and driving his fingers in and out of me.

"Conor, I can't... not again," I pant.

"You can. You can give me way more than that," he murmurs against my skin.

"I c-can't," I cry out as a second orgasm bursts through me, way more powerful and violent than the last one.

"That's my girl," he chuckles as he draws his fingers out of me.

My head rolls back as stars cloud my vision.

"Look at me, Jessie," he growls and I lift my head, just in time to see him place his two fingers into his mouth and suck them clean. "So fucking good," he hisses before he sinks them back inside me again.

"Conor," I groan loudly, the sound filling the gym as he starts to finger fuck me again. "Please?"

"Please what, angel?"

"I need..." I whimper, unable to finish my sentence and tell him that I need even more of him, because he starts to pepper kisses over my stomach. Then my head starts to swim and my brain is no longer able to form any coherent thoughts, let alone string a sentence together. When he reaches my breasts, he sucks one of my pebbled nipples into his mouth before letting it go with a wet pop.

"You need me to fuck you, right?" he chuckles as he moves to my other breast.

"Umm," I mumble as I nod my head.

"So fucking greedy for my cock. But I don't think I should fuck you yet."

That works to snap some sense back into me. "Please, Conor?"

"Aw, angel. You regretting making me crawl on my knees like a dog to you now?" he laughs darkly.

"Not like a dog," I breathe. "I was just teasing you."

"Hmm," he murmurs against my skin. "Maybe I'll just keep teasing you?"

"No," I whimper shamelessly as he curls his fingers inside me again, rubbing that sweet, tender spot deep in my pussy that is making every cell in my body tremble.

"C-Conor!" I moan as another orgasm threatens to overwhelm me.

"So fucking wet, angel. Can you hear how wet you are for me?" he groans as he slides his fingers out before driving them back inside at the same time as he bites down on my sensitive nipple.

I come apart around him. My climax bursts out of me, splashing onto the canvas below and if I had any dignity left I might feel a little embarrassed about how much cum he just wrung out of my body.

My head rolls back, hanging back between my shoulder blades while I gasp for breath. I can't take any more. My body is aching. My limbs are tired from being stretched so wide. But my devilish husband obviously doesn't agree. He grabs onto my hips as he edges closer to me, holding onto my waist and pressing the crown of his cock against my entrance, making my thighs tremble in the process.

"You're so fucking tight, Jessie," he hisses as he pushes in further. "Even soaking wet and stretched wide open I can see my cock stretching your sweet pussy."

Holy fuckballs! When I look back at him he's staring at the place where our bodies are joined. "Such a good girl the way you take my cock," he growls as he sinks deeper and my pussy walls squeeze around him, wanting him further inside me even after the orgasms he's already given me. Even after I was sure I couldn't take any more.

I rock my hips as much as I can to meet his thrusts, because the feeling of his huge cock filling me sends new waves of pleasure and need coursing through my body. He turns me into some sort of raging, desperate for cock demon.

"God, you feel so good," I moan as he pulls almost all the way out before driving inside me again.

"Fuck," he mumbles as he sinks so deep inside that I gasp in a breath. Our bodies are flush together now as he wraps his arms around my waist and rolls his hips against me while he buries his face against my neck. His warm breath dances over my skin as he whispers, "I remember the first time I got inside this sweet pussy. I knew right then I was never gonna let you go, angel."

He sucks a finger into his mouth and lifts his head so he can look into my eyes again. Then with his dark eyes fixed on mine, he winks at me while he slides that same hand over my hips and between my ass cheeks. "And this ass too," he growls as he pushes a finger inside me, making me cry out a garbled word that even I don't understand. "So fucking perfect. So fucking mine."

"Yours," I agree as warmth and heat floods my pussy, slicking his cock so that we're making loud, wet slurping sounds as he fucks me relentlessly. I pull at the ropes but it only makes them tighten on my limbs.

"Fucking mine," he snarls as he cups my ass with his free hand. His fingers dig into my soft flesh as he pulls me further onto his cock, clawing at my skin as though he can't get enough of me and I know exactly how he feels. I can't get enough of him either.

If I could free my arms I would wrap them around his neck and use him as leverage to grind my hips and take him even deeper.

"I need more, Conor," I groan and his fingers grip my ass cheek so hard I know they'll leave a mark but I don't care.

"I'm giving you everything I got, Jessie," he growls as he drives into me, sinking even deeper while he adds a second finger to my ass and pushes further inside.

"Oh! Holy f-f...," I sputter out as he pulls another orgasm from my body. It crashes over me in a long, undulating wave. My head drops onto his shoulder as I shudder and tremble in his arms.

"There's my good girl," he whispers in my ear. "But we're still not done, angel."

I can't even argue with him. I can't tell him that I can't take any more because I'm about to slip into blissful unconsciousness. He pulls his cock out of me and a torrent of cum comes with it, making an audible splat on the canvas.

"Fuck, Jessie. You know that's still all you, right?" he chuckles.

I'm vaguely aware of him moving away from me because the cool air rushes over my body when he does, making me shiver uncontrollably. Then I feel his warm arms around me from behind, and his chest pressed against my back. He must have climbed out of the ring.

"Let's get you out of here, angel," he whispers in my ear as he frees my arms from the ropes before he does the same to my legs. When I'm loose he scoops me into his arms.

"Are you finally taking me to bed to have your way with me?" I murmur as my senses start returning.

"Nope," he chuckles softly. "I got everything I need to have my way with you right here."

I open my eyes and stare into his handsome face. What the hell is he planning on doing now?

I find out a second later when he walks us to the weight bench and sits me on it.

"Lie on your front, Jessie."

I blink up at him.

"That wasn't a suggestion, angel," he growls. "I told you I wasn't done with you. Now lie down."

I swallow hard. Damn, he's so hot when he's bossy. "This bench is kinda small to lie on," I protest as I spin around and do as he asks. Pressing my face against the cool leather.

"It's big enough," he chuckles as he takes hold of my hips and pulls me toward him. Sliding me further down the bench, he positions me so that my ass is hanging off the edge before he pushes my legs either side and I have to rest my knees on the floor. The result of which leaves me once again spread wide open for him.

"Perfect," he says as he drops to his knees behind me.

He brushes his fingers over my sensitive folds and I whimper.

"Feeling a little tender, angel?"

"Yes," I whisper.

"That's okay," he chuckles as he rubs some of my cum over my asshole. "I want your ass now anyway. You come so hard for me when I fuck you here."

I gasp out loud when his tongue sweeps over me too, instinctively clenching my thighs together and meeting the resistance of the bench.

"Conor," I squeak but he is undeterred and when I start wriggling he takes hold of my wrists and pins them behind my back.

"Stay still or I will set you free and chase you through this goddamn apartment, Jessie," he warns. "And when I catch you..." He doesn't need to finish that sentence.

I stop wriggling. Being chased by Conor is hot — and high on my list of favorite activities, but right now I'm too spent and he knows it. I don't think I could run if the gym was on fire. So instead I relax against the bench and focus on his warm soft tongue as he licks and sucks my sensitive skin. When he's starts to trail kisses over my ass cheeks and along my back, I feel his cock nudging at my pussy again and I moan softly.

"I just need a little lube, angel," he groans softly as he pushes inside me. Everything burns but it feels so good too. I love a little pain with my pleasure.

"Conor," I gasp as I squeeze around him, trying to keep him inside me even as he pulls out.

"If I fuck your pussy again, you're gonna end up sore, and then my brothers will never forgive me," he chuckles darkly.

"Spoilsport," I grumble, but I love that he knows my limits. I would let this man do anything to my body even if I knew I was going to regret it later.

"You're fucking insatiable," he growls as he sinks his thick cock into my ass. His earlier teasing there has me ready for him and he slides in almost all the way. My pussy is so tender that it throbs as he slowly fucks my ass. I feel him everywhere.

"Conor," I whimper.

"You're so fucking tight like this," he hisses as he grabs onto my ass cheek with one hand while he goes on holding my wrists with the other.

"You fuck me so good," I cry as tears start to run down my cheeks. My body is overwhelmed and I need more release but he's not going to let me have another one just yet.

"Fuck, I can't get enough of you. You know that, right?" he asks as he slides even deeper. "I'm almost balls deep in your ass, angel, and it's not enough. How the fuck do you do this to me?"

I don't answer him. I can't. All I can do is suck in stuttered breaths as he fucks my ass to a delicious and relentless rhythm. Taking my hands, he places them on the bench above my head so that he can lean over me. Then he presses his lips against my ear, growling filthy things that make my pussy flutter and my insides contract. But he doesn't let me come — not yet. He keeps me teetering on the edge of oblivion.

60

"I'm s-sorry I-I made you c-crawl," I whimper.

"I'm not," he laughs as he grips my hips with his powerful thighs and sinks all the way inside me, making me cry out his name as my orgasm tears through my body until I have no sense of anything other than the wave after wave of pleasure that courses through every single part of me.

I'm vaguely aware of Conor grunting and cursing in my ear and a warmth between my thighs before his strong arms are wrapped around me as my eyelids flutter open. "You still with me, angel?" he asks softly.

"Uh-huh," I murmur as I look into his eyes and see that he's carrying me out of the gym now. I'm pressed against his hard chest and I rest my cheek on his shoulder. "Did you just make me pass out?"

He arches an eyebrow at me. "Maybe. Am I that good?"

"Hmm. You know you are," I whisper as I snuggle against him. "Where are we going?"

"For a bath," he says, pressing a soft kiss on my forehead. "We're both very sticky."

"Well, it was a hell of a workout," I giggle.

"Told you," he says with a wink.

"I love you," I whisper.

He kisses my forehead and holds me tighter to him. "Love you more."

A RYAN REVELATION

A NEW YORK RUTHLESS SHORT STORY

CHAPTER 1
JESSIE

"Babies?" Mikey asks as he takes a bottle of tequila from the highest cupboard in the kitchen.

"Bathed and in their pajamas. Conor is putting them both down now," I say with a smile as I take a seat at the kitchen island.

"Babysitters?" his twin, Liam asks as he places the lemon wedges, shot glasses and salt cellar on the island in front of me.

"They'll be here at nine-thirty."

"Car?" Mikey adds, heading over to us with the bottle of Cuervo in his hand.

"Booked for ten," I reply.

"Incredibly short, tight-fitting, sexy dress?" Liam asks with a wink.

"Laid out on the bed and ready."

Mikey arches an eyebrow. "Ridiculous green shamrock hats and glasses that Conor and Shane are going to hate but will wear anyway because you're going to ask them to?"

"Locked and loaded and ready to go," I reply with a triumphant smile.

I have them stashed in a bag in the basement, because

where is the fun in being married to four incredibly sexy Irish men if I can't make them dress up for St. Patrick's Day?

"Then seems like we have plenty of time for a game of Never Have I Ever then?" Mikey gives a wicked grin and pours three shots of tequila.

"Okay, but this time you can only say things if you don't know for certain one of the other people hasn't done them," I warn him and he laughs out loud. "Because last time I got so drunk I almost passed out and Conor had to carry me to bed—and not in the good way."

"True, bro. Jessie passing out drunk before nine p.m. is not going to end well for any of us."

"Is it my fault that our wife here is way more sexually adventurous than us?" Mikey replies.

"I am not," I protest.

"Hmm," Mikey murmurs as he runs a hand over his beard as though deep in thought. "Pretty sure you're the only person in this room who needs four people to keep them satisfied, Red."

"I do not..." I start to say but both Liam and him laugh so hard that I don't bother protesting further. "Just don't get me drunk, Mikey Ryan."

"I won't, Red. Promise." He leans over the island and gives me a soft kiss on the lips. "I'll even let you go first."

I sit back, and my nose wrinkles as I try to come up with my first statement. "Never have I ever cheated on a partner," I say with a smirk.

"Fuck," Mikey grins and takes his shot.

"Dammit," Liam groans as he does a shot straight after.

I stare at him, open-mouthed. "Liam Ryan!"

"What, baby? Mikey had a shot too."

"Yes, but I kind of expect it from him," I say making Mikey laugh again and Liam shake his head as he pretends to be offended.

Mikey is still laughing when their eldest brother, Shane walks into the room a moment later. Upon noticing the open bottle of tequila and shot glasses on the counter in front of us, he rolls his eyes. "You three need to pace yourselves. Especially you, sweetheart," he says as he slips an arm around my waist and gives me a brief kiss on the cheek. Then he presses his hot mouth against my ear. "Because the only thing I want you passing out from, is me fucking you too hard."

A shiver runs the length of my spine, but I don't get a chance to respond before he turns his attention to Liam and Mikey. "And I'm not cleaning up your puke all night."

"Yes, Dad," Liam says with a roll of his eyes.

"Sure, Daddy," I whisper. I intended it to sound all purring and seductive but instead I'm giggling like a naughty teenager.

Shane's entire face darkens and he glares at me, running his tongue over his lip. The entire room crackles with tension. Without another word, he picks me up and hoists me over his shoulder. When I protest he smacks my ass—hard.

"Hey, we were kind of the middle of something and we're going out in three hours," Liam yells as Shane walks out of the room.

"I'll be done with her in one. Two tops," Shane replies.

Mikey makes a clicking sound before he adds. "New kink unlocked." Both he and Liam burst into laughter while my head spins from hanging upside down.

"Can I walk to wherever you're taking me?" I ask.

"No, because naughty little brats are carried," he growls and smacks my ass again, making me squeal.

As he heads down the hallway I hear footsteps coming toward us.

"Babies are sound asleep," Conor says after he's just walked out of our children's nursery. "Would take an earthquake to wake those two now."

"Good, because I plan on making their mother scream this goddamn building down," Shane says making his younger brother chuckle.

"Let me see her," Conor says, and Shane turns sideways so Conor can talk to both of us. He cups my chin in his hand and arches an eyebrow. "Were you drinking tequila with the twins?"

"Well, I was going to, until I got forcibly removed from the kitchen."

"So what did you do?"

"Um," I chew on my lip. "I called Shane daddy."

Conor looks at his older brother then, amusement all over his face. "I see," he says with a knowing nod.

"Yeah," Shane agrees with him although I'm unsure what he's agreeing with. I feel like I'm out of the loop. I swear these two can read each other's minds just like Liam and Mikey can.

"I gotta grab a shower and something to eat but then maybe I'll join you," Conor says, his wicked grin flooding my body with heat and desire.

"We'll be in the end room," Shane tells him and I shiver. That room is where he takes me when he either wants to punish me, or fuck me like a demon – or both.

Conor laughs darkly before he gives me a sweet kiss on the lips. "Good luck, angel. Try not to pass out before I get there."

"I'll do my best," I flutter my eyelashes and Shane resumes carrying me down the hallway to the end bedroom. It used to be Conor's bedroom but now we all share a room so we had it sound proofed. It's kind of become our grown up play room. It can only be accessed with one of our fingerprints to ensure no guests can enter—or tiny toddlers when our kids get older.

As soon as we're inside the room, Shane kicks the door closed and sets me on my feet beside the huge chaise lounge—or sex sofa as Mikey has aptly named it. He looks down at me, his eyes narrowed and his six foot two frame towering over me.

"You want to call me that again, sweetheart?" he asks, his deep, low voice melting my core.

"Daddy?" I whisper, my legs trembling in anticipation. I've never had daddy issues, despite having good reason to, and I have never *ever* had a daddy kink. Neither has Shane, as far as I'm aware. So I have no idea why the hell he's looking at me like that or why I'm about ready to melt into a goddamn puddle on the floor.

He steps closer until his body is touching mine and trails his fingertips over my cheek. "What have I warned you about drinking with those boys, Jessie?" he growls.

My brain takes a few seconds to compute what he's saying and then I realize we're actually doing this.

"I'm sorry," I whisper, fluttering my eyelashes.

He dips his head, ghosting his lips over the shell of my ear. "You know those boys are only interested in you for one thing."

"But they're my friends."

"Friends who only want to fuck you, sweetheart. Did you let them fuck your tight little holes?"

I gasp as wet heat sears between my thighs. Damn, this is way hotter than I thought it would be. But then Shane Ryan makes everything hot. "I'm sorry, Daddy," I purr.

"Hmm?" He rubs a hand over his jaw. "What shall I do with my naughty little slut?"

I nibble on my bottom lip as he slips off his suit jacket and rolls up his shirt sleeves. I swear if my pussy could talk she would shriek with delight at the sight of his thick, tattooed forearms and the promise of the spanking I'm about to get.

Shane sits on the sex sofa. "Take everything off except the panties," he growls and heat blooms across my chest.

I keep my eyes glued to his as I peel my dress over my head and toss it onto the floor beside me. I take off my bra, and his gaze drops to my hard nipples for a moment before his eyes meet mine again. When I'm left in only my panties, he holds out his hand. My heart rate kicks up about two hundred gears as I curl my fingers around his and allow him to pull me onto his lap—but I'm not sitting on him. He pulls me forward until I'm lying across his huge thighs.

I breathe faster and harder as his hand glides over my ass and he kneads the soft flesh of my cheeks in his huge palm. The weight of his hand disappears, and I suck in a breath and prepare for what's about to happen. He smacks my ass hard and I mean to play along with his little game and shriek in feigned horror, but I moan instead because Shane Ryan's spankings are a gift from the heavens.

He spanks me again, and I bite my lip but another moan escapes anyway.

"Sounds like my naughty slut is enjoying her spanking a little too much."

"I'm not. I promise," I giggle.

Tension vibrates through every muscle in his body, and a deep groan rumbles in his chest as he rolls my panties down over my ass cheeks until they're resting at the top of my thighs. The next smack is way harder and I squirm on his lap.

"Did you let those boys touch you, sweetheart?" he growls as he slips his hand between my thighs. Finding me soaking already, he sucks in a sharp breath. "Who made you all wet like this?"

"You did, Daddy," I whimper.

He smacks my ass hard with his other hand and slides his middle and pointer fingers up through my folds. "Did you let those two boys in the kitchen touch you here?"

"Yes."

Smack!

He pushes two thick fingers deep inside. "Did you let them put their fingers in you?"

"Yeah," I whimper as wet heat slicks his fingers and earns me another sharp slap on my ass.

"So who made you this wet, sweetheart?"

"Only you, Daddy," I whisper.

He slides his fingers out of me and I whine in frustration. "Only good girls get to come," he growls before he spanks me again.

His slaps grow harder and faster until my ass is throbbing and he has to press one hand on the small of my back to keep me in place as I squirm. He could simply order me to stay still like he usually does, and I would, but I guess that doesn't fit into this little scenario we're playing. Pleasure and heat and anticipation burns through my body. Every time his palm connects with my ass it makes me wetter and more needy for him.

"How many times did you let those boys fuck you, sweetheart?" he asks, taking a quick break to rub a soothing hand over my inflamed skin.

"I don't know."

"You don't know?" he hisses, dragging his fingernails over my sensitive flesh.

"I lost count," I whimper. "I'm sorry, Daddy."

"Such a naughty fucking slut," he groans as he starts spanking me again with one hand as he presses the tip of his finger against my asshole. "Did they fuck you here too?" He edges inside me.

"Y-yes," I gasp as waves of pleasure roll through my core. "P-please. I'm sorry," I cry. "I won't do it again."

"No more drinking with those boys in the kitchen?" *Smack.*

"No."

"No more letting them touch you or fuck you?" *Smack.*

"No, Daddy."

"Goddammit, Jessie," he roars, tearing my panties all of the way off before he grabs hold of me like I'm as light as air. Then he sits me on his lap so I'm straddling him.

I swallow as I look into his eyes and they are so dark with heat and passion and longing that I already feel like I'm going to have to be carried out of this room on a stretcher. I think I've unleashed something in him that I might never be able to put back—but I am one hundred percent here for it.

"Who is the only man who gets to fuck your tight little pussy?" he asks and the deep growl of his voice makes me shiver all over.

"Only you," I whisper, catching my bottom lip with my teeth.

"Yeah? So take out my cock and sit on it," he hisses. "Use that tight little cunt of yours to make me come ."

"Yes, Daddy," I purr, grasping for his belt and zipper so that I can work his cock free and do as he asks as soon as humanly possible. I am so hot for him I think I'm going to implode as soon as I feel him inside me.

Wrapping my hand around his thick shaft, I squeeze and he sucks in a stuttered breath that makes me smile to myself. So he thinks he's the only one in control?

"I said sit on it, not play with it," he growls.

"You're so bossy," I protest as I shift my position, lining my pussy up with the crown of his cock.

"You have no fucking idea, sweetheart," he says as he places his hands on my hips. "Now sit." He pulls my hips down until I sink onto him, taking him to the hilt as he stretches me wide open.

"Jesus," I gasp, my body adjusting to accommodate him filling me so completely.

He holds me still, staring into my eyes with a wicked look of deviance in his. Running his nose over my neck, he grunts in my ear. "I bet those boys didn't fill your sweet pussy this good?"

I trail kisses over the thick column of his throat, working my way up and brushing my lips over his ear, I squeeze his cock with my pussy muscles and whisper. "They kinda did, Daddy. They made me come real hard too."

He bites down on his lip and I see the internal struggle he's having between tossing me onto the bed and spanking me with his belt, and making me ride him until he comes. He wraps his huge arms around me, pulling me closer. "Well, I hope it was worth it, sweetheart, because you won't be coming for the rest of the month," he says with a wicked grin.

I blink at him. There's another two weeks in this month. We're still just playing, right?

"Now make me come like my good little slut," he demands.

I roll my hips over him and the sensation of him deep inside me makes my core turn to molten lava. Shane might try and stop me from coming but I'm so close to the edge after his spanking, he'll have a pretty tough job.

My eyes roll in my head as my slick pussy coats him. Every time I move, his thick cock massages those parts that make my thighs tremble.

"That feel good, sweetheart?"

"Uh-huh," I moan as he holds me tighter and takes control of my movements, pulling me down onto him as he lifts his hips slightly until he's pressing against my G-spot and my entire body shivers with an impending orgasm.

"I can get so deep into you like this."

"Yes," I agree, rocking my hips for more friction.

"Yeah?" he grunts.

"Yes, Shane," I cry out as my orgasm is about to hit.

"No," he laughs darkly, grabbing hold of my hips and lifting me off him until my incredible, life altering orgasm ebbs away like waves on a shoreline.

"Why did you do that?" I protest.

"I already told you, sweetheart, no coming for the rest of the month."

"But that's —" I don't get to finish my sentence before he pulls me back down on top of him, slamming into me at the same time until my teeth rattle in my head.

"You're still gonna make me come though," he growls.

"What if I refuse?" I pant, staring into his dark eyes.

He's still holding onto my hips and he rolls me over him again. "Then I'll just use your sweet cunt to make myself come." He winks at me and my ovaries almost burst.

I place my hands on his firm shoulders. "Can I come if I promise to be a good girl from now on, Daddy?" I purr.

"No," he shakes his head.

"You're so mean." I pout.

"Yeah," he grinds out the words as his cock pulses inside me. I widen my thighs, sinking lower as I grip his shaft with my inner muscles. Squeezing and releasing until his eyes start to roll and his jaw ticks with tension.

He's about to learn that two can play at this teasing game. Right when he's on the edge, I stop.

But it only makes him hold me still and fuck me instead. Driving his hips upward and hitting that sweet sensitive spot deep inside me over and over again until I'm about ready to explode in a flurry of starlight and electricity.

"Fuck," he grunts, his fingers digging into my hips as he grinds his own climax into me whilst leaving me teetering on the edge of absolute oblivion. My ass and pussy are throbbing and my entire body is pulsing with heat and energy – and all he has to do is flick the switch and I'll be gone.

But he doesn't. Asshole!

"Shane, please?" I whimper, my hand sliding between my thighs so I can get myself off instead. But he catches my wrist and holds me tight, pulling me toward him until our foreheads are pressed together.

He breathes hard and I rest my free hand on his cheek until his eyes lock on mine again. He lifts me off him until I'm sitting on his lap, dripping his cum all over his suit pants. "That was..." he shakes his head as though he can't find the word.

"It was epic until the end," I pout and he laughs softly.

"I'll make you come now, sweetheart. Just give me a minute."

"Are you okay?" I ask with a frown.

"Yeah, but I think I just blacked out," he laughs harder and the sound soothes every frayed edge and nerve in my body, making me laugh too. "Maybe give me a heads up if you ever plan on calling me Daddy again, yeah?"

"Hmm. You kind of got a little feral on me there," I whisper. "And mean."

He brushes my hair back from my face. "I'll make it up to you." He stands and carries me to the giant bed before tossing me into the middle. "You want my fingers or my mouth, sweetheart?"

"Um, both?" I say with a frown. "Given that you just almost blacked out and all because I rode you so hard, I figure I deserve it."

Shane glares at me as he starts removing his clothes. "Don't be a brat, Jessie, because I will happily still spank your ass instead and that threat of not letting you come for the rest of the month will become a promise."

Just smile at him sweetly, Jessie. Say sorry, Sir because you know he's in one of his controlling alpha-hole moods. "Your brothers wouldn't allow it," I say instead, my tone dripping with sass.

"Oh, so you want my belt, is that it?" he asks as he unbuckles it.

Dammit, yeah, I do. "No."

"Too bad, sweetheart," he growls as he pulls it off and the sound of the soft leather against the fabric makes my pussy drip with need. "On your hands and knees. Now!"

I mumble a fake protest but I flip over and push myself onto my knees.

"Your ass is fucking beautiful, Jessie," he says right before he brings his belt cracking down right across the middle of my ass cheeks, making the already tender skin sting. Tears prick my eyes as a rush of pleasure washes over me. "And this pussy..." he growls as he trails the tip of the leather through my folds, making me whimper. When he flicks it lightly, grazing my clit, my knees buckle.

"Easy sweetheart," he says softly. "You pass out on me tonight and my brothers will be super pissed." Then he smacks my ass with his belt again until I moan his name.

I lose count of the number of times he spanks me but by the time I hear the familiar sound of the buckle dropping to the floor, I'm about ready to slip into unconsciousness or come on command. The bed dips behind me as he crawls onto it, rubbing his huge, soothing hands over my ass cheeks.

"Such a good girl," he whispers before he slips two fingers inside me. Wrapping his free arm around my waist, he gently lowers me to the bed as he finger fucks me. "Spread a little wider for me."

I can barely move my legs but I shuffle them further apart, allowing Shane to slide deeper inside. When he brushes my clit with his thumb, my climax rips through my body like black powder is running through my veins and he just lit the fuse.

It's a good thing I was already lying on the bed because my entire body trembles and shudders as he rips a sound from me that I didn't even know I was capable of making. My orgasm is still skittering through my body when he lies over me, pushing my thighs wider apart before he sinks his cock into me.

"Shane," I moan, my cheek pressed against the mattress as he starts to nail me into it.

"I know, sweetheart," he growls in my ear, driving into me harder. "Spanking you makes me so fucking hard."

My head spins as my next orgasm builds so quickly, catching the sparks of the last one and igniting into a full blown inferno as it sears through my body.

"I can't," I cry out, unsure of what it is I'm telling him I can't do— speak, think, control my bodily functions?

Shane presses almost the full weight of his body on mine, his lips on my neck as he kisses and bites the soft skin. "You squeeze me so tight when you come, sweetheart," he grunts and I go off like I just went supernova, screaming so loud I swear I made a glass shatter somewhere.

"Fuck, Jessie," he groans as my pussy squeezes him for dear life, tipping him over the edge along with me.

I'm still seeing stars when he rolls off me, wrapping his arm around me and pulling me close to him as I remain lying on my front and trying to learn how to breathe again.

"You're a devil, Shane Ryan," I mumble when I finally regain the ability to speak.

"And you are fucking hellfire, Jessie Ryan," he says before he presses soft kisses over my shoulder.

"Hmm. My ass feels like it's been bathed in hellfire," I giggle.

He rubs his hand over it softly. "I'll take care of it as soon as I can feel my legs again," he says drily making me laugh out loud. "It looks beautiful."

"Like a candy cane?" I ask.

"Better," he replies before he bends his head and trails kisses over the tender skin there. "I didn't intend to be so rough because we're going out later. Will you be able to sit down okay?" he asks, his voice tinged with a concern I rarely hear post spanking and making me wonder just how red and belt striped my poor ass is.

"I'm sure I'll be fine. And I kind of pushed you. What can I say? I guess I needed that belt of yours," I purr like a contented cat.

"I love my naughty little brat," he laughs darkly and then his lips disappear and he jumps up from the bed, leaving me lying alone.

SHANE IS RUBBING arnica gel onto my ass when the door opens and Liam walks into the room. I smile at him as he strolls toward the bed. "What the fuck, Shane?" he says with a sigh as he gets closer and notices my belt striped behind.

"I'm fine," I assure him as he lies on the bed beside me, rubbing his warm, strong hand gently over my back.

He narrows his eyes at me. "Are you sure, baby?"

I hear Shane chuckling softly as he goes on rubbing the soothing gel onto my ass. Liam is such a sensitive soul – my gentle giant.

"I'm sure."

He looks up at his older brother. "Did you have to leave your hand prints and your belt marks all over my wife's beautiful ass, Shane?"

"She likes my marks on her, don't you sweetheart?"

"Kinda."

"Only kinda?" he asks, grabbing a handful of my ass cheek.

"Okay, a lot," I squirm in his grip, giggling as Liam slaps Shane's hand away.

"Leave her poor ass alone, bro," Liam says with a roll of his eyes. "I have plans for it later."

"You do?" I ask him, my eyes widening with excitement.

He grins at me, his dark brown eyes twinkling with deviant

delight as he leans close and gives me a soft kiss. "I *always* have plans for your ass, baby," he whispers, sending shivers of pleasure and anticipation skittering around my body.

"I can't wait," I tell him as he lays down next to me, our noses tip to tip as Shane goes on rubbing cool gel into my skin.

"Me neither," he growls before inching forward and sealing his lips over mine. I moan softly as he slips his tongue inside my mouth and his hand to the back of my head, crushing me against him as he deepens our kiss.

He tugs my hair at the roots as he claims my mouth, making heat bloom beneath my skin and soft, desperate whimpers escape my throat. Liam is still kissing me when the bedroom door bursts open and Mikey walks in before loudly announcing that we have a problem. "Babysitters have canceled. Chester has stomach flu."

Liam groans as he breaks our kiss and we both look up to see Conor walking into the room after his younger brother and closing the door. His eyes land on me, raking over my naked body as I lie between his two brothers.

"You call it a problem. I call it an opportunity," he says, placing his hand on Mikey's shoulder and grinning widely.

Mikey frowns at his older brother while the rest of us wait for his explanation.

Conor rolls his eyes before he goes on. "We all have the night off. We have two sleeping babies who are unlikely to wake until morning, and a naked wife who looks to me like she just had the spanking of her life. And we all know how fucking feral that makes her."

Mikey starts grinning while Liam laughs softly.

"I am not feral," I protest.

"Um, you kind of are, baby," Liam says as he gives me a soft kiss on the forehead. "But we love it."

"Man's got a point," Shane adds, pushing himself up into a

sitting position. "And now we don't have to wear those God-awful St Patrick's day hats you bought."

My mouth drops open in shock. "You knew about them?"

He leans down and presses a soft kiss on my ass. "When are you going to learn that I know everything, sweetheart?" he growls.

"You must know I also got us huge green glasses with shamrocks on them?" I say with a giggle.

"Yeah, we found them too, angel," Conor adds as he starts pulling off his t-shirt.

"You would have worn them though, right?" I ask. "I mean just in the car. Just for me?"

Shane cups my jaw in his hand and tilts my head back so I'm looking into his deep green eyes. "We would do anything for you, sweetheart," he whispers before giving me a quick kiss on the mouth and jumping off the bed.

Conor pulls his sweatpants off, revealing his already hard cock. Then he climbs onto the bed and lays down on his back beside me. "You okay with her ass, bro?" he asks Liam who nods his agreement. "Come here, angel," he says to me, taking hold of my hand and pulling me up until I'm straddling him. He grabs onto my hips as his cock twitches against my pussy. "You're so fucking beautiful," he hisses as one hand glides over my ribs and he palms one of my breasts in his other, squeezing softly and making me gasp.

"Did you and Shane work out some daddy issues?" he laughs softly as he grabs a handful of my ass.

"Hmm," I chew on my lip. "I don't have any daddy issues, but I think I tapped into a new kink for your older brother. He let his animal side loose."

"I can hear you, sweetheart," Shane growls and I turn my head to see he's sitting on the sex sofa watching his brothers and me while Mikey is busy pulling off his clothes too.

"I know," I smile sweetly before turning back to Conor who's suddenly no longer smiling. His eyes are dark as he stares at me, his tongue darting out as he licks his bottom lip.

He holds onto his cock with one hand and gives it a quick tug until precum seeps from the crown. I lick my lips because I want to taste him, but he grabs my jaw. "No," he says with a shake of his head. "Sit on my cock, angel. Let me feel how wet your spanking made you."

I shift myself into position, lining the tip of his length at my entrance while he holds still. I sink down onto him a little, easing the tip inside me and reveling in the tormented look on his face as I tease him. My upper hand lasts all of three seconds before Conor grabs my hips again and pulls me down onto him.

"Jesus, Conor," I moan as he hits my G-spot and my pussy flutters around him. "You boys are so impatient tonight."

"I told you to sit, angel, not fucking hover," he grunts as he rolls my hips over him, causing warm waves of pleasure to roll over me.

I arch an eyebrow. "I'm pretty sure I remember you telling me that many times before."

"Hmm. And I'm gonna make you sit on my face later too. After I clean you up in the shower."

"I'm not dirty," I feign my indignation.

"You're about to be, baby," Liam says, crawling onto the bed behind me with a bottle of lube in his hand.

"Yeah, you're gonna have four lots of cum in you soon, and I only want to taste yours, angel."

"Me too. I only want to eat pure, uncumtaminated pussy," Mikey laughs. Then he crawls onto the bed beside us, one hand behind his head as he strokes his cock with the other. He watches me intently while one of his brothers fucks me and the other is coating his cock with lube. I reach for his free hand and he laces his fingers through mine, lifting our joined hands to his lips, he dusts them over my knuckles.

Liam places one of his huge hands between my shoulder blades, pushing me down gently onto Conor, who slides his arms around my waist and holds me tight against his chest.

"You okay?" he asks, his breath dusting over my hair.

"Yeah," I breathe out as Liam pushes the tip of his cock into my ass. He rubs my still tender skin as he edges deeper inside. "I'm almost in, baby," he grunts with the effort of holding himself back. "Relax a little more for me."

"I got you, angel," Conor soothes, pressing my face into the crook of his neck before he palms my ass cheeks and spreads me a little wider, allowing his younger brother to slide in deeper.

"Oh, God," I moan against Conor's skin as my ass and pussy burn from the stretch of them both inside me. But it feels so good to be so full of them. Warmth pools in my core and I slick Conor's cock with a rush of release.

"Come here to me, baby," Liam growls as he pulls me up, pressing my back against his chest and wrapping his arms around me while Conor grabs onto my hips again.

Liam's hand dips between my thighs and he rubs my clit softly, making my entire body tremble.

I place one hand on the solid muscle of Conor's chest to keep myself steady as he drives his hips upwards while Liam rocks into me at the same time. Mikey holds onto my other hand while he grips his cock in his other. My gaze locks on his and the heat in his eyes as he patiently waits his turn makes me shiver.

"Mikey, why are you just lying there watching?" Shane's deep, rumbling voice grabs my attention and I turn my head to see he's moved to the side of the bed. Dressed in only his suit pants, which are tented with his erection, he looks as equally hot and delicious as his three brothers.

"She has three holes, right? So why aren't you filling the other one?" Shane looks past me and at his younger brother with a wicked grin on his face.

"I-I," I stammer as heat sears my cheeks.

Shane cups my face in his hand. His thumb pressed against the underside of my jaw, he angles my head so that he's looking down into my eyes. "I want to see you taking all three of my boys, sweetheart," he growls.

His boys. Why is that so hot? I mean he all but raised his younger brothers, he's more like a father than a brother, but when he calls them his boys, it does something to me—turning my internal organs to molten lava.

I try to swallow. "Could you maybe get me a drink of water please?"

I love sucking Mikey's cock and the thought of having all three of them inside me is beyond hot, but my mouth is so dry.

His eyes narrow. "You need some lubrication, sweetheart?"

"Yes, please," I breathe.

Liam and Conor slow their movements, rocking gently while my attention is on Shane.

Shane's eyes don't leave mine as he changes his grip on my jaw, until he's squeezing my cheeks, opening my mouth wide for him. He tilts my head back further and then he leans down, bringing his face a little closer to mine.

My heart beats wildly against my chest. Conor, Liam and Mikey have their hands all over my body while their older brother holds my head still.

"Is your throat dry?" Shane asks with a wicked glint in his eyes.

"Uh-huh," I breathe out, open-mouthed.

He leans a little closer, purses his lips, and then the devil spits into my open mouth. His fingers grip my cheeks tighter so

I can't swallow and his saliva runs over my tongue and down the back of my throat.

He arches an eyebrow. "Better?"

Better? That was hotter than hell. I make a noise that sounds vaguely like yes and he releases me from his grip.

"Good girl, now suck Mikey's cock and make them all come. If you do a good job, I might allow them to let you come too."

I nod my understanding, too sensitive and close to orgasm to argue with him. Then I turn back to Mikey who is kneeling beside me with his cock in his hand.

He threads his fingers through my hair, guiding my head while he pushes his cock into my open mouth until he hits the back of my throat. "Fuck! Me!" he hisses. "You're so fucking good at that, Red."

I almost melt into a puddle as the three of them fuck me at the same time. I swear if they weren't all holding onto me then I would fall into a trembling heap. Every cell in my body is desperate for release. They are everywhere. Their hands on me, their cocks filling me, their scent blanketing my body as they take what they want, but there is something reverent in the way they hold me. Hard and gentle at the same time. They grip me tightly—fingertips digging into my skin—but I feel their love and protection coursing through them and into every fiber of my body.

And while they're fucking me, Shane and Conor tell me what a good girl I am. Liam kisses my neck while Mikey brushes away the tears being squeezed out of my eyes from gagging on his huge cock. His fingers tighten on my scalp and he tugs my hair as I suck him harder. A few seconds later, he comes hard against my throat. When he slides out of my mouth I don't even have the energy to wipe the saliva and cum that escapes my lips, but Mikey wipes it for me as Liam and Conor grunt and groan letting me know they're close to the edge too.

"Aw, we got to let her come, Shane," Mikey says.

"Hmm," Shane cups my jaw in his hand, turning me to face him again. "You want to come, sweetheart?"

I mean is that even a question. "Yes. Please?"

"What do you think, boys?" he says to Conor and Liam.

"I'm always in favor of making my wife come," Liam groans, his lips pressed close to my ear.

"She's been such a good girl taking all three of us," Conor says, brushing my hair back from my face.

Shane winks at me. "Then you'd better take care of her then."

"Fuck," Liam grunts as he pushes deeper while rubbing on my clit.

At the same time Conor holds me steady while he circles his hips, rubbing the crown of his cock against my G-spot. And the very second Mikey grabs my face and slides his tongue into my mouth, I come apart. A billion tiny explosions go off in my body at the same time. Flickering starbursts of electricity that converge in one spot between my thighs as I soak the four of us with my cum.

"That's my girl," Liam grunts as Conor roars my name.

Then I hear muffled voices but they're drowned out by the blood whooshing in my ears and my own labored breathing as my head spins. Mikey releases my mouth from his and I suck in deep breaths.

By the time I can focus again, I'm lying on Conor's chest with his arms wrapped around me while Liam and Mikey lie either side of us with their hands resting gently on my back.

"You still with us, angel?" Conor asks with a soft chuckle.

"I don't know," I admit.

"So much better than going out," Mikey says with a contented sigh.

"And we're only just getting started, baby," Liam adds.

"Hmm. I definitely need a drink now though," I protest.

"Refreshment break before round two," Mikey declares.

"Hmm," I close my eyes and nestle my cheek against Conor's chest. "I'll just wait here."

Then I feel another hand on my back and the scent of Shane's cologne as he leans over me and kisses the back of my head. "You relax with Conor, sweetheart and we'll be back with some food and drink soon."

"Sounds perfect," I purr.

A RYAN RECON

A NEW YORK RUTHLESS SHORT STORY

CHAPTER 1
JESSIE

A familiar black SUV rolls to a stop in the basement as I duck out of the nightclub exit and head to the elevator that leads to the safety of the penthouse above. As well as having a club down here, we also have a huge parking garage full of expensive, high end cars.

The doors open and the occupants jump out, laughing loudly at some private joke between themselves because they haven't seen me yet. I eye them suspiciously as they make their way across the concrete floor, their heavy, black boots stomping on the ground. They're dressed in black military gear and each of them has an AK47 slung over their shoulders, carrying them as casually as I would do a purse. The fluorescent lights highlight the dark, purple patches of dried blood on their clothing as they move purposefully through the garage – all muscle and masculinity and sex.

I cross my arms over my chest as they approach, suddenly feeling in the mood for a little fun. Upon seeing me, they falter for a second. They look at each other, then without another word they pull their masks up from beneath their jaws until the lower part of their faces are covered. The two of them would be almost indistinguishable from each other, except that one has a killer clown smile on his mask, while the other has a vampire's mouth on his – fangs bared and blood dripping from his lips.

"That's quite the look," I say with a pop of one eyebrow as they approach me.

The clown tilts his head, his dark eyes roaming over my body hungrily. He grabs hold of his dick, readjusting himself in his pants and I roll my eyes.

"You shouldn't be hanging around a place like this all on your own," the vampire says, his voice deep and smooth.

I shrug. "Pretty sure I can take care of myself."

The clown steps around me, circling me like a hunter would his prey. He bends his head low, running his nose over my hair before he pulls it aside, exposing my neck. He stands directly behind me, his fingers still threaded in my hair and the heat from his body penetrating the thin fabric of my dress. His hot breath dusts over my skin, making a shiver run the length of my body. "I bet I could take care of a pretty little thing like you."

I glance back at him, to see his dark eyes dancing with mischief. "Well, you could try."

His teeth snap together beneath his mask. "I think we found ourselves a live wire here," he growls, his voice low and full of menace.

The vampire takes two steps toward me, until I'm sandwiched between their two hard bodies. My breathing grows heavier. My pulse thrums against my skin. Warmth pools in my core. I tilt my head up so I can look him in the eyes.

He gives me a cheeky wink that makes heat coil up my spine. "Hmm. I figure it might take the two of us to handle this one."

"I'll handle her right here, right now," the clown growls in my ear, pressing his hard cock against my back. His free hand glides down my body, over my ass until his fingers are playing with the edge of my dress.

I glance back at him again. "Let me guess, you're supposed to be the funny one, right?"

He snarls in frustration, grabbing hold of my jaw and titling my head so he can stare into my eyes.

"Well, you are dressed like a clown," I purr, pressing my ass back against him.

He glances down, appraising his attire before his dark eyes lock on mine again. "You think I'm a clown? Just here for your entertainment?"

"Well, surely you don't think I'm going to let you two blood-soaked mercenaries upstairs where my children are sleeping, do you? So I figured you can only be here for me."

He grabs a fistful of my hair, tilting my head back further and exposing the delicate skin of my neck.

"Then you'd be right. Why the fuck would I want to get upstairs when we can have you all to ourselves down here?"

The vampire presses his body closer, one hand skimming over my hip and down between my thighs.

"You think we should show her exactly how much fun we'd like to have with her, bro?" the clown asks.

The vampire's eyes burn into my skin as he pulls up my short dress, exposing the bare skin of my legs as well as my panties. He rubs his index finger over the triangle of fabric and my cheeks burn with heat as he finds it damp. "Uh-huh," he grunts.

The clown brings his face close to mine, his breathing heavy and harsh through his mask. "You think you can handle being our little fuck-toy for the night?" he grunts, before running his nose up the column of my throat.

"Pretty sure I can handle anything either of you have to give me, *clown*."

The vampire laughs darkly as the clown's grip on my hair tightens. His lips are pressed against my ear. "You seem to have a death wish tonight," he whispers.

"You couldn't hurt me and you know it. Not even a little bit," I say, wanting to push him until he snaps like a tightly wound piece of elastic. Because I'm also in the mood for danger tonight and I'm pretty sure these guys are so pumped up from whatever they've been out there doing, they are just the men to give it to me.

A deep animalistic growl rumbles in the clown's throat and the sound vibrates through every cell in my body. I let out a soft whimper – needy and frustrated. Then without any further warning, he picks me up and hoists me over his shoulder. Smacking my ass hard, he carries me to one of the basement rooms with his brother following close behind us.

Once we're inside the small concrete cell, the clown sets me on my feet. He doesn't bother to close the huge steel door because there is no way anyone but them or my husbands could get in here anyway. Then he hands his AK47 to his brother, who leans both guns against the wall before standing beside us.

"You got any rope left?" the clown asks.

The vampire unhooks a thick coil of heavy rope from his utility belt and hands it to his brother with a wink. Then he lies back on the bed in the center of the room, hands behind his head as he and watches us intently.

"You seriously need to tie me up?" I ask with a pop of one eyebrow. "Are you that afraid I can take you down?"

The vein in his temple throbs as he narrows his eyes at me. "Don't need to tie you up," he grunts as he spins me around, pinning my wrists together before securing them with the rope. "I just want to," he adds with a wicked chuckle, pulling the rope tighter as he finishes his final knot. I gasp in a breath as the thick cord bites into my skin.

Once he's satisfied that the bindings are tight enough, he spins me back around. "On your knees. Now," he snarls as he unbuckles his belt and unzips his trousers.

I sink to my knees, watching him freeing his cock from his pants as I wait for further instructions. He grabs my jaw between his thumb and forefinger, tilting my head as far back as it can go as he stares down at me. "You still think you can take everything I have to give?"

I lick my lips. "And then some."

He arches an eyebrow. "We'll see about that. Yeah?"

"Mmm," I murmur, leaning forward without waiting for any further permission, I lick the bead of precum from the tip of his cock before opening my mouth wide to take him inside.

"Fuck me, you're dangerous," he groans, rocking his hips until I swallow the crown. Pressing the flat of my tongue against his shaft, I suck softly and his moans turn to grunts as he pushes deeper. Both of his hands fist in my hair, tightening at the roots so that he can hold my head still while he fucks my mouth. "You keep sucking my cock this good and I might just keep you."

"Hmmf," I mumble, my mouth stuffed full as he rams his cock against the back of my throat so hard that drool dribbles down my chin and onto my chest.

"She good, bro?" the vampire asks.

"Fuck yeah," the clown hisses, fingers digging even tighter into my scalp as he fucks my face with deep, punishing thrusts.

"I wonder how wet you're making her fucking her throat like that."

The clown tilts his head so he can look me in the eye, pulling his mask down and revealing his familiar handsome face. "You're soaking, aren't you, Red?"

I bat my eyelashes to signal that yes, I most definitely am. My entire body is trembling with anticipation and excitement. I love pushing their buttons, and I especially love when they get into a little role playing with me. He winks before he puts his mask back in place. "Yeah, I definitely think we can find a few uses for this one, bro," he grunts as he sinks deeper, slipping further down my throat.

I wish my hands were free so I could hold onto his muscular thighs as he punishes me, throat fucking me relentlessly as his fingers dig into my scalp and his rope cuts into my wrists. My knees are aching from the force of him thrusting into me while I'm kneeling on the cold concrete floor, but my pussy is dripping wet for him and his brother. Desperate for them both to use me in any way they want.

"Maybe we will keep her then," the vampire's soft laugh drifts through the room but it's almost drowned out by the blood rushing in my ears.

"Jesus. Fuck!" the clown roars as he grinds his hips one last time, shoving every single millimeter of his cock down my throat, and I lap it up, sucking and licking him as he slowly slips out of my mouth, greedy for every single drop he'll give me.

He wipes some drool and cum from my chin, and I smile up at him, desperate for his approval now that I've got what I wanted from him. His dark eyes twinkle, and I can tell he's smiling behind that mask but he doesn't speak the words I'm waiting for. Not yet.

He pulls me up and I stand on shaky legs. Then he takes a huge hunting knife from one of the pockets of his pants. "Such a shame to ruin this pretty dress."

"So don't. It's one of my favorites," I remind him. In fact, he bought me it.

But he takes no notice, taking hold of the neck of my dress, he uses the blade to slice a clean cut straight down the center until it's hanging from my arms .

His gaze drifts down to my panties. They are black lace – his favorite kind. "And it's a damn shame to ruin these," he adds right before he cuts the panties off me too. The remaining scraps of fabric slide down my legs, landing in a pile at my feet.

"You could have just taken them off," I fake my indignation as I kick off my sneakers along with the remaining fabric. But the truth is every cell in my body is desperate to have his hands on me again.

"Don't forget the bra," the vampire pipes up from his spot on the bed where he has a ringside seat to this particular show.

"I'm on it," his brother replies before slicing through the front of that too until it's hanging off my arms along with my dress.

"Her clothes are still in the way," the vampire says with a sigh.

The clown rolls his eyes, but then he cuts through the remaining fabric until it all slips from my body, leaving me standing naked with my arms tied around my back. "Better?" he asks.

"Yes," both me and the vampire say in unison.

The clown narrows his eyes at me as he pockets his knife. Then he slips a hand between my thighs and I lean into his body, seeking the heat and warmth of him in the cold room. His fingers glide through my slick folds, eliciting a soft moan from my lips.

"So wet," he hisses, the pads of his fingers rubbing firmly over my swollen clit. "Did one of your husbands just fuck you?"

Heat flushes over my chest and neck. "No," I whisper truthfully.

He dips the tip of one finger inside me and a rush of wet heat makes my legs almost buckle. "So is this all for me and my brother?" he asks with a cock of one eyebrow.

"For your brother," I pant, teasing him. "I have a thing for fangs."

"Oh yeah?" he snarls.

"Yeah," I whimper.

He wraps one of his huge arms around me, holding me close as he thrusts a second finger inside me. He's rougher now and I suck in a breath as he gives me exactly what I need from him.

I press my body into his, my face against his neck as I inhale the scent of his skin, mixed with the scent of blood and dirt on his clothes. The thick material is rough against my soft flesh as he holds me tighter, and I moan loudly as my senses threaten to overwhelm me. He finger fucks me harder, forcing me onto my tiptoes as he drives deeper and rougher. The pads of his fingertips press against the sweet spot inside me that has my legs trembling and my heart pounding in my ears. I would do anything right now for the promise of what he can deliver and he knows it.

"You hear how wet she is?" he groans as his fingers grow slicker with my arousal.

"Yup."

"Oh, fuck," I moan as heat furls up my spine and pleasure sizzles through my nerve endings. And right when I'm about to fall off the edge, the clown stops. Pulling his hand from between my thighs, he leaves me a trembling mess.

"Mikey," I whimper in protest

"Who the fuck is Mikey?" he laughs darkly before slipping his fingers beneath his mask and sucking them clean. "Besides, it's my brother's turn to have a little fun with you now."

"Sure is. Come here," the vampire, says, holding out one hand to me while he has the other wrapped around the base of his thick cock.

"Go make him come as hard as you just made me and maybe you might get a little something in return," Mikey says as he turns me, guiding me toward the bed.

My eyes focus on his twin, Liam – and I don't think I have

ever seen him look hotter than he does in his black camo gear. My pussy is aching to have him inside me.

As soon as I'm in touching distance, Liam grabs hold of me, pulling me down onto the bed until I'm straddling him. He pulls his mask down, tucking it beneath his chin. "Come sit up here." He traces his fingers over his lips. "I want to taste you."

Oh yes please! My legs tremble violently as my body screams for some release. With the help of Liam's hands on my hips, I shuffle up the bed until I'm sitting directly above his face.

"You smell delicious, baby. He got you nice and wet for me, huh?"

"Yeah," I gasp as he pulls me down, until his mouth is on my sensitive flesh. He mumbles appreciatively as his mouth settles over my clit. He flicks the sensitive bud with his tongue, and soon enough I can't help from grind against his face.

"Don't make her come," Mikey says, causing Liam to stop what he's doing.

He twists his head so he can speak, leaving me panting and breathless as tremors wrack my body. "The fuck?"

"You think she deserves to come?"

"It wasn't me she was giving attitude to, bro," Liam laughs softly before he goes back to eating my pussy. I close my eyes, focusing on Liam's expert mouth as the familiar tightening of my impending orgasm builds in my core.

My eyes fly open as Mikey tugs my hair again, but the sharp pain in my scalp only intensifies the pleasure his brother's tongue is bringing me. He presses his mouth against my ear. "Yeah, why was that? Why did I getting all your attitude, Red? You think I'm just a clown, is that it?"

"N-no," I whimper.

He yanks my hair harder just as Liam sucks on my clit with the perfect amount of pressure, nudging either side with his tongue until I'm exploding like a million tiny fire-bursts of energy. I close my eyes, rocking my hips over Liam's face as he sucks and licks me through my climax.

And as I'm coming down from the high and Liam goes on softly nuzzling my sensitive flesh, Mikey keeps his lips pressed close to my ear. "Enjoy him fucking you, Red, because as soon as he's done, you're mine." His tone is so low and menacing, Liam won't have heard what he said. And it's so unlike how Mikey has ever spoken to me before, that it makes a shiver run the length of my spine.

My head spins as I try to process what's going on with him, while still reeling from the orgasm Liam just gave me, so when Liam lifts me off his face and pulls me down the bed, impaling me on his huge cock instead, I gasp in surprise. He fills me to the hilt, groaning loudly as he sinks balls deep inside me.

"Oh, fuck," I cry out, biting on my lip to stop from screaming the entire basement down.

"I got you, baby," he soothes, brushing my hair back from my face and I stare down at his handsome face, trying to avoid the heat of Mikey's gaze as he watches us – waiting his turn.

"You feel so good," he groans, holding my hips still while he drives up into me, taking all of the control while I battle to stay upright. I wrestle against my restraints, desperate to touch him and hold on to something as he rails into me. Hitting a spot deep inside me over and over again until I'm about ready to beg him to never ever stop.

Sweat beads over my skin and my eyelids flutter as he brings me close to another orgasm quickly, as though the last one never quite had the time to ebb away completely and the next one caught it's flickering coat tails.

"Fuck, baby. Can you come for me again?" he grunts, his fingers digging into my hips.

"Yeah," I whimper.

"That's my girl."

His words tip me over the edge and I slump forward, my forehead pressed against his hard chest as another orgasm tears through me. Tears run down my face and my body shakes uncontrollably as the aftershocks roll through me.

I melt into Liam's body as he keeps his strong arms wrapped around me while he drives into me until he finds his own release. "You did so good, baby," he groans in my ear, "you feel so good squeezing my cock when you come."

I breathe him in, my face buried in his clothes as my senses are overwhelmed with him. I feel him everywhere, like a blanket over my skin.

"You two done?" Mikey asks impatiently, reminding us he's still in the room.

Liam brushes my hair back from my face and narrows his eyes at me. "We done here?"

I nod my head, unable to form a coherent word right now.

"Good girl," he says before giving me a soft kiss on the forehead.

"Flip her onto her back," Mikey orders.

"Let me cut her arms free—"

"No. Leave her arms as they are."

Liam looks at me, his brow furrowed in concern now. Mikey seems super pissed, but maybe I kind of want him to be, and I can handle him.

"It's fine," I assure him. My arms are uncomfortable tied like this, but I'm nowhere near my pain threshold yet.

"Whatever you say," Liam says with a wink.

Then he slips out from under me and rolls me onto my back, until I'm lying with my bound arms tied behind me looking up into the brooding, sexy, if slightly angry, face of Mikey Ryan. Him being dressed entirely in black gives his already formidable appearance an even more sinister edge, and I swallow hard as the heat from his gaze sears my skin.

Liam zips up his pants and leans against the wall, his arms folded across his chest as he watches his brother and me with interest.

"So I'm just a clown to you, am I, Jessie?" Mikey growls as he crawls over me on the tiny bed until his knees are pinning my thighs together and his forearms are either side of my head.

"You had a clown mask on," I whisper a reminder.

"But that's not what you were talking about, is it?"

I blink at him in confusion.

"Is it?" he barks.

"I don't think you're a clown."

"No?" He frowns, pulling the huge knife from his pocket again.

I glance at the blade as the metal flashes beneath the fluorescent light. "No."

He pushes himself up until all of his weight is on one forearm before trailing the tip of the blade down over my chest. I draw in a sharp breath that makes my breasts shudder and my pebbled nipples graze the thick fabric of his clothes, causing heat to bloom beneath the skin there. The tip of the blade gets lower and I squirm beneath the delicate taunt of the metal as he traces it over my skin. I steal a glance at Liam, who remains watching intently, his muscles tense as he waits to see whatever his twin has planned.

"You know what I think?" Mikey dips the tip of the blade between my thighs and I freeze on instinct.

"Mikey!" Liam warns but his brother doesn't acknowledge that he's spoken. Instead he goes on staring at me, his dark eyes burning into mine. Every muscle in his body seems to vibrate with the effort of holding himself back.

"I think that you were talking about way more than the mask, Red. You come to me when you're looking for a little fun, right? Sometimes, I wonder if me being that for you has made you forget who I really am."

My heart kicks up another gear as he slips that blade a little lower, pressing the flat of the tip against my clit. I glare at him, hoping the fire in my eyes matches his. "I have never forgotten for a second who you really are, Mikey Ryan."

He runs his teeth over the curve of my jaw before he asks, "and who is that, Red?"

"A man who comes home to his wife and children soaked in the blood of his enemies."

I gasp as he presses the blade a little firmer, but Mikey simply smirks at my reaction. He's a man of many talents, and one of them is being a skilled chef, which means that he handles knives like no-one else I've ever known. I'm not in any danger with him. I don't know what's going on with him right now – whether he's pissed or hurting – but I can be whatever he needs, just like he would do for me.

"Just because you make me laugh more than any other person I know, and because you're my best friend..." I suck in a breath and his eyes soften a little at those words. "That doesn't mean I don't know the kind of man you really are – the same kind you've always been."

"Hmm," he murmurs, pressing soft kisses over my throat as he holds the knife still against me. "Now I think maybe you're just trying to make me go a little easier on you."

"I don't need you to go easy," I pant as the blood thunders around my body. My clit throbs against the pressure of his blade and I want to rock my hips against it despite how dangerous that would be.

"You don't, huh?" he teases me as his lips dust over my collarbone, making me shiver.

"No," I groan, frustrated at being unable to move. I want to touch him. Weave my fingers through his hair and wrap my legs around his waist as I grind myself on his huge cock.

"Shall I fuck you with my knife?" he whispers softly.

"Fuck me with anything you want, just fuck me," I hiss, my skin burning with fire and need.

"You're such a needy little hostage," he laughs darkly. "But I think I want to feel that tight pussy for myself." He tosses the knife onto the floor and my entire body sags against the mattress as my muscles relax.

The sound of his zipper opening makes wet heat sear between my thighs – dammit these boys play me like a violin. Mikey shifts his position so that he can lift my legs up in the air, until the backs of my calves are pressed against his chest and my feet are either side of his head. My arms burn as all my weight rests on them, and I wince as the rope digs into my wrists.

"You sure you don't want me to take it easy on you?" he asks with a grin.

I glare at him, refusing to back down because I can take whatever he can give me and then some. "Give me everything you got."

That devilish grin he had on his face turns downright sadistic as he slams into me, knocking the air from my body and making my teeth rattle in my head.

"Holy fuck."

"Fuck, you're so tight like this," he groans as he pulls out and slams into me again.

"Is that all you got?" I pant even as my internal organs feel like they've turned to molten lava.

"You want more?"

"Much more."

He leans down, planting his hands either side of my head and folding me like a pretzel before he drives into me again, and my eyes almost roll out of my head. "Fuck, Red, you're going to fucking kill me," he growls as he nails me to the tiny bed with so much force the small metal frame ricochets off the wall.

My core tightens and my walls clench around his cock, squeezing him deeper as he rails into me with everything he has. The bed squeaks and rattles but the noise is mostly drowned out by Mikey's growling and grunting in my ear as he fucks me mercilessly.

He doesn't ease off when I scream his name as my orgasm crashes into me like a freight train. He doesn't ease off when the metal legs break under the force of his thrusting and the entire bed crashes to the floor. He wraps my legs around his waist instead, burying his face into my neck as he fucks me like a man possessed. When he finds his own release he roars my name as he grinds out every drop of himself into me.

I pant for breath, his heavy weight on top of me causing my arms to start feeling completely numb.

"Fuck, Jessie," he groans as he pushes himself up onto his forearms allowing me some room to move. Then he seals his lips over mine, slipping his tongue into my mouth and kissing me so hard I almost lose my breath again. He tastes so good. Of fresh air and mint and a little bourbon.

I'm left wanting when he pulls back, grinning at me like he knows exactly what his kisses do to me.

"Good girl," he says softly and my face breaks into a huge smile.

A second later, Liam is crouched down beside us, with his knife in his hand. "Sit up, baby."

Mikey pushes himself onto his knees, helping me to sit up so that Liam can cut the ropes binding my arms. As soon as my limbs are free, they each take hold of an arm and begin to rub, soothing my aching muscles and increasing the blood flow.

Liam leans in and kisses me softly too, his tongue exploring my mouth like his twin's just did. He tastes of fresh air and bourbon too, and a hint of cinnamon from his favorite gum.

"You okay?" Liam asks me, his eyes full of concern as he breaks our kiss.

"Of course," I assure him before I turn to Mikey. "Are you?"

He pushes a damp strand of hair from my face as his eyes search mine. "I am now. I guess I had some anger to burn off."

"I guess you did."

Mikey maneuvers into a sitting position, his legs outstretched in front of him before pulling me to straddle his lap. Then Liam moves in behind us, kneeling between his twin's legs and pressing his chest up against my back. He pulls my hair to one side, peppering soft kisses over my neck while Mikey goes on rubbing my arms and my wrists.

"Those outfits are super hot, by the way," I say with a contented sigh.

"They're not outfits," Liam says.

"They're work attire," Mikey adds.

"Whatever. They're hot."

"Yeah, we kind of figured that, Red. You're a fucking deviant."

"Yeah," Liam agrees as he wraps his arms around me. "You almost made Mikey lose his shit."

"I did not," I insist.

"Yeah, you did," Mikey groans. "I almost fucked you with my knife."

"Well, if you're going to come home dressed like that and carrying guns..." I shrug.

"You hate guns, baby," Liam reminds me.

"Yeah, but not when you two are holding them like that."

"See? A deviant?" Mikey says with a wink.

"Well if I am, it's because you boys make me that way."

"I'll take that," Liam says as his hand dips between my

thighs again. "And I'll take you again too, as soon as we've all had a shower, baby."

"How about a hot bubble bath instead?" I suggest, leaning back against him as his fingers soothe my throbbing pussy.

"Sounds like fucking heaven. So let's get you upstairs," Mikey replies.

Liam stands first and then he lifts me into his arms. I wrap my arms around his neck while Mikey grabs the guns, and then the three of us head to the elevator.

"If Shane and Conor see us like this then they are going to crash our tub," Mikey says with a soft chuckle.

"Fine by me," I giggle.

"Deviant," Mikey mutters.

"You love it," I remind him.

"I fucking love you, Red."

"I love you both too," I sigh contentedly, nuzzling my face against Liam's hot neck. I think I might just be the luckiest girl in the whole damn world.

A RYAN REVIEW

A NEW YORK RUTHLESS SHORT STORY

JESSIE

Heavy bass music thumps in my ears. Two thick arms band around my waist, pulling me closer until my back is pressed up against his firm chest. I wiggle my ass, rubbing it over his hard length and earning myself a warning nip at my neck. Then his lips ghost over my ear.

"If you want to watch the rest of the show, you'd better behave yourself, baby. You know I don't do the public fucking thing." His warm breath dusts over my skin, making me shiver in anticipation.

"I know," I say with a wicked smile, as I push my ass back against him, settling into a comfortable position in his arms as I keep my eyes fixed on the stage in front of us. The dull ache between my thighs grows more insistent as I watch the couple in the center of the room.

The woman wears nothing but a pair of crotchless panties, and a thick leather collar around her neck, while her Dom is dressed in black suit pants and shirt. She's kneeling at his feet, drool dripping from her chin as he fucks her mouth with his fingers after he made her crawl to him. I'm so impressed by her confidence and her focus. With at least a hundred pairs of eyes on her ass and pussy, she crawled the length of the twenty feet of stage to get to him, never once taking her eyes off his face. And the way he looks at her... wow! It's all super hot.

"Fuck," I whisper, sinking my teeth into my bottom lip as I grind myself against Liam, making him groan as his cock twitches against my ass.

"You like what you see, baby?" he says in my ear.

"Fuck, yes," I pant as heat blooms beneath my skin.

"You should. The first theme night has been a hit." He kisses my neck and I drop my head back against his shoulder, taking my eyes off the scene on the stage for a few seconds as I allow him easier access to my throat. "You did a good job, baby. I'm so fucking proud of you." He kisses me again, this time trailing his teeth tantalizingly over my sensitive skin and making wet heat sear between my thighs.

"Thank you," I say with a soft purr. I love running our private clubs and I'm so relieved that my worries over the first theme night were entirely unfounded, because we sold out within hours of tickets going on sale, and it has been a phenomenal success. The 'show' on stage is just one of the many unscripted ones that's taken place tonight. Anyone can get up there and perform, but this couple are clearly very well versed in public displays, and the connection between them is fire.

He skates a hand over my abdomen, dangerously close to my pussy. "Liam," I whimper.

"I know, baby," he groans in my ear. "I want to fuck you just as bad as you want me to, but we can't leave just yet."

I groan in frustration because I know he's right. This is our big night. Along with our dedicated team of staff we've put a ton of work into it. A lot of important people have come here tonight and we owe it to our team to remain here for the duration of the evening. I wish we'd reserved ourselves one of the private rooms for a few hours though. I should have known spending time with any of my husbands in this place would leave me feeling wet and needy.

I snake an arm around Liam's neck, pulling that delicious mouth of his closer. "We do have an office here."

"Yeah, and it's currently being used as a green room for the *talent*," he reminds me.

"Damn!" Of course it is. I agreed to allow the dancers we booked for tonight to use the room to take a break, and to change.

He dips his hand a little lower until it's resting at the very base of my abdomen, directly above where I want to feel him the most. He pulls me tighter, making hot pleasure pulse through my core. "We have two hours until I can take you home."

"Mmm," I murmur as my eyes drift back to the show on stage. "I guess I'll just watch someone else get fucked for now then."

"And while you do, you can think about how fucking hard you make me, and how hard I'm going to fuck you as soon as I can get you alone," he says with a deep throaty growl.

I blow a stray strand of hair out of my eyes. Yeah, that's not going to make this any easier at all.

"The boss told me he wants to see you downstairs. Room twelve." Rochelle, our club manager, says, lips quirking in a knowing smile.

I arch an eyebrow at her. The club will stay open as long as people are still here having fun, but it's two am and that means Liam and I can leave without feeling like we're abandoning the team. "The boss, huh?"

She tilts her head, eyes twinkling with amusement. "That's what he said to tell you."

"I thought all of the rooms were booked tonight?"

"Room twelve was reserved earlier and has been thoroughly cleaned to your exacting standards."

"Room twelve, huh?"

She nods her head. "I'll let the team know you're no longer available, Mrs. Ryan," she says with a soft purr as she unclips the thick velvet rope granting me access to the stairwell.

The bouncers standing at the bottom of the stairs nod to me in greeting as I pass. What the hell is Liam up to? I mean I can take a pretty good guess that it involves me getting naked given that he's waiting in one of the private rooms, but we could have easily done that in the car on the way home to our penthouse apartment, where his three brothers—my other husbands—are waiting for us.

The Boss? My lips curl into a smile, even if I am little confused, because while Liam Ryan fucks like a demon and has the body of a god, he's not usually into playing games.

My stomach flutters with excitement and anticipation as I push open the black door and step into the room. Liam sits in the large leather wingback chair, legs spread wide. His tie hangs loose around his neck and the sleeves of his white dress shirt are rolled up, revealing his thick tattooed forearms as he rests his chin on his hand. He's half shrouded in shadow but I can see his dark eyes raking over my body. He is one of the most handsome men I've ever laid eyes on, but I don't think I've ever seen him looking so damn fine as he does right now. Electric sexual tension crackles in the air between us.

"You wanted to see me, Sir?" I ask with a soft purr, closing the door behind me and playing into whatever game it is he has in mind.

"Hmm," he murmurs as his eyes lock on mine. "I believe it's time for your performance review."

Oh, so that's his angle? Warmth pools in my core. "Yes, I believe it is, Sir," I whisper, fluttering my eyelashes. "Are we doing it in here?"

His eyes twinkle with wicked deviance. "We sure are. So strip," he orders, his voice so low and commanding that it makes my thighs tremble and my pussy clench with need.

Reaching behind me, I pull down the long zip at the back of my dress and shrug it off slowly, while Liam watches me so intently I can almost feel the burn of his gaze on my skin. As I shimmy the dress past my hips and reveal my panties, I have to roll my lips to suppress a smile when I hear the animalistic growl that rumbles in his throat at the sight of them. They are plain white cotton. All four of my husbands have different taste in panties and the plain white cotton kind drive this one crazy.

He adjusts his cock in his suit pants. "You wear them for me?"

I smile sweetly. "Yes, Sir."

"Leave them on. Take off everything else," he commands and the deep timbre of his voice makes me shiver.

I continue undressing, taking off my bra and slipping off my heels until I'm standing a few feet away from him in only a scrap of white fabric. I sink my teeth into my lower lip as I watch him, his eyes still full of fire and his muscles tense as he stares at me. "What now, Sir?"

He licks his bottom lip and then one corner of his mouth curls in a half smile. "Crawl to me."

I blink at him in surprise. Of all of the words that I expected to come out of that man's mouth, those were not even on the same page.

"Don't make me repeat myself, baby," he says, his voice a low raspy growl that makes my knees weak.

Holy fuck! With trembling limbs, I sink to the floor and fall forward until I'm on all fours. My eyes never leave his face as I watch a devious, sexy smile spread across his face.

Sucking on my bottom lip I slowly crawl forward, keeping my eyes on him as the sexual tension ratchets up about three hundred levels. My clit pulses with need and wet heat slicks between my thighs.

"That's it, baby, all the way," he says with a throaty growl as he squeezes his cock through his pants. I edge closer until I'm just a couple of feet away from him and I catch the scent of his expensive cologne. "Let's soak those sweet little panties of yours."

Holy mother, why is this so damn hot?

I look up expectantly when I reach him and he grabs hold of my jaw, pulling me up into a kneeling position. I shuffle closer until I'm wedged between his hard thighs and the heat from him warms me from the inside.

I bat my eyelashes. "What now, Sir?"

He narrows his dark eyes as his tongue darts out to moisten his lips and I have to stop myself from lunging forward and kissing him. "Well," his eyes twinkle with devious intent, "this performance review will involve all three of your holes, and as you're already on your knees," he slides his thumb into my mouth and I swirl my tongue around the tip, "maybe we should start with this one."

I suck his thumb hard before releasing it with a wet pop. "If that's what you want, Sir."

Without taking my eyes off his I unfasten his belt and zipper before freeing his huge hard cock from his boxers. I wrap my hand around his shaft and he hisses out a strained breath that makes me smile. I love seeing my strong, powerful husband coming so easily undone.

"Let's see just how much you've learned since you started here, huh?" he says with a groan.

My pleasure. I squeeze his cock before licking the precum that weeps from the crown. "You taste so good, Sir," I moan softly before I wrap my lips around his shaft and suck him into my mouth until he hits the back of my throat.

He fists his hand in my hair, tangling his fingers through the strands at the back of my head as he shifts his hips until I take his entire length.

"So fucking good," he says with a groan. "You trained that gag reflex right out, huh?"

"Mmhmm," I murmur as I hollow my cheeks and suck him hard, because the quicker I can get him off like this, the sooner he'll fuck me and I was ready for him to do that about two hours ago when we were watching the couple on the stage.

"How'd you get so good at sucking cock, baby?" he says with a deep groan that rumbles through his entire body.

He threads his fingers tighter into my hair as he rocks his hips, fucking my mouth while I lick and suck his beautiful cock. I plant my hands on his powerful thighs, squeezing his muscles as he rocks into me and reveling in the control he allows me to have over him in moments like these.

I swallow, squeezing the crown of his cock in my throat and making his eyes roll back in his head. "Fuck, baby," he grits out the words, pushing my head down further as he drives his hips upward. I take a deep breath through my nose, saliva dripping down my chin and wetness seeping into my panties as I suck him to a climax.

He releases his grip on my hair and sinks into the chair as I let him slip from my mouth, swallowing as much of his cum as I can, but some still drips down my chin and he brushes it away with his thumb. "You're so fucking beautiful," he rasps.

"Did I pass my review, Sir?" I ask with a flutter of my eyelashes.

He arches an eyebrow at me, gripping my jaw between his thumb and forefinger. "We didn't cover all aspects of your performance yet, baby."

I bite into my lip, clenching my thighs to stem the growing ache between them. Liam stands, his six foot four frame towering over me. He tips my head back, eyes raking over my body as they darken with heat and desire. "Crawl to the bed," he orders.

Heat coils up my spine. He rarely shows this side of himself, at least not with me. He's my best friend and my sweet, caring teddy bear, and given that his brothers, particularly the oldest one, have the whole bossy asshole routine down perfectly, I love how different my relationship with him is. However, I can't deny how much I love it when he lets this side of himself out to play.

I do as he asks, crawling to the bed and making sure to wiggle my ass as much as possible and give him a show as I do. He rewards me by slapping my ass hard as he drops to his knees behind me as soon as I reach the huge four poster bed in the center of the room.

"Liam," I groan out his name as wet heat sears between my thighs.

"Bend over the bed," he says with a growl and another smack.

"Ow." I pout dramatically as I lay my face against the crisp cotton sheet.

"Don't pretend like that hurt, baby," he says with a dark laugh. "I know you can take way more than that." He curls his fingers in the waistband of my panties. "These are so fucking sexy on you," he grunts the last words as he tugs them roughly over my behind until they're sitting at the top of my thighs. "You know I love fucking you in these."

"I do," I giggle.

He spanks me again and warm pleasure rolls through me. "Is that why you wore them?"

"Yes," I admit on a moan.

"You knew I was going to fuck you before we got home?" He smacks my ass harder and I cry out. "Because I can't keep my goddamn hands off you, baby, can I?"

He doesn't give me a chance to reply before he slides two thick fingers inside me, ripping a guttural groan from deep in my core.

Liam groans too. "You know how much I fucking love how wet sucking my cock makes you, baby?"

"Uh-huh," I pant as he drives his fingers deeper, rubbing the tips against the sweet spot inside me while he spanks my ass again.

"Because your tight little pussy is so wet, you're dripping down my hand."

"Liam!" I cry out his name as my inner walls clench around him and pleasure coils deep in my core, spiraling out until it winds through my limbs.

"Or is it the spanking making you soaking like this?" He spanks me again to emphasize his point and I bite into the covers as my hands fist in the soft cotton bedsheets. "Fuck," he grunts as my pussy squeezes him like a vise and my climax tears through me like black powder.

"Liam," I pant his name as I struggle to breathe.

He slaps my ass again. "Sir," he reminds me with a growl.

"Sir," I breathe.

He slides his fingers out of me and I hear him sucking them clean as he rubs his free hand over my back. "Time to see how well this sweet pussy can take my cock, huh?"

"Please, Sir," I whimper, already needy for more of him.

Grabbing hold of my hips, his fingertips dig into my soft flesh as he lines the tip of his cock at my entrance.

"So tight, baby," he grunts before he drives all the way inside me, making me moan loudly. He slams into me, pinning me to the bed. Heat and pleasure coil around my spine and I push my hips back against him, desperate for everything he can give me. "Your pussy feels so good wrapped around my cock," he says with a deep, rumbling groan.

Leaning over me, he presses his hot mouth against my ear. "Let's see how hard I can make you come with just my cock." He rolls his hips, hitting the perfect spot inside me that makes me whimper desperately.

"Oh, fuck, Sir."

"Fuck, Jessie," he grunts as he drives harder. "Your pussy... you take my cock so fucking well, baby."

"Yes," I whimper as hot, pulsing pleasure rolls through every part of my body. And my sex god of a husband goes on railing me relentlessly, until I cry out his name and almost pass out with the strength of the climax he wrenches from my body.

I lay my face on the bed, panting breathlessly and craning my neck so that I can watch Liam. He pulls out of me, leaving a trail of my cum to drip down my thighs. He scoops some of it up with his pointer finger and then sucks it from his fingertip. "You taste so fucking sweet too, don't you? Too fucking sweet to resist?" He spanks my ass again when I don't answer. "Don't you?"

"Yes," I groan.

He grabs my hair at the nape of my neck, yanking me backward until my back is pressed up against his chest. I whimper as pain burns through my scalp, making more wetness slick between my thighs.

"You're doing so well, baby. You want to be a good girl and let me fuck this juicy ass now?" He slides his wet fingers between my cheeks, pressing the tip of one inside me.

"Y-yes," I gasp, rocking back against him.

"Yes what?" He drives his finger deeper and I melt against him. Damn, he plays my body like he can read my freaking mind.

"Yes, Sir."

"Good fucking girl," he grunts in my ear before pushing me back down onto the bed. "But I think we need to get these panties all the way off you first, huh?" He tugs them down over my thighs. "These are fucking soaking." He pulls them off and holds them in front of my eyes. "And this is all you. See how wet you got for me, baby?"

"Yes." My cheeks burn with heat.

Then with a low growl, he presses them against my face. "Smell how fucking hard I make you come."

Holy fuck! The scent of my own arousal fills my nose and I groan loudly.

"You want to taste too?" He wads them into a ball and wipes them over my lips. "Open."

I press my lips together, wanting to see how far I can push my usually sweet, sensitive husband.

"Open. Your. Fucking. Mouth," he growls.

The deep, commanding timbre of his voice sends pleasure and excitement skittering up my spine. A deep, aching heat rolls in my core and I open my mouth, allowing him to stuff my wet panties inside.

Then without any further warning, he pushes the tip of his thick cock into my ass. The sensation of him stretching me open with only my own cum as lube makes pleasure and a delicious burning pain snake up my spine, each sensation fighting for control of my body. And when he bites down on my neck as he pushes his cock deeper inside me, pleasure wins out and I moan, the sound muffled by the damp fabric.

He leans over me again, his chiseled chest pressed up at my back and his muscular thighs flush against mine as he pins me flat to the mattress "Jesus, fuck, your ass is tight," he says with a grunt. "Your review is going so well, baby, I think I might just keep you."

Yes please, Sir.

"How about you become my personal assistant, huh? My own personal fuck-toy to use whenever I feel like it."

Holy goddamn fuckballs, who is this guy and what has he done with Liam? I nod my head, my words of agreement far too muffled by my panty gag for him to understand.

"Yeah," he grunts, teeth trailing over my shoulder blades. "Keep you locked in this room so I can fuck you all day and all night?"

"Hmm," I mumble before taking a deep breath through my nose as he drives into me even harder until tiny specks of light pepper my vision and molten heat sears though my body. He pulls out slowly before driving back in hard again. And he does it over and over, relentless and frustratingly steady, keeping me on the edge of complete oblivion.

I moan as loudly as the gag allows, wishing I could beg him for more—or less—or to go harder—or stop—anything other than the delicious, slow torture of the way he's fucking me.

I try to push backwards against him, but he holds me in place with his huge, powerful frame, laughing darkly at my efforts. "Aw, you want to come again, baby?"

"Mmff." I nod as tears roll down my cheeks.

He pulls out slowly again. "You think you passed your review?"

I nod again.

"Yeah?" He drives back inside and I almost black out with the strength of the tremors that wrack my body.

"I dunno, baby," he whispers hoarsely. "Maybe I'll need to go another round or two before I decide." He licks a tear from my cheek before burying his face in the crook of my neck. Then he places his huge hands over mine, uncurling my fingers from the sheets, before he raises them above my head and pins my wrists to the bed.

I whimper because I know he's about to nail me into the afterlife, or at the very least a coma.

"You. Make. Me. So. Fucking. Hard," he grunts close to my ear, punctuating each word with a thrust of his hips.

I take a deep breath through my nose. My heart races. Blood thunders through my veins. Electric pulses of pleasure vibrate through every cell in my body.

"I love you so fucking much," he groans as he rolls his hips, rocking them slowly and sinking deeper into me than before. And it's my undoing. I come hard, shaking and trembling as a torrent of arousal rushes between my thighs, making Liam groan loudly and appreciatively as I soak his suit pants. I struggle to breathe and he pulls the wadded up panties from my mouth, allowing me to suck in deep, bone shuddering breaths while he fucks me through the last tremors of my orgasm until he comes too, shouting my name loudly as he does.

"You did so good, baby," Liam soothes as he cradles me in his arms and lies on the bed, pulling me snug against his chest. I nestle into him, completely naked while he's still in suit, but feeling warm and spent.

"Thank you, Sir," I whisper softly making him laugh.

"You liked that, huh?"

I sigh contentedly. "Yes I did."

He drags his knuckles over my cheek. "My pants are soaked in your cum."

I smile, draping my leg over his hip and ensuring our bodies as close together as humanly possible. "I know. But that's all your fault."

"Damn fucking right it is," he says with a possessive growl as he bands one arm tighter around me, while tipping my head up so he can look into my eyes.

"I loved calling you sir," I say with a flutter of my eyelashes.

He arches an eyebrow at me. "Yeah, I got that."

I narrow my eyes in response. "It was super hot, but I hope you don't do all of our staff performance reviews like this?"

That makes him laugh out loud, his chest rumbling with the sound and making me laugh too. God, I love him so freaking much it hurts.

"No, only yours, baby," he assures me. "But I saw how hot that little show with the Dom and his sub got you, and well..." He traces the pad of his thumb over my cheek. "I would have been a fucking idiot not to take advantage of it."

Before I can answer him, the door to the room opens, making Liam tense. Only three other people would be allowed to enter this room while we're in here so I keep my head nestled against Liam's chest, too tired to turn around and see which of his brothers have come looking for us.

"You two were supposed to be home hours ago," Shane says and I smile. I should have known it would be him.

"I sent you a text, bro," Liam replies. His arms tighten around me and he drops a soft kiss on the top of my head.

"Saying you'd be a little late," Shane replies. Then the bed dips beside us and he places a warm, rough hand on my back.

"That was over two hours ago." He nuzzles my neck, making me squirm and giggle in Liam's arms. "Hey, sweetheart."

"Hey," I purr in response.

"We got a little sidetracked," Liam says with a shrug.

"I was worried," Shane murmurs, his warm breath on my skin making goosebumps prickle over my forearms.

"I can take care of our girl, Shane," Liam snaps defensively.

"I know that, son," Shane replies, his voice laced with a hint of a warning. "But I'm still going to worry about you both when you're not home when you say you're going to be."

"He was undertaking my performance review," I add, trying to dilute a little of the alpha male energy in the room.

"Your performance review?" Shane asks, running a hand over my back before squeezing my ass cheek.

"Yep."

"Seeing as how you're both covered in cum, I assume it went well?" he growls.

"I passed with flying colors," I giggle.

"Yeah, she's good. I'm keeping her," Liam says with a grin.

"You know," Shane trails kisses over my back, "as the official head of the family, I have to approve any performance reviews."

"You do?" I ask as he moves that hot, sinful mouth lower and my insides contract with anticipation.

"Yeah," he growls before addressing his younger brother. "So maybe I need to check out just how good she is for myself before I can let you sign off on that review."

A growl rumbles through Liam's chest. "What do you have in mind?"

Shane slips a hand between my thighs, making me gasp. "What have you already done?"

"Fucked her everywhere," Liam says with a wicked laugh.

"Hmm," Shane murmurs appreciatively. "And you said she was good, right?"

I close my eyes and stifle a moan as Shane slides one thick finger inside me.

"She was very fucking good," Liam groans.

"You didn't come in her pussy though." Shane says as he slides in deeper.

My cheeks flush with heat. "How do you know that?"

"You know I can tell the difference between his cum and yours, sweetheart," he reminds me as he slips his hand from between my thighs. "Hold her still for me," he orders his younger brother and the next thing I hear is the sound of his zipper being opened. The ensuing rush of arousal between my thighs makes me gasp for breath.

"Come here, baby," Liam says as he pulls me flat against his chest, keeping his arms wrapped around my back as he hooks his feet over my calves, spreading my legs wide open for his oldest brother.

"Oh, fuck," I moan softly as Shane holds himself over me, nudging the crown of his cock at my entrance.

He places his lips against my ear. "I'm desperate to know if you're as good as he says you are." Then he sinks inside me, right to the hilt, filling me completely as he presses my body into Liam.

"Shane," I whine his name as he rocks into me slowly while Liam holds me tightly.

"Fuck, my brother made you real wet, sweetheart," Shane says with a grunt as he pulls out and slams back inside, hitting that sensitive spot inside me over and over.

"Sure did," Liam chuckles, slipping a hand between our two bodies and rubbing on my throbbing clit.

My inner walls squeeze around Shane as he fucks me hard.

He grunts and growls in my ear, his hot breath warming my skin. "He was right, you are good, sweetheart."

Liam presses harder on my sensitive clit. "Told you, bro."

I suck in a lungful of air. "Oh, God."

"What have I told you about calling for him when I'm inside you," Shane says with a menacing growl that makes my thighs tremble.

"Shane," I moan his name instead.

"Good. Fucking. Girl." He drives into me with each word and my aching pussy squeezes him like it will never let him go. "How many times you been fucked tonight and you still need more."

"I-oh, fuck," I whimper as the pressure of Liam's fingers and Shane's cock drive me to the edge of madness. I feel them both everywhere, as though my body has become a part of theirs and no longer my own. My head spins. Pulse thrums against my skin. I'm going to pass out.

"God, she's fucking beautiful isn't she?" Liam groans as he fists his free hand in my hair, tilting my head so that he can seal his lips over mine. His tongue slides into my mouth, possessive and all consuming, dominating me as much as his brother.

"She's fucking perfect," Shane growls in response.

And that's it. I'm done. Coming apart in their arms as my entire core lights up like a firework display, sending heat and pleasure skittering through every nerve ending in my body. I come loudly, shouting a combination of both of their names—a word that sounds unidentifiable even to my own ears.

"There she is," Shane grunts. "My little hacker." He goes on fucking me, while Liam holds me in his arms and I think I must black out because the next thing I know Shane's pulling out of me and warm cum is running between my legs.

"Holy fuck," I whisper as my eyes flutter closed again.

"So can we keep her?" Liam asks and it makes me smile,

because it was him and his brothers who convinced Shane to take me home instead of killing me the day they first found me.

"I think we gotta," Shane replies breathlessly as he rolls onto his back, pulling me to lie between the two of them. "I'm not sure I could live without this pussy now I've had a taste."

"You didn't taste it," I remind him with a soft, sleepy giggle.

He slaps my ass. "I was speaking figuratively, hacker."

"It's sure fucking sweet tonight, bro," Liam says with a soft appreciative groan.

"I ate earlier in my office." Shane grabs my jaw and turns my head before kissing me softly. "Didn't I?"

"You did," I say with a smile, recalling how he spread me out on his office desk while I was on a call and ate me out while I was trying to negotiate a contract with a whiskey supplier.

Shane checks his watch—the inscribed Breitling I bought him for his fortieth birthday. "We'd better get home before everyone wonders where we are."

"Yeah," Liam sighs his agreement. "Who's up with the tiny demons in a few hours?"

Meanwhile, I snuggle between their two hard bodies, smiling widely as I drift off to sleep in a state of pure bliss while I listen to my incredible husbands talk about our beautiful children.

Have you read Sadie's latest series yet?
You can find Dante here

This is a novella connected to the New York Ruthless series, set after the end of Ryan Renewed. If you haven't read the series yet, you can find them on Amazon and Kindle Unlimited
Ryan Rule
Ryan Redemption
Ryan Retribution

Ryan Reign
Ryan Renewed

Or if you're looking for more spicy short stories, you can find them here

A Ryan Reckoning
A Ryan Rewind
A Ryan Restraint
A Ryan Revelation
A Ryan Recon
A Ryan Halloween
A Ryan Christmas
A Ryan New Year

A RYAN HALLOWEEN

A NEW YORK RUTHLESS NOVELLA

JESSIE

I turn down the small dirt road that leads to the house by the lake. The moon is full tonight, bathing the tree tops in an eerie pale glow which I suppose is fitting for Halloween. This used to be my favorite holiday when I was a kid, but I haven't celebrated it since I was fifteen. I suppose being kidnapped by a psychopath when I was sixteen kind of put a dent in my enjoyment of the holidays in general. Given the hell I went through for the two years afterward, fake ghosts and monsters didn't really hold the same appeal, not when the real ones are so much scarier.

It was my declaration that I could no longer be scared by cheap tricks, Halloween masks or scary movies that has me driving down this dirt road alone. You see, my husbands love Halloween, and they have made me a bet that they will prove me wrong about the whole not being scared thing. So, while our twin babies are being looked after by their great aunt Em, as well as a team of ex Navy SEALs, I am on my way to our house by the lake, in the middle of the woods.

My pulse thrums against my skin as I draw nearer. I have no

idea what the guys have planned, but there is nothing those men could do that I wouldn't love.

As I pull up to the house, I peer through the windshield. It's in darkness. Not a single light on in the whole place. The guys should be here by now though. I laugh to myself. It's going to take more than a dark house to rattle me.

Turning off the engine, I grab my small purse and climb out of the car. Sodden leaves squelch beneath my feet. It's been raining on and off for days, although it's stopped for now. I fix my purse over my shoulder and smooth down the fabric of my mini skirt before pulling my pigtails tighter. The moonlight gives me enough light to check out my outfit. A red and white cheerleader's uniform, complete with white cotton panties and a skirt that barely covers my ass.

The guys didn't go to high school in the States so they missed out on the whole dating a cheerleader experience. I bet they could have dated the head cheerleader too, because I'm pretty sure even in high school they were hotter than hell and could have had their pick of any girl they wanted.

As I walk toward the house, four orbs of light come into view. It's only when I draw nearer I can see they are faces. Four masks that are glowing with LED lights in the darkness. From here, it looks pretty eerie — four disembodied heads floating through the night toward me. They stop on the decking, standing beside each other in a line. It's only once they are still that I can clearly see them. They are dressed entirely in black, except for their faces. Each of them wears an illuminated Halloween mask.

A clown.

A demon.

A vampire.

A devil.

I edge closer to them, looking around me and half expecting

something to pop out or spring up from the ground like a cheesy haunted house trick, but nothing happens.

"Hey, guys," I say with a grin and a wave but they don't respond.

Suddenly, an outside light comes on, temporarily blinding me. Holding my hand over my eyes, I blink, trying to adjust to the sudden brightness. I'm frozen to the spot now. What the hell are these guys up to?

Then one of them speaks, in a creepy voice that I don't recognize. He says only one word and it sends a shiver of fear skittering along my spine.

"Run!"

I will my legs to do that very thing, but my body betrays me as my feet don't seem to get the signal from my brain that I need to move. And so for a few seconds, I stand there as though my feet have taken root like the trees around us. Then I hear a loud grunt as the four dark figures start to move and finally my feet remember what to do.

Turning in the opposite direction, I pump my arms and start to run as fast as I can for the cover of the trees. My little purse flapping wildly against my hipbone reminds me that I have my cell with me if I need it.

I'll be fine.

I got this.

Right?

Adrenaline courses through my veins as I propel myself forward, but my feet slide in the wet mud, costing me vital seconds. I feel them closing in behind me. I hear their heavy breathing. Their heavy footfall as they chase me down. One of them is laughing and the sound sends a chill through my bones.

My heart pounds. Blood rushes in my ears. My brain screams at me to look back to see how close they are, but logic and experience remind me that I can't. It will lose me vital time that I can't afford. Instead, I dart into the trees. I know these woods and they're my best chance of evading my masked pursuers.

As I head into the trees, I see a faint glow of white light darting off to my left. The clown. Then a green light to my right. The demon. So where the hell are the devil and the vampire? I listen intently as I keep moving, dodging the trees as I make my way through the undergrowth. The light from the moon grows dimmer as the branches thicken, and my heart starts to race a little faster as my breathing grows heavier. I suck in a breath, reminding myself that the darkness will work in my favor because the light of their masks makes them more visible to me. I listen for their footsteps but they seem to have faded. Allowing myself a moment, I take a glance backward, feeling a surge of relief when I don't see any of them.

I slow my pace slightly. Now that I'm in the cover of the woods, I can take a minute to think about my best move. Maybe I should circle back to the house? Or would one of them be waiting there for me? Climb a tree and watch them run around looking for me? I press a hand to my mouth and stifle a giggle. Now that would be funny. Looking up at one of the huge trunks, I consider how easy – or not – they are to scale and decide against that option. No doubt those crafty fuckers have night vision goggles in those fancy masks of theirs.

Soft droplets of rain fall onto my face as I stare up and I close my eyes and enjoy the sensation, forgetting for a second that I'm being chased through the woods by four masked men. I love the rain. I love the fall. It's my favorite season.

The snapping of a twig pulls me back to the present and I take a deep breath and start moving again, feeling my way through the trees. My hands brush over the wet bark as I move past each one and I imagine some animal tracing me by my scent. If they were I would lead them straight to me and the thought makes me shudder.

I glance around again but I see no light. What if they turned off the light from their masks though? I mean they're not stupid. They would know how visible that makes them in the darkness. Damn! I hadn't thought of that.

Where the hell are they?

My foot catches on a branch and it snaps — loudly. I freeze, wondering if that is going to draw them closer to me. Listening intently I wait for some signal that one of them is near but all I hear is the sound of my own heavy breathing and my heartbeat in my ears.

I keep moving and the light from the moon grows a little brighter as the trees thin out. My face breaks into a smile because I know this spot near the lake. There is a huge fallen oak somewhere nearby that I like to sit on when we go for walks.

The thought of that is comforting in the darkness, and maybe I am feeling a little too comfortable because I don't hear him approaching until it's too late. The sound of his breathing right behind me shocks my heart like a defibrillator and I start to run again, but I'm not fast enough. My feet slip in the damp leaves as he reaches me, taking me down until I'm lying beneath him.

"Fuck!" I hiss as the breath leaves my lungs and he chuckles softly.

"Got you," he says in that eerie computerized voice and I wonder if the voice changer is a part of the mask too.

My face is inches from the mud as the weight of his body presses me into the damp ground. My heart beats so fast it feels like it's going to hammer straight through my ribcage. I try to shake him off but he is far too heavy to move.

I glance behind me to see that it's the demon who's caught

me first. The light from his mask is softer now but it glows faintly in the darkness, bathing us in a soft green glow. I suppose it might even be slightly romantic if he didn't have me pinned in the mud after chasing me down. I struggle beneath him, reaching back to pull his mask off, but he takes my wrists and pins both of them behind my back with one large hand. I feel his hot breath against my ear and it makes me shiver.

His hand glides down the side of my body until he finds the edge of my tiny cheerleader skirt. "I love your outfit by the way," he says as he slips his hand beneath while he forces my thighs apart with one of his knees.

His hand feels warm against my cold skin as it skates up the inside of my thigh until he reaches my panties. Tugging them roughly to one side, he gives himself easy access to my pussy.

Icy tendrils of fear curl around my spine, making my entire body freeze. I stop breathing and close my eyes tightly. *What if this is real?*

He freezes too. His breathing less steady than before and I wonder what's going through his mind. Then he lets go of my wrists, but he keeps them pinned against my back with the weight of his body. I feel him tugging at his mask and then his lips dust over the shell of my ear.

"You should have run faster," he growls and the deep timbre of his real voice rolls through my body, warming my core and turning the ice cold fear into pulse throbbing heat. "I think you wanted me to catch you."

"No, I didn't," I lie and he chuckles softly before he replaces his mask.

He slides a finger through my folds until he reaches my clit and warmth starts to build in my core as he rubs it softly.

"Oh, fuck," I hiss as I spread my legs wider.

"Oh, you want this?" he says, the voice I don't recognize back now. "You want to be fucked in the mud in the woods?"

"Yes," I gasp and he laughs, the chilling sound echoing through the darkness. I wonder if the others heard it. I wonder if they are here too. Watching us?

"Yeah you do," he says as he drives two fingers inside me. I moan softly as wet heat surges between my thighs. He thrusts them deeper and harder, making me cry out in pleasure. My walls squeeze around him, drawing him further as he finger fucks me roughly. Then his weight leaves me as he pushes himself up. He leans down, his head close to my pussy and I hear a soft sucking sound and wonder what he's doing before he lies on top me again. When his thumb starts sliding between my ass cheeks, I realize he was lubricating it.

"You like being fucked here too, little cheerleader?" he asks as he slides his thumb into my ass and to my shame, I practically purr like a kitten. Damn, he can work my body so well.

"I guess so, huh?" he laughs again as he starts to fuck both of my holes now until I'm rocking my hips and ass against his hand, chasing the orgasm that I know he's so very capable of delivering. "You want me to make you come now?" He drives deeper and harder and I gasp loudly.

My cheek presses against the mud but I don't care. I can't hold my head up any longer while he's teasing me like this.

"Yes," I whimper as my thighs tremble with my impending release.

"Beg me and I'll let you come."

"Please? I'll do whatever you want," I plead with him as he pushes his thumb deeper while he curls his fingers inside my pussy, pressing against that spot deep inside me that would make me agree to absolutely anything.

"Whatever I want? What if I want to keep this pretty ass and pussy for my own?" He thrusts deeper. "What if I want to fuck them every single day? Over and over?"

"Yes."

"Yeah?" he works his fingers harder inside me, rubbing at those sensitive spots until stars are flickering behind my eyelids and every nerve in my body is screaming for release.

"Yes," I scream as he finally tips me over the edge. My body shudders beneath him as he goes on rubbing me, coaxing every last tremor and tremble from my body.

"I think my buddies just heard you coming for me," he says as he pulls his fingers out of me and my cheeks flush with heat. I would bet my life that they did. "They're going to be over here wanting some of this sweet pussy for themselves now."

"Then let me go," I pant as the tremors of my orgasm ebb away.

"Let you go?" He pushes himself up and grabs hold of my hips. "I've barely even started."

CHAPTER 2

DEMON

G rabbing hold of her hips, I pull her up so that she's on all fours. Her body is still shaking from her orgasm and her knees are trembling as I push them further apart, spreading her wide open for me.

Fuck, she is a beautiful sight. Her tiny red cheerleader skirt pushed up over her waist and those sweet cotton panties all dirty from the mud. I pull them to one side exposing half of her juicy round ass to me. I want to fuck her ass and her pussy but there isn't time now. The others are patiently waiting their turn and the rain is getting heavier. We don't have much longer before we'll need to get her out of the cold.

Reaching for my zipper, I open it and pull out my cock while she waits there for me. I rub my free hand over her ass. "Such a good girl waiting for my cock, angel," I say and she shivers, making me smile.

I am so fucking hard for her. I've been desperate to bury myself inside her since I saw her getting out of the car in this damn cheerleaders outfit. And the pigtails too? Fuck, my cock was weeping just looking at her.

I line myself up at her entrance. She pushes her ass back

slightly and I slap it. Hard. The breathy little moan she lets out makes me close my eyes and suck in a breath. I'm going to last all of five seconds in her sweet little cunt if I don't calm down.

Something about chasing her through the woods, then pinning her down and making her come when I caught her makes me feel like some kind of animal. I want to nail her into oblivion. I want to fuck her so hard she won't be able to get up and run away when I'm done. But that would spoil the other's fun, and what can I say, I'm a team player.

I grab an ass cheek with one hand and her pigtails with the other and then I drive my cock into her. She moans loudly and her pussy squeezes me like a vise as I sink deep into her smooth, wet heat.

"You feel so fucking good," I hiss as I pull out and drive back into her even harder.

"So do you," she pants as she wiggles her beautiful ass against me. So, she thinks she can tease me, does she?

I pull her pigtails hard, tilting her head up so that I can lean over and press my face against her neck. She smells so fucking good. If I didn't have this mask on, I would sink my teeth into her neck and suck her so hard she'd have a bruise as big as an apple.

Her tiny little whimpers vibrate through her body as I rail into her. Taking my own pleasure with no thought for hers this time. No doubt she'll come anyway, because she loves my cock and the way she's milking me with her greedy little squeezes tells me she's on the edge already.

"Oh, fuck," she hisses as she comes and my balls draw up into my stomach. I pick up my pace, sinking into her over and over as she coats me in her slick juices.

I grab her ass harder, letting go of her hair so that I can slide my other hand down to her pussy. I palm her mound in my hand. "Who does this belong to?"

"You," she breathes and she tips me over the edge until I'm filling her with my release. I hold her against me, pumping every last drop into her so that when she runs off in a moments time, my cum will be dripping out of her.

I pull out of her even though I'd prefer to pin her on the ground and fuck her senseless as soon as my cock is hard enough again — which would be in about two minutes flat.

Sitting back on my heels, I drink in the sight of her. Freshly fucked. Her clothes and legs covered in mud. Her neat pigtails now falling out of their braids.

She pushes herself to her knees. Her breathing hard and fast. I sense her about to make her escape, but I'm not going to stop her. There is no escape from us. She knows that too. But it is so much fun chasing her down.

We know exactly where she is at all times. She's carrying her cell in her purse and we track that. She also has a tracker in her arm and we can monitor that on an app on our cell phones too. Not to mention we have night vision lenses in our masks.

The hot little cheerleader belongs to us and there is no way we would ever let her go.

CHAPTER 3
JESSIE

The demon kneels behind me. I straighten my purse on my shoulder, careful not to make it too obvious because I don't want him to take it from me. I hear him breathing heavily as he fastens his trousers and know that this is the best moment I have to make my escape.

I rock back onto my heels before jumping up and making a run for it.

"I'll just catch you again," he shouts after me.

"Then do it, asshole," I shout back as I weave through the trees, smiling to myself at my own genius at escaping his clutches. My triumph doesn't last long though as I run straight into a pair of giant arms attached to a solid chest.

Damn!

Suddenly, his face is illuminated and I am staring up at the face of a super creepy looking clown. I'm not scared of clowns at all, but I do wonder why anyone, especially kids, would find them funny. I mean they are so freaking weird looking.

"Gotcha," he whispers as he wraps his arms around me. I struggle in his grip and he laughs at my effort. He has biceps like boulders and I'm not going anywhere.

"What do you want?" I scowl at him.

"Oh, a feisty little cheerleader," he says as he loosens his grip slightly.

I snort as I glare up at him.

Then he bends his head low, so his fake clown mouth is near my ear. "What I want is for you to suck my cock."

"What?" I blink at him.

"Do it and I'll let you go."

I imagine him smiling behind his mask as he says that.

I arch an eyebrow at him. "Promise?"

"Cross my heart," he chuckles as he unwraps his arms from around my body and places a firm hand on the top of my head.

I swallow hard and allow him to push me to my knees. The rain is getting heavier now. My clothes are wet and my skin is cold but my insides are on fire. Reaching for his zipper, I undo it and reach into his boxers to pull out his cock. It is hard already and precum glistens on the tip. I lick my lips unconsciously which makes him chuckle.

"You want me so bad, little cheerleader," he teases me.

"Whatever, asshole," I say with a slight shake of my head.

Then I dip my head forward and swirl my tongue over the tip of his cock. The groan vibrates through his entire body. He palms the back of my head with his other hand, threading his fingers through the top of my pigtails. I open my mouth wider, allowing him to push my head onto his cock until he hits the back of my throat. I gag slightly before I adjust to the intrusion and then I start to suck him softly, making him groan as he rocks his hips into my mouth.

"You suck cock so fucking good," he says in that creepy robotic voice.

I bite back a smile as I swirl my tongue over the length of his shaft, closing my eyes and savoring the taste of him. Placing my hands on his ass, I take him further into my mouth and the guttural noises that he makes when I do make warmth pool in my center.

I'm so lost to the act of sucking him off that I don't hear anyone else coming up behind us until there are more hands on my waist.

"Are you two having fun here?" someone says behind me.

I open my eyes but I can't turn my head to see. It is the same creepy ass voice that the others have but the light from his mask is a soft yellow, so I figure it's the vampire. I wonder if he's here to suck my blood? His hands slip beneath my skirt and onto my ass.

"I want to fuck her while she's sucking your cock," he says to the clown.

"Fuck, yeah," the clown agrees and then he starts to slowly drop to his knees while the vampire holds my hips, coaxing me backward until I'm on all fours.

"I'm not sure we're going to be needing these sexy little panties," the vampire says as he starts to work them off over my ass and down my legs. "So why don't I just hold onto them for you?"

I shift my legs as he takes them off me, while the clown keeps his hands on my head ensuring that I don't get so distracted that I stop sucking his cock.

As soon as my panties are off, the vampire runs his fingers through my dripping folds. "Fuck me, she's soaking here," he says and the clown grunts appreciatively.

Then with no further warning, the vampire drives his cock into me, forcing the clown deeper into my throat. I moan around him as my inner walls contract at the sudden, but welcome invasion.

"Your pussy is so good, cheerleader," the vampire says as he slowly drives in and out of me before pulling out completely and leaving me feeling empty. "But I want your ass."

Wet heat rushes between my thighs at the thought. We have no lube out here, do we?

He answers my question when he parts my ass cheeks with his strong hands and spits on my ass. The sound alone makes my thighs tremble in anticipation. Why the hell is this so hot?

"My cock is already slick from your cum," he says as he grabs my hips again. "I'm sure we'll be fine." Then he slowly pushes into my ass. "Fuck, you're so tight, baby."

The sensation of their hands holding me in place, his cock filling me while the clown keeps fucking my mouth makes me feel like I'm about to pass out from how turned on I am.

All I can do is moan as the pleasure rolls through my body.

"Hey, if you're fucking her ass, is that sweet pussy free?" the clown says.

"Uh-huh," the vampire grunts.

The clown pulls out of my mouth and saliva runs down my chin.

"How do you want to do this?" the vampire asks, talking about me like I'm not here while he goes on railing me as I'm on my hands and knees in the mud.

"Stand up with her," the clown replies.

"You hear that, we're gonna stand?"

Strong arms wrap around my waist as the vampire stands up, carrying me with him so he can remain inside me. My head falls back against his shoulder as the clown stands too and reaches for my legs. Lifting them, he wraps them around his waist until I'm sandwiched between their two hard bodies. He rubs the tip of his cock over my clit and I whimper softly.

"Oh we're gonna fuck you so hard, little cheerleader," the clown chuckles before he slides his cock inside me too.

"Oh, God," I cry out as my pussy clenches around him, making him groan.

"I don't think you're gonna find him anywhere in these

woods," the vampire laughs now too. Then the two of them hold me still between them, driving into me over and over as they fuck me together. They talk dirty to me the whole time, making wet heat flood my pussy.

"You are so fucking hot."

"You take our cocks so good."

"So fucking wet."

Then the clown pushes my wet hair back from my face. "Such a good girl," he whispers as both he and the vampire drive deep inside me and I lose it. My thighs tremble violently as my orgasm bursts out of me and my eyes roll back in my head.

"That's it, coat us in your sweet cum," the vampire says as he grinds his cock deeper. A few seconds later, the clown roars as he thrusts harder, pressing me tighter against his buddy as he rocks his hips, pumping his release into me.

"Fuck, I feel you squeezing him," the vampire says as he falls over the edge too and I sit, boneless in their arms as they both grind out the last of their orgasms into me.

When they're done, they each pull out of me slowly before they lower my legs to the ground. My legs shake as I'm forced to take my own body weight and my head spins. They both stay close to me, making sure I don't fall before they step back and allow me to breathe.

They're going to let me run. Now I realize that the demon let me run too, and here was I thinking I was smart escaping him. But they want to chase me through these woods. They want to hunt me down. That's why they told me to run. The fun is all about the chase, right?

I brush some of the mud from my clothes as best I can and then I hold out my hand to the vampire. "Can I have my panties back?"

He shakes his head. "Not a chance."

"What?" I scowl at him. "I can't run around here with no panties."

"Not my problem," he says with a shrug. "And if you don't want to be held down in this mud and rain and be fucked by both of us again, I suggest you run, little cheerleader."

I swallow hard as I look between him and the clown. Being held down and fucked by these two actually sounds pretty hot. But the rain is falling harder now. The ground is getting muddier. I want to go take a soak in the tub — and then maybe be held down and fucked.

"You got five seconds to haul your ass out of here before I take you down," the clown says.

Taking a deep breath, I turn and head off in the direction of the house. I know I haven't ran into the devil yet, but he can catch up with me there – preferably in the tub. I make my way through the trees. The house can't be too far now. Can it? I think I'm heading in the direction of it anyway. But it's hard to tell in the dark. Maybe I should just check my location on my cell.

I reach for my purse but it's gone.

Oh shit! It must have fallen off me. Do any of them have it? Fear starts to creep into my bones, making me shiver. What if I get lost in these woods?

What if a bear gets me?

Are there bears here?

Or wolves?

Shit! The wolf? The man who stole me and kept me prisoner.

I know he's dead but he has haunted my dreams for so long that sometimes I fear I might dream him back into reality. My heart starts to beat faster and I gasp for breath as I start to panic for real now. What if I'm lost?

What if I never see my babies or my husbands again?

CHAPTER 4
JESSIE

I'm spiraling into an anxiety attack and so freaked out by the thought of dying alone in these woods that I almost cry with relief when a hand reaches out of the darkness and grabs my wrist. But instead, I shriek with fright before the soft red glow of the devil's mask lights up the space around us.

"I was wondering where you were," I say, breathlessly.

His fingers dig into the skin of my forearm as he grips me tightly. Then his free hand slides beneath my tiny skirt until he reaches my ass. Cupping my bare cheek in his hand, he squeezes hard.

"Where the fuck are your panties?" he says against my ear. "Bad things are going to happen to girls who run around the woods not wearing panties?"

"Yeah," I breathe as he squeezes my ass harder. "Well I was wearing panties but one of your buddies stole them."

"They did, huh?" he sneers as his hand slides between my thighs instead.

"Yes," I gasp out loud as his fingers glide through my folds.

"They all fuck you too?"

"Y-yes," I stammer as he pushes a finger inside me.

"Feels like they made you come pretty hard as well," he says as he drives deeper.

"Maybe that's not mine," I pant as I rock my hips against his hand.

He presses his masked mouth against my ear and laughs softly before he speaks in that eerie voice. "You think I don't know the difference between your cum and theirs?"

"You do?"

"Hmm," he murmurs as he adds a second finger and I clamp my lips together to stifle a moan. "Yours is like liquid silk. I love the way it slicks my fingers." He pushes deeper until my walls squeeze around him. "And I know how it's going to coat my cock when I fuck you," he growls, his mouth brushing over the shell of my ear and making a shiver run the length of my spine.

Then his fingers are gone and I groan at the loss of his touch.

"But girls who run around here with no panties need to be punished, no matter how much I might want to bury my head in your cunt and eat that sweet cream you're dripping."

He grabs my hips, pushing me back until we reach a nearby tree. It's a familiar one to me. Not too far from the house, it was almost blown down in the wind at one point in it's long life and now grows at a forty-five degree angle. It's absolutely perfect for climbing and I imagine our kids having so much fun here one day. The devil spins me around until I'm facing the trunk before he presses me flat against it. His hard cock presses against my lower back for a few seconds before he moves back a little.

"Put your arms around the tree," he orders and I comply. I can just about wrap them all the way around the trunk so that my fingertips are touching.

He moves to the front, working quickly to secure my wrists with a piece of rope he must have had in his pocket, until I'm bound to the tree. I press my cheek against the cool damp bark as I wait for whatever he has planned.

He's behind me again now and he taps the back of my thighs. "Spread them," he orders and I do as he commands. He helps me along, nudging my thighs with his knee until my ankles are at either side of the thick trunk, before he lifts my skirt so that my ass is exposed to the cold air. I turn my head to see him but I can't make out what he's doing now.

"You want to be punished, little cheerleader? Is that why you're not wearing your panties?"

"No," I lie.

"Too bad."

The sound of him sliding his belt off makes my entire body shiver in anticipation.

A soft whooshing of the leather slicing through the air is the only warning I have before he brings his belt down over my ass cheeks with a loud crack.

"Oh, fuck," I hiss, before I bite on my lip.

"You like that?" he says before he does it again, this time a little harder.

I don't need to answer him. He knows that I do.

"Did you let my buddies fuck all of your tight little holes?"

"Yes," I gasp.

Smack.

"Did you come real hard?"

"Yes."

Smack.

"You gonna come for me?"

"No."

Crack. The leather stings my ass cheeks as he brings it down harder than before.

150

"You sure about that?" he asks.

"Damn sure," I tease him before he smacks my ass again so hard that my eyes water.

"We'll see," he chuckles. "Because we both know how hard I can make you come, don't we?"

I figure that's a rhetorical question so I don't answer. Instead I lean against the tree as he goes on spanking my ass with his belt until my pussy is slick with longing for him. When he's done, he drops his belt to the ground and rubs his hands over the hot, throbbing skin on my behind.

"The way you take my belt makes me hard as fuck. You know that?" he growls.

"Yes," I whisper as he begins to wrap a piece of soft material around my head until I'm blindfolded too.

My thighs tremble in anticipation and when I hear the sound of his zipper opening a few seconds later, wet heat surges between my thighs. He straddles the tree until he's directly behind me. Pressing the tip of his cock against my entrance, I bite on my lip to stifle a deep groan.

"Your cunt is fucking dripping for me," he hisses as he drives his cock deep inside me, pushing me a few inches up the tree until I'm stretching onto my tiptoes.

"Oh, God," I cry out into the darkness and he starts to laugh.

"Now you are definitely calling out for the wrong team," he chuckles as he nails me against the tree.

His chest is pressed against my back and his warm breath at my ear as he takes what he wants from me. His lips brush over my ear and I realize he's removed his mask. His mouth trails over my skin until he's nuzzling my neck as he drives his cock into me over and over again until I'm struggling to stand. If it wasn't for the tree supporting some of my weight and the devil pressed against me, I think I'd collapse into a heap on the floor.

I whimper shamelessly as he keeps me teetering on the edge

of my climax. He remains silent though without his mask. His heavy breathing and soft grunts are his only response until I can't take any more.

"Please?" I plead with him.

"Fuck, you beg like such a good girl even when you run around the woods with no panties like a slut."

Oh, sweet Jesus! His voice. His words. My orgasm rips through my body like I'm filled with black powder and he just lit the damn fuse.

"You like that, huh?" he growls.

"Yes," I gasp as he rolls his hips, hitting the spot deep inside me over and over until he grinds out his own release and comes with a loud groan.

When he pulls out of me, I whimper softly in frustration at the loss of contact.

He pulls my skirt back over my ass and then I hear him zipping up his pants and putting his belt back on. I wait for him to untie me, but then his footsteps are disappearing.

"Hey! Can you untie me?" I shout.

"Nope."

Asshole!

I wait, expecting one of the others to come untie me instead, but minutes pass and I'm still blindfolded and tied to a tree.

I strain to hear what is going on around me. The rain hitting the leaves. Some sort of insect making a noise.

Oh fuck! What if they start crawling over me? What insects are even out here? I mean, I'm not scared of bugs, but I don't want any crawling over me while I'm tied to a tree. And what about other animals?

My heart starts pounding again and I twist my wrists trying to break free of the rope binding my hands. I don't like this any more. I don't like feeling helpless. But the devil has bound me tight.

I think about shouting for help but my pride won't let me. I can hold out a little longer. They would never let anything bad happen to me, right?

I lean against the tree and sigh. Someone will be here soon.

CHAPTER 5
VAMPIRE

I stand in the darkness and watch her. She is struggling with the ropes around her wrists and I can feel the anxiety in her from here. I fight the urge to go to her and tell her everything is okay.

Five minutes. That's how long I need to leave her there. It gives everyone else time to get back and pretend like we were never out here. If she keeps struggling though, I'll go to her. I'll stroke her hair and tell her she's safe, because I can't bear to see her afraid.

But then she stops. She rests her cheek against the tree trunk and the softest smile plays on her lips. She knows we would never let anything bad happen to her. That we would all die to protect her.

So I keep watching. She is fucking beautiful. She is mine.

When the five minutes are up, I go to her. Her head snaps up as I start to untie her. I rub the red skin on the inside of her wrists softly and then release her hands. Immediately, she reaches for her blindfold.

"No," I tell her, trying to disguise my voice as best I can. I've taken off my mask and I don't want to ruin the illusion. She knows who we all are, I'm sure, but still.

"Okay," she whispers and drops her hands to her sides. Fuck me, she is so compliant. I don't usually give a fuck about her doing what I tell her to do, that's kind of my older brothers' deal, but I do love her submissiveness when it comes to her body.

My cock twitches when I think about being out here alone with her and the things she would let me do. For a few seconds, I seriously contemplate pushing her back against that tree and fucking her again, but I should shower first. Not to mention, she looks cold and tired and her legs are shaking.

Instead, I scoop her into my arms and head back to the house. She smiles and snuggles her head against my chest as she snakes one arm around my neck and curls some of my hair around her fingertip.

"Thank you," she whispers.

My only reply is a soft kiss on her forehead.

CHAPTER 6
JESSIE

He smells so good as I press my face against his chest. I guess he doesn't have his mask on as he warned me not to take off my blindfold, but I still know this is my vampire. His hair is a little longer than normal and it reaches his collar. I curl a wet strand of it around my finger as he carries me through the trees.

I hope we're heading back to the house. As much fun as this has been, I need some warmth, a soak in the tub and some food.

A few moments later, he stops and sets me down on my feet.

And then he is gone. I wait for further instructions but there are none. With trembling hands, I reach for my blindfold and untie it. Blinking as I remove the soft material from my eyes, I see I'm standing on the decking of our house. The lights are on now and the place looks warm and inviting.

I walk through the open double doors and into the lounge. My purse is on the coffee table and I breathe a sigh of relief because now we won't have to go looking for it tomorrow.

My clothes are torn and soaked through. My knees are scratched and bleeding and I have cum dripping down the inside of my thighs. My hair is dripping with rain. I reach up and push a wet strand from my forehead, pulling out a stray twig that's tangled at the roots. I caught a glimpse of myself in the glass door on the way in and figured I looked like I'd just stepped straight out of a horror movie.

Shane is sitting on the sofa with his cell phone in his hand. He looks up when he hears my wet sneakers squeaking on the polished wooden floor. "Rough day, sweetheart?"

I arch an eyebrow at him. "You could say that."

Mikey stands in the kitchen doorway, his arms crossed over his bare chest and his legs crossed at the ankles. He lets out a soft whistle, making me turn my attention to him.

"You really went all out on your costume, Red. What is it? Like, zombie cheerleader or something?" he grins at me.

"Just a cheerleader, actually," I try to blow a piece of hair from my forehead but it remains stubbornly in place, stuck with the weight of the water.

He narrows his eyes at me as he rubs a hand over his beard. "Hmm. I like it anyway," he finally says before he turns and heads back into the kitchen.

"Where are Conor and Liam?" I ask Shane.

"No idea," he says with a shake of his head. "Why don't you go see if you can find them? Dinner will be another hour."

"They're not going to jump out on me with an axe or anything, are they? I think my heart has had enough drama for one night."

"Now, why would they do that, sweetheart?" he asks with a grin.

WALKING THROUGH THE MASTER BEDROOM, I can see the steam coming from the bathroom. I don't hear the shower running so there must be a full, hot tub in there.

Yes!

I am going to soak in it for at least forty-five minutes. I pull off my wet clothes as I walk through the room, tossing them into the laundry hamper as I pass it. I'm naked by the time I step into the bathroom and see Conor sitting in a tub full of bubbles. He has his arms spread out on the edge of the bath with his head hanging back and his eyes closed.

I'm already stepping into the water when he finally hears me.

"Hey, angel," he says with a smile.

"Hey, big guy."

His eyes scan over my body, landing on my scraped knees. "Are you okay?"

"Yes," I say as I sink into the delicious hot water. "I just ran into a few issues getting here, is all."

He holds out his hand to me and I take it, curling my fingers around his. "You did, huh? Anything I should know about?" He grins wickedly. My super hot demon.

"No. I took care of it."

He pulls me toward him and wraps his arms around my waist. I straddle his lap, curling a wet lock of his hair around my fingertip as I stare into his deep brown eyes.

"You sure you're okay?" he whispers.

"Yes, I'm more than okay," I assure him.

"Good." He presses a soft kiss on my throat and I shiver in his arms.

"Why did you talk to me earlier? I mean, without the voice changer?"

He brushes my hair back from my face. "Because I was about to slide my fingers inside you and I felt you freeze, angel. And I never want you to feel that kind of fear again."

"But wasn't the whole idea of tonight to scare me? I mean we made a bet and all," I whisper.

"Yeah, but I don't care about no bet. I care about you. I never want you to be afraid of me when I fuck you. And you froze, Jessie. I felt it."

"I did," I admit. "For a second, I thought what if it wasn't you guys chasing me. But I didn't think you'd notice. You always know exactly what I need Conor Ryan. How do you do that?"

He rubs his nose along the column of my throat, making me tremble. "I told you before, angel, we're the same, you and me."

I stare into his eyes. "We are, huh?" I whisper as I shift on his lap, until his cock is nudging at my entrance. My pussy throbs with a heartbeat of its own after tonight's events in the woods, but despite that I still want more. I want him. All of him. All I have to do is drop my hips lower and he'll be inside me.

He grabs hold of my hips, shifting me slightly so that his cock is between us now. "Uh-uh," he says with a shake of his head and a wicked grin. "You've been fucked enough for now, Mrs. Ryan."

"That's so unfair," I pout. "I mean we're both ready to go. We both want it. We could just take it easy?"

He throws his head back as he laughs loudly and I can't help but giggle too. "No," he finally says. "You are fucking insatiable, angel."

"So you keep telling me," I whisper in his ear. "But you're the one with the raging boner, big guy."

He palms the back of my head, his hand fisting in my wet hair as he pulls me back so he can look into my eyes. "You're rubbing that sweet pussy over me, Jessie. Of course I'm hard, but I'm not fucking you."

"Conor, please?" I whimper as I bite on my lip, doing my best to seduce him.

"You're a fucking deviant," he says with a sigh before he grabs my waist and lifts me, spinning us around and sitting me on the edge of the tub. He pushes my thighs apart so that his body is nestled between them. "Lie back, angel," he growls, his brown eyes as dark as coal.

I do as he says, pushing myself back onto the ceramic tiles. We have underfloor heating and they are warm to the touch, but despite that, I shiver when my skin is flat against the floor. Conor lifts my legs out of the water, pulling my knees over his shoulders until my ass is almost touching his chest.

"You want to come, angel?" he says as he starts to trail soft kisses over the inside of my thighs.

"Yeah," I pant as I writhe beneath his expert mouth. "But what about you?"

"Me?" he chuckles softly and the sound vibrates through my body. "Don't worry about me. I could come just from eating your sweet pussy."

Then his tongue dances over my skin until he reaches the apex of my thighs. "So fucking good," he murmurs against my delicate flesh before he licks the length of my folds, making me shudder.

"Conor," I whimper, bucking my hips slightly as he swirls his tongue over my sensitive clit.

"I got you, angel. Close your eyes and let me take care of you."

"Fuck," I groan softly as warm waves of pleasure begin to roll through my core as he works me with his expert tongue. I close my eyes and focus on him gently licking and sucking my delicate flesh, sending sparks of pleasure skittering around my body until I'm blanketed in a warm fuzzy glow.

"I-I'm gonna..." I stammer as my orgasm crests a wave, but he moves lower, lapping at my opening instead as he eases me back down.

"Eating your pussy makes me hard as fuck," he groans and I

hear the telltale sound of the water sloshing around the tub that tells me he is giving himself some much needed relief as well as me. The thought of him jerking off while he eats my pussy makes my inner walls contract. I lifts my hips slightly, trying to chase the orgasm he's withholding and my skin is slippery on the tiles.

"Keep those eyes closed, angel," he warns as he continues torturing me with wave after wave of exquisite pleasure.

"Conor," I groan, half in pleasure and half frustration.

It's then that I feel a warm, wet mouth on my nipple, sucking me softly as a firm hand slides over my abdomen. I know it can't be Conor because his tongue continues tantalizing my pussy. As I open my eyes and tilt my head, Liam's eyes lock on mine and he winks at me. I reach out and run my fingers through his wet hair. He smells of expensive shampoo so I figure he must have taken a shower after he left me on the decking. My vampire.

"Hey," I breathe as warm heat floods my body.

"Hey," he says as he moves his face close to mine, lying beside me on the warm tiles. "Is Conor eating your pussy good, baby?"

"Y-yeah," I gasp as his older brother sucks harder on my clit, making stars flicker behind my eyelids.

"He's making you so wet, Jessie. I can smell your cum from here," he whispers against my ear and wet heat floods my entire body. "Make her scream, yeah, Con? I want to feel our girl come hard."

"Hmm," Conor agrees, his tongue buried in my pussy.

I suck in a breath as Liam seals his lips over mine and when his older brother finally tips me over the edge, I groan into Liam's mouth and he swallows every sound I make, drawing out my pleasure as I buck my hips against Conor's skilled tongue. When every last tremor has rippled through my body,

SADIE KINCAID

Liam breaks our kiss and Conor lifts his head from between my thighs and his eyes lock on mine.

"You okay, angel?" he asks with a wink.

"Yeah," I pant. "Are you?"

He wipes his mouth and chin with his hand. "Finished right after you did."

"You are so fucking beautiful when you come, baby," Liam says as he brushes his fingertips over my cheek. "I can't wait to fuck you later."

"You can fuck me now," I pant and Conor laughs softly.

"Dinner and scary movies first," he says with a wink before he jumps up and pulls me with him.

CHAPTER 7
CLOWN

I look up from chopping strawberries to see the sexiest woman I have ever met in my entire life walking into the kitchen wearing one of my t-shirts and nothing else. I have no idea how I got lucky enough to call her mine, but she is and she always will be.

"I have a bone to pick with you, Mikey Ryan," she says as she walks toward me.

"Yeah?" I grin at her, popping a strawberry into her mouth when she reaches me. "What's that, Red?"

She swallows the strawberry and then pops an eyebrow at me. "Where the hell are all of my panties?"

Fuck! She's onto me. I should have coated that strawberry in chocolate to sweeten her up a little more. "You're not going to be needing any tonight," I say before kissing her softly, tasting the sweet fruit on her tongue.

"You didn't have to hide them all," she breathes when she breaks our kiss.

"Hey, I don't take chances with things that are so important, Red. You know this."

"Me not wearing panties is that important to you, is it?"

"You know it." I smack her on the ass. "Now let me finish dessert. We're eating in front of the TV so we can watch all our favorite scary movies."

"Sounds perfect. You need any help?" she asks with a sweet smile.

I bend my head so that my lips are pressed against her ear. She smells so fucking good it makes my cock twitch in my shorts. "If you stay here and help me, I'll end up lifting you onto this counter and eating your pussy instead of making dinner," I whisper in her ear.

I feel the shiver running through her body and it makes me smile.

"Sounds good to me," she giggles.

"I knew you two would be up to no good in here," my older brother, Shane says as he walks into the kitchen.

"I can't help if I have an incredibly sexy wife who can't keep her hands off me, bro," I say with a shrug and she giggles.

He comes up behind her and kisses her neck. "She is pretty fucking irresistible," he agrees and the skin on her neck and cheeks turns pink. She is so fucking adorable.

"Mikey hid all of my panties," she says, expecting me to get a telling off.

Instead, Shane holds up his hand for a high five. "Nice work, kid."

"You're all as bad as each other," she purrs and the twitch in my cock turns into a throb.

"And you're badder than all of us, Red." I wink at her and her cheeks flush a deeper shade of pink.

I look at Shane. We could fuck her together right now. I'll take her pussy and he could take her ass. And she'd let us too. Catching her out there in the dark tonight made me so fucking hard for her. Everything she does makes me hard for her. I loved fucking her with my twin earlier, but I love taking her with any of my brothers.

I can almost see Shane's thoughts as he considers it too. The way he's looking at her and then me — he is one hundred percent thinking about fucking her too. But then he pulls back from her.

"We all need to eat," he says with a sigh.

My big brother — the voice of reason and currently cock-blocker extraordinaire.

CHAPTER 8
JESSIE

The credits from Friday 13th roll over the screen and I lean back against Shane's chest as I sit between his legs on the sofa.

"Part two next or something else?" Mikey asks as he picks up the TV remote.

"Something else," Liam replies.

"Chainsaw Massacre," Conor suggests.

"No," I protest. "I want something less gruesome. How about Hocus Pocus?"

"That's a kid's film," Conor and Liam protest.

"So? It's my turn to choose, isn't it? I've sat through two of your guy's choices."

"Lady has a point," Shane says and the other three roll their eyes.

"Thank you," I whisper as I wiggle my ass against his groin.

"Stop it," he warns in my ear.

"What? I'm just getting comfortable," I giggle.

"Hmm," he murmurs before kissing the top of my head. His hand is resting on my stomach and I shuffle my body up so that it falls between my legs instead. I smile as he slides his fingers beneath Mikey's t-shirt that I'm wearing.

Mikey puts the movie on and we all settle back to watch it as Shane starts to toy with my clit. He rubs it softly, drawing slow teasing circles with the pads of two fingers while I watch the giant screen. He kisses my neck, his stubble tickling my skin while he presses the tips of his fingers more firmly against me. I tilt my head back, closing my eyes and moaning softly as a familiar warmth starts building in my core. When I open them again, his three younger brothers are no longer watching the movie but have their eyes firmly fixed on us, specifically his fingers working my pussy.

"So wet, sweetheart," he breathes as he slides his fingers through my folds and then pushes one inside me.

"God, Shane," I hiss as I hold onto his forearm while he slides in and out of me.

"Haven't I already told you he's not here tonight," he whispers, adding a second finger and making me gasp out loud as I release a rush of slick heat.

The sound of his fingers working in and out of my dripping pussy is so loud and it makes the heat creep over my cheeks.

Liam is sitting by us on the sofa and he edges closer. "Fuck, I can smell you, baby," he growls. "I'm gonna need to fuck you if Shane keeps doing that."

"Then do it," I beg him.

"If Liam fucks you then we're all fucking you, sweetheart," Shane warns. "Can you handle that after your adventure in the woods?"

"How do you know about my adventure in the woods?" I half chuckle, half pant as I rock my hips against his hand.

"We know everything, Jessie," he murmurs against my neck, his teeth grazing my soft skin.

"Then you know I can take so much more."

"Let me fuck her, Shane," Liam pleads.

Shane pulls his fingers out of me and slides them back to my clit and that is all the permission Liam needs. He kneels between my thighs, pulling his sweatpants down a little and allowing his hard, thick cock to spring free.

With his hands on my knees, he pushes them further apart until I'm spread wide for him. "Fucking beautiful, baby," he whispers.

Then he slowly drives his cock into me and I suck in a breath. The feeling of being filled by him while Shane rubs my clit is exquisite.

"So. Fucking. Hot," Liam hisses as he drives in and out of me, burying his cock as deep inside me as he can get as he pushes my thighs further and further apart.

"You have any idea how good you look when you're being nailed by my brothers, sweetheart?" Shane whispers in my ear as he goes on rubbing my clit.

"Baby, stop milking my cock," Liam groans. "I've been dreaming about being inside this pussy all night and you're going to make me come."

"I can't help it," I moan as the two of them bring me to an earth shattering climax. I buck and shudder so much that Shane has to hold me down with his free arm.

"Oh, fuck!" Liam shouts as he drives deeper and fills me with his own climax.

He pulls out of me when he's done while Shane goes on softly massaging me with his fingertips, coaxing every last tremor from my body. When Liam climbs off the sofa, his twin, Mikey is already waiting to take his place. He looks at Shane with a wicked glint in his eye.

"You want to take her together?" Shane asks and I almost pass out.

"Yup," Mikey replies with a grin as he pulls his cock free

from his sweatpants and kneels between my legs where Liam just was.

Shane taps my ass. "Lift up," he says and I do as he tells me, allowing him some room to pull his own sweatpants down enough to take his cock out.

"Here, bro," Conor says as he tosses him a bottle of lube from a drawer in the table next to him.

Shane coats his shaft quickly before he guides me back down onto him, pulling my back against his chest as he pushes his cock into my ass until I cry out.

"Okay, sweetheart?" he checks in on me.

"Yeah," I pant.

"You ready for me too?" Mikey asks and I nod my response.

"Hold her for me, bro," he says to Shane, who obliges by wrapping one huge arm around my waist and pinning one of my thighs down with the other.

"We're gonna fuck you so hard, Red," Mikey growls as he slips his cock into my pussy until I'm full of him and his brother. "You're so fucking tight like this."

"Oh! Fuck me!" I groan loudly and the two of them laugh softly.

"With pleasure, sweetheart," Shane says against my ear.

CHAPTER 9
DEVIL

I feel Jessie's orgasm rippling through her body as I drive my cock as deep into her as I can go while my younger brother fucks her pussy.

"Shane. Mikey," she groans our names as we fuck her together in a relentless rhythm. She's been teetering on the edge for a while now, but I still can't allow her to tip over because I love to keep her here, bordering on oblivion before I allow her the release she so desperately craves. I love to hear her beg. The way she says my name makes me feel like a fucking God and I will never, ever get enough of her. Being buried inside her is my peace and my chaos.

"I can't hold on," Mikey hisses as he slams into her so hard that she's pressed tight against me. He grinds his hips against her pussy, making her take every drop he has to give her and she whimpers because she was about to come just as he stopped fucking her. When he realizes that, he starts to fuck her slowly again.

"Please?" she begs and I take pity on her too, reaching between her and my brother and rubbing on her clit until she explodes between the two of us, bucking and trembling through her orgasm and the aftershock.

"Your pussy is addictive, Red," Mikey groans as he pulls out of her, allowing me to push a little deeper into her ass.

"So is this juicy ass," I say, sitting up and flipping her onto all fours so that I can get deeper inside her. Her cheeks are striped pink and white from my belt earlier and it makes me want to fuck her even harder.

"Are you saying my ass is fat?" she asks.

I slap her behind hard and she yelps. "No I'm fucking not," I growl, reaching for her hair and pulling her head back so she can look at me. Then I rub her stinging skin before palming her round cheek in my hand. "I said it was juicy, so don't put words in my mouth, sweetheart."

"I'm sorry," she whimpers.

"I should make you feel my belt for even thinking that."

"You should," Conor agrees with me, a scowl on his face.

"I said I'm sorry," she whispers.

I push her down again so her face is against the sofa cushions and her perfect ass is in the air. Then I fuck her ass as hard as I have ever fucked anyone in my life while my brothers watch me. And when I'm done, I sit back, taking her with me and pulling her onto my lap. I brush her hair from her face and kiss her soft lips. She opens her mouth, allowing my tongue inside so that I can taste her.

Sliding my hand between her thighs, I cup her pussy and leave my hand there, resting possessively so that there is no doubt she belongs to me. When I let her up for air, I frown at her. "You okay because you still got one brother to go."

"I know," she whispers before she looks over at Conor who holds out his hand to her.

"Come here, angel," he says, winking at her and she dutifully obeys.

CHAPTER 10
JESSIE

I stroll across the room and allow Conor to pull me onto his lap so that I'm straddling him. Mine and his brothers' cum drips out of me and onto his lap but he doesn't seem to care at all.

"You can suck my cock if you're sore?" he offers.

"No," I shake my head. "If that's okay?" I wanted this from him when we were in the tub earlier and my desire for him overrides any feelings of soreness I might have.

"Of course it's okay. Given the choice between your mouth or your pussy," he slides his hand between my thighs and strokes between my folds, "this wins every fucking time."

"Conor," I groan as I shift on his lap.

He starts to trail feather light kisses along the column of my throat. "Shall I take it easy with you, angel? Fuck you nice and slow?" he murmurs.

"Yes please."

"Slide onto my cock then. Show me how you much want it."

I reach for his sweatpants and pull his cock free, wrapping my hand around his hard shaft and squeezing hard until he moans before I lower myself onto him. I sink deep, allowing him to stretch me so deliciously slowly that it makes tears prick at the corners of my eyes.

"Fuck, Conor. You feel so good," I gasp.

"Because your pussy is molded to my cock, angel," he says as he stares deep into my eyes.

Grabbing hold of my hips, he rolls me over him, taking back control after he allowed me it for a moment. "You were made for us Ryan boys, weren't you?"

"Yeah," I agree.

"What's your name?"

"Jessie Ryan."

"Yeah it is," he pushes his hips up, hitting deeper. "Are you our good girl?"

Oh fuck! "Yes."

"Did you enjoy our Halloween surprise?"

"Yes," I gasp. "A lot."

Laughter ripples around the room.

"I'm gonna make you come now, angel and then we're going to bed for some movies and sleep. Okay?"

"Yeah," I say as he goes on rolling my hips over him as his cock pulses in my pussy and my walls squeeze around him.

I wrap my arms around his neck and he pulls me closer as he fulfills the first part of his promise.

A RYAN CHRISTMAS

ONE

Five days to Christmas

M y fingers are trembling as I press the button for the elevator of our penthouse apartment. If I just keep taking deep breaths, I'll be okay, right?

You can do this, Jessie. Just breathe. It's all gonna be fine.

"Where did you say you were headed, angel?" His deep voice carries across the hallway.

Shit!

I have four husbands, Shane, Conor, Liam and Mikey Ryan. Of all of them, he had to be the one to come out here and ask me that They're pretty much all possessive alpha-holes who like to be made aware of my every move. I also suspect they all know me better than I even know myself, but Conor – well he sees right through me, no matter what.

Taking a breath in and forcing a smile, I turn and face him. "I told you. I'm not leaving the building. I'm going to the basement. I'm going to be perfectly safe."

He narrows his dark brown eyes at me as he steps closer. "Yeah, I heard that part. But why?"

"I also told you all it was something I had to do. It's Christmas related," I remind him. "I'll be back up here in two hours."

My breath stutters in my throat as he reaches me. I turn my head, averting my eyes from his intense gaze, but he catches my jaw in his fingers, tilting my chin so there is no escaping him.

"Why are you trembling, angel?" he growls and the sound travels through my bones.

Damn! Now I feel sick too.

"I-I'm not," I stammer. *Idiot!*

His jaw ticks as he glares at me. He knows I'm hiding something from him. Even if I wasn't shaking like a leaf in the fall, he would know.

"What are you up to, Jessie?" his already deep voice drops an octave, making a shiver skitter along my spine.

I gasp in a breath and an unexpected tear pricks at my eyes. I so wanted to do this. It was supposed to be a surprise. I imagined their faces when I showed them and how brave they would say I was to finally overcome my phobia of needles.

"I was going to get a tattoo," I whisper.

His handsome features are pulled into a frown. Relaxing his grip on my jaw, he brushes a single tear from my cheek with the pad of his thumb. "A tattoo? In the basement?"

"Yeah," I sniff. "Gia is downstairs. Chester let her in for me."

"Gia?"

"Yeah." Chester is one of our security detail, and Gia Fenton is the woman who did most of Conor's and his brothers' tattoos. Her designs are stunning and she is a true artist. When I spoke to her about the idea I had, she came up with a beautiful, simple design that would take no more than ninety minutes to complete. I figured I could handle that, but my needle phobia has other ideas. "I don't think I can do it though. And it was going to be so good too."

I reach into the pocket of my sweater dress and pull out the sketch she made me. Handing it to Conor, I watch as he unfolds the small piece of paper. It's a simple rose, but the thorns are his and his brother's names. They wind around the flower, furling into each other until they reach the top where our children's names, Ella and Finn, are the petals.

"Fuck. It would look incredible on you," he whispers, looking between me and the paper in his hand.

"It'd beautiful, right?"

"But you hate needles?"

"I know. That's why it's just simple black ink. She said the coloring in takes longer. I thought I could..." a sob wells up in my throat.

He places a strong hand on the back of my neck — both calming and possessive. "You want to do this, angel?" he asks as he hands me back my sketch.

"Yeah."

"Then let's do it. I'll be with you every second, okay? I'll hold your hand, or whatever you need."

I rest my forehead on his chest and suck in a breath, letting his comforting scent wash over and through me. As though somehow I can take some of his strength and imbibe it into my bones.

"I would never let anyone hurt you," he says, running his hands over my arms before pressing a soft kiss on the top of my head.

I know that he speaks the truth. My fear of needles is rooted in the fact that I have been stuck with them, drugged and kidnapped more times than any one person should ever have to. I mean most people go through their entire lives without having that happen, right? Not me.

This must be hard for him too. It would be so much easier for him to tell me that I don't need to do this. He could go and pay Gia for her time and tell her that I've changed my mind. Then he and I could curl up on the sofa and watch a Christmas movie. That would be the easy option. Easier for both of us. His instinct is to protect me. But he knows that what I need is for him to push me to be better. Stronger. Faster. No longer afraid. It's why he and his younger brother almost kill me in the gym four times a week.

"You'll hold me the whole time?" I whisper.

"Anything you need, angel."

AFTER CONOR TOLD his brothers he'd be accompanying me to the basement for a couple of hours, we headed down to his office in the nightclub which makes up the lower floors of this building. Gia is already set up when we walk inside.

"Hey," she greets me, arching an eyebrow as she sees Conor walk into the room behind me. No doubt wondering why he's here when I made her promise that this would be our secret.

"I need him to hold my hand," I explain with a wince, feeling foolish that I'm being such a baby about a needle.

"I figured you might need some back up," she says with a chuckle. "You couldn't even watch Liam getting his last tattoo."

"I know." I place a hand over my mouth as the memory makes me want to hurl. He was in the chair for six hours and I had to leave after fifteen minutes.

"I'm proud of you, girl," she adds. "Getting a tattoo when you're terrified of needles is a big deal. You're a fucking warrior."

"Yeah, well I don't feel like one," I whisper as I eye her instruments.

A wave of nausea washes over me and I sway on my feet.

Conor's warm hands grip my waist and he moves his lips close to my ear. "You're okay. You got this."

"Uh-huh," I mumble, not as convinced as he is.

"Just sit yourself down here," Gia says, patting the seat of Conor's large office chair.

I look at the chair and then at her, and then her needles.

Fuck! I'm going to pass out.

Heat creeps over my skin and perspiration prickles over my brow. I stand rooted to the spot.

Gia looks past me at Conor. "How about I give Conor here a little ink to start with and you can watch exactly what happens this time. Okay?" she suggests.

"Yeah," I breathe out the word. Knowing exactly what to expect will calm my nerves — won't it?

"Where do you want it, big guy?" she says with a grin.

If I wasn't about to throw up into her lap, I might give her some sass for flirting with my husband. Gia flirts with every single person she meets — no matter their gender or sexuality.

Conor pulls his t-shirt off over his head and tosses it onto his desk before taking a seat on the chair. He taps his collarbone, right next to the tattoo of my name. "Right here. Give me a heart next to Jessie."

She grins at me as she picks up her artists needle. "You watching closely?"

I step closer to Conor and he reaches for my hand, lacing his fingers through mine. When Gia pierces his skin for the first time, I flinch but Conor doesn't even flicker. He winks at me as he squeezes my hand in his.

"Just a scratch. It doesn't go all that deep, see?" he nods toward Gia's hand as she draws over and over the tiny heart.

"Yeah," I whisper.

He knows I'm not afraid of pain. It is the act of the needle piercing my skin that terrifies me.

181

I force myself to watch as Gia drags the needle repeatedly over Conor's skin to create a small heart the size of a pea. A few minutes later, she sits back with a proud smile on her face. "Not bad for freehand, right?"

Conor looks down at his tiny new ink. "Hmm," he nods his agreement before he looks back at me. "You ready, angel?"

"Uh-huh," I murmur but I stand rooted to the spot.

"Where are you having your tattoo?" he asks.

"On m-my shoulder."

He tugs my hand, still clasped in his. "Come here." His words are soft but his tone is commanding and my body obeys him even though my brain is telling me to run from the room and far away from the small pointy instruments of torture.

I edge closer until my thighs are touching his.

"Here!" he looks down at his lap.

With shaky legs, I straddle him on the chair, placing my hands on his solid chest and feeling how he grounds me. My fingertips flex over the tattoos on his chest. The myriad of dark colors swirling and coiling into beautiful patterns on his skin.

Grabbing hold of my waist, he shifts his position slightly. "You okay there?" he asks.

I swallow hard. My groin is directly over his cock and the memories of the many times I have sat with him like this on this chair makes wet heat pool in my core.

"Yes," I whisper as I stare into his eyes.

He sees it too, as though he's watching the thoughts in my head like a movie. His eyes darken as a low growl rumbles through his chest.

"You wanna take your dress off or just pop your arm out, Jessie?" Gia asks as she readies her equipment for her next victim — me.

"Arm out," Conor growls, glaring at me in warning. "I'm barely gonna get through this with you fully clothed."

CHAPTER ONE

Despite my nerves, that makes me giggle. I pull my arm through my sweater dress and pull down my bra strap, exposing my right shoulder to be Gia's canvas.

When she wipes my skin with alcohol a few seconds later, the unexpected touch of her fingers on me makes me instinctively edge forward, causing me to rub my pussy over Conor's cock.

"Fuck!" he hisses.

"Sorry. Should have warned you," Gia laughs softly.

"That's okay," I reply, my eyes locked on Conor's.

His length hardens against me until it's nudging at my folds through my panties. Under almost any other circumstances that would be enough to distract me from anything. And I want to focus only on the feel of his body against mine, but the familiar feelings of pleasure, comfort and warmth that he usually evokes remain frustratingly close, yet too far to reach.

I FLINCH every single time Gia touches my skin and the longer she works, the more my entire body starts to tremble with fear.

"You're gonna have to do something to calm your girl, down, Conor," she says with a sigh. "She's shaking like a goddam jell-o shot in a virgin's belly button here."

I understand what she's saying but I can't stop my body from quivering. I need something to focus on. Something to distract me. Something all consuming.

"What do you suggest, Gia?" he says as his fingertips dig into the soft flesh of my hips.

"Whatever she needs, right?" she purrs while I stare into Conor's eyes, hoping he's willing to go that far.

His cock twitches against me and I roll my hips just the tiniest amount but it's enough to make me whimper with need.

Gia puts her instruments down on the metal tray with a

183

clatter. "I tell you what's gonna happen. I'm gonna go use the ladies room. And when I come back you two can be in whatever *situation* you need to be in to make this happen. Okay."

"Situation?" Conor snaps at her. "Are you-?"

"I don't care what you do, man. Pretty sure I have already seen and done everything that you are worrying about right now. Just get your girl to relax so we can get this done, because right now she has half a tattoo and we've been at this for almost an hour. Okay?"

Then without another word, she walks out of the office to find the ladies room, leaving Conor and me alone.

"Tell me what you need, angel," he breathes.

I bear down on him, pressing my aching pussy against his cock and making heat sear between my thighs. "This, Conor," I whimper. "I need to get out of my head."

"Fuck!" he mutters. "You know if Shane were here with you now, he'd already be inside you?"

"I know," I say with a smile. His older brother would love to fuck me with an audience, but Conor has always been so against it that Shane has held off from doing it so far. "But I'm still glad it's you here with me."

"Fuck! You know I'll always give you what you need," he grinds out the words as though they pain him to say.

"I know that."

He pinches the bridge of his nose. "So take off the damn panties," he says with a deep sigh that rolls through his entire body.

"Are you sure?"

"I don't think this tattoo is gonna get finished otherwise, is it?"

"Probably not," I admit.

"So do as you're told and take off your panties," he growls as his hard cock twitches against me.

I climb off him and reach beneath my sweater dress. Hooking my fingers into my panties, I peel them off over my legs.

"Give them to me," Conor orders and I place them in his outstretched palm.

He wads them into a ball and stuffs them into the pocket of his sweatpants. Reaching for my hand again, he pulls me back onto his lap. "Take what you need, angel," he growls.

Reaching between us, I tug his sweatpants down and release his huge cock. The crown glistens with precum and I bite back a smile but he sees it anyway.

"You seriously think having you sitting on my lap, grinding yourself on my cock would have me any other way, Jessie?" he groans. "Now slide your hot pussy onto me before Gia comes back in here."

I wrap my hand around his thick shaft, causing a deep groan to rumble through his chest, before sinking onto him. He slides easily into my wet heat and I sink all the way down until our bodies are flush together. The sensation of being so full of him makes warmth and relief curl around my spine and flutter through my body.

"You feel so good," I hiss as I roll my hips over him.

"Fuck!" he mutters, his teeth catching on his bottom lip as he grabs my waist and holds me still. "You can't ride me while you're getting a tattoo, Jessie, you're gonna have to stay still."

"I know," I whimper as a rush of wet heat slicks us both. "But I'm not getting a tattoo right this second."

The sound of the door opening makes Conor's grip on me tighten and I close my eyes and still my hips. Despite how much I want to grind on him right now, I know that he's right and I need to remain as still as possible while Gia has the instrument of torture pressed against my back. And having him inside me is calming enough for now.

"We ready to proceed?" Gia asks with a knowing smile. She can't see thanks to my dress — but, oh she knows - if only by the pained expression on Conor's face.

"Yep," I say.

"Uh-huh," Conor grunts, narrowing his eyes at me in warning.

I bite my lip to stop myself from laughing at the look on his face but at least it distracts me from Gia's needles and I barely even notice when she starts tattooing me again.

I concentrate on Conor's fingers digging into my hips. His huge cock throbbing inside my pussy as I force myself to keep still. But then as Gia switches from the quiet pen back to her gun, the sound of the tiny motor makes me flinch.

"It's okay, angel," Conor says softly, his deep voice rolling through my core.

But my body starts to tremble slightly.

"Keep her still," Gia warns.

His gaze holds mine as he slides his hand beneath my dress and starts to rub the pad of his thumb softly over my clit, making endorphins flood my body.

I hiss out a breath but it stops the trembling as I focus on his expert fingers soothing me. He doesn't apply enough pressure to get me off yet, just enough to make the pleasure coil up my spine and into every nerve ending in my body.

My walls squeeze around him and a growl rumbles through his chest. "Don't," he warns me.

I stare at him, my eyelids fluttering as he goes on gently rubbing my clit.

"Hold it, Jessie," he grinds out the words.

I smile at him. He thinks I'm the only one about to come. That is so sweet.

I squeeze my walls around him again and again. Squeezing

and releasing. Over and over. I see his eyes rolling in his head as he fights to maintain control.

"Jessie!" he hisses, but it's too late. My walls ripple around him as I bring us both to the edge.

His eyes press tightly closed and his jaw sets in a grimace, his fingers digging deeper into the soft flesh of my hips as he comes inside me with a deep, but almost silent grunt. And the sight of my usually cool, calm husband losing control tips me over the edge too. With his strong hands holding me, I manage to stay completely still while my orgasm rolls through my body in a long, intense wave. I clamp my lips together to stop myself from moaning loudly and the effort of staying still and quiet makes the climax even more intense. It implodes inside me, sending aftershocks of pleasure skittering through all of my nerve endings.

A tiny whimper escapes and I hold my breath, wondering if Gia is going to laugh or give any indication that she knows what just happened, but she goes on working diligently on my tattoo — seemingly lost in her art and being a complete professional.

TWO

S taring up at my deviant wife, I watch the relief wash over her beautiful face as Gia finally says those words she's been waiting for.

"All done."

"Really?" Jessie breathes.

"Yup." Gia holds up a small mirror and Jessie cranes her neck so she can see the work of art that's just been permanently tattooed onto her shoulder. I look too. It's fucking perfect, just like her.

"Oh," Jessie gasps. "I love it, Gia. It's beautiful."

"It looks hot," Gia says with a proud grin. "Just let me cover it."

Gia cleans Jessie up and takes a clear plastic wrap that's also used for burns from the table beside her and places it on Jessie's shoulder. She always covers her tattoos with them and they work way more effectively than anything else I've seen. You just leave it on for a few days and then peel it off, leaving a perfect tattoo with no scabbing.

The smile on Jessie's face makes my cock throb inside her. I'm so fucking proud of her. I'm also pissed that she made us both come in front of Gia. I mean what the fuck was that thing she did with the squeezing? I had no fucking control at all. She took it all.

She played me.

She looks down at me, her face flushed pink and her eyes shining with happiness. My cock is still inside her and I'm still hard as fuck.

"Gia, I'm gonna need you to go," I grunt.

"Okay," she says as she starts collecting her stuff. "So, Jessie, you're gonna need to-"

"Now, Gia!"

She turns and blinks at me. "I need to go through the aftercare."

"Pretty sure I know how to take care of a tattoo," I breathe out the words as my fingers dig into Jessie's hips. Half my body is covered in ink.

"Fine," she says with a sigh and roll of her eyes. "Just let me get my stuff."

"I'll have someone bring it to your studio," I hiss, making Jessie giggle softly.

"Whatever," she says with a shrug. "This was my last job before the holidays anyway. Have someone deliver it after ten tonight, yeah?"

"Will do," I say, staring into Jessie's bright blue eyes. She licks her lip and my balls twitch.

"Okay, well, Happy holidays, I guess," Gia says with a soft laugh.

"Bye, Gia. Happy holidays and thanks again," Jessie says sweetly, as though she's not currently gripping my cock in her pussy.

"You're welcome, girl."

"Go!" I bark.

"I'm going," Gia sighs and then makes her way out of my office. She turns and winks at Jessie before she leaves.

As soon as the door is closed I sigh with relief. "You are so gonna pay for that," I say, grabbing the edge of Jessie's dress and pulling it off over her head.

"Pay for what?" she purrs, fluttering her eyelashes at me.

God, I fucking love her. "For making me come in front of Gia."

She doesn't deny it. Instead she bites on her bottom lip and I can't take another damn second of her teasing. Grabbing onto her hips, I push myself up out of the chair, my cock still inside her as I walk her to my desk.

She wraps her legs around my waist and I narrow my eyes at her, brushing a loose wave of her hair behind her ear. "Did you just fuck me?"

She raises her eyebrows in amusement. "Kinda."

"You know that is not how this works, right? I fuck you, angel."

"Yeah?" she stares into my eyes, challenging me. The fear that she felt just two hours ago completely dissipated now. And I can't even describe how much I love that I can do that for her.

"Yeah," I growl as I pull her off my cock and spin her around, bending her over my desk.

I push her thighs apart with my knee and take a second to stare at her almost naked body. She's only wearing knee high boots and a bra. Her sweet pussy is dripping with our cum. Wet, warm and pink, and begging to be filled. Then there's her ass. Her perfect peach of an ass. I swear half the time I don't know whether to eat it or worship it.

I rub my hand over it and she shivers. "You need me to remind you who is in control here, angel?"

It's her. It's always fucking her. One word and I would be on my knees at her feet and she knows it. But that she allows me the illusion that it's me is one of the many, many reasons I adore her.

"You are," she whimpers. "I'm sorry."

"It's a bit late for sorry now, Jessie," I growl as I open my desk drawer and pull out my belt. I keep it in here as a spare — for occasions like this when I'm not wearing one and I want to spank her beautiful ass.

"Conor," she moans softly as she hears the familiar jingle of the belt buckle.

I spank her with my hand first, leaving a satisfying red hand print on her skin as she hisses out a breath.

"Why did you make me come even when I warned you not to?" I ask as I bring my hand down again.

"I couldn't help it," she giggles, making me spank her harder.

"And now you're lying to me?"

"I-I," she stammers. "I really couldn't stop."

"You could, you just didn't want to." Palming the buckle, I wrap the leather around my fist. "Isn't that right?" The belt slices through the air as I bring it down over her ass cheeks with a satisfying crack.

"Ah," she cries, wriggling her ass until I spank her again.

"Answer the question, Jessie."

"Yes," she moans. "I didn't want to stop."

Crack!

"So why did you disobey me, angel?"

Crack!

"Because I wanted to see you lose control," she whispers, half giggling despite the fact she has pink and white stripes all over her backside.

"And how has that worked out for you?"

Crack!

"Pretty damn perfect if I'm honest," she breathes as she closes her eyes and presses her face against the desk.

I can't help but smile at her. My horny little angel.

I drop my belt to the floor, desperate now to fuck her. Pressing my hands on the tops of her thighs and her ass cheeks, I spread her wide open for me and she shivers at my touch.

"You're so fucking beautiful," I whisper as I push two fingers inside her.

"Please, Conor," she whimpers as I finger fuck her slowly, readying her for the absolute pounding I'm about to give her.

Only when her thighs are trembling and she's whimpering with need do I pull my fingers out and drive my cock into her instead. She cries out my name and it makes my balls tighten.

I bury myself in her. Over and over again. Driving further and harder inside her.

Bending her over always allows for hitting that sweet spot deep in her pussy that makes her come real hard. I fuck her until our bodies are slick with perspiration and our thighs are wet with her juices. I've made her come already but she's teetering on the edge again. She squeezes me tight, wanting to take me with her.

"Conor," she breathes out my name as another orgasm rolls through her body, softer this time. Her eyes roll in her head as she rides the waves and I thrust deeper as my own climax tears through me, searing heat in my balls and my spine.

I lean over her, careful to avoid the hot, tender skin where she just got her first tattoo and press my lips against her ear. "I'm so fucking proud of you, angel."

"Thank you for making me strong enough to go through with it," she whispers.

"You were already strong enough. You just needed a little reminder, is all."

. . .

WHEN WE WALK BACK into the apartment, we head for the kitchen where my brothers are gathered with our babies. Ella is crawling around the floor with Liam while Finn sits quietly on Shane's lap playing with a toy cell phone.

"Where have you two been for so long?" Mikey asks with a frown.

He's making dinner and wearing his Kiss the Chef apron.

"I got a surprise," Jessie says excitedly.

"What?" my three brothers say in unison.

She walks over to Shane who is closest and pulls down the sleeve of her sweater dress to reveal her brand new tattoo.

"You got a tattoo?" Liam asks, scooping Ella up before he walks over to her. He traces his fingertips lightly over the plastic wrap.

"Is that all of our names?" Mikey asks as he comes closer and peers at her shoulder with a huge goofy smile on his face.

"Yes." She smiles back at him.

"It's beautiful, baby," Liam says, kissing her shoulder softly.

She looks at Shane, waiting for his reaction. "You got a tattoo?" he eventually asks.

"Yep." She blinks at him, desperate for his approval too.

His brow furrows in confusion and then he looks at me. "You fucked her while she was getting a tattoo."

I swallow while Jessie's mouth hangs open in shock. "How do you even know that?" she says. "Did you watch on the security camera?"

"No," he shakes his head and laughs. "But you are terrified of needles, sweetheart, and that is the quickest and surest way I know to calm you down."

"True," Mikey adds with a nod.

Shane is staring at me again, a wicked glint in his eyes. I groan inwardly because I know what he's thinking.

"So you did fuck her?" he asks.

193

"Yeah," I sigh. Closing my eyes to avoid the smug look on his face.

"You fucked our wife and made her come in front of another person?"

"It was Gia," Jessie adds, as though that somehow makes this better.

"Interesting," he says with a nod as he slips an arm around her waist. "Your tattoo is beautiful by the way, sweetheart. I love it." He kisses her shoulder softly and she beams with pride.

"This doesn't mean it's open season for you two to go nailing our wife in public," I say to Shane and Mikey who are exchanging glances that let me know that is exactly what they are thinking about.

"You started it, bro. You fucked Jessie in front of Gia," Mikey replies, his arms crossed over his chest.

"Can we all stop saying the word 'fuck' in front of our children?" I suggest as Finn and Ella stare up at us.

"Yes," Jessie agrees.

"So what do we say?" Liam asks with a frown.

I look around the kitchen and suggest the first object that grabs my attention. "Balloon?"

"So you ballooned Jessie in front of Gia then?" Mikey says with a grin, making Jessie and Liam snigger.

"Actually, it was more like Jessie ballooned me," I reply.

"How is that?" Shane asks.

Liam raises his eyebrows. "Oh, she do that squeezing thing?"

"You know about that?" I ask him.

"Course," he says with a shrug.

"What squeezing thing?" Shane demands as he looks between me and her.

"Ah, the squeezing," Mikey says with a contented sigh.

"What is this fu-" Shane starts to say before he remembers

the 'no fuck' rule we just made, "ballooning squeezing are you talking about?" His scowl deepens.

Jessie laughs harder, placing her hand on his face. "You wouldn't know about this because you never, ever, give up enough control to let me do it to you," she says with a shrug. "Neither does Conor usually."

I nod my agreement. I have never been so still inside her that she's been able to do that to me before. Unless she's sucking my cock, I'm all about making her come, not the other way around.

"So, what is it?" Shane snaps.

"So, basically while you're... ballooning," I laugh now. I couldn't have chosen a better word? "You stay completely still and Jessie just squeezes and releases until..."

"Until..." Mikey mimes an explosion.

"Like the fourth of July," Liam adds.

"It was pretty intense," I agree.

Shane narrows his eyes at her. "I need to try this, sweetheart."

"I doubt you could handle it," she whispers in his ear and the vein in his neck starts to bulge. I swear if he wasn't holding our son he would bend her over the breakfast island, spank her and then fuck her.

A timer goes off behind us. "Dinner is ready," Mikey declares. "Sit your asses down and let's eat."

"Saved by the bell, Jessie," Shane says, scowling at her.

She takes his face in her hands and kisses him softly. "I can show you later if you like though."

"I have to work after dinner."

"Perfect. I'll help you. And then..."

"Fourth of July," he finishes for her, smacking her on the ass before he walks to the dinner table.

CHAPTER
THREE

JESSIE

4 days to Christmas

Conor frowns as he listens to whoever is talking on the other end of his cell phone.

"You've tried everyone?" he asks with a sigh. "For fuck's sake, isn't this why I pay you, Bianca? To manage?"

A few seconds later, he says. "Leave it with me," before ending the call.

"Problem?" Shane asks.

"Apparently half of the bar staff have some kind of stomach bug meaning we are seriously short staffed. It's Christmas week and the place is going to be busting at the seams with no fucker to serve them."

"I could work the bar," I suggest.

"No," Conor snaps.

"What?" I ask with a frown. "I've worked in bars for years. I know what I'm doing. At least it's one more body down there."

"Maybe I don't want your body down there," Conor says making Shane chuckle.

"Oh, don't be ridiculous. I'll be perfectly safe. It's your club. One of you can even come be my bodyguard for the night."

"I'll watch her," Shane offers.

"If she's going to work in our club, don't you think I should watch her?"

"No, because you will snarl at every guy she serves and end up throat punching half of them," Shane replies.

"True," I say with a smile.

"And you won't?" Conor challenges him.

"Anyone makes a pass at her and they'll get a punch in the mouth, but asking her for a drink I can handle."

"So, it's settled then. Tell Bianca I'll help out. I'll start at ten and stay until they need me."

Conor frowns as he considers my request.

"All hell will break loose down there if people can't get their beer," Shane says. "I'll take care of her."

"Fine," Conor grunts as he calls the manager of our night-club back.

"Thank you," I whisper to Shane who winks at me.

I'm actually looking forward to a night behind the bar. I always loved working in them when I was younger. I love drunk people. I love the club. I love Christmas. What could possibly go wrong?

CLOSING THE CASH REGISTER, I turn back to the sea of faces waiting to be served at the bar. I've been down here for three hours now and the club just keeps getting busier and busier. I, along with the other bar staff, have been working flat out to keep up with the rush.

I love it though. The music. The buzz of it all.

"Jessie? Jessie Heaton is that you?" A voice that sounds vaguely familiar shouts loudly. Turning to face the direction of the noise, I see a guy with a dark goatee wearing a Santa hat.

"It's me, Jason," he says with a big grin, launching himself across the bar with his arms wide open as though he's about to drag me in for a hug.

He is stopped by a large hand grabbing the scruff of his neck, pulling him sharply backward and making him yelp in surprise. That's when I realize who I'm looking at. Jason Donegan. I haven't seen him in ten years. A ghost of Christmas past if ever there was one.

"What the hell, man?" he snaps at Shane who glares at him, practically foaming at the mouth.

"You do not fucking touch her," he snarls. "Never fucking touch her."

Jason shrugs himself free from Shane's grip. "Who are you? Her bodyguard?"

Oh, crap!

Shane's jaw is clenched tightly shut and I see the telltale drawing back of his shoulders. Jason is about to get a punch in the mouth — or much worse. But the club is packed. It's almost Christmas. Everyone is drunk and happy — the last thing we need is my possessive husband tearing off someone's head at the bar.

"Jason, this is my husband, Shane," I shout, wishing I could get out there and stand between the two of them and diffuse some of the anger that is radiating from Shane in waves. But two feet of mahogany and ebony is in my way. I reach out instead, placing my hand on Shane's arm.

Jason holds his hands up in surrender. "I just wanted to say hello. I knew Jessie way back, is all," he says.

"I don't give a fuck when you knew her, or how, you do not

touch what belongs to me," Shane snarls. "Touch her and I will break your hand. Do you fucking understand me?"

"She's not your property, man," Jason scowls at him.

"Shane?" I plead. "He's just an old..." I stumble over the word. Fuck, what is he? "Friend," I finally say. Deciding that is the best description I can offer right now.

Shane grabs him by his collar. "She *is* my property, asshole. Every single inch of her. So stay the fuck away." He pushes Jason backward and a few seconds later he's swallowed by the huge crowd.

I roll my eyes, watching the Santa hat bobbing away through the throngs of people. When I look back at Shane, he is glaring at me, his eyes narrowed. "Who was that asshole?"

"Just some guy I knew a long time ago," I say with a shrug before I look at the woman dressed as a sexy Mrs. Claus who has just sidled up next to up him, and is waiting to be served.

"Knew him how?" Shane asks, speaking loudly enough that I can hear him in the club, but somehow keeping that low, menacing tone that turns my insides to warm butter, and also lets me know that this conversation isn't over.

I glance back at him, unable to stop my eyebrows from pulling my face into a frown even though I don't want to start anything with him right now. But I don't know what to say. I can't lie to him, but if I tell him the truth he might just run after Jason, pull off his arms and beat him to death right on the middle of the dance floor.

I falter for way too long before I reply. "I stayed with him for a few weeks one Christmas, that's all. There's nothing else to know."

Then I turn back to sexy Mrs. Claus. "What can I get you?"

Clearly that is not an acceptable answer to my husband's question and the next thing I know, he is vaulting the bar like a goddamn Olympic gymnast. Mrs. Claus stares at him open mouthed — a mixture of surprise, awe and desire on her face. I mean he is a pretty fine ass man and he just cleared a bar in one jump to get to me.

"Sha-" I don't even get his full name out of my mouth before he is on me. One hand gripping my waist and one in my hair as he crashes his lips over mine, making my legs tremble. His kiss is brief but full of fire and when he pulls back I'm left gasping. The fact that he only did it to mark his territory, showing everyone in this club who I belong to, doesn't make it any less hot.

He takes my hand and pulls me to the room behind the bar where the glasses are washed. He leads me to the back toward the storeroom, ignoring the looks of surprise on the two young glass collector's faces as they pass us with full trays. Once we're inside the small room, he closes the door.

I take a step back, pressing myself flat against the wall and trying to create a little space between us in this tiny room, because he looks a little pissed right now.

"Who is he?" he demands.

I fight every instinct in my body, willing my eyes not to roll — but they do anyway. Damn!

"Did you just...?" he snarls, advancing on me until he has me pinned against the wall. Placing one of his huge hands on the back of my neck, he runs the pad of his thumb along the curve of my jaw, causing goosebumps to break out all over my body.

He sucks in a breath and licks his lip, trying to control his temper. Meanwhile I'm trying to control the urge to push his buttons even more and make him fuck me over a stack of beer. It would be exactly what we both need right now, but I have to get back out to the bar before the crowd become a baying mob. There's nothing as demanding as a bunch of drunk people at Christmas, who are intent on getting even more drunk.

"Do not make me ask again," he says quietly, but there is no mistaking the threat implicit in his tone.

"His name is Jason. I met him in Virginia and I stayed with him for a few weeks when I needed a place to crash."

"How many weeks?"

"Six."

"Did you fuck him?"

"Yes," I whisper, trying to avoid his intense gaze but being unable to.

He narrows his eyes at me. "Okay. But I know you fucked other people before I met you, Jessie. Why are you being so vague about this guy? Did you love him?"

"God, no!" I wrinkle my face in disgust.

"So? Why so sketchy about him?" He pushes his body against mine, making warmth pool in my center and coil around my spine. He presses his thumb on my jawbone, tilting my chin slightly so he can stare directly into my eyes.

"I'm not being sketchy. I just don't want you to go all Shane on him, is all."

He frowns at my use of his name as an adjective. "I swear to God, if you don't tell me what the fuck happened between you two right now I will drag him in here and ask him myself. And you know I'm not gonna go about that politely."

"Promise you won't kill him?"

"Depends what he did."

I arch an eyebrow at him. "Nothing worth killing him for."

"I'll be the judge of that. Now talk."

"I was eighteen. It was a few weeks before Christmas. I needed a place to crash. I met him in a bar where I was working..."

Shane narrows his eyes in confusion.

"I pretended to be twenty-one. I had a fake ID, but the owners weren't the kind to check anyway — you know what I mean? As long as I was a hit with the customers and I didn't give them any trouble, they were happy to have me," I'm babbling now.

"You're stalling, sweetheart."

"I'm telling you how I met him," I say with a sigh and I don't miss the annoyance that flashes over his face. "So, I told Jason I needed a place to stay for the holidays and he offered me one. He seemed like a nice guy so I took it."

"And?"

I close my eyes and take a breath. This is the part he won't like. "After a day or two, it became clear that staying there came with some..." I struggle to find the right word for a few seconds, "expectations."

His frown deepens into a scowl. "He forced you to have sex with him?"

"I wouldn't say forced," I scrunch up my eyes. I am not handling this well at all. Jason is going to have his head on a spike if I don't stop making him sound like a rapist. "He just made some suggestions about what I could do to repay him for his kindness, and because I was trying to lie low, I went along with them. But I was a willing, if not enthusiastic, participant."

"He made you have sex so you could keep a roof over your head? That is not willing, Jessie," he snarls.

I cup his face in my hands. "No. He never threatened to throw me out. He just suggested that I could sleep in his bed and stuff..."

"Stuff?"

"You know what I mean, Shane. Besides, he didn't know I was on the run from the Wolf and how desperate I was for somewhere to stay. I genuinely think he thought he was helping me out and that I was into him. I mean, he was a nice looking guy with a nice place and a hot car. He was rich — or his parents were. I'm pretty sure he got laid whenever he wanted."

"Yet he still pressured young women into sex?"

"He's an asshole. He was then and no doubt he is now. Can we forget about him? Please?" I whisper, standing on my tiptoes to pepper soft kisses over his face.

He grunts his response, the hand on my neck now fisting in my hair while his free hand slides to my ass. He squeezes hard, making me moan, my lips twitching against his jaw. When he dips his head low and runs his nose over the soft skin of my throat, I whimper with need, rocking my hips and rubbing myself over his hardening cock.

"You belong to me, Jessie. Every fucking inch of you is mine."

"I know, Shane."

"How much longer do you need to work in this damn bar before I can take you to bed and fuck your brains out?"

Oh my God! "Until three, maybe? It should quiet down a little after that."

"Fuck. That's two more hours."

"I know." I grab hold of the lapels of his jacket, pulling him closer to me.

He growls in my ear, dragging my body over his thick cock as it bulges in his suit pants. "You make me feel like a goddamn animal."

"You are an animal," I whisper, dusting my lips over his. "And I can't wait for you to mount me later."

"Fuck, Jessie! You're not helping here," he groans loudly, making me giggle.

"Sorry. It's not exactly easy resisting you when you have me pinned against a wall with your huge cock. Not to mention having to watch women drool all over you while you sit at that bar."

He drags his teeth over the shell of my ear. "Sitting at that bar watching you," he whispers, making me shiver. "Besides, you think I like watching guys looking at your ass every single time you turn around? You wonder why all the guys ask for the Bud Light, sweetheart? It's because it's on the bottom shelf of the refrigerator and you have to bend to get it."

"Bud Light is just a very popular drink," I whisper, wrapping my arms around his neck.

"Really? If we don't get out of this room in the next five seconds, I'm gonna have to bend you over that stack of it, and you won't be going anywhere but bed because you won't be able to walk after. *One.*"

"That sounds kinda hot."

"*Two.*"

"How quick can you be, because I gotta get back to work?"

"*Three.*"

"You know that door has no lock, right?"

"*Four,*" he growls, his grip on me tightening.

I grab hold of his hand and pull him toward the door before he can get to five, opening it wide before he has a chance to pull me back inside and make good on his promise.

It's just before 3am. The club has quieted down a little and I figure the bar staff can manage without me for the next three hours.

Shane is deep in conversation with one of the club bouncers and I need to pee. I start to head in the direction of the ladies room.

"Where are you going?" he shouts after me.

I walk back to him because I don't want to announce to the

entire club where I'm headed. "I'm just going to the ladies room. Then I'll cash up my register and we can go home?"

"Give me two minutes and I'll come with you."

I cross my arms over my chest. "I need to pee. I can go to the bathroom on my own."

He looks to another bouncer who is standing nearby. "Watch her," he barks.

"I'll use the bathroom in Conor's office. It's like thirty feet away. I'll be fine," I say with a roll of my eyes.

He simply scowls at me in response as his employee talks in his ear about something which appears important. So I leave him to it and head off to the office with the other bouncer's eyes burning a hole into my skin.

I'm through the door when I feel someone behind me. A hand between my shoulder blades gently guiding me into the room.

"I can't believe you couldn't even let me go to the bathroom alone," I say with a chuckle as the door closes behind us. But when I turn around, it's not Shane who just shoved me into this room. "J-Jason," I stammer. "What the hell?"

He grabs my wrist, his fingers pressing into the soft skin of my forearm as he holds me a little too tight. His eyes are glassy but they are fixed on my face.

"Jessie," he says and there is something in his tone that I can't work out. "Are you okay?"

"Well, not right now, I'm not," I snap. "Get your damn hands off me."

He releases his grip at the same time as the pounding starts on the door behind him. Startled by the noise, Jason stumbles forward and onto me. He smells of alcohol and cigars and I wrinkle my nose at the offensive stench.

"Jessie! Open this fucking door!" Shane shouts while the banging continues.

I look behind Jason. "You need to open that door, right now," I say, aware of the tremor in my voice.

"Jessie. You're shaking," he reaches for me, brushing his fingertips over my cheek and making me flinch.

"Open this fucking door or I will tear your fucking head off!" Shane yells behind him.

Jason glances back quickly. "I can help you get away from him, Jessie. I know people."

I blink at him. "I don't want to get away from him. It's not my head he's about to tear off. What the hell are you talking about?"

The banging grows louder and the door rattles as though is about to come off its hinges.

"The way he talked about you," he says with a sneer. "You *belong* to him?"

"Jason. Listen to me. If you do not open that door right now and he has to break it down, he is going to kill you."

"I can protect us, baby," he whispers as he reaches for me again.

I dodge past him, elbowing him in the stomach as I run for the door and wrench it open, coming face to face with the wall of rage that is an incredibly pissed off Shane Ryan.

He pulls me straight into his arms, wrapping them tight around me and kissing my head. He walks into the room, kicking the door closed behind him and only then does he release me from his embrace. "Are you okay, sweetheart?"

"Yes, I'm fine," I say with a nod.

His eyes burn with anger again as he looks past me and at Jason. "What the fuck?" he snarls, his teeth bared.

"I-I," Jason stammers.

Meanwhile Shane's eyes drift back to me and his gaze lingers on the red fingerprints on my arm. "Did he fucking touch you?" he rages.

"He just grabbed me. I'm fine," I say, subconsciously rubbing at the skin.

"I was protecting her. She's fucking scared of you."

Jason may have well just poured gasoline over an open flame as Shane's anger rips through him like an inferno. In one swift move, he has Jason by the throat. Spinning him around, he presses him against the door.

"What did you just fucking say to me?"

"She's fucking scared of you," Jason snarls. "She was shaking when I came in here."

I close my eyes and pray for Jason to pass out or something because I cannot believe how one person can be so utterly stupid.

"Because you just locked her in a fucking room, you stupid cunt!" Shane squeezes Jason's throat tighter, making his face turn purple.

"She's not your property, man," Jason croaks. "You don't get to treat her like that."

Instead of tearing his throat out like I expected, Shane lets him go. And then he starts to laugh, and I can't imagine any scenario where this is a good thing.

"Come here, sweetheart," Shane says to me as Jason rubs at the raw skin on his throat.

Obediently, I take a few steps until I'm standing by his side.

"Tell this fuckwit who you belong to."

I look Jason in the eyes as I take hold of Shane's hand. "I belong to him and I like it that way. You're not rescuing me from him, asshole."

Jason blinks, looking between me and Shane.

"You think she's fucking scared of me?" Shane laughs again.

"She can say what she likes now, but she was trembling when she heard you coming through that door."

Shane grabs his throat again. "Yeah? That's because my girl

is a nice person and she doesn't want me to rip your fucking heart out and feed it to you while it's still beating," he snarls before pushing Jason onto a chair nearby.

Picking up some of the Christmas lights we had left over from decorating the club from the floor, Shane starts to wind the length around Jason's chest, tying him to the chair. He struggles and curses but he's no match for a determined Ryan brother and a moment later, Jason's arms are pinned to his sides and he's bound tightly.

He struggles for a few moments longer, panting for breath as he tries to work himself free. But Shane can tie a knot better than anyone else I know. I have had plenty of first hand experience of his binding skills and there is no way Jason is getting out of those Christmas lights unless Shane wants him to.

Finally, accepting defeat, he mutters under his breath and stops wriggling, glaring at the two of us instead.

"Shall I show you how scared my girl is of me, Jason?" Shane snarls, taking my hand and leading me over to the desk.

I swallow hard as his fingers grip mine, wondering what the hell is going through his devious mind.

He taps the edge of Conor's huge desk. "Sit here, sweetheart."

I look into his eyes, trying to read his mind, but I do as he tells me because I trust him completely. When I'm perched on the edge of the desk with my back to Jason, Shane presses his lips against my ear. "I won't let him see anything."

"Okay," I whisper.

He nudges my thighs apart with his knee until he's standing between them. Sliding one hand beneath my skirt and up my inner thigh, he keeps his eyes on Jason. Then he brushes his free hand up my arm and over the curve of my breast, pushing me slightly. "Lean back for me."

I plant my palms on the desk and lean back a little as his

208

hand between my thighs glides higher. When his fingertips brush my panties, my breath hitches in my throat. He tugs the fabric aside, sliding a finger through my slickness.

"So fucking wet," he hisses as he pushes one finger inside me.

"Shane," I moan softy as my walls ripple and squeeze around him.

"Fucking terrified of me, aren't you, sweetheart?" he chuckles darkly as he starts to lazily finger fuck me.

I tip my head back as the waves of pleasure start rolling through my core.

"You hear that, Jason?" Shane asks as adds another finger and the sound of my arousal fills the small room. "You hear how wet my girl is?" he growls as he drives deeper.

"Shane," I whimper, holding onto his forearm as he drives deeper, pressing against my walls and sending deep, throbbing pulses of ecstasy through me.

"Come here," he growls, wrapping an arm around my waist and pulling me close to him. He presses his lips against my ear. "You feel so fucking good squeezing my fingers, Jessie," he whispers as he pulls them out of me.

He keeps my body pressed tight against his but he is glaring at Jason. "You got a hard on for my girl, asshole?"

"Fuck you!" Jason spits.

Shane puts the fingers he just had inside me into his mouth and sucks them clean. "Fuck, you taste so good," he looks at me again for a second before training his glare back on the other side of the room. "You remember how sweet she tastes?"

My cheeks flame with heat and I scrunch my eyes closed because I can't believe we're about to have this conversation right now. "He never..." I whisper.

"What?" Shane says and I open my eyes to find him staring

at me. "You spent six weeks in his bed and he never tasted your pussy?"

Jason grumbles in the background, but I try and tune him out and focus on Shane. "No. He was more into receiving than giving."

Shane shakes his head and stares at Jason. "You are the biggest fucktard I have ever met in my life. Do you still fuck women without eating pussy? You must be a real hit with the ladies."

"Fuck you, man. We were just kids back then," Jason protests.

"He older than you?" Shane frowns at me.

"Yeah. He was twenty. His parents paid for his apartment and car," I reply, my cheeks still pink.

"Twenty? You weren't a kid, asshole, and even if you were... Fuck, I've been eating pussy since I was fifteen."

A sharp stab of jealousy pierces my chest. "Hey!" I nudge him in the ribs.

Realizing what he just said, he smiles at me and gives me a soft kiss on the forehead. "I have never enjoyed eating any as much as yours, Jessie, nor have I partaken so frequently as I do with you."

"You're such a poet," I say with a sigh, making him smile wider. His hand slides beneath my dress again, and for a moment there is only me and him in the room as he drags his pointer finger through my wet folds before circling my swollen clit. "Ah," I whimper, clinging to his neck.

"What the fuck?" Jason hisses, struggling in his bindings and reminding me he's there.

"Did he ever make you come, sweetheart?" Shane growls as he goes on rubbing the sensitive bud of flesh.

"No," I breathe.

"Yes I fucking did," Jason snarls.

"My girl said you didn't," Shane laughs softly.

"She's fucking lying," Jason insists. His bruised ego clearly winning out over his survival instinct because Shane's face turns dark with anger.

"Did you just call my wife a fucking liar?" he snarls.

"She's not gonna tell you I made her come, is she?" he goes on, digging himself deeper into a hole.

"Pretty sure she would, asshole," Shane snaps. "Because she doesn't fucking lie to me."

I curl my hand around his neck and press my cheek against his chest. That means so much to me given our incredibly shaky start when I had to hide who I really was from him and his brothers. Shane hates lying above anything else and it took him a long time to forgive me and to trust me again.

Jason grunts and grumbles in response.

"I tell you what, asshole," Shane says as he slides two fingers deep inside me, making me gasp as I coat him in a rush of slick heat. "I'll make my girl come right now, and you can hear what her actual orgasms sound like, rather than the ones she faked for you just to get you to leave her the fuck alone? How's that?" He spits out the last words — laced with anger and rage.

I feel it coursing through him but despite that, his fingers are gentle inside me, as though he's purposely holding back all of the emotion that is trying to spill out.

"Shane," I whimper as he brings me close to the edge.

He brushes the pad of his thumb over my clit and presses his mouth against my ear. "I know, sweetheart. I got you."

"I c-can't," I bury my head against his shoulder. "Not in front of him."

"You want me to stop?"

"No," I rock my hips against his hand. "I just can't let go."

"You can. Just focus on me, Jessie," he whispers as he works his fingers deeper, pressing against my G-spot and making my entire body tremble.

I breathe in the scent of him, inhaling his familiar cologne and that something else that I can never put my finger on, but which is just so uniquely him. I rub my cheek against his hard chest, taking comfort in its firm, reassuring warmth. His hand flexes on my waist, reminding me that he is holding onto me tight — that he's got me and that I have nothing to fear when I'm in his arms.

I curl my fingers in his hair, winding a strand around my fingertip.

"Shane," I breathe as my walls pulse around his fingers.

"Show him how hard you come for me," he orders, loud enough for Jason to hear and in that deep, commanding tone that vibrates through my bones and seems to be hardwired to my brain.

My body responds on instinct and my climax washes over me in a deep, bone shuddering, wave.

"Good girl," he whispers before he kisses the top of my head, massaging his fingers inside me until he has wrung out every last drop. "You hear that, dipshit? That's how to make my girl come," he says to Jason.

"Fuck you," Jason hisses.

"Is that the only comeback in your repertoire?" Shane laughs darkly, his fingers still inside me as he taunts his captive audience.

"Now if I thought you were worthy of such a show, I would spread my wife out on this desk and eat her pussy. Show you how to really make her scream," he says as he slides his fingers out of me, sucking them clean again before he goes on. "From the bulge in your jeans, I'd say you'd enjoy that a whole lot. But you're not fit to see her like that — not even close."

"You're sick," Jason spits.

"I'm sick? Says the man tied to chair with a raging boner," Shane laughs harder. Then he fixes my skirt and takes my hand, pulling me into a standing position. "Go to the restroom, sweetheart. Get yourself cleaned up while I have a word with Jason here."

I look back at Jason for the first time since Shane had me sit on the desk. He's red in the face. He struggles against his bonds. He's an asshole, yes. But he looks kind of pathetic sitting there like that.

I place a hand on Shane's cheek and he presses his face into my palm. "Don't kill him."

He glares at me. His jaw twitching as he maintains his temper a little while longer. I'm pretty sure Jason is going to bear the brunt of his wrath as soon as I walk into the restroom. "I won't," he eventually agrees. "For you."

"No, not for me," I push onto my tiptoes and brush my lips over his. "For you. Because he is not worth the blood on your hands."

Shane Ryan might be one of the most ruthless men I know, but I also know that it always costs him to take someone's life. No matter how easily and skillfully he appears to do it.

"I love you," he breathes out the words as though it pains him to say them.

"I know," I reply with a smile. That's usually our standard reply when the other one says I love you. It all started because he used to be an arrogant asshole, but now it's kind of our thing.

He grabs my elbow, pulling me closer until our bodies are pressed tightly together. "No. Not tonight, Jessie. Say the words."

I blink at him. Is he feeling insecure? Shane Ryan? I stare into his dark green eyes. "I love you, Shane. We were written in the stars."

213

That makes a smile flicker over his face before he pulls my face closer and kisses me. Hard. His teeth clash against mine as his tongue claims my mouth. I melt against him as he pours some of the anger in his veins out into me instead. And I swallow it all gladly. Letting him take whatever he needs.

FOUR

SHANE

As soon as she is in the restroom, I walk over to the piece of shit sitting tied to a chair in the corner. I lean over him, my hands on the armrests.

"Why did you follow her in here?" I snarl.

"I thought I w-was helping her," he stammers.

"Helping her how?"

"You're kind of a controlling..." he doesn't finish the sentence.

"So what? You were going to rescue her from me? Is that it?"

"I thought she was scared of you," he says, avoiding my eyes. Useless sack of shit.

"I warned you I would break your hand if you touched her," I remind him.

"I know," he snivels. "But I never hurt her."

I press my face closer to his, anger burning in my chest. "No, because if you had you would be screaming in fucking agony right now. I would peel your skin from your body while you were still alive, you fuck!" I spit the words and he flinches at the venom in my tone. He has no idea who he's dealing with. On another night, I might show him, but I made her a promise. And she is all I want. Dealing with this waste of oxygen would only keep me from her.

I free his right hand from the cable binding him to the chair.

"W-what," he whimpers as I thread my thick fingers through his, pushing back until I hear the satisfying crunch of bone.

He screams so loudly that I have to punch him in the mouth to shut him up. He blinks up at me, blood running from his lip and tears in his eyes.

"If you ever come to my club again. If you ever go near her again. Speak to her. Touch her. Jerk off while you're thinking about her, I will find you and I will crush every bone in your body. Do you understand me?" I squeeze his broken fingers harder and his face twists in agony.

"Yes," he nods as tears run down his cheeks.

When I let his hand go, it drops limply to his side. I untie him quickly and pull him to his feet before opening the door and signaling one of my bouncers. "See this piece of shit out and never allow him in here again."

"Of course, boss," he says with a nod as he takes hold of Jason by his good arm and leads him through the club.

I'M LEANING against the desk, hands shoved in my pockets as she walks out of the bathroom.

"Where is Jason?" she whispers.

"He left."

She makes her way toward me and places her hands on my chest. "Did he walk out of here or was he carried?"

I arch an eyebrow at her. "He walked."

She nods her head and smiles at me.

"You're not gonna though," I slide my hands to her waist, my fingertips gripping her tightly.

"I'm not?"

"No." Standing up, I spin her around so she's facing the desk. Pressing my lips against her ear, I inhale the smell of her — shampoo and the citrus perfume she wears. I could fucking eat her. "You won't be able to walk once I'm done with you."

My cock is aching for her. I press it against her backside, dragging her over my length.

"You think?" she breathes.

"I know. But don't worry. I'll carry you," I whisper in her ear as I start to unbuckle my belt. "Because your legs are gonna be shaking, sweetheart."

"Shane," my name leaves her lips on a breathy moan.

I pull her tiny mini skirt up over her ass before I push her down to lie face down on the desk. I love taking her like this. Driving myself into her and watching my shaft as it gets coated in her thick, creamy cum. Pulling my cock out of my pants, I nudge her legs further apart with my knee and line myself up at her entrance.

"You make me so fucking hard, Jessie." She wiggles her ass, trying to make me slide inside her but I hold back. "I've had this all damn night, sweetheart. You have any idea how uncomfortable this has been?"

"No," she giggles.

I slap her ass hard, making her suck in a breath. I glance down at the red mark on her perfect cream skin and it makes me smile. She is mine.

"Shane, please," she whimpers and my cock throbs.

I love how much she loves a spanking. How much she loves my hands on her. The way her body responds to every single touch.

Sliding myself deep into her, I moan even louder than she does at the relief of being inside her. Her silky heat swallowing my cock and squeezing me in her tight channel. There is no better feeling in this world than being buried in her.

I grab onto her hips and drive deeper, making her cry out.

"You wore this tiny skirt to drive me crazy all night, didn't you, sweetheart?" I growl as I rail into her. "Because you knew I would fuck you like this as soon as I could get my hands on you."

"No," she whimpers. "It was…" she trails off, groaning loudly as I slam into her even harder.

"You feel how hard you make me? I can't get enough of you, Jessie," I groan as my balls tighten and heat pools at the base of my spine.

"Shane!"

"Who do you belong to, sweetheart?"

"You," she pants as her walls tighten around me and I feel her orgasm cresting.

"Say it louder," I grunt, fucking her harder than she deserves, but I'm feral for her. The thought of that prick's hands on her, of all of the jackasses in here tonight who looked at her and thought that they might have a shot, it makes the rage burn inside me. I am a possessive asshole when it comes to her and I know it. I allow people to look at her, to want her, to want to taste and touch what is mine. Because the knowledge that she belongs to me and they will never have her makes me feel invincible.

She makes me invincible.

"You," she screams as her climax rips through her, making her hot little pussy squeeze my dick, wrenching my own orgasm from me as she milks me.

I lean over her, my lips pressed against her ear. "Damn fucking right you do," I hiss as I empty myself into her.

When I'm done, I tuck my cock back into my pants, pull down her skirt and scoop her into my arms, holding her still trembling body close to my chest.

She snakes an arm around my neck, her warm fingers curling a strand of my hair.

"I love you," she whispers as she nestles her head against my chest and I carry her out of the office and through the club.

It's not as crowded as it was an hour ago, but it's still busy enough for us to draw attention as I walk through to the exit that leads to the basement at the back of the club. It consists of two doors. One has a passcode and the other can only be accessed by our fingerprints.

I notice the concern in some of the faces as we pass by, and I hold her closer, not wanting any drunken hands to touch her to check if she's okay. I mean if they asked me, I'd happily tell them she can't walk because I just fucked her brains out.

She buries her face in my neck, her breath hot on my skin.

"Almost home, sweetheart."

"Hmm," she murmurs contentedly.

A FEW MOMENTS LATER, I step out of the elevator that leads to our penthouse apartment. Conor is standing in the hallway waiting for us, his hands stuffed into the pockets of his sweatpants.

"You see all that?" I ask him.

He can watch the feed from the security cameras in the club from up here, and he also has cameras in his office. And he is always watching her.

"Yeah," he grinds out the word, his jaw clenched tightly shut.

Jessie lifts her head and blinks at him. I feel the tension creeping into her body as she stiffens in my arms. She thinks he's pissed at her, but I know him better than that.

He walks over to us. "Give her to me."

I kiss her head softly before I allow him to take her from my arms.

"Are you, okay, angel?" he asks, running his hand over her hair as he squeezes her tight. He turns and starts to walk down the hallway to our bedroom and I fall into step beside him.

"Yes. And I can walk if you like?"

"I don't like," he snaps.

"Are you mad?" she whispers.

"Not at you," he replies, giving me the side eye.

"Please don't be mad at Shane. I don't want you to fight," she says, placing her hand on his face.

"We won't fight, angel. Promise," he reassures her before kissing her forehead.

Liar!

"Good." Jessie yawns. "Are we all going to bed?"

"Soon. I just need to talk to Shane first. Mikey and Liam are waiting for you."

"You said you wouldn't fight," she reminds him.

"We won't," I tell her. I have no intention of fighting with him over this.

"You sure you're okay?" he asks her again and the simmering anger bristles beneath my skin.

Of course she's okay. She was with me. Like I would let anyone hurt her. But I don't say any of those things right now because I don't want to argue in front of her.

He carries her to bed where Liam is lying awake waiting for her.

"Hey, baby," our younger brother says with a smile, seemingly unaware of what took place downstairs.

"Hey," she says as Conor sets her on her feet.

"Get in here, Red," Mikey grumbles, half asleep.

"I just need to freshen up first," she whispers

I want to tell her no. I want my cum running out of her while she lies between my brothers, but maybe it's not me she's washing away? So, I remain silent.

She looks between Conor and me, worry etched on her beautiful face.

"I just want to talk to him," Conor says quietly.

She narrows her eyes at us. "Okay," she finally says with a sigh. "But you'll come to bed soon, right?"

I place my hand on her waist and drop a soft kiss on the top of her head. "Very soon, sweetheart."

"Yeah," Conor agrees and together we watch her walk to the bathroom, her hips and ass swaying seductively in that skintight skirt.

Only when she's disappeared from view do Conor and I walk out of the room.

"What the fuck, Shane?" he snarls as soon as we're out in the hallway.

"He didn't see anything."

"He saw her come. He heard her," he snaps, his brow furrowed in anger.

"It's no worse than what you did in front of Gia. In fact it's less so."

He spins on his heel, glaring at me. "I did that for her. Because she needed me to. What you just did..." he scrubs a hand over his beard. "That was only for you."

I glare back at him. The rage is still bubbling inside me, just beneath the surface. Even fucking her didn't get it out of me. I should have killed him. I should have worked out every bit of anger and jealousy on him. He touched her.

He said...

Fuck! Conor is right.

SHANE

"I know," I admit and he blinks at me in surprise. I doubt he was expecting that admission so easily. "He said she was scared of me, Con. He said he was protecting her from me."

"Jessie?" he frowns. "Scared of you?"

"That's what he said." I swallow hard.

"But you know she's not."

"Yeah, I do. But, I dunno, Con," I shake my head. "I needed him to know it. I needed him to see how much she trusts me. I would have fucked her too, but I knew you'd be watching."

"Fuck," Conor says with a sigh, his anger at me seeping out of him as his shoulders drop. "Who the fuck was he?"

"Some guy she met when she was eighteen."

My younger brother listens intently as I tell him everything Jessie told me about Jason Donegan.

"You should have killed him," he snarls.

"I know," I admit.

"She asked you not to?" he says with a faint smile.

"Yup."

"Simp," he laughs and shakes his head. But he would have done exactly the same and we both know it.

"Besides, I half expected you to come down there and kill him yourself."

"You seemed to have it handled," he says with a shrug.

I smile at his trust in me. He never undermines me even when he doesn't agree with my methods. He backs me one hundred percent and then argues with me about it later. Just the two of us. It's the way it's always been.

"You want a nightcap or shall we just go to bed?" I ask, looking at the door a few feet away from us where she and our younger brothers are sleeping. I'm still on edge and I won't be able to sleep yet.

"Whiskey or Jessie?" he says, sucking on his top lip as though he's deep in thought.

I think about which of those two things is going to make me feel better about what happened tonight. There is only one answer. She's the answer to everything. "Bed then?"

He nods his head and puts an arm around my shoulder and we head back to the bedroom.

FIVE

Three days before Christmas

I press a soft kiss on Finn's cheek as he sits contentedly in Mikey's arms sucking on a chunk of pineapple, before bending and scooping Ella up for a cuddle. She grabs my hair and pulls with an excitable squeal before wriggling to get back down to the floor where she can continue crawling around and causing mayhem. I place her back down and she gives me a beautiful smile in return.

"Our little girl is gonna turn us all gray by the time we're thirty, Red," Mikey whispers.

I crouch down on my heels and take Liam's sneaker from her, just before she sticks it into her mouth. "She is not!" I insist. "She's just spirited, aren't you, baby girl?"

"Spirited? That's what we used to call Mikey, and look how that worked out," Conor laughs as he comes up behind me, picking Ella up from the floor again. She doesn't resist him though. She giggles as he hoists her high up into the air. Such a Daddy's girl.

"She's gonna be a warrior princess, aren't you, baby?" Conor says and she squeals in delight.

Meanwhile, her twin brother looks on, happily eating his pineapple. They have such different temperaments.

Conor tucks Ella into the crook of his arm and gives Finn a kiss on the head too before he focuses on me.

"Where are you going?" he says, looking me up and down. I usually don't wear shoes, or many clothes in the apartment, but I am bundled up ready to brave the New York winter.

"Going to collect my dress for tomorrow night from Callie," I say with a grin.

I am so excited to see it and even more excited to wear it tomorrow night for the masked ball. Callie owns a boutique in Manhattan and she is an artist when it comes to clothes. She knows what suits me and my coloring way better than I do.

"I'll come with you," Conor says with a wicked glint in his eye. No doubt remembering the very first time he and I had sex in Callie's dressing room — and the many times since.

"No you won't," Liam says as he walks into the room wearing only one sneaker. "I'm taking Jessie shopping."

"But taking her shopping is kind of my thing," Conor says with a frown.

"I've been looking for that," Liam says, spying his stray sneaker on the floor.

"The pint sized terror stole it," Mikey says, indicating Ella, who has started to wriggle now that she doesn't have Conor's full attention.

"Sorry, bro. I haven't spent any time alone with my wife for three days," Liam says as he pulls on his shoe. "I get the shopping trip."

"Fuck!" Conor mutters just as Ella starts to cry and hold out her arms to me.

"Oh, you want your mama when you're upset," I chuckle as I take her from Conor and give her a quick squeeze before placing her back on the floor where she wants to be.

"Besides, we have to go to The Peacock Club after to make sure everything's set up for tomorrow," Liam adds as he stands up straight.

The Peacock Club is one of a string of exclusive, private clubs we own across the States and Europe. They are sex clubs which cater to every kink imaginable. Every year they hold a Christmas Eve masked ball and they are the hottest tickets in the city. We didn't go last year because I was eight months pregnant, and I had thought we wouldn't make this years either. None of us wanted to miss our children's first Christmas Eve, but Shane insisted that they move the ball to the day before – a Christmas Eve, Eve masked ball – so now we are all going.

Liam, Mikey and I mostly look after The Peacock Clubs, while Conor handles the main nightclub, The Emerald Shamrock, which makes up half the basement and the entire first floor of our building.

"I can come with you to the club," Mikey says with a flash of his eyebrows, never one to miss out on an opportunity to visit and make use of one of the basement rooms while we're there.

"No. They're going to work, you fucking deviant. Besides, you're watching the babies," Conor reminds him. "I have some work to do."

"Why can't you watch the babies and let me have an afternoon of fun with my wife too?" Mikey suggests with a wicked grin.

"Because I have to work."

"But you were going to take the afternoon off to go shopping with Jessie?" Mikey reminds him.

"Yeah, well shopping with Jessie is worth taking an afternoon off for."

"But looking after our beautiful children isn't?" Mikey teases.

"Of course that would be worth it if they didn't have a perfectly good father right here already."

"You think I'm a good father?" Mikey pretends to choke up and wipes a fake tear from his eye.

"You're an asshole," Conor says with a roll of his eyes.

"Shall we go, baby?" Liam cuts through their bantering and slides an arm around my waist.

"Yes," I say with a smile.

"Will you buy some new panties please? Just for me?" Mikey asks me with a wink.

"Of course," I reply giving him a quick kiss.

"And get something for me, angel," Conor growls as he comes up beside me, pressing his lips against my ear. "Something you don't mind me tearing in half later."

LIAM SITS IN THE PLUSH, purple velvet chair in the dressing room of Callie's boutique. His legs sprawled and his hand resting on his chin as he watches me intently.

"I picked everything you asked for, Jessie," Callie says with a smile as her eyes sweep the room and land on a pile of underwear. "And also Conor called me a half hour ago and added to the list," she adds with a soft giggle.

"I bet he did," I laugh too.

She places a soft, manicured hand on my arm and sucks in a deep breath as though she's holding in her excitement. "But first, your gown," she squeaks, clapping her hands together. "Shall we try it?"

"Yes," I give a little squeal of excitement too. I am so pumped for the ball and Callie has promised to find me the perfect gown.

"It's behind here," she says, pulling back the thick velvet curtain a little and ushering me to step inside.

"Um, I thought you tried on clothes out here, baby?" Liam says.

I turn and smile at him. "I do, but not my gown."

"No," Callie agrees, shaking her head at him.

His brows knit into a frown. "Why?"

"Because you're not allowed to see it until the ball," I admonish him.

"So fucking unfair," he grumbles.

"Your Jessie has plenty of beautiful clothes to try on for you after her gown," Callie tells him with a wink.

AFTER I TRY on my gown, which is exquisitely perfect, Callie zips it into a bag and hangs it for me. When we're done, I step out of the small curtained area in just my underwear. She bustles around beside me, sorting clothes into piles. Liam, however, simply stares at me, his dark eyes roaming over my body and making me blush.

"Would you like me to stay and help?" Callie asks as she stands straight, blowing a stray curl from her forehead.

"No," Liam says immediately, making her laugh.

"He is so like his brother, no?" she says to me with a pop of one perfectly manicured eyebrow.

"He is," I agree.

"You both have one hour before the store opens again," she adds with a smile before she slips out of the room, leaving us alone.

"So now you try on all of these?" Liam asks, his eyes narrowed as he glances around the room.

"If you'd like me to?" I offer. I have no doubt that all of it will fit me perfectly because Callie knows my size and what suits me. "Where should I start?"

His Adam's apple bobs in his throat as he swallows hard. "The workout gear," he says with a low growl.

I smile as I walk over to it. His tastes are so different to his brothers. Conor would have gone straight for the black mini dress, while Mikey and Shane would have chosen the sexy underwear.

Fingering the soft, lilac material I flutter my eyelashes at him. "You know I don't usually wear underwear with my workout gear?"

"Yeah," he grunts.

"Okay," I whisper as I unhook my bra, keeping my gaze fixed on his as I peel it off and over my arms.

His eyes darken and he licks his lips.

Dropping my bra to the floor, I slide my hands over my stomach and hips, hooking my thumbs into the band of my panties before slowly working them down my legs.

"Fuck, Jessie," he groans as he pushes himself out of the chair. In a few swift moves he has me wrapped in his huge arms, my back against his chest and his face in my hair. "You know what you do to me, baby," he growls in my ear.

"I thought you wanted me to try on the clothes?" I whisper, aware that I won't be doing any such thing now, and that's fine with me.

"Is there any chance Callie will come back in here?"

"No. She knows not to disturb us."

"Fuck!" he hisses.

Unlike Shane and Mikey, he prefers privacy. Even the

thought of someone other than his brothers hearing us, would bother him.

"Does Conor fuck you in here?" he asks as he starts to unzip his jeans, keeping his other arm wrapped tightly around me.

"Yes."

He sucks in a deep breath and I feel him pumping his cock behind me before he picks me up with one arm and carries me across the small room until we're standing in front of the full length mirror. I drop my eyes instinctively and he grabs my jaw, tilting my head up so that I'm looking at our reflection. "Look how fucking beautiful you are, baby."

I look at him instead, staring into his eyes in the mirror.

"I said look at you, not me."

"I'd rather look at you," I whisper.

His lips dust over my ear. "Then watch me, baby. Watch my hands worship you."

I look at his hand gripping my jaw and follow it as he rubs it down my neck, onto my chest before he squeezes one of my breasts, making me moan softly. Then the other slides from my waist where he's holding me, gliding over my stomach. Over the gentle roundness in my lower abdomen that I can't seem to flatten no matter how hard I work out.

I close my eyes as his fingertips trace over the silvery stretch-marks I have now.

"Open your eyes, Jessie," he orders.

"You're so bossy," I protest as my eyes flicker open and I look at his huge hands on my stomach and breasts. Who am I kidding though? I love bossy Liam.

"Yeah?" he says, his warm breath on my neck making me shiver. "And you are even more beautiful now than you ever were. You gonna grow some more of my babies in here?" he growls, splaying his fingers across my abdomen.

"Hmm," I murmur as his fingers slide lower.

CHAPTER FIVE

"Spread those legs for me, baby."

I do as he asks me, allowing him to slide his hand between my thighs. He cups my pussy as he tugs on my nipples with his other hand and wet heat pools in my center.

"Who was the first out of us to kiss you?"

"You were," I breathe, remembering the night on the sofa with him and Mikey. It feels like just yesterday but also a lifetime ago.

"And who was the first one of us to taste this beautiful pussy?"

"You," I gasp as he starts to circle my clit with the tip of his pointer finger.

"You've always been mine, Jessie," he squeezes possessively.

"You were the first man I ever kissed for real," I remind him.

He brushes his lips over the sensitive skin on my neck. "I know, baby. And now, I want you to watch yourself while you fall apart for me. And then you're gonna watch me fuck you. You think you can keep quiet while I do that?"

"I'll try," I promise.

"You'd better do more than try, baby. Nobody else gets to hear you come but me, okay?" He slides a finger inside me while he goes on squeezing and tugging my nipples and I have to bite on my lip to stop myself from crying out as a wave of pleasure rolls through me. I moan softly instead.

"Good girl," he whispers as he rubs the knuckle of his thumb over my clit while he adds a second finger.

"Liam," I whimper. "You feel so good."

"You too, baby. Your pussy is dripping for me. I can't wait to slide my cock inside you too."

Dear God. His filthy talk really isn't helping me be quiet.

"Please?" I beg, pressing my hands flat against the mirror as my legs tremble. "I want you inside me."

231

"I am inside you, baby," he chuckles as he drives his fingers deeper. "Don't you feel that?"

"Ah," I groan as wet heat slicks his fingers.

"Yeah you do," he growls and the sound vibrates through my body. "You were made for me, weren't you?"

"Yes," I whimper as he massages my inner walls and rubs my clit while he rolls my sensitive nipple between his finger and thumb.

"Fuck, Liam!" I hiss as quietly as I can as the first waves of my orgasm pulse through my core.

"Look how beautiful you are when you come for me," he growls as he works his fingers expertly.

I look at myself in the mirror. My skin flushed pink. My body cradled in his strong hands. This is the body that he loves. The one that his brothers love. It is an irrefutable fact. One that I know in my bones.

His huge frame almost dwarfs me. His powerful thighs either side of mine. His thick biceps cocooning me — full of warmth and strength. He is strong and I am soft.

But my body is strong too. I grew two babies. Two incredible tiny humans who are going to change the world.

"I love you," I breathe as my climax bursts through me, coating his fingers as he wrings the last drops with his skilled hands.

"Love you too, baby," he whispers in my ear, sliding his fingers out of me. "Now lean forward and spread a little wider for me."

I widen my stance, dropping my head between my shoulders slightly as he grabs hold of my hip with one hand and his cock with the other. He presses the crown against my opening and I draw in a deep breath. I still want more of him. I always want more.

"Keep your eyes in the mirror. Watch how I fuck you."

I look in the mirror, my eyes on him rather than myself and watch his almost roll back in his head as he drives his cock into me.

"Fuck. You feel so good," he growls. "So. Fucking. Good." He thrusts on every word, rocking me forward onto my tiptoes every time he does and hitting me at the perfect angle.

Over and over again he rails into me. His eyes never leave my body as he fucks me relentlessly.

"Liam," I pant, my breath fogging the glass.

"Come for me again, baby. Squeeze my cock with your tight pussy so I can I fill you with my cum."

Oh sweet Jesus!

"Oh, God!" I shout out and he clamps a hand over my mouth, pulling me back so that my back is flush against his chest again.

"I warned you to keep quiet," he groans in my ear.

Lifting me from the floor, he carries me to the huge purple chair and drops me onto my knees on the seat. Pressing a hand between my shoulder blades, he pushes me forward so my face is pressing against the back cushion.

"Bite down, baby. Because I'm giving you another one of them."

"Liam, I can't," I whimper. "If you make me come again, I might ruin this chair."

"You won't," he soothes, holding my hips in place as he slides deep inside me. "Just let me fuck you."

"If you make me squirt all over this beautiful chair..." I trail off because he starts to trail kisses over my shoulders as he reaches in front of me and starts to rub my clit.

I squeeze my eyes tightly shut as my third orgasm crests and my entire body starts to shudder. Stars flicker behind my eyelids as he maintains his relentless fucking and rubbing and kissing. I'm so sensitive. I'm going to pass out or...

"Liam," I whimper again.

"I said bite down," he reminds me.

I press my face into the deep velvet cushion, muffling my moans as I come.

Hard.

I soak his jeans and the cushion I'm kneeling on while Liam sucks on my neck as he grinds deeper into me, filling me with his own release.

When he finally stops, he pants in my ear and I look down at the mess we've made. The chair is soaked in my cum.

"I told you we'd ruin the chair. Callie is going to kill us."

"I'll buy her a new one," he chuckles as he peppers soft kisses over my back, making me squirm.

"She's going to know what we were doing in here," I tell him, even though I'm pretty sure she already does.

He looks down too. "Fuck," he mumbles. "I'll tell her I spilled a drink."

"What drink would that be, Einstein?" I ask with a roll of my eyes.

He slaps my ass. "Don't be cheeky," he growls and I giggle.

He pushes himself up and zips up his jeans.

"You're in so much trouble, Liam Ryan. If Callie bans us from her boutique, Conor is going to be so pissed at you."

That makes him falter and he screws his eyes closed. "We'll take the cushion and I'll have someone come pick up the rest of it and deliver a new one by the end of the day."

"Why are we taking the cushion?" I turn and frown in confusion. "Maybe we could just flip it to the dry side?"

He shakes his head. "No. It's soaked in your cum, baby. It's coming with us."

"You're serious?" I ask as I search for my discarded underwear.

He hands me my panties. "Deadly."

Taking them from his outstretched hand, I arch an eyebrow at him. "You happen to know a guy who sells giant purple velvet chairs then?"

Pinching the bridge of his nose, he sighs deeply before he says, "I'll get something else for today. Just get dressed so we can plan our escape."

I laugh, wondering how he's going to explain his way out of this. Once I'm dressed, Liam calls Callie into the room. He's flipped the cushion so the huge wet patch can't be seen. His jeans are also wet but he hides that with his coat.

"We'll take all of the clothes," he says. "And the chair."

"The chair?" Callie blinks at him in confusion.

"Yup. It's going to be Conor's Christmas present."

"You can't have my chair," Callie laughs softly.

"I'm gonna need it," Liam replies. "I'll have a replacement one sent within the hour and then if you let me know where to get the purple one from, I'll have it here as soon as possible."

"But that's not possible. It was custom made. The designer doesn't make them any longer. It cost me fifteen thousand dollars."

"I'll give you fifty thousand for it," Liam offers and I suppress a grin. That chair is from a chain store and they still sell them now.

"But it was a family heirloom," she adds.

Liam frowns at her. "But you just said..."

Callie and I burst out laughing at the same time and Liam shakes his head.

"You can take the chair. But yes I want a new one. Jessie knows where to buy them," Callie says with a giggle as she wanders out of the room.

Liam turns and trains his gaze on me. "You know where to buy them?"

I chew on my lip, trying to look sweet and adorable. "Yeah," I whisper.

He crosses the room in two strides, pulling me into his arms. "If I was into spanking..." he breathes, brushing my hair behind my ear. "Your pretty ass would be red by the time we left here."

"You've spanked me plenty of times," I remind him.

"A slap on the ass is not a spanking, baby," he growls, making a shiver skitter along my spine.

"I would love a spanking from you."

He narrows his eyes at me. "Haven't you had enough fun for one afternoon?"

"Not nearly enough," I whisper and he laughs softly.

SIX

JESSIE

Two days before Christmas

I adjust my green and gold mask and take a deep breath as I grip the door handle. Looking down at the deep emerald green material of my dress, I blink back an unexpected tear. I have never been to a ball before. I've never worn a dress as exquisite as this one. Even my wedding dress was simple. This is made of the softest velvet I have ever felt — softer than a baby's skin. It's strapless and studded with Swarovski crystals all along the split up my thigh, which is so high it's almost indecent. They sparkle every time I move.

I feel like a princess.

I can't even imagine what it cost because Callie wouldn't tell me and my husbands insisted on paying for it. I hope they love it as much as I do.

I walk out of the bedroom and the four of them are standing in the hallway in their matching tuxedos waiting for me. It's a good thing I'm not wearing panties because they would have just burst into flames.

"Fuck, baby," Liam says with a low whistle.

"That dress is hot, Red," Mikey says as he walks straight over to me and slides his hands around my waist.

"You look beautiful, Mrs. Ryan," Chester says and I realize I hadn't even noticed him standing in the hallway too. I was too mesmerized by the four hot devils in the finest suits I have ever seen.

Chester is the brother's longest serving and most trusted employee, and along with his wife, Rosie, he is our babysitter for the evening. There is also a team of four ex Navy SEALS in the basement making sure that nobody can get to the apartment.

"What did you say?" Conor growls as he glares at Chester.

"Relax, Con," Shane laughs. "She's pretty hard not to look at."

"I'll just go check on the twins," Chester mumbles apologetically.

"Thank you," I say to him with a smile.

"Call us for anything at all," Conor reminds him as he walks down the hallway.

"Will do, Boss," he calls back. "Have a great time."

Conor watches after him. It took us a long time to trust anyone with our children's safety, but Chester and his wife are almost part of the family now, and his small unit of security do an amazing job.

When there is just the five of us in the hallway, Conor, Shane and Liam walk toward me until I'm standing in the middle of all four of them.

Conor looks down at the split in my dress, his dark eyes twinkling. But it's Shane who slides his hand inside and brushes his fingers over my bare pussy.

"She wearing panties?" Conor asks him.

"Nope," Shane grins. "Freshly shaved too."

I blush and Conor closes his eyes. "Dammit, angel," he hisses.

"I can't really wear underwear with this dress," I protest. "It's so tight."

"Fits you like a second skin, Red," Mikey says appreciatively as he runs his hands over my ass.

"Can we just stay home?" Liam groans as he trails his lips over my bare shoulder.

"No," I say, but his brothers laugh.

"We have a room booked too," Shane reminds him.

Mikey rubs a hand over his beard. "And now that Conor has given the green light for public-"

"It's not a green light," Conor snarls.

"But some public fuckery must be permissible after what you did, bro?" Mikey winks at him. "And I mean, we all came prepared, right?"

"Prepared?" I blink at him.

He pulls his pocket square out and reveals it's actually a large white handkerchief. "For any spillages," he says with a wicked grin.

I look at the three of them and they all nod to confirm they too have white handkerchiefs.

"Can't have you spoiling that beautiful dress, sweetheart," Shane whispers.

"Maybe I should wear panties too?" I suggest, wondering if I'm going to able to sit down at all tonight without staining this dress.

"No," Mikey and Liam reply.

"We need to leave," Shane says, checking his watch.

"Wait. Where are your masks?" I ask.

"We've got them," Liam says, patting his breast pocket. "We'll put them on outside the club."

"Let's go before I tie you to my bed instead, angel," Conor says with a sigh, placing his hand on the small of my back and guiding me to the elevator.

MIKEY POURS CHAMPAGNE as we sit in the back of the limo. I sit on Liam's lap. I rarely get my own seat but that's fine with me because I'd much prefer to have one of them holding onto me.

"Just a small one for me, please. You know I get giddy when I drink bubbles."

"Yeah, and you're kinda giddy enough already, Red," Mikey says with a grin as he hands me my glass.

"I can't help it. It's Christmas. We're going to a masked ball. All of us at The Peacock Club," I shiver in anticipation.

"You need me to help you relax, baby?" Liam whispers in my ear, making goosebumps prickle over my forearms.

"How is that not gonna make her even more excited?" Conor asks his younger brother with a frown, but Liam's hand is already trailing up the inside of my thigh through the split in my dress.

"But she looks so damn good in this dress," Liam groans as he trails kisses over my throat.

Conor sighs but it's Shane's voice that stops Liam's fingers as they are just millimeters from my pussy. "If you make our girl come now and she starts moaning in this car, then someone is gonna fuck her. And if one of us fucks her..."

"We'll all want to fuck her," Conor finishes for him.

"And then we never get to the club," Mikey adds.

"Jessie's call," Shane says. "You want to go to the ball or you want to drive around the city all night being nailed in this car?"

I swallow. I mean on any other night the car option sounds good too. "I want to go to the ball," I whisper.

"Then your wish is my command, Cinderella," Liam says with a wink as he slides his hand from inside my dress.

Conor takes my hand and lifts it to his lips, brushing them over my fingertips while Liam dusts his lips over my ear. "Besides, we got all night, baby."

We do. A whole night with them in the club. With the use of a private room in the basement. My insides turn to molten lava at the thought.

It's going to be perfect.

CHAPTER
SEVEN
JESSIE

I actually gasp out loud when we walk into the club. Our manager, Evelyn, has done an incredible job with the place. At first glance it is decorated with elegantly tasteful Christmas garlands and ornaments, but on closer inspection, most of them have some kind of cock, pussy or something kinky on them. It is perfect for a masked Christmas Eve, Eve ball in a sex club.

I look at Liam who holds onto my hand. "It's perfect, isn't it?"

He nods his agreement.

"We should go find Evelyn and tell her."

Shane slides a hand onto my ass and whispers in my ear. "You can do that tomorrow, Mrs. Ryan. Tonight there will be no shop talk. We're just regular customers here."

I smile at him. I love that idea. And being here with four guys isn't that unusual for this place. Anything and everything goes.

"If we're just regular customers then I would like to take my wife for a dance," Mikey says, taking my other hand and nodding toward the dance floor.

Just as he says that the opening beats of *Pony* come on and I roll my eyes. There is no way he didn't plan that to happen.

"Look out, Magic Mikey is in the house," Liam laughs softly.

"Come on, Red, dance with me?" he says, tugging my hand.

"Just dancing, right?" Conor says with a frown.

"Oh, bro, we are gonna do so much more than dance," Mikey winks at him before he pulls me off into the crowd and finds us a dark spot on the dance floor.

"You shouldn't push his buttons like that," I giggle as I wrap my arms around his neck.

"Oh, but Red," he whispers in my ear. "I can guarantee he's going to be over here within ten minutes and then you're gonna have both of us here finger fucking you in the middle of this club."

"Mikey," I gasp as he steps back and starts busting out his best moves. His hand slides over his stomach as he rocks his hips and I bite on my lip as I watch him. Damn, he is so fine.

When he notices I'm not dancing, he wraps his arms around my waist. "Dance with me, Jessie."

"I hate dancing on my own," I whisper. "I feel self-conscious."

He frowns at me. "But I'm right here with you."

"I know, I mean... I like dancing like this. With you," I say as my cheeks flush pink.

He raises his eyebrows at me. "You mean you like my hands on you at all times?"

"Yes," I laugh.

"Then consider it done," he growls as he rocks his hips against mine. "But know I'm gonna have a raging boner the whole time."

"Yeah?" I bite on my lip and press my lips to his ear. "Watching you bust out your Magic Mikey routine gives me a lady boner."

"Fuck!" he groans in my ear.

Then he's walking me backwards until we're tucked away in a corner. His hand slides into the split in my dress until his fingers glide over my pussy and I shiver at his touch.

"Remember when I made you come in The Shamrock, Red?" he groans, reminding me of an evening we spent in our other nightclub as he slips a finger between my folds.

"Yes," I hiss.

"And remember how mad we made Conor?" he chuckles.

"Yeah," I whimper, remembering the aftermath of that whole event.

"Well, he must have seen me sneaking off into a dark corner with you because he's on his way over here right now."

With his final word he slides a finger inside me and my walls tighten around him.

"Oh, fuck," I gasp as strong hands slide over my abdomen and a hard chest is pressed against my back.

"You're a fucking deviant, Mikey," Conor says gruffly.

"Never claimed to be anything else," he replies with a grin as he leans his face closer to his older brother. "But you should feel how wet she is, bro."

Conor grunts in response, stepping closer to me and pinning my body against Mikey's until I'm sandwiched between the two of them. Mikey looks down at me and gently pumps his finger in and out of me. "You okay, Red?"

"Uh-huh," I mumble as slick heat coats his fingers and warmth spreads through my thighs.

My body shudders and Conor's hard cock digs into my back. He's so rigid and tense. I feel it in his arms and chest, as though he's holding back from something — either he wants to punch his little brother in the face, or he wants to touch me too.

When his hand slides over my abdomen until he reaches the

split in my dress, I realize which temptation he was fighting. Pulling the soft fabric aside to allow his hand inside too, he brushes the pad of his middle finger over my clit and I whimper with need.

Mikey palms the back of my head and presses my mouth against his neck. "Stay right here. We got you," he whispers.

God do they got me. The two of them work their fingers in and on my pussy like they each know what the other is thinking. I moan into Mikey's neck as he pushes deeper and Conor presses harder. Then in the space of one single song they have me coming on their hands and shuddering between them.

"Good girl," Conor whispers in my ear.

"Such a good fucking girl, Red," Mikey adds as he brushes back my hair.

"How long do we have to stay up here before we can make use of that fucking room downstairs?" Conor growls as he slides his hand from my dress.

Mikey does the same, sucking his fingers clean in full view of the crowd.

Meanwhile Conor takes his handkerchief from his pocket. "Keep her covered," he barks to Mikey as his hand slips between my thighs again.

"As if I wouldn't," Mikey says with a scowl.

"I can go to the rest-" I start to say but Conor is already wiping the soft cotton between my folds.

"I don't want you spoiling your beautiful dress, angel," he whispers in my ear.

"Then thank you."

"But I hope you don't ever plan on wearing it again after tonight, because I'm going to fucking ruin it later," he adds.

I gasp out loud. "You can't. It's too expensive, and it's way too gorgeous to ruin."

"Not as gorgeous as you, Red," Mikey grins.

"And we're going to ruin you too," Conor growls, making my insides turn to Jell-o.

I blow out a shaky breath. "As hot as that sounds, we only just got here and we can't go to the room downstairs yet."

"Fuck!" Conor grumbles.

"Shane has reserved us a booth anyway. Pretty sure he just watched us make you come on this dance floor and will be wanting to push some more boundaries tonight," Mikey adds with a laugh.

AN HOUR LATER, Shane, Liam and I are making our way back to the booth after I wanted to see the displays in the other rooms. As we pass the stairs to the basement, I stop them.

"I need the powder room," I say.

We just passed the customer restrooms and the line was enormous but there's a staff bathroom downstairs that I could use.

"Shane Ryan?" a guy with gray hair wearing a red and black mask comes up beside us and says.

All of my husbands are wearing masks too but they are pretty recognizable anyway. Shane clearly knows this man and likes him because he smiles.

"Alfred," he says as he shakes his hand.

"And Mikey?" the man I now know is Alfred says to Liam.

"Liam," he corrects him.

"Sorry. You look even more alike with a mask on," Alfred laughs.

"And this is my wife, Jessie," Shane introduces me and I smile too. But now I am busting to pee.

"I need to use the ladies' room," I say, excusing myself.

Shane frowns at me.

"I'll go with her," Liam says and we both say goodbye to Alfred and make our way downstairs to the basement.

"I can go to the restroom alone, you know?" I say to Liam, reminded of a similar conversation I had with Shane a few evenings before.

"I know, but it's more fun with me," he says with a wink.

As we reach the bottom of the stairs, there is some kind of commotion going on in one of the rooms because a woman runs out crying and a half naked man comes running after her and bumps straight into Liam.

"What the fuck?" Liam snarls as he pushes the man off him.

"Cassidy!" he shouts after the fleeing woman.

"Did you do something to her?" Liam snarls.

"No," the man scowls at him.

Oh my God, I'm going to pee.

The hallways starts to fill up with people who are either startled by what's going on or simply on their way down here to use one of the rooms. There is usually a bouncer at the top of the stairs but I imagine he may have gone running after the crying woman. I hope she's okay.

Damn. Now I really need to pee.

"Liam. I gotta go now. I'll be right back," I say as I head off to the bathroom.

"Jessie, wait."

"I'll be right back," I call, turning the corner as I head to the staff restroom and straight into a bearded man in a Santa mask.

"Jessie Heaton? Twice in one week? This must be fate, right?" the familiar voice sneers. "And lucky for you I have a room here."

Jason!

I shout for Liam but there is too much noise down here now. People are jostling through the hallway. Jason grabs my arm, opening the door to the nearest room which he has clearly just come out of and pushing me inside.

There are three other men in there and they all look up as he walks in. They all wear masks. The Grinch, an elf and a reindeer.

"Where are the girls? One is no good to us?" The Grinch barks.

"Oh, but this one is even better," Jason sneers as he takes off his Santa mask. "She's the one who did this." He holds up his hand which I now see is in a cast.

"I didn't do that," I say but he pushes me further into the room and I stumble forward in my heels.

"Shut up. Fucking whore!" he spits.

"But where are the girls we were supposed to be hooking up with?" the elf asks.

"Couldn't fucking find them. I think they stood us up," Jason says with a shrug.

"So what? We all take turns on her?" The Grinch asks with a sneer as he removes his mask too. He has a dark goatee too and his eyes are similar to Jason's.

"Exactly, bro," Jason says, confirming they are brothers.

"Take turns on me?" I spit. "Have you lost your tiny fucking minds?"

"Did she just..." The Grinch looks at his brother. "Who the fuck is this bitch?"

I stare at The Grinch. Clearly he thinks he is somebody special. He's dressed in a finely tailored suit. Expensive leather shoes. He wears a fancy watch too. From here it looks like an Omega. Jason's parents were very wealthy. I remember how much he used to go on about how rich his family were. He always thought he was somebody special too.

The other two men in the room are dressed pretty similarly. I imagine they all think they have the balls to do what they're about to. I also imagine they probably get away with crap like this all the time. But clearly they have no idea who I am.

"I told you. That whore who used to fuck me for a place to stay. The one that had her asshole, psycho husband make me watch him finger fuck her," Jason answers The Grinch's question.

"If her husband is a psycho is this the wisest move?" the elf asks.

"Like he could touch us," the Grinch replies with a smug grin.

"Are you really that stupid that you think he won't annihilate every single one of you?" I say with a shake of my head. "You don't think he's looking for me right now?"

The Grinch shrugs. "He can look all he wants, princess. He ain't gonna find you down here. These rooms are private and soundproof. Those doors are made of solid steel. There are no cameras. Nobody gets in without a special keycard."

"Yeah, I know asshole, because I-"

Before I can finish that sentence and possibly save their lives by telling them who I am so they can let me go, Jason grabs me by the throat.

"You call my brother an asshole. Do you know who he is? He has friends, bitch. Powerful fucking friends."

"I guarantee none of them are powerful enough to save you if you don't let me go," I croak and he squeezes tighter.

"Let you go? When we haven't even started yet. You're gonna pay me back for the other night, you fucking slut! You think you can humiliate me and get away with it?"

He pushes me backward, letting go of my throat as he does. "Humiliate you? How exactly did I do that?"

He holds up his bandaged hand. "This! Making me watch you and him..." he spits out the words.

"I believe it was my husband who did both of those things.

Why don't you take this up with him?" I snarl as I take a step closer to him. "Because you are a fucking coward, that's why. He humiliated you, but you want to take that out on me?"

He presses his face closer to mine. "No. He will feel what I'm going to do to you, you filthy fucking whore!" he hisses. "Every time he looks at you, he's going to know what I did. Know that we all fucked your pretty little holes." He pulls a flick knife from his pocket and flashes it in front of my eyes.

I don't flinch. I glare at him instead. "You lay one finger on me and he will kill you, Jason. And he won't do it quickly. He will make you scream for mercy."

He seems to find that funny and he throws his head back with laughter. "I think I can handle him."

"I really don't think you can," I spit. "You certainly couldn't the other night."

He glares at me again, his teeth bared like a rabid animal. "I'm not on my own now though, am I?" He nods toward his three friends. "You have no idea who you've been fucking with, whore!"

I glare back at him. I think he is the one who has no idea who he's dealing with, but I don't say that. I let him go on thinking he's a big man — it all buys me some time until one of my husbands gets in here.

"Stop calling me a whore," I say instead.

He drags the tip of the blade over the soft skin of my neck. Fear prickles along my spine but I stay rooted to the spot, determined not to show any fear to this stupid asshole. "But you are a whore, Jessie," he snarls. "You slept with me for a place to stay."

I narrow my eyes at him. "Kind of makes you a sick, twisted piece of shit then!"

"And I saw you up there in the club. Oh yeah, I saw you. I hoped we might get a chance to talk alone. Letting your husband's buddies slide a hand inside your dress. Does he know that they do that? Does he like to pass you around?"

My nostrils flare as I suck in a breath. "He does not *pass me around,* asshole. They are not his buddies, they're his brothers, and they're my husbands too."

That certainly gets his attention. "You can't have more than one husband. It's illegal."

"Pretty sure my husbands don't give a crap about the law, as you're about to find out to your detriment if you don't let me go right now."

"You got four husbands?" Jason's brother asks me.

"Yes," I snap.

His face turns whiter than Santa's beard as he realizes who I am. He looks back at Jason before slapping him across the back of the head. "You fucking stupid prick. You said this was just some chick who fucked you over."

"Sh-she is," Jason stammers as he frowns at his brother.

"You have any fucking idea who she's married to?" his brother asks as he runs a hand through his hair. "Fuck!" he mutters, pacing back and forth while Jason stares at him.

"Who?"

"The Ryans, you fucking reject!"

"Who the fuck are they?" Jason snarls.

His brother stops pacing and glares at him so hard it's a wonder he doesn't burst into flames. "Only the goddamn Irish." He slaps Jason again. "Fucking." Slap. "Mafia."

"W-what?" Jason stammers.

"Yeah, dipshit," I say. "So let me go right now and they might not cut off your balls and make you eat them while I watch."

"We can't let her go, man," the reindeer says. "We need to get her out of here. Like now."

Oh, fuck!

"No. You need to let me go and get yourselves out of here," I say. "Before they find you."

"So you can tell your husbands what we did and have them come looking for us?" Jason's brother scowls.

I fold my arms over my chest. "How the hell do you expect to get me out of here without them noticing?"

"We could knock her out. Pretend she's drunk," the elf suggests.

"You'll never get past the bouncers. You think they don't know me?"

Jason's brother looks at his two buddies. "Where was that fire escape?"

"End of the hallway," the reindeer replies.

"You take me out of here and they will come for you," my voice trembles but I tip my jaw in defiance. I have dealt with scarier and tougher men than these before. "That is an inescapable fact. But you let me go back upstairs and you at least have a chance."

"Shut her the fuck up," Jason's brother orders.

Jason makes a grab for me but I dodge him and knee him in the balls, causing him to drop to the floor.

"You shouldn't have done that. Dumb bitch!" His brother snarls as he wraps a thick, tattooed hand around my throat and his two buddies close in on me too.

He squeezes tightly, making my head spin. I claw at his arms and try to suck in a breath as I prepare to try and fight my way out of this. I would rather die than let them take me away from this club. Because if they do manage to get me out of here, they only have one option and they know it. They need to make me disappear.

"You *really* shouldn't have done that, asshole," Mikey's voice washes over me and I almost pass out with relief. His fingers curl around Jason's brother's wrist as it's wrapped around my throat, and he squeezes hard enough that I hear the crunch of bone. The elf jumps on Mikey's back but he shrugs him off as though he's made of air.

When the grip on my throat loosens, I stagger backward, stumbling against the wall and rubbing the reddened skin on my neck.

"One of them has a knife," I croak but Mikey already has Jason's brother on the floor. He stamps on his head and the sickening crunch of bone almost makes me retch.

My eyes flicker closed as blood thunders around my body and I sway on my feet, feeling like I'm about to faint. That's when I feel the two strong arms wrapped around me and I sink against his chest, seeking the comfort and warmth of him. The familiarity of his touch, his smell, his arms — they all soothe me.

"Liam," I murmur.

"I got you, baby," he says, stroking my hair as he holds me tight.

"Get her home. Now!" Shane's deep voice fills the room and I look up to see him and Conor running inside.

"Come on. Let's get you out of here," Liam whispers as he picks me up and cradles me to his chest.

"I'm sorry," I rasp, my throat raw.

"Don't, Jessie," Shane barks as he grabs Jason by the jaw and pushes him back against the wall. Then he starts to pummel his face with his fist and Jason screeches in agony. Meanwhile Conor grabs both the elf and the reindeer by the throat at the same time. He doesn't even look at me and that makes me want to cry.

I have ruined the whole night.

"I said get her out of here, Liam," Shane barks again and the harshness in his tone makes me bury my face in Liam's chest.

Before we leave the room, I take a final glance back at Conor and Shane and the scene is like something from an action movie.

Conor has the reindeer in a headlock while he kicks the elf in the chest, sending him flying across the room and landing near Shane's feet. Shane still has hold of Jason, whose face is a bloody pulp, by the throat, but he looks down and kicks the elf in the head like he's kicking a soccer ball.

I want to help. I want them to know I didn't mean for this to happen, but then Mikey closes the door and they're gone.

"Keep the hallway clear. Escort any guests to and from the rooms for the rest of the night," Liam says to the two bouncers who are standing in the hallway.

"Yes, Boss," they reply.

"Nobody is to know anything has happened. Make sure the customers have a good night, right?" Mikey adds.

"Always," one of them replies.

"Are you okay, Mrs. Ryan?" the other one asks me, his face full of concern.

"Yes, thank you," I say, forcing a smile.

"Shane and Conor will debrief you when they're done," Liam adds. Then he tucks my face back into the crook of his neck and walks down the hallway to the fire exit.

"The car is here, baby," he whispers. "We'll be home soon."

Mikey holds my hand while I sit on Liam's lap on the car ride home. Liam has his arms wrapped so tightly around me that I can barely move. We have hardly spoken since we left the club.

"I'm sorry I ruined our night," I whisper.

"No, baby. You didn't," Liam says softly, brushing my hair from my face. "You didn't ruin anything. I should never have let you out of my sight for even a second."

"I should have waited for you," I sniff. "Was that woman okay?"

"What woman?" he frowns at me.

"The woman who was crying earlier."

"I have no fucking idea, Jessie," he says with a frown. "The minute I realized you were missing my whole fucking world stopped turning."

Mikey puts his hand on the back of Liam's neck. "It wasn't your fault either, bro," he says.

"What are Shane and Conor going to do to them?"

"You already know, Red," Mikey replies.

I wipe away a tear that falls down my cheek. "It's my fault they have to do that."

"No. It's not," Liam says, hugging me tighter. "Those men hurt you, Jessie. They would have done way worse if we hadn't found you."

"Thank fuck we got to you so quick," Mikey says with a deep sigh.

"I'm so glad you did," I say with a shudder thinking of the threats Jason and his buddies made to me.

"Well, I knew you had to be in one of those rooms. We just had to get the keys and work our way through them," Liam tells me.

"Yeah, we saw some interesting sights opening the other doors before we found you, Red," Mikey says with a soft chuckle.

I smile at him but my heart is heavy with worry. Laying my head against Liam's chest, I hope that Shane and Conor are home soon.

As soon as we got home, Liam and Mikey briefed Chester on the evenings events while I took a quick shower — trying to wash away the reminder of Jason and his brother's grubby hands on my skin. I'm so relieved that it was only my neck they touched.

I rub the skin there subconsciously. My throat is a little sore but otherwise I'm fine. I just wish that Conor and Shane would come home so that I know they're fine too.

I climb into bed, pulling the covers over myself and a few moments later, Liam and Mikey walk into the room. Both of them are dressed in only their boxer shorts and Mikey carries a tray of hot chocolate.

"I put a little something special in for you, Red," he says with a wink. "It will help your sore throat."

"Irish whiskey, perhaps?" I ask and he smiles at me.

"Of course," Liam says as he climbs into bed beside me while Mikey sets the tray down on the nightstand before he slips beneath the covers too.

"You okay, baby?" Liam asks as he wraps a huge arm around me.

"Yeah," I lie. "I'm sorry I ruined Christmas."

"You did not," Mikey admonishes me. "Of all my Christmases, this doesn't rank in even the top twenty-five worst ones."

"Yeah. This Christmas is still epic and it's only just Christmas Eve," Liam adds with a chuckle.

I snuggle between them both. "I'm sorry you never had good Christmases growing up," I whisper.

I have only happy memories of my family before I was kidnapped by a psychopath when I was sixteen. Sometimes I forget how difficult my husband's childhoods were, particularly Liam and Mikey. Their mom was murdered by the man they believed was their father when they were just babies. Then he neglected, abused and mentally tortured them until Shane took them away from him when they were sixteen. Leaving Ireland and moving to New York.

"We did have that one Christmas, remember," Mikey laughs. "When Shane bought the house in Carrickfergus?"

"Yeah," Liam says with a smile. "How old were we?"

"Eleven," Mikey replies. "He was nineteen and Conor was fifteen."

"Oh, yeah. Conor was annoyed because he wanted to spend Christmas with his new girlfriend but Shane made him come with us. Poor kid had just discovered the joys of fucking," Liam laughs.

"So it was just the four of you for Christmas?" I ask.

"Yeah. We left on Christmas Eve. Shane had a tree and presents and everything. We had a great two days," Mikey replies.

"Yup. Until boxing day," Liam says with a shudder.

"Patrick found you all?" I ask them. He is Shane and Conor's biological father but not the twins, which they only found out about two years ago when Patrick died.

"Yeah. Shane had gone out for something and Patrick must have waited for him to leave because he showed up as soon as he left. He beat the shit out of the three of us and took me and Liam home," Mikey says matter of factly.

"It was the last time he ever laid a hand on Conor," Liam adds. "Because he stood up to him that day."

"Evil fuck stopped Shane coming into the house for about two months after, didn't he?" Mikey asks his brother.

Liam nods. "Uh-huh."

My heart aches for them and what they endured as children. Shane all but raised them. He was their protector. He and Conor were the only people to ever give them any love and affection and I can't imagine how hard it must have been for them all when their oldest brother wasn't allowed to see them.

"I'm sorry," I whisper.

"Don't be, baby. It was a long time ago," Liam says as he kisses my forehead. "And now we have you and our beautiful babies. You made Christmas magic for us again."

"You have for me too," I breathe.

There was a time when my only focus in life was finding the man who murdered my family and kept me prisoner for two years. All I wanted was to make him pay — and after that I had no future plans of happiness or family. Then I met my incredible Ryan brothers and my life changed forever.

"I love you."

"We love you too, Red," Mikey says softly.

I swallow the ball of emotion in my throat as I lie between the two of them, feeling safer and more loved than I have since I was a child. I only hope that their older brothers are safe right now, and that they can forgive me for what they're currently doing.

EIGHT

Christmas Eve

I lay awake for hours but must have drifted off to sleep because I don't hear Shane and Conor come into the room.

"Everything okay, bro?" Liam asks and the sound of his voice rouses me.

"All sorted," Conor replies as he and Shane start undressing. They're wearing jeans and t-shirts rather than their tuxedos and I can't help but think of the reason why.

"I think I heard one of the twins waking up," Shane says. "Can you?"

"Sure," Liam says, nudging Mikey awake before rolling out of bed.

I check the clock and notice it's almost seven a.m.

Pulling back the covers, I go to climb out of bed too.

"Not you, sweetheart," Shane orders. "Stay right where you are."

"But I should help," I insist as uncertainty settles into the pit of my stomach. Shane looks super pissed while Conor is so quiet and can barely look at me.

"Yeah. You didn't get much sleep, Red," Mikey says with a yawn. "I felt you tossing and turning all night."

"Okay," I whisper as I lie back against the pillow and watch Shane and Conor pulling off the last of their clothes.

My heart races. Are they going to punish me? Together? I mean usually that's hot, bur right now I feel too fragile. Besides, it's not like I asked to be manhandled into a room with those creeps.

Mikey and Liam walk out of the room, closing the door behind them and my pulse quickens further. When they are naked, Shane and Conor climb into bed, one either side of me.

"I'm sorry," I almost cry.

"Don't, Jessie," Shane snaps, taking hold of my chin in his strong hand, he turns my face so he can look into my eyes. "I'm sorry, sweetheart. We all fucked up. Not you."

"W-what?" I stammer, aware of Conor's hand sliding onto my stomach.

"We never take our eyes off you, angel," he says before he kisses my shoulder softly. "That's the rule."

"But you can't always-"

"You should never have been in a position where any of those fucks could lay a finger on you, sweetheart. I'm sorry that they did."

"That's not your fault," I whisper as emotion balls in my chest. I thought they were mad at me, but they were mad at themselves.

"It will never happen again," Conor murmurs against my skin.

"Did you..." I don't finish the question.

"They're taken care of," Shane says before he slides his hand to my waist. "Turn on your side."

I shift onto my side until I'm facing him. Conor splays his hand on my stomach, pulling me against him so his chest is at my back as Shane presses a soft kiss on my lips.

"Can you forgive us, angel?" Conor asks as he nuzzles my neck.

"There's nothing to forgive."

"Thank you, sweetheart," Shane mumbles as his eyes close. "I'm so fucking tired."

"Me too," Conor yawns.

"What time do we have to be up for the Christmas Eve activities?" Shane asks and I smile.

Before I came into their lives they never really celebrated Christmas and I love how they are embracing my holiday spirit.

"Midday would be good," I suggest.

"That gives us five solid hours," Shane groans.

"Sounds like fucking heaven," Conor agrees.

"I should go help the twins with the twins."

"No," they say in unison.

"You're staying right here. Because I never sleep as well as when I have your gorgeous fucking body against mine," Shane adds.

"He speaks the truth," Conor agrees sleepily.

"Okay," I whisper, relieved to have them both home safe and not mad at me.

Smiling, I close my eyes and snuggle between the warmth of their hard bodies.

NINE

MIKEY

"Dada. Dada," Ella chants as she waves her chocolate frosting covered fingers in the air.

"Mo. Mo," Finn squeals for more before he stuffs another fistful of frosting into his mouth.

"These babies will never sleep tonight," Jessie laughs as she wipes a blob of goo from Ella's hair. "They've eaten more sugar this afternoon than they have in their entire lives."

"Well, it was your idea to make Christmas cookies, Red," I remind her with a wink.

"It's a Christmas Eve tradition," she says as her cheeks turn pink.

Fuck, I love how she blushes at the slightest thing. As though she's not a deviant sex maniac under that sweet exterior.

"And is us wearing more cookies than we make part of our tradition, angel?" Conor asks as he looks down at his t-shirt and jeans which are covered in frosting, flour and cookie dough.

"Well, you do look kind of cute," she says with a shrug.

"And these babies look goddamn adorable," Liam adds as

he picks Ella up from her chair and she shrieks with laughter as she wipes more chocolate into his beard.

"They sure had fun," Shane laughs softly as he peels a squashed M&M from his jeans.

"They did," Jessie beams with pride.

She had a list of things she wanted us all to do on the twin's first Christmas Eve, including watching Elf, which the babies were less than impressed with. But they had fun rolling around the floor with Shane and me instead while Jessie watched the film with Liam and Conor. Then we went to the roof and made a snowman. After that we had hot chocolate and made Christmas cards, which Ella and Finn enjoyed because they got their hands and feet covered in paint. If that wasn't exhausting enough, then we made Christmas cookies. The result of which is now stuck to all of us and also scattered around the entire kitchen.

"I think they need a bath now though," Conor chuckles as he picks Finn up from his high chair, who protests at being parted from the chocolate frosting on his tray that he's yet to eat.

"Hey, buddy," Conor says calmly, rubbing his thumb over our son's cheek. "You can't eat any more sugar today, okay?"

Finn stops yelling, as though he understands what Conor is saying. He's not as vocal as Ella yet. She can say more than a dozen words, but all he can say is Ma, Da, no and mo — which means more, but damn that kid is as smart as a whip. He's gonna be just like his mom. He has her bright blue eyes and our dark hair, while Ella looks just like us Ryan boys, and she's as mischievous as us too. I can already tell that girl is going to give us a whole world of trouble, and I am so here for it.

I look at my brothers holding our kids - Jessie pulling more frosting out of Ella's hair while she tells her what a beautiful girl she is as Liam gently bounces her in his arms. Conor passes

Finn to Shane while he cleans some frosting from his beard and Finn giggles at the face Shane pulls at him. Of all of my brothers, I never thought I'd see Shane with kids of his own. I mean, he pretty much raised Liam, Conor and me, and I figured that would have been enough to put him off for life. But then we met Jessie and she turned our entire fucking worlds on their axis — in the best possible way. She has given me everything I didn't even know I wanted and then some.

"You okay?" she asks as she looks up at me and I realize I'm staring.

"Yep. Just wondering who's going to clean this kitchen up with me, is all."

"I'll help you, obviously," she says with a smile.

"Let's get these monsters cleaned up and in their Christmas pajamas," Liam says.

"You all have pajamas too," Jessie giggles, biting her lip in that adorable way that makes us unable to refuse her anything.

"Jessie!" Shane says with a roll of his eyes. "I'm not wearing pajamas, sweetheart."

"Me neither," Conor agrees.

"But they're Christmas pajamas. We all have to match. Please?" She clasps her hands together and flutters her eyelashes.

"We'll see," Shane grunts but we all know he's wearing the pajamas. And Conor will too. They would do anything to make her happy, just like Liam and I would.

My brothers took the twins for a bath about ten minutes ago and Jessie and I started tackling the mess that is the kitchen immediately after. We've made quick work of it together and all that's left to clean is the kitchen island.

She walks up beside me with a wet cloth in her hand and a bottle of organic cleaning spray that she makes herself because she doesn't want too many chemicals around our babies. She is way too fucking smart for me and I love every single fucking thing about her. And suddenly I realize I am alone with her. It's going to take my brothers at least another twenty minutes to bath our kids and then get themselves cleaned up.

And now I have zero interest in cleaning.

I pick up a giant blob of green frosting on my forefinger and smudge it onto her neck.

"Mikey!" she shrieks.

"Sorry, Red, my hand slipped," I say, grinning at her as she stands there pretending to be mad at me. "Here, let me get that for you," I offer, resting my hand on her hip and turning her to face me. I bend my head low, running my tongue over her collarbone and then up the soft skin of her throat until I collect all the frosting.

A tremor ripples through her body.

"Mmm. So fucking sweet," I murmur against her skin.

Her hands are in my hair now as she purrs like a kitten while I trail kisses over her neck. "Mikey," she whispers. "We're supposed to be cleaning."

"I am cleaning," I chuckle. "Cleaning you. You are very dirty, Red."

"So are you."

"About to get a whole lot fucking dirtier," I say, grabbing her by her ass cheeks and lifting her onto the counter, pushing myself between her thighs.

"Mikey. No," she laughs, trying to bat my hands away as I tickle her while I pull her dress up and off over her head.

I arch an eyebrow at her. "No?"

She stares at me, her eyes twinkling with mischief and delight as she chews on her bottom lip. I put a hand on her chest and push her to lie down flat on the counter top before dragging a stool over so I can sit down. Grabbing her ankles, I hook her legs over my shoulders.

She leans up on her elbows, staring at me with those beautiful blue eyes. "What are you doing?" she whispers.

"Oh you already know that, Red," I grin at her as I hook her panties to one side. I slide a finger through her silky wetness and she sucks in a stuttered breath that make her perfect tits jiggle for me. "You make me so fucking hard, you know that, right?"

"Y-yeah," she pants as I slip a finger inside her.

"And you're always so wet and ready for me." I thrust deeper. "Such a good fucking girl."

"Oh," she moans, lying flat on her back as I add another digit and rub her inner walls.

"You know what's sweeter than all this frosting?" I ask as I start to pepper kisses along the inside of her thighs.

"No."

"Your pussy, Red. You already knew that though." I nip her thigh lightly and she whimpers. "So fucking sweet," I growl as I breathe in the scent of her wet heat. I could fucking eat her all day every day. Every fucking meal and snack.

My cock throbs in my shorts, desperate to be inside her. But I gotta taste her first. Hooking a second finger into her panties, I pull them further aside, exposing her entire beautiful pussy to me. The soft, sucking sound of her wetness as I pump my fingers in and out of her makes my mouth water.

"God, Mikey," she breathes.

I bend my head closer and swirl my tongue over her clit while I keep finger fucking her. She gets wetter every time I thrust back inside her and I lap at her opening, drinking her in before I suck on her clit again.

Her sweet, salty arousal runs over my tongue and I swear

it's the best damn thing I ever tasted. Thighs trembling, she moans softly and suddenly my balls are tightening and my spine is tingling and I feel like I'm gonna come just from eating her.

Reaching into my shorts, I grab hold of my cock and squeeze.

Sweet relief floods my body. *Fuck!*

Nothing beats being inside her hot, wet pussy, but right now she's on the edge of oblivion and I want to keep her here for as long as I can — with my name on her lips and in her head.

"Mikey," she groans my name again. "You feel so good."

"You taste so fucking good, Red," I growl as I start tugging on my rock hard dick, pumping the shaft to the same rhythm I'm drilling my fingers into her pussy.

"Fuck!" she hisses, threading her fingers through my hair. "So. Good."

I pull my fingers almost all the way out and seeing them thick with her cream makes my cock almost explode. Sliding them back in slowly, I tease her, sucking on the sensitive bud of flesh and keeping her teetering on the edge.

"Please?" she gasps, tugging on my hair as she rides my face and I take pity on her. Curling my fingers inside her as I suck harder, rimming her pretty little clit with my tongue and squeezing my dick harder until she is bucking and shaking and falling apart around me.

Her soft, breathy moans make me come apart, and as she's still grinding her sweet pussy on my mouth, I climax too, spilling cum all over my hand.

"Fuck!" I growl, my teeth nipping at her sensitive flesh.

She looks up at me, her skin pink and her eyes dark. "Did you just jack off while you were eating me?" she whispers wickedly.

I hold up my hand and show her the thick white ribbons

streaked over my knuckles. "I thought you were supposed to be helping me clean. You went and got me real messy."

She pushes herself up, a devilish grin on her face. "I can help you with that."

Then she takes my hand in hers and starts to lick my knuckles clean. Murmuring softly as she's cleaning me up, savoring the taste of me the way I just did her.

"Fuck, Red, that looks so fucking hot," I whisper.

Finally she sucks my thumb into her mouth, her tongue swirling around the tip as she stares into my eyes and now I'm sorry I didn't make her suck my cock. Her long dark lashes flutter and she looks so sweet and innocent — well she would be if she wasn't sucking my cum off my thumb.

"Keep sucking like that, Red, and I'll give you something else to put in that beautiful mouth of yours instead."

She releases my thumb from her mouth with a wet pop. "Fine by me," she purrs.

"You are a horny fucking minx, Mrs. Ryan," I say, wrapping my arms around her waist and lifting her from the counter. "And we need to finish cleaning this kitchen."

"I was trying to when you accosted me," she says, her eyes narrowed as she pretends to glare at me.

"I didn't hear no complaints," I say with a grin before I start to kiss her neck again. She still smells of chocolate frosting and cookies. I brush my fingers along her jawline and over her throat — the ones I just had inside her, so now she smells of her cum too.

"We should finish up and get ourselves cleaned up," she breathes even as she rakes her nails down my back, making me shiver.

"Goddammit, Jessie. I'm gonna bend you over this counter and fuck you instead."

"I knew you two would be fucking," Shane says with a sigh as he walks back into the kitchen.

I keep my arms wrapped around her and glare at him. "Clearly, we're not fucking."

He narrows his eyes at me in suspicion. "You just did though."

"No, we didn't," I insist.

He walks toward us, ignoring the fact that she's in my arms, he takes hold of her jaw, turns her head and kisses her. "You did something," he says, licking his lips and staring into her eyes.

"How do you know that?" she whispers.

He traces his pointer finger over her cheek. "Because your neck is all pink the way it is when you've just come."

"Maybe I'm just a little hot from you two kissing me?" she says with a shrug.

He shakes his head and then runs his nose along her jawline. "I can smell your cum on you, sweetheart, which means Mikey must have at least had his fingers in you."

I can't help laughing as her cheeks flush bright pink now. "Busted," I say to her with a wink. "We didn't fuck though. I mean I was about five seconds away from bending our wife over the nearest thing I could find and doing that, but we didn't."

Shane takes a deep breath as though the thought of doing that is distracting him from what he actually came in for.

"Did you need something?" Jessie asks him, trying to change the subject before one of us bends her over something.

He blinks at her. "I think Finn and Ella are about to crash after all that sugar. Their baths have wiped them out. I was gonna get them some milk and put them down a little early tonight."

"Yes, and then the adults Christmas Eve activities begin," I say with a grin.

"And they are presents, eggnog, hot chocolate and *A Christmas Carol*," Jessie says, shooting me a warning look.

"I know, Red."

"I'll come help with the twins," she says to Shane.

He arches an eyebrow at her. "We got it. Besides, I think you two need a shower."

A wicked grin spreads across my face.

"Separately," Shane adds.

"You are such a fucking buzzkill sometimes," I say to him.

He knows I'm joking but it doesn't stop him from slapping me across the back of my head.

"We'll finish up here, say goodnight to the twins and shower. Then we can all meet in the den in half an hour?" Jessie says excitedly.

God, I love how much this woman loves Christmas. She's like a shiny, sexy little elf.

"You think you can manage that?" Shane says to me.

I roll my eyes. "Like you wouldn't be buried in Jessie right now if it had been you two left on your own here?"

He sucks on his top lip as though he's deep in thought. "No. I would have taken her to my office instead where no-one would walk in on us," he finally says with a shrug.

"I'm standing right here, you know," Jessie protests.

"Don't pretend that you don't fucking love it, sweetheart," he says to her and her face breaks into another smile.

WHEN I'M SHOWERED, I pick up the Christmas pajamas Jessie has chosen for us. I suppose they're not that bad. The bottoms are red and white stripes and the top is like a Santa suit. I'm sure our kids will love them when we all wear them tomorrow, but for tonight I toss the t-shirt onto the bed and just pull on the pants. When I walk into the bedroom we all share, I see my brothers have had the same idea and are only wearing the bottoms too.

"Where is Jessie?" I ask.

"Just checking on the babies," Liam replies.

A few seconds later she walks into the room behind me and I spin around to see her dressed in a head to toe Mrs. Claus onesie with a hood.

"Where are your pajamas?" she asks us.

"Um. Wearing em," I say, pointing down at the ridiculous pants.

"You're supposed to wear the whole ensemble," she says with a roll of her eyes. "Now you don't look like Santa, just..." she chews on her lip as her eyes roam over the four of us.

"Just what, angel?" Conor asks.

"Just four super hot..." She waves her hand dismissively. "Don't worry. I can work with it," she adds with a soft sigh.

"But what the hell are you wearing, baby?" my twin asks as she walks toward the four of us.

"I'm Mrs. Claus," she whispers.

I pull her into my arms, spinning her around so I can check out her outfit. I look for snaps. Buttons? A zipper? A gap somewhere that I can get my hand in, but there isn't a single fucking one. "What fucking devious trickery is this, Red?" I growl.

"It's my onesie," she giggles.

"But how do I get into it?" I ask her as my brothers laugh — like this is funny.

She pulls a tiny flap near the base of her throat. "It's a concealed zipper, see?"

"I don't like it," I say with a shake of my head. "It's impenetrable."

"It's just for Christmas," she laughs.

271

"I still don't like it," I say as I wrap my arms around her and kiss her neck. "I like my hands on your skin."

She shivers in my arms and my cock twitches. "I like your hands on my skin too," she purrs.

Fuck! I didn't get enough of her in the kitchen. Not nearly enough. I want to fuck her so bad, but we have to go through her activity list first. I would much rather peel this goddam onesie off her, lay her down on that bed and do filthy things to her sexy little body all night long. I can guarantee my brothers will be thinking the same too. But she's so fucking excited about Christmas Eve and all of the things she has planned for us.

I can wait.

For her, I can.

For her I would wait a goddamn lifetime.

CHAPTER

TEN

JESSIE

After the twins have fallen asleep we head to the den to exchange presents. None of us are in need of much, and the boys never even used to exchange gifts at all, so we have agreed on one present each. They still didn't buy each other gifts though, which means I'll end up with four, and they only get one. They don't know about the extra ones I sneaked under the tree from the twins though.

I smile to myself when I think about tomorrow morning – Christmas with them and our babies is going to be something else. Last Christmas was magical. I was eight months pregnant and they spoiled me in so many ways. But I know that this one is going to be even better.

I sit cross legged on the floor and wait for them to open their gifts. "One at a time," I insist because I want to watch them all as they see what I got them.

They have more money than they could spend in three lifetimes and don't need anything at all — so I tried to choose gifts that would make them smile instead.

"Me first," Mikey insists, already tearing into the paper before the others have agreed, not that they would deny him.

He's an excitable little toddler at heart and it is one of the many reasons I love him. He pulls the soft fabric out of its wrapping and unfurls it, holding it up so he can see it in its full splendor. I can't see his face because it's hidden but then I hear him laughing loudly. He places the gift beside him and crawls across the floor to me.

"I fucking love it, Red," he grins before he kisses me on the lips.

"What does it say?" Conor asks as Liam picks it up.

"Don't kiss the chef," Liam chuckles as he turns the apron around to show everybody. "Unless your name is Jessie Ryan."

"Well your old one was getting a little worn. And that one seemed much more fitting," I say with a smile. Mikey always wears his 'Kiss the Chef' apron when he's cooking.

"It's perfect," he says with a wink.

"Me next?" Liam asks as he holds his own wrapped gift in his hands, and Shane and Conor nod their agreement.

He opens the paper carefully and pulls out the framed map and certificate before he reads it. "You named a star after me?" he asks with a smile so big that it makes me feel warm and fuzzy all over. He is such a sensitive soul.

"Yes. And the map is of where it was in the sky the night you first kissed me and changed our lives forever." I blush at the memory making his brothers laugh.

He shakes his head and stares down at the frame in his hands.

Shane catches my eye and winks at me. *Written in the stars.*

"I love it, baby," Liam says when he looks up again. "It's the best gift I've ever gotten."

"Might I remind you of the fucking red Porsche I bought you when you were twenty-one?" Mikey asks incredulously.

"Nothing compared to this, bro. Sorry," Liam laughs as he places the frame on the floor beside him.

"You're up next, Con," Shane says.

Conor smiles at me as he unwraps the paper. When he pulls out the book, he runs his hand over the soft leather. I see his Adam's apple bob in his throat as he swallows.

"It's the Maude translation. First edition," I tell him. "I know you wanted to read it to the babies now that you've finished *The Grapes of Wrath*."

Some people might question his choice of reading material, but I swear he could read those babies a takeout menu and they'd still be mesmerized by his deep, soothing voice. I love when he reads to me too and he used to read me this book, *Anna Karenina*, when we first met.

"It's fucking perfect, angel. Thank you," he says as he looks up at me, his eyes shining with happiness.

"Shane's turn," Mikey says excitedly and my heart flutters in my chest. This is either going to be as funny as hell or a complete disaster. Suddenly, I'm worried it's going to be the latter.

I press my lips together so that I don't giggle as I watch Shane unwrapping his gift. He tears at the red glittery paper and tosses it onto the floor before opening the small black cardboard box.

When he pulls out the contents I have to pinch the inside of my thigh to stop myself from laughing out loud. His brows knit into a frown as he rolls the thick rubber ring between his thumb and forefinger.

"It's a cock ring," I whisper, biting down on my bottom lip to stop the giggle escaping.

He looks up at me and arches one eyebrow. "I know what it is, sweetheart, but what I don't understand is why you bought it for me."

"They make erections harder and last longer," Mikey says nonchalantly and the look Shane gives him almost makes me pee my onesie. My cheeks hurt with the effort of not laughing.

"So why didn't everyone get one?" he asks me.

"Well, you did turn forty this year," I whisper and his entire face darkens.

"What the fuck?" he growls and I'm starting to wish I'd just given him his actual present instead of this one which Mikey convinced me would be too funny to pass up. His brothers stare at him and I can't stop myself. I am going to burst if I hold this in any longer. The look on his face is priceless.

I hold onto my sides as a snigger escapes my lips. Before I can tell him that I have his real present under the tree, he pounces on me from halfway across the room, pinning me flat to the floor with his hands clamped around my wrists.

He rocks his hips against me, his hard length digging into my abdomen as I giggle uncontrollably. "Does this feel like I need help getting hard, Jessie?"

Conor, Liam and Mikey start laughing too and I snort hysterically, squirming in Shane's grip as he rubs his jaw over my neck, tickling my soft skin.

"Does it?" he asks as he presses me flatter to the floor before one of his hands slides over my ribs and he starts to tickle me.

"Shane!" I shriek with laughter. "Stop! It was Mikey. He made me do it."

"Wow. Way to throw me under the bus, Red. Remind me never to take you to a negotiation," Mikey says with an exaggerated sigh.

"I'm not surprised this was your idea," Shane says as he looks at his younger brother. He's still holding onto the offending rubber band and he tosses it at Mikey. It bounces off his head and rolls under the sofa.

"What? I'd wear it," Mikey says with a shrug.

"It would be way too big for you, son," Shane laughs darkly

before he turns his attention back to me as I lie beneath him on the floor barely able to control myself. He shifts between my thighs until his cock is nudging at my pussy. "Did you think that was funny, sweetheart?" he whispers, his hot breath dusting over my cheek.

"Kinda," I grin at him.

"You looking for a spanking? Is that it?"

"You can't spank me on Christmas Eve," I protest.

"No?" He narrows his eyes at me.

"No. It's not on the permitted list of activities," I snigger.

"You're right it's not," he runs his nose along my jawline "So how about I fuck you instead? Right here, right now, sweetheart? Because if you think I need a cock ring clearly I need to remind you that I can fuck you longer and harder than any man in this room."

Sweet baby Jesus! Yes please! "We can't," I say instead even as I grind myself against him. "You haven't had your real present yet."

"And Jessie hasn't had hers," Liam adds.

"Jessie is about to get hers," Shane says as his eyes burn into mine.

I swallow hard. I can't figure out if he's amused, mad, horny — or all three. "Your real present is under the tree," I whisper. "The cock ring was just a joke. I promise."

He narrows his eyes at me, but there is a wicked glint in them that makes my insides melt like warm butter. He's not mad at all.

"Here it is," Liam says as he rummages under the tree and pulls out another gift wrapped in the red glittery paper.

Shane releases my wrists and pushes himself up, taking the gift from Liam, he starts to unwrap it, but he remains straddling me the entire time. His knees pinned against my hips so I can't move. When he unwraps this one he grins at me.

"It's Italian. They only make a dozen of them a year. Feel how soft it is?" I say.

"Hmm," he murmurs his agreement as he runs his hand over the soft, black leather. "You'll be feeling how soft it is."

Heat pools in my core at the meaning behind that statement. "Now you will always think of me when you take off your pants."

"Already do," he says with a smile before leaning down and kissing me. "Thank you, sweetheart."

My breath catches in my throat. As much as I enjoy pushing his buttons, I love to see that smile even more. "You're welcome."

"Time for Jessie's presents," Mikey says excitedly, interrupting the moment.

"I don't know," Shane says as he sits up and then pulls me onto his lap. My very own sexy Santa. "I don't think our Jessie has been a good enough girl for presents."

I roll my eyes. Did I say Santa? More like sexy Satan.

"I have been good," I insist and Conor and Liam laugh softly in the background while Mikey starts to rummage beneath our huge Christmas tree.

Shane tucks my hair behind my ear. "Well, not even counting that bratty little eye roll, shall we add up all of your little misdemeanors from the past few days?"

"What misdemeanors?" I say with a flutter of my eyelashes.

He arches one eyebrow at me. "The tattoo?"

"How is that a misdemeanor?"

"You kept it from us, angel," Conor says.

"Because it was a surprise," I insist.

"Yeah? But rigging the security feed so that we wouldn't see what you were doing wasn't, was it, sweetheart?"

My cheeks flush pink.

"You think we didn't know about that?" Conor chuckles.

"Oh, you're in trouble, baby," Liam adds with a soft laugh.

"Naughty, Red," Mikey says. "More of a felony than a misdemeanor, I'd say, bro."

"Hmm," Shane agrees as he rubs a hand over his jaw.

"How did you know about that?" I ask.

"Because you know we always watch you. How else would you have gone through with your little surprise if you didn't do something to the feed downstairs?"

I open my mouth to respond but nothing comes out. I have no comeback and should have known he would realize what I'd done.

"That was incredibly dangerous, sweetheart. What if something had happened to you?" Shane goes on.

"I was in our basement. Chester was going to be there," I protest as my blush deepens.

"I don't care. One of us has eyes on you at all times. That's the rule."

"Yeah, baby," Liam agrees with him.

I look at the concerned faces of Conor and Liam and then back at Shane. "So why are you only bringing this up now? Why didn't you say something the other day?"

Shane trails his fingertips over my cheek. "Because Conor was with you. You would never have gotten to that basement alone. Besides, then you went and floored me with that beautiful tattoo and..." he trails off and looks at Conor.

"That leads us to your other little indiscretion," Conor says, narrowing his eyes at me. "Making me come in front of Gia when I warned you not to."

I stifle a giggle. "I don't think I can be held accountable for your inability to control yourself," I say, trying to keep a straight face.

Shane laughs, the sound rumbling through him and making me shake on his lap.

Conor narrows his eyes at me. "Really, angel?" he challenges me.

"Really."

"Not to mention wearing the tiniest, tightest mini skirt possible when you went to work at the club the other night, and giving me a three hour boner," Shane goes on.

"It's the only black mini I own," I say with a shrug. "Conor chose it for me."

"I did," Conor admits with a wicked grin.

"You realize how many guys saw her in that sexy little skirt the other night, Con?" Shane asks and suddenly Conor's face darkens.

"Fuck," he growls.

"Am I wasting my time pulling all these gifts out?" Mikey asks as he sits back on his heels. "Because our girl has been so bad."

"I have not," I insist.

"Then there was the incident at Callie's," Liam adds.

I scowl at him. "I am definitely not responsible for that."

"I kinda think you are, baby," he says, winking at me and making heat coil up my spine.

"And now we have a hideous purple chair in our guest bedroom," Shane laughs.

"I quite like it," I say with a shrug.

"And the dress," Shane goes on.

"Oh, the dress," Mikey groans as he pokes his head back under the tree and both Liam and Conor voice their agreement.

"The dress?" I blink in confusion.

"Yes, the dress, sweetheart. The one that you wore last night. The one that hugged every inch of you?"

"It was just a dress," I whisper.

"That was not *just* a dress, angel. It was fucking..." Conor shakes his head.

"It was way too distracting," Shane growls as he presses his lips close to my ear.

I swallow hard.

"Then there's the pajamas," Liam adds as he pulls at the waistband of his red and white striped pants.

"And let's not forget that fucking monstrosity," Mikey says as he crawls out from under the tree and looks at me.

"What monstrosity?" I ask with a frown.

Shane grabs a wad of my pajama fabric in his fist. "I think he means this, sweetheart."

"Oh," I giggle.

"So, what are we gonna do with all these then?" Mikey asks as he looks down at the pile of wrapped gifts beside him.

"Are they all for me? There are way too many. We agreed one each," I say.

"Like you stuck to that rule, Red," Mikey laughs. "I see our other gifts under there too."

"They're just little ones from the babies."

"These are just little," Mikey replies as he picks up a small gold parcel before he looks at his brothers and grins wickedly. "Are we gonna let her open them?"

I look at Shane. "What do you say, Santa?"

He cups my face in his hands, his eyes dark as they burn into mine. "Are you our good girl?" he asks in that low timbre that has a direct path to my ovaries.

Holy fuck!

"Yes," I purr.

"Then I suppose we are," he slaps my ass and shifts me off his lap.

Then I sit cross legged on the floor and my husbands watch as I start to unwrap the first of my gifts.

~

I'M SITTING on the floor, my back against the sofa, surrounded by swathes of glittery paper and gift tags and with a pile of gifts on my lap. Eight new sets of underwear — two from each of them. A pair of leopard print Louboutins with a six inch heel. Eight, yes eight, tubes of lube in a variety of different flavors. A flogger. A paddle. A vibrating egg that is controlled by a remote app they have already installed on their phones. Massage oil. And a silk blindfold. There is definitely a theme here. Though I don't know why I expected any less.

"Thank you so much," I say, my cheeks hurting from smiling. "I love them all."

"Good," Liam leans across and kisses my cheek.

"These are just your naughty presents, Red," Mikey says with a grin. "You can open your real ones tomorrow."

I stare at him. *My real ones?* "What? No. We agreed one gift each and you already bought too many. We said tomorrow would be about the babies." I protest.

"I believe you agreed to that all on your own, angel," Conor says.

"No. We all said one gift each."

"We agreed you would get us one gift," Shane reminds me.

"But that's not fair. I didn't get you guys hardly anything."

"We don't need anything, Red," Mikey says with a shrug.

"Neither do I," I protest.

I'm about to go on protesting when Liam jumps up and pulls me into his arms. "You have given us everything we have ever wanted, baby. Please let us spoil you a little. It makes us happy."

I stare into his beautiful dark eyes. How the hell do I stay mad at him, or any of them?

"You won't fool me next year," I say with a fake scowl.

"We already know what we want next year," Mikey mumbles, earning him a withering look from Shane.

"Eggnog?" Conor shouts as he pushes himself to his feet and the conversation changes before I have a chance to ask Mikey what he means.

"And cookies," I say with a smile.

"Eggnog and cookies," Mikey rolls his eyes.

"What? I'm sure they'll be perfect together," I say with a shrug.

"I want some of the cookies Mikey made," Shane says, winking at me.

I put my hands on my hips and glare at him. "Are you saying you don't want the cookies me and our children made?"

"I'm saying exactly that, sweetheart," he laughs.

Liam wraps his arm around my waist and kisses my neck. "I'll have your cookies, baby," he whispers.

"Later, sex pest," Conor says giving him a nudge on the arm. "Let's get this cleared up."

"I'll go help Mikey." I smile and then he and I head to the kitchen while Conor, Liam and Shane tidy up the wrapping paper.

CONOR TAKES the glass of eggnog from my hand and then pulls me to sit on his lap, wrapping his huge arms around me and nuzzling my neck, I practically purr in contentment as I snuggle against his hard chest.

"Hey, I forgot to tell you all, I had a call from some magazine wanting to interview me," he says nonchalantly before taking a sip of his drink.

I open my mouth, about to ask him half a dozen questions, but his brothers get there before me.

"What magazine?" Mikey asks.

"What did you say?" Shane says as at the same time.

"I said, fuck no," Conor replies with a frown. "Why the hell would some magazine want to put me in it?"

"Um, because you're a super successful, handsome owner of the hottest nightclub in New York," I say.

"Part owner," Mikey adds.

"Yeah, well when I said no, she asked if any of you were available. I said fuck no on your behalf too."

"You sure it was a magazine and not someone fishing for information?" Shane asks with a scowl — always so suspicious, although I suppose he has reason to be.

Conor shrugs. "Seemed legit. Said she was from that magazine Jessie reads. Ten things I want to know about you, or some shit."

"The *Ten things you didn't know* column," I squeal. "I love that feature. It's one of my favorites. I can totally see why they would want to interview one of you guys for it."

Liam reaches forward and shuffles through the magazines beneath the coffee table before he finds the Christmas edition of Fever magazine. I have it on a monthly subscription and love to read it at night lying on the sofa with my head on Mikey's lap.

"I would so do that interview," Mikey says with a chuckle.

"You will not," Shane says with a scowl.

"It's not like they ask anything deep and meaningful. It's all pretty lighthearted stuff," I tell him.

"I don't want anyone knowing anything about any of us," Shane says and Conor nods his agreement while Liam flicks through the magazine before he finds the regular feature.

"So, Michael Ryan," Liam says in a thick New York accent. "Successful businessman. Father of two. Sex god?"

Mikey sits forward in his seat, puffing out his chest as he prepares for his big interview. "Yup."

"What do you wear in bed?" Liam asks in his regular voice.

"My wife," Mikey replies without a seconds thought, making his brothers laugh.

"Favorite thing to eat?" Liam asks.

"My wife's pussy."

"Mikey," I say as my cheeks turn pink.

"It's true, Red," he frowns at me then he turns back to his twin. "Next question."

"Favorite drink?"

"The sweet stuff that comes out of my wife's pussy," Mikey answers and my cheeks redden further.

"That's not a drink," I say.

"I drink it," Mikey insists. "I'd bottle it and take it in a flask to work with me if I could."

"You have to choose an actual drink. My pussy can't be your answer to everything."

"But your pussy is the answer to everything, sweetheart," Shane says with a wicked grin.

His words make warmth roll through my core, but I keep trying to argue my point anyway. "It's not a drink," I whisper.

"Then let's put it to a vote," Mikey suggests. "A drink is a liquid, right? Best liquid you've ever tasted?" He looks between each of his brothers and then back at me.

I fake a scowl at him and he flashes his eyebrows at me.

Conor sips his eggnog. "This stuff is pretty good, actually," he says, running his tongue over his bottom lip as he stares into my eyes. "But nowhere near as sweet as you, angel."

"I agree, baby," Liam adds while Shane sips his eggnog and winks at me over the rim of his glass.

"Favorite thing to do at Christm-"

"My wife," Mikey says before Liam has even finished the question.

Shane grins wickedly while Liam tries to keep a straight face, meanwhile Conor is chuckling softly and the sound rumbles through his entire body. Mikey winks at me and I roll my eyes.

"You're my favorite thing to do on any holiday though, Red," he insists. "Any season. Any time really."

I can't help but smile at him. "Can you answer the next ones properly?"

"I am answering properly," he says with a frown before he looks to Liam again who is scanning the magazine page with a devious look on his face.

"Favorite travel destination?" Liam asks.

"My wife's pussy," Mikey replies without missing a beat and his three brothers burst into laughter.

"That is not a travel destination!" I exclaim, which only makes his brothers laugh harder.

Conor's entire body is shaking now as he keeps his arms wrapped around me. It's a good thing his eggnog glass is empty or it would be spilling all over the two of us.

"It is," Mikey insists. "If I wanted to be inside it right now, which I do, obviously, then I would have to stand and walk across the room to get there. That is the very definition of traveling, Red."

I shake my head as a soft laugh bubbles in my throat. Seeing my four husbands so relaxed and happy is the best Christmas present I could ever ask for. "You're a deviant, Mikey Ryan."

He stands and walks over to me, bending his head and brushing his lips over my cheek. "But I'm your deviant, Jessie Ryan," he growls in my ear. His hand slides over my neck until he finds the zipper of my onesie and flicks the tip of it between his thumb and forefinger.

"We haven't watched the movie yet," I whisper.

"I know," he says, his warm breath dusting over my cheek and making me shiver. "I was just on my way to fill everyone's eggnog."

286

He stands tall again and takes Conor's glass from him. "Then can I have a hot chocolate please?" I flutter my eyelashes at him.

"Sure."

"With marshmallows?"

"Anything for you, Red," he leans and gives me a soft kiss on the lips before leaving the room.

~

Mikey switches off the TV and suddenly I feel all of my husband's eyes on me.

"That was the final thing on your list of Christmas Eve activities, baby," Liam says with a smile.

"Hmm," Conor agrees as he fingers the zip of my onesie. "Now it's time for our list."

"Your list?" I whisper as he starts to pull down my zipper. "But Christmas Eve is almost over."

"Oh it's not a big list, angel," he chuckles as he slips a hand inside my pajamas, cupping one of my breasts and squeezing gently. "You'll have time to get to sleep before Santa comes."

Shane has crossed the room now and is kneeling in front of us. "But only if you're a good girl, sweetheart," he adds with a grin. "You gonna be a good girl for us?"

His words vibrate through my entire body as Conor pulls my zipper all the way down.

"Y-yes," I whimper as wet heat sears between my thighs and my entire body starts to tremble.

"She's always a good girl, aren't you, angel?" Conor whispers in my ear as he turns me on his lap so I'm facing frontward before he begins peeling my onesie off over my arms.

I blow out a long breath as Shane takes hold of the fabric and starts to pull it over my hips and thighs. His dark green eyes burn into mine as he works the soft material over my legs and a few seconds later I'm completely naked as I sit on Conor's lap.

"No panties, Red?" Mikey asks.

"Not with pajamas," I whisper as my eyes stay fixed on Shane's and I wonder what's going through his devious mind.

"I'm gonna need you to hold her for me, Con," Shane growls as his hands slide up my inner thighs. "I don't want her to be able to move."

Holy fuck!

Conor chuckles softly as he spreads my legs wider apart and hooks my feet beneath his calves. When my legs are secure, he takes hold of my wrists and places them behind my back, before wrapping his arms around me tightly so that I'm completely restrained. When Shane presses his palms against the top of my inner thighs, I can barely move at all.

My heart hammers against my ribcage as Shane dips his head close to my pussy. "You smell so fucking good, Hacker," he breathes. "Why are you soaking wet already?"

"Because Conor was kissing my neck and grabbing my ass through the whole movie."

"I was," Conor admits.

"Can't say I blame you, bro," Mikey says as he sits on the sofa beside Liam watching me and his brothers intently.

"Hmm," Shane mumbles before he starts to pepper soft kisses over the top of my thighs. I try to squirm in Conor's grasp but I'm held still by the two of them.

"Why don't you want me to move?" I whisper.

Shane looks up at me. "You know why, sweetheart." He presses a soft kiss directly on my clit and I shudder. "Because I want to wear Mikey's favorite drink."

I hear Mikey laughing but the sound seems far away as I focus on Shane's expert tongue as he swirls it over my sensitive flesh. "Shane," I groan his name softly.

"I know, sweetheart," he murmurs against my skin.

Conor nuzzles my neck while Shane sucks and nibbles on my pussy and my head starts to swim as pleasure builds in my core and starts to coil through my limbs.

"Tell her what we were going to do to her in the basement of the club, Con," Mikey says.

"Fuck yeah," he hisses. "We were gonna tie you up, angel. And then we were just gonna take turns fucking you and making come all night."

"Oh my God," I moan. That sounds so hot. "I wanna do that."

"We'll do it soon," he promises as he kisses my neck.

"I'm gonna..." I come unexpectedly, my body shaking and shuddering in Conor's arms. Shane growls his appreciation as he laps up my juices.

"Damn, angel, I need to fuck you right now," Conor grunts in my ear and I shiver. "I'm gonna have to let her move while I get inside her, bro," he says to Shane who mumbles his agreement while he goes on sucking my clit.

Conor snaps his fingers and Liam tosses him a bottle of lube from the coffee table. He coats his shaft quickly and expertly before lifting me slightly and spreading my legs wider using his feet. His cock presses against the seam of my ass and I whimper as he breaches my opening.

"I know," he whispers in my ear, "Focus on Shane while I slide inside you, okay?"

"Yes," I gasp as he sinks deeper while his older brother slips a finger inside my pussy. "Oh, God," I whine, trying to buck my hips but the two of them hold me firmly in place.

Shane swirls his tongue over my clit and sucks my sensitive flesh at the same time as he massages his finger against that spot inside me that makes me whimper shamelessly — all while Conor fucks my ass. It's too much sensation. I can't handle any more...

"Oh, holy fuck," I groan as my orgasm bursts out of me so violently that I hear it splashing onto the wooden floor.

"That's my good girl," Conor growls in my ear as he goes on fucking me through it and the deep groan that rumbles through his chest tells me he's found his own release too.

Shane pulls back, wiping his jaw with a sweep of his huge hand.

"Look at me, sweetheart," he says, the low timbre of his voice rumbling through my bones.

I stare at him, my eyes locked on his.

"Look at me on my fucking knees for you."

I suck in a stuttered breath.

"Do you see what you do to me? To all of us?" he goes on.

"You make us fucking feral, Red," Mikey adds with a low growl as he walks over to us. I look up at him now and his eyes darken. His muscles flex as he crosses his arms and I stare at his hard, tattooed body.

Liam crosses the room too until he's standing beside his twin. "We know you were hoping for a some sleep tonight," he says with a wicked grin.

"But that's not happening," Conor says.

"You're getting fucked by all of us," Liam adds.

I lick my lips as my heart starts to flutter in my chest and my internal organs turn to liquid chocolate. I'm surrounded by these four huge, powerful, violent men who are all staring at me like they want to eat me alive. Conor is still holding me so tightly that I can barely move.

I tremble in his arms. I guess I must look like a frightened rabbit in a lion's den.

Except I am not a rabbit. I am a lion too.

ELEVEN

L iam holds out his hand to me. "You remember where this all began, baby?" he says, his eyes sparkling with mischief and happiness. "This den."

"That sofa," Mikey adds with a wicked grin as he nods toward the huge couch he and Liam were just sitting on.

Conor releases me from his embrace and I take Liam's hand and allow him to pull me up onto shaky legs until he has me wrapped in his arms.

He trails his lips over my ear. "You remember how nervous you were about taking us both together?"

"Yes," I blush at the memory.

"And now you take us all," he chuckles.

"And so fucking well, Red," Mikey says as he presses his body against my back.

"You gonna take us all in here tonight?" Liam whispers as his hand slips between my thighs and he rubs my swollen, throbbing clit with the slightest of pressure, but it's enough to make my legs buckle and Liam has to hold me up.

"Yes," I pant against his neck and he lifts me, wrapping my

legs around his waist and carrying me over to the rug in front of the fire.

He lays me down on it and then pushes himself up, standing over me as Mikey and Shane walk over and join us. Conor leaves the room and I figure he must be going to clean up so he can fuck me again too.

How is it that I can never get enough of these men? My limbs ache. My pussy throbs. My ass is tender, but I still want more. I want everything they can give me.

The three of them stare down at me, still dressed in their Christmas pajama pants.

Mikey rubs a hand over his jaw. "We were gonna tie her up last night, right?"

"Yep," Shane replies as his eyes roam over every inch of my body.

"I still wanna," Mikey says and when I look at him, he's pulling a huge swathe of thick green tinsel from the mantelpiece. He holds it up for his brothers to inspect and they both nod their approval.

"Our girl does look good in green," Shane laughs.

I arch an eyebrow at them. "You're going to tie me up with tinsel?"

"Looks like," Liam laughs too as Shane and Mikey drop to their knees beside my head.

"Hands," Shane orders and I hold them out in front of me, allowing Mikey to wrap the tinsel around my wrists.

I squirm and giggle as the strands dance over my breasts ever time he loops the length through my arms.

"Stop it, Red," Mikey grins at me.

"I can't help it. It tickles," I laugh harder.

"A little help, bro?" he says to Shane.

Shane rolls his eyes. "You're such a fucking amateur," he

says with a shake of his head as he places his huge hands on my waist and holds me still.

But as Mikey resumes tying me up, Shane wiggles his fingers against my sides and I squeal with laughter, curling my knees up to my chest as I try to stop him from tickling me.

"Shane!" Mikey sighs. "I'm trying to fucking tie her up here."

Tears roll down my cheeks as I writhe on the floor as Shane goes on pressing his fingers into my incredibly ticklish ribs.

"I'm not doing anything," Shane protests.

Mikey lets the tinsel go and sits back on his heels. "Is this about the cock ring?"

"Of course not," his older brother replies with a smug grin. This is so about the cock ring. "It's not my fault you don't know how to properly restrain our wife."

"You do it then, smart ass," Mikey challenges him.

"Fine," Shane says, winking at me as he lets go of my waist and takes hold of the end of the tinsel which is dangling from my wrists.

He has it tied securely almost before I can take another breath let alone have another fit of giggles.

Mikey looks on in admiration at his eldest brother's handi-work while I lie here waiting for whatever is coming next.

"And that's how it's done, son," Shane says to him with a wink.

"You are a cocky fucker, you know that?" Mikey says with a shake of his head.

"I sure am," he laughs as he grabs hold of the tinsel binding my wrists and lays down. "Come here, sweetheart and we'll remind my little brother just how much of a fucker I am."

He pulls me up and I straddle him, placing my bound hands on his chest as he pulls his striped pajama pants down enough to free his cock. I whimper with need as I press myself against it, coating him in the slick juices he just wrung from my body.

"You gonna ride me like my good girl?" he growls as he grabs my hips and shifts my position so that he's sliding into my pussy.

"Yeah," I groan, sinking all the way down and letting him fill me.

Mikey kneels behind me, between Shane's legs. "You look so good when you're being fucked, Red," he whispers in my ear. "I'm gonna fuck you with him, okay."

I nod my agreement, overwhelmed by the sensations of his hands on me and his mouth on my ear while Shane rocks his hips deeper inside me.

"You want the lube?" Conor says as he comes up beside us.

"Nope," Mikey laughs softly. "I'm not gonna need any where I'm going."

"Jesus!" Shane hisses as my pussy squeezes around his cock.

"Are you both...?" I whimper as heat floods my entire body. I'm going to pass out any moment now and miss the rest of Christmas because I'll be in an orgasm induced coma.

"Yeah. You can take us both, can't you?" Mikey growls as he slides a hand over my hips and onto my stomach, holding me still as he presses his cock against my pussy opening. I am so full of Shane I have no idea how he's going to fit too and my whole body tenses.

"Relax, sweetheart," Shane soothes, pulling me to lie flat against his chest and looping my bound wrists over his head and around his neck. "We would never hurt you."

"I know," I whisper as I press my cheek against his hard chest.

Mikey nudges the tip of his cock inside me and I suck in a deep breath at the burning stretch.

"That's my good girl," Shane whispers and my entire body

melts against him. Damn devil knows exactly what those words do to me.

"Oh fuck, Red. You feel so good like this," Mikey groans.

"Oh, God," I whimper as he pushes deeper until I'm so full I feel like I can hardly breathe.

Shane wraps both of his arms around me, holding me tight to him as he starts to rock his hips up slightly. The pressure of Mikey's cock tight against his as he moves makes me feel every single millimeter of him. And when Mikey starts moving too, their thick lengths massage my inner walls, rubbing against every nerve ending inside me and the feeling is so exquisite – so much, that I sob.

Both of them stop moving immediately.

Shane cups my chin in his hand and looks at me, worry darkening his handsome features. "Sweetheart?"

I suck in a shaky breath that vibrates through my body. "I'm good. It feels so good. But it's just so... much."

"You want us to stop?" Mikey leans over me, pressing a soft kiss on the back of my neck.

"No, I just need a second," I say.

Suddenly Conor and Liam are lying either side of their brothers. Conor leans in and brushes his lips over the tears on my cheek. "You're incredible, angel."

"Yeah, baby," Liam adds. "You're taking those cocks like a champ."

That makes me laugh and then Shane and Mikey start to laugh too, and the sound vibrates through their bodies and into mine until I'm sandwiched between them feeling completely boneless.

"I'm ready," I breathe.

"Good, 'cause I'm about to come from being squeezed so tight in your pussy, sweetheart," Shane says, giving me a kiss on the forehead before he presses my face against the crook of his neck and then starts to fuck me again.

The euphoria tears through my body, wave after wave of pleasure and pain and pleasure again as I have another squirting orgasm that soaks all of us.

I lie between them, unable to move or even speak as they fuck me through every delicious second.

"I'm gonna come," Shane grunts and Mikey pulls out as his older brother finishes deep inside me.

"Fuck, Red," Mikey growls as he finishes on my backside, leaving warm ribbons of his release on my ass cheeks. "You look so good covered in my cum." Then his hands are on me, massaging my lower back and rubbing his arousal into my skin like it's lotion.

I moan softly as his strong hands work gently into my muscles. Shane cups my chin and tilts my head so he can kiss me, lazily tongue fucking me as his hands glide over my back and shoulders. Between him and Mikey they make me feel completely boneless. Like a giant pile of Jell-o.

I don't know how long we stay like that with Shane kissing me while him and Mikey soothe my aching muscles. I'm in some kind of space that I can't explain. That blissed out place between sleeping and waking where you're aware of everything but remain in a cocoon of warmth and happiness.

"You okay, Red?" Mikey asks, pressing his lips to my ear.

Shane breaks our kiss and I drop my head back to his chest. "Yes," I purr.

"Good, because you know we're not done yet," Shane whispers as he slides his cock out of me and releases a rush of our cum that soaks him. "Fuck, sweetheart," he groans. "You're gonna need to hydrate before round two."

Mikey chuckles and I feel him pushing himself to a standing

position. "I'll go grab the Gatorade and meet you all in the bedroom."

"You can come with me, angel," Conor whispers as he pulls me from Shane's arms and scoops me into his.

I loop my still tinsel bound arms over his head and around his neck as I press my face against his skin. Damn! He smells so good I could lick him from head to toe. "Sounds good to me."

TWELVE

LIAM

T railing soft kisses over her stomach, I brush my fingers over Jessie's sensitive clit and it makes her back arch in pleasure as she moans loudly.

"Liam," she hisses as I press a little firmer.

"I know, baby," I murmur against her skin.

She is lying on Conor, her back against his chest as he fucks her. He starts to rub her clit now and she bucks in his arms. She's almost taken as much as she can handle from all four of us but she has a little more to give. We push her so hard but she handles it all so well.

I look up at my older brother. I want inside her. For as long as I've been fucking women, I've shared them with my twin, but never with my two older brothers before we met Jessie. Despite that we're all as in tune when it comes to her.

Conor slides his cock out of her pussy and she whimpers in frustration.

"Only for a second, angel," he chuckles as he pushes inside her ass instead, already lubricated from the four us fucking her tonight.

I slide two fingers into her hot pussy at the same time.

298

"Oh, fuck!" she hisses.

"Good girl, sweetheart. You take us all so fucking well," Shane says as he and Mikey watch us, their hands kneading her breasts.

I feel the effect of my older brother's words in her pussy as she squeezes me tight. Our girl has a massive praise kink and we all know it.

I'm the last to fuck her pussy tonight but that's fine with me. It means I get her to myself for a little while and I can savor every tremor and moan that my cock in her pussy will wring from her body.

"Fuck, angel," Conor groans as he thrusts deeper inside her and the sounds he makes tell me he's just blown his load.

"Conor," she whimpers his name now as he pulls his cock out of her ass.

As soon as Conor is done, Shane and I slide her off him and onto the bed and she groans in frustration as I pull my fingers out of her. Chasing her next orgasm despite how many times we've already made her come tonight. I love keeping her on the edge of them and then watching her bright blue eyes roll in her head as she comes apart for me.

"Soon, baby," I chuckle as I nestle between her thighs, my cock at her opening. Pushing the tip into her silky wet center is all I need to do to make her wrap her legs around my waist and her arms around my neck. It's just me and her now. My brothers watch but the next time she comes it will all be for me.

I sink all the way inside her, relief flooding through me at being encased in her tight pussy. "You're still so fucking snug, baby," I groan as I drive deeper. "Even after all my brothers fucked you."

"Oh! Liam. You feel," she gasps. "So. Good."

"I love fucking you, Jessie," I grunt as I bury my face in her neck and nail her to the mattress, finally tipping her over the edge.

My balls almost explode when she screams my name and I pound into her, emptying every last drop of cum inside her.

When she's stopped shaking, I lift my head and stare into her eyes. "Merry Christmas, baby."

"Merry Christmas," she breathes with a smile.

I roll onto my side, allowing Conor to slide in next to her so she's nestled between the two of us.

"I love you all so much," she mumbles sleepily as her eyes flutter closed.

"Shall we tell her what we want next Christmas?" Mikey asks with a chuckle.

"We'll tell her tomorrow," Shane says as he sits on the edge of the bed staring at her.

"I think we fucked her into a coma."

I have never seen my older brother so at peace in my whole life as he is when he's with her or our kids. But then she has the same effect on all of us. She is the light to our shade. The eye of our storm. Where we begin and end.

"God, she's fucking beautiful," Conor says with a soft sigh as he lays his head next to hers.

"She sure is," Mikey and I agree.

"Merry Christmas, boys," Shane says as he crawls into bed and lies next to me.

"Thank you for letting us bring her home," I whisper to him, remembering the day we found her hiding beneath a desk in a Russian gangster's mansion.

We were supposed to kill everyone in that house. But then we found her inside. It still makes me smile when I remember the way she fronted him. This pint-sized redhead in a hoody standing on her tiptoes to face off with my grumpy big brother.

"Thank you for making me, kid," he says with a wink.

CHAPTER

THIRTEEN

JESSIE

Christmas Day

Today has been the most perfect day in the history of Christmases. Although they're a little young to fully understand, Ella and Finn loved tearing into their presents. And having their daddies and I playing with their new toys all morning made them squeal with laughter the entire time. We only had one tantrum from Ella when Conor stopped her from trying to climb the Christmas tree.

My husbands spoiled me with presents, even though I'd told them not to, making the cologne, socks and candy I got for them pale into insignificance.

I have a huge dopey grin on my face as I watch them now. Finn crawls to the sofa and reaches beneath it before putting something in his mouth.

My heart almost stops beating. "Oh, Jesus! Mikey!" I shout, pointing at our son. "He's chewing on the cock ring."

Mikey scoops Finn into his arms as he laughs loudly. "Aw he's enjoying it."

"Please take it off him," I say, wincing at our poor innocent child sucking on a sex toy.

"It's just a rubber ring. It doesn't become a cock ring until someone has actually worn it on their cock."

Conor walks up behind him and slaps Mikey lightly across the back of his head before taking Finn from his arms. "Stop saying 'cock' in front of my son," he says as he takes the offending item from Finn's grasp.

Our son's lower lip starts to tremble, but Conor swaps the ring for a rubber teething ring instead and Finn gnaws happily on it.

"It's Shane's fault for leaving his sex toys lying around the den," Mikey says, rubbing the back of his head.

"I will kick your ass Mikey," Shane says good naturedly as he walks up behind me and grabs a handful of my backside with his free hand while he holds Ella in his other arm. He bends his head low so he can whisper in my ear. "And I haven't forgotten about the spanking I owe you for that whole cock ring stunt, Mrs. Ryan."

A shiver of excitement skitters along my spine. "I said I was sorry," I whisper.

"Not good enough," he says with a wicked grin. "And I believe I get you all to myself next Thursday, right?"

My knees almost buckle as heat sears between my thighs. He's right. It's our date night next week. Just me and him.

"I'm gonna enjoy making you squirm so much, sweetheart," he growls before pressing a soft kiss on the nape of my neck and walking over to where Conor and Finn are sitting on the rug.

Mikey and Liam sit too. And then the six of them sit there, with smiles on their faces as my husbands talk and the babies play.

This is perfect.

Nothing could top this.

Nothing.

"Hey, Red, we were talking the other day about what we want for next Christmas," Mikey says and suddenly all eyes are on me. Even our children are looking at me.

"And what's that?" I ask, a hand on my hip as I wonder what devious scheme the four of them have concocted now.

They glance at each other, Mikey suddenly lost for words it seems.

"You tell her," Liam nudges Shane who rolls his eyes.

But then he looks at me and nods to Ella and Finn. "How about some more of these?"

A RYAN NEW YEARS

With my hand pressed against the bottom of Jessie's back, resting just above her perfect ass, I guide her through the crowded club. People move out of our way as we weave through the mass of bodies.

My three brothers and I, along with our beautiful wife, own this club and have kind of become well known around here. And while pretty much anything goes in The Peacock Club, Jessie Ryan is completely off limits. Even the briefest brush against her skin without our permission is likely to incur either mine or my brothers' wrath.

I'm happy for people to watch though — to watch me with her and to long for something that they will never have. Because whilst we are more than happy to share her with each other, we are incredibly possessive, bordering on psychotic, when it comes to anyone else.

She turns as I guide us toward our booth at the back. "Everyone looks so amazing, don't they?" she says with a huge smile.

Her eyes are shining almost as much as the Swarovski crystals that are shimmering on her dress. Conor picked it out for her and she almost cried when she saw it. It fits her like a second skin and is so short it barely covers her ass — but when she's out with all four of us, she doesn't need to worry about anything like that.

I press my lips against her ear. "Not as amazing as you, sweetheart," I whisper and she giggles softly, making my cock twitch.

"Where is our table?"

"At the back. Out of sight," I tell her with a wink.

"Oh," she breathes before chewing on her bottom lip, because she knows what a table out of sight means.

"Yeah. So move your ass," I tell her as I slide my hand lower and palm her ass cheek.

"Yes, Sir," she purrs like a goddamn kitten and now I'm hard as iron for her.

My brothers got caught up in a little business when we first walked in here — nothing important but enough to keep them busy for the next twenty minutes or so and allow me some time alone with my wife. Usually, I'd handle any business problems myself but our date night last night got cancelled because of some work drama, so I'm being selfish for a change and taking whatever time with her I can get.

"Mr. Ryan, Mrs. Ryan," a bouncer nods in greeting as he unclips a thick velvet rope that leads to an exclusive VIP area the very back of the club, reserved for only a very few select guests.

This part of the club was Jessie's idea, and getting access to it isn't about money, but a place for our most loyal and regular patrons to play. Anyone can apply to get a booth here, but the entry requirements are strict. It allows for a greater sense of security and privacy than in the regular booths which can be reserved around the rest of the club. I like that the exclusivity of this place isn't about money and it's exactly the kind of thing

Jessie would come up with. You could be the richest man in the country, but if you're an asshole too, you ain't getting back here.

"Thanks, Kurt," Jessie says sweetly before I guide her to our booth. She and my twin brothers oversee this club and she makes a point of knowing all of our staff members by name.

I take a seat first, sliding along the plush velvet and leather bench before taking her hand and pulling her to sit on my lap.

She wraps her arms around my neck and wiggles her ass against my groin as she gets comfortable. Now my already hard cock starts throbbing with the need to be inside her. We haven't even opened the champagne which is sitting in a bucket of ice waiting for us yet, but I'm already about ten seconds away from fucking her.

"Unless you're going to do something about that situation you're creating down there, sweetheart, I'd suggest you stop your wriggling."

"Well, maybe I want to do something about that *situation*," she purrs and every drop of blood in my body feels like it rushes to my groin.

"Can I?" she whispers, running her tongue over her soft, full lips. Fuck me, they're gonna look good wrapped around my cock in a few seconds.

I shift in my seat, my eyes narrowed as I search her face. We've never done this in public before — not that this secluded booth is exactly public – but I need to know she's fully on board. The devious look in her eyes and that flush on her skin tells me she wants it as much as I do.

"Be my guest, sweetheart," I say as I look down at the bulge in my pants.

She smiles at me, so happy for my permission before she drops to her knees. Like I would ever say no to an offer like that from her. I palm the back of her head as she positions herself beneath the table and begins working to free my cock. Once she has, her fingertips trail over my shaft and I hiss out a breath. "Fuck, Jessie!"

She giggles softly before wrapping her fingers around my length and flicking her tongue over my crown. She murmurs appreciatively as she collects the precum before teasing me again with her skilled tongue. Her eyes are locked on mine, her beautiful blue irises obscured by the dark orbs of her pupils.

"Suck my cock, sweetheart," I command. "Because as soon as you're done, I'm gonna slide my fingers into your wet little cunt and make you ride my hand as you scream my name in this booth."

"Shane," she breathes as her cheeks flush pink,

I cup her face with my free hand, rubbing the pad of my thumb over her cheek. "I love that you blush like a virgin even when you're on your knees in a sex club desperate to suck my cock."

She narrows her eyes at me but then she wraps her perfect pink lips around my dick, swirling her tongue over the tip as she starts to suck.

I tighten my grip on the back of her head, my fingertips threaded through her thick hair and digging into her scalp as she gives me the best head I have ever had in my life.

"Jesus, sweetheart," I growl as I push her further onto me while I rock my hips slightly. "You are so fucking good at that."

She grabs my thigh with her free hand as I hit the back of her throat, struggling for a few breaths before she is able to accommodate every single inch of me.

Tears run down her cheeks as I fuck her hard. There is only so much control I'm willing to give her during sex and I reached my limit pretty much as soon as she started sucking.

She groans and sucks, and the sounds she makes are so damn beautiful as she devours my cock like she enjoys it as much as I do.

"Such a good fucking girl for me," I say as my other hand slides to the back of her head too.

She mewls around my cock and sucks harder — spurred on by the praise – her pretty head bobbing up and down as she brings me to the edge of fucking heaven.

I close my eyes as I come hard, spurting down her throat. She sucks eagerly, pulling every last drop from me as though I'm the best thing she's ever tasted.

"Jesus, fuck!" I groan as the heat pulses through my entire body.

When I open my eyes again, my younger brother is standing awkwardly in front of our table. The look on his face makes me want to close my eyes again and pretend he's not here.

I rub my hand over the back of Jessie's head as she goes on softly suckling on my cock. "Liam? Something wrong?"

"Declan Boyle is here," he says with a heavy sigh. "He's with his wife."

"Fuck," I groan and Jessie looks up, releasing my dick from her pretty lips.

I hand her the handkerchief that I use instead of a pocket square. She takes it from me and wipes the corners of her mouth. "Who are they?" she asks.

I roll my eyes in annoyance and pull her up from beneath the table to sit on my lap again. "You remember why Mikey isn't invited to weddings any more?"

She blinks for a few seconds before she realizes what I'm talking about. As the head of the Irish families here in New York, we get invited to plenty of weddings. Years ago, at Declan Boyle's, my delinquent little brother decided it would be a good idea to nail the virgin bride at the wedding reception.

When they were discovered by Declan himself, he tried to cut off Mikey's head with a butter knife. That was until Liam knocked him out before both he and his twin stole Declan's new

Maserati as a getaway car. I remember Declan being distinctly more pissed about the car than his wife. Needless to say, it took a hell of a lot of smoothing over.

Fortunately, Declan's old man, Roy, is a lot more level headed and rational than his hot-headed son, and between us we've managed to keep the peace over the years.

"Oh no," Jessie says, covering her mouth with her hand but still unable to hide the smile tugging at the corners.

"Is Roy with him?" I ask Liam.

"Nope," he says with a shake of his head. "Just Kian and Evan."

"Fuck!" I mutter. Kian and Evan are his brother and cousin. At least Roy would have kept them all on a leash.

"It was all okay and then she squeezed Mikey's bicep and..." Liam shrugs.

That certainly wipes the smile off my girl's face. "She what now?" Jessie snaps.

"Relax, my little wildcat," I say with a laugh, wrapping my arms tightly around her.

"He only has eyes for you. Red," Liam assures her before his eyes lock on mine again. "Things are getting a little *tense* down there, bro."

I blow out a breath. Can we never just have a quiet night out? "I'll sort it."

Taking Jessie's chin in my hand, I turn her head so she's giving me her full attention. She blinks at me, her eyes still a little watery from having my cock rammed down her throat. I wish I could repay her right now for that because I hate to leave her wet and needy. Instead, I brush my fingertips over her cheek, my brows knitted into a frown as I stare at her. "I'll take care of you later, sweetheart. I promise."

"I know you will. Go do what you need to do. I'll wait right here," she says with a smile.

"No. I want you to go wait downstairs with Liam. Okay?"

She frowns at me. "Why? Is everything-?"

"Everything will be fine. This isn't that kind of trouble. I promise," I assure her. "I just need to have a talk with a few people and then we'll all join you both."

Liam holds out his hand to her. "Come on, baby," he says with a wink. "Shane will sort this out in no time and we can get back to our evening."

She nods at him and gives us both a faint smile as though she doesn't quite believe us.

CHAPTER

TWO

MIKEY

Declan Boyle is glaring at me with so much hatred, I swear he would slit my throat right now given half the chance. Not that he'd ever get it.

I can handle him though. What I don't like is the way that his wife, Heather, is looking at me — like she wants a repeat of what happened six years ago. God, I was so fucking drunk I barely remember it, but what the hell was I thinking? She's not even my type. All false tits, pouty lips and fake hair.

Still, now that I got a wife of my own, I completely get why Declan tried to decapitate me with a piece of wedding silverware — and why he's still kind of pissed about it. There is a vital difference between me and him though — if anyone other than my brothers ever did touch my wife, I would cut out his heart with a fucking spoon. No matter who told me that I couldn't.

Declan and his brother, Kian, along with their cousin, Evan are staring me down. Two women dressed in sequined dresses stand beside Declan's wife, Heather, and they all stare at me too. How the hell they got tickets to this event without me noticing I don't know. They must have booked them under one of the girl's names. Kian and Evan aren't hitched yet so I assume the other two women are their dates.

Conor stands between us all in no mans land while we wait for Shane. Nobody who knows him would dare pick a fight with Conor Ryan, but tension is ratcheting up. Declan's father, Roy Boyle, is well respected and he has a lot of loyalty and good men behind him. The last thing any of us need is a war with his family.

Suddenly Shane walks up behind me.

"Gentlemen," he says in greeting. "Do we have a problem here?"

"Ask your little brother, Shane," Declan snaps.

"I already know he doesn't have a problem. I'm asking you," Shane snarls at him. "You got five seconds to answer me before I have you all thrown out of here."

"We didn't do nothing wrong," one of the women squeaks, her huge lips pulled into a pout.

"Declan?" Shane asks as he steps closer.

"Tell him to stay the fuck away from my wife," he points a finger at me.

I pull a face in disgust but that only seems to make Declan even more pissed at me.

"He has no interest in your wife, I assure you." Shane takes a step closer, grabbing Declan by the wrist.

From an outsiders viewpoint, it doesn't look like he's doing much at all, but the pain on Declan's face says otherwise.

Shane is a strong fucker. He is the only man I know who can tear a man's ear off with his bare hands. My brothers and I have tried to emulate that particular party trick many times over the years but have never been able to come close.

He bends his head closer to Declan's. "Now either fuck off to your own little booth and stay out of our way, or leave. The choice is yours. But you ever point a finger at one of my brothers again and I will cut it off. Do you understand me?"

Declan glances between his wife and me. She's clearly drunk — but I suppose you kind of have to be to get through being married to her boring, fat fuck of a husband. He's a sleaze-bag too. Hitting on any woman within a two mile radius when he thinks nobody is looking. The fact that she walked straight up to me when she saw me and tried to give me a kiss didn't exactly help matters. I pushed her away obviously – I mean I am only interested in one woman, but still, this asshole seems to think it's my fault.

"We'll stay away," Declan mutters.

"Good boy," Shane replies as he releases him from his grip and Declan immediately rubs his wrist. "And keep your wife away from him too."

"Yeah, I'm very happy with my own wife, thanks," I add, just because I feel like I need to say something.

Shane rolls his eyes at me and inclines his head toward the basement stairs, telling me it's time to walk away.

"I hear you all are," Evan laughs. He clearly thinks it's funny. He thinks that he's funny — that is until he sees the murderous look that flashes across my oldest brothers face as Shane stops in his tracks.

"What the fuck did you just say?" Shane snarls as he advances on Evan.

"I-I," Evan stammers. "You all share her, right?"

Shane grabs him by the throat and lifts him an inch off the floor. "We do not fucking *share* her. What do you think she is, a fucking condo?"

The three women start to wail and shriek and suddenly all eyes in the club are gazing in our direction. Declan and Kian bristle with nervous energy, ready to fight if they need to, but they know they don't stand a chance.

CHAPTER TWO

Evan opens his mouth to protest but Shane has him in such a chokehold that he can't speak.

"He didn't mean anything, Shane," Kian pleads. "It's an unusual arrangement is all he meant. Just let him go."

Shane trains his glare on Kian now while Evan turns a deeper shade of purple. "Do you enjoy having the use of your legs, Kian? Because if you do, I'd think very carefully about anything you say about my wife."

Kian swallows hard and looks at Declan and the two of them clearly have no idea what to do. Neither do I. There aren't many people who can handle a super pissed Shane.

Conor runs a hand through his hair and shakes his head. "For fuck's sake," he mutters as he takes a few steps until he's standing beside our older brother. "You know I'm down with whatever, bro, but this is our place of business. It's Jessie's club," he says softly and it's that realization that makes Shane release his grip on Evan's throat.

If this was The Emerald Shamrock, he wouldn't give a fuck about drawing attention — but these clubs are Jessie's babies. She's worked so hard on them.

Evan drops to the floor, rubbing his neck and gasping for breath.

"All of you need to leave. Now!" Conor says.

Kian helps his cousin from the floor and the bouncers who have been slowly gathering start to usher them all from the club.

"Well, that escalated quickly," I say with a grin but Shane is clearly not in the mood. He walks right past me with a look of thunder on his face and heads toward the stairs that lead to the basement rooms.

"That wasn't my fault, Con," I say as he stands beside me. "I didn't do anything. I was good, right?" I kept my mouth shut

317

and my hands to myself when I really wanted to smash Declan's face in and call him a cunt.

"No it wasn't your fault, kid," Conor assures me. "He'll be fine."

"Hmm," I say but I feel kind of sick. I hate it when Shane is pissed at me.

"Come on. Jessie and Liam must be downstairs," he says, wrapping an arm around my shoulder and together we make our way through the club.

THREE

I sit on Liam's lap in the huge wingback leather chair. He rubs his beard over the delicate skin of my neck as he kisses me softly, making me squirm in his arms as I giggle.

"You're so damn ticklish, baby," he chuckles.

"You're so damn distracting, Liam," I say as I take his handsome face in my hands. "I know what you're trying to do."

"And what's that?" he grins at me.

"Make me forget that your brothers might be in trouble upstairs."

"No, baby," he shakes his head before he resumes kissing my neck as his hand slides up my dress. "If I wanted to distract you, I'd be fucking you right now," he murmurs against my skin.

"So this is...?" I purr as I run my fingers through his thick dark hair.

"This is me being alone with you and not being able to do anything but fucking touch you," he groans as his fingers brush my panties.

"Well, I know that feeling," I whisper as I drop my thighs open and I rock my hips against his hand.

"Hmm," he smiles his appreciation against my skin.

As his fingers curl around the edge of my panties, the sound of the door opening startles both of us. We look up to see Shane walking into the room with Conor and Mikey close behind him. Liam pulls his fingers back and rests his warm hand on my thigh instead.

"Everything taken care of?" Liam asks.

Shane grunts as he starts to pace the small room.

"Yeah," Conor says, winking at me before his eyes drift to his older brother and he frowns slightly. Shane seems super pissed about something.

"Probably better that we stay in here for the rest of the night though, Red," Mikey adds with a grin.

"Fine by me. But will we ever have a night out here in The Peacock Club and not have some trouble?" I say with a sigh as I rest my head against Liam's chest, recalling the incident at the Christmas Eve masked ball when an ex-boyfriend of mine tried to assault me. "At least it wasn't me who caused it this time."

"You didn't cause it last time either," Conor says, walking over and pressing a soft kiss on my forehead.

"This is he life we live, Red. Trouble kind of finds us wherever we go," Mikey adds.

"I know, and I've kind of been thinking about that," I say and suddenly I feel all of their eyes on me.

Crap! Why did I have to bring that up right now?

Liam's muscles tense as his arms wrap around my waist protectively and his three brothers stand staring at me expectantly as they wait for me to finish my thought.

I take a deep breath and go on, trying to explain what I mean without causing a drama. "Especially now we have our babies to think of, and if you guys want more..." I chew on my lip, aware that I still haven't given them an answer to their suggestion on Christmas Day that we have some more children.

Shane frowns at me. "Just what exactly have you been thinking, Jessie?" he barks, speaking for the first time since he entered the room.

"I was thinking about our future and whether this is it for us. Is this the kind of life we want for our children?"

"Are you suggesting that you're thinking of leaving? Taking our kids away?" Shane snarls and the venom in his voice catches me off guard. "You really think we'd let you walk out with our babies in search of a different life?"

I blink at him, my cheeks flushing red. That's not what I meant at all. How can he think for even a second that it was?

"That's not what she said, Shane," Conor says with a sigh.

"Sure fucking sounded like that's where she was headed," he snaps.

I open my mouth to tell him how wrong he is, but Liam speaks first. "I kind of agree with Jessie. If we have more kids then maybe New York City isn't the best place to raise them."

Shane's face almost turns purple with rage as he turns his attention on his youngest brother. "Are you fucking shitting me?" he snarls. "You have any idea how hard I worked to get us where we are? How many people I had to step on? How much blood is on my hands?"

"It's on all of our hands, Shane," Conor says, his eyes narrowed as he searches his brother's face for a clue as to what's causing this outburst.

"You all think it's so easy just to up and walk away from all this. You think if I could, I would have fucking done it before now?" he barks.

"Shane?" I say, jumping off Liam's lap and reaching for his hand.

He shrugs me off. "Ungrateful bastards," he mutters under

his breath before turning on his heel and marching out of the room, slamming the door behind him so hard that it rattles the walls, and leaving the four of us standing staring after him and wondering what the hell has just happened.

"What the fuck?" Mikey mumbles.

"I'll go after him," Conor says.

I put my hand on his arm. "No. Let me. Please?"

"He's super pissed, angel."

"Yeah, I kinda got that. I can handle him. Let me go speak to him."

"Fine," Conor agrees. "If you're not back here in ten minutes I'm coming to get you myself."

I lean onto my tiptoes and kiss his cheek softly. "I'll be back soon."

"And if she's not, it's because Shane's bent her over something and is fucking his bad mood away," Mikey chuckles and I roll my eyes at him.

Conor opens the door into the hallway for me and I see the bouncers standing outside. "He went that way," one of them says, indicating his head to the fire exit at the end of the hallway.

"Thanks," I reply with a smile.

"I'll be right here watching that door," Conor says with a kiss on my forehead. "If he's not out there, you come straight back here to me. You got that? Do not go out there alone."

"I won't," I say, resisting the urge to roll my eyes because I know he's just being protective. And let's face it, he kind of has good reason to be.

A few seconds later, I push open the huge steel door and see Shane pacing the alleyway, running his hands through his thick hair. I turn and give a thumbs up to Conor to let him know I'm okay before I step out into the cool night air.

"Shane," I say, stopping him in his tracks.

"Go back inside, Jessie," he hisses through gritted teeth.

"Only if you're coming with me," I reply as I walk over to him, standing so close that I can smell his expensive cologne as I stare into his dark green eyes and they burn into mine.

"I said go back inside," he growls.

I stand my ground. "No."

He glares at me like I'm his enemy rather than his wife before he spins me around until I'm facing the wall. His hand fists in my hair as he holds my head still and presses me against the cool damp bricks. "I'm not fucking playing, Jessie," he growls and his words roll through my body.

"What are you gonna do, Shane? Fuck me in this alleyway?" I challenge him as I push my ass back against his groin. "Because if that's what it's gonna take, then go ahead."

His fingers thread through my hair and he tugs my head back causing a sharp pain in my scalp that makes me gasp in a breath.

"I'm warning you, Jessie," he growls.

I smile even as he keeps pinned to the wall. "You know I'm not even a little bit scared of you though. So, what exactly are you warning me about?"

He presses his lips against my ear. "Not scared of me?" he hisses. "Yet you want out of this life with me?"

His words are like a knife twisting in my heart. "I never said that, Shane. I never said anything about wanting away from you."

"No?" he asks as his free hand slides down my thigh until his fingers reach the edge of my dress. "Cause it kinda sounded like you did."

"I didn't," I whisper, heat coiling around my spine as his hand snakes further up my dress and between my thighs.

"When you question this life, Jessie, you question me. This is who I am."

"This is what you do, not who you are."

"Same damn thing," he growls.

"No, it's not," I insist.

He rubs his jaw over the delicate skin of my neck, making me shiver as his fingers brush my panties. "Do you regret not accepting my offer now?"

"What offer?"

He tugs my panties to the side and I moan softly as his fingers brush my wet folds. "My offer to marry Conor and live a normal life?"

I suck in a stuttered breath. He may as well have just slapped me in the face. "Shane! How could you even ask me that?"

"Really? The woman who just told me she wants no part of this life. My life," he growls as he slides a finger inside me.

"Fuck you!" I hiss.

"You think I would ever let you leave me?" He thrusts his finger harder and my walls squeeze around him.

"I never said that, Shane," I breathe. God, he's so blind sometimes. "Stop putting words into my mouth. I said that I was worried about this always being the way things are for us."

He goes to argue but I cut him off.

"All of us. Because in case you hadn't noticed, there is no us without you. There is no me without you," my words catch on a sob in my throat.

His lips ghost over the shell of my ear as he pushes deeper inside me and wet heat slicks his finger. Then just as quickly, he withdraws his hand and I whimper in frustration.

"Fuck, Jessie," he groans as he spins me back around to face him. Then he bends his head and presses his forehead against mine.

I place my hands on his beautiful face. "I'm sorry if I hurt you. I never meant to do that, I swear. I know this is what we all do. I just wonder if there might be a future where we don't have to worry about running into an old enemy every time we leave the house. Not just your enemies, but mine too." I slide my hands beneath his suit jacket, over his strong abs and onto his back. Pressing myself closer to him, I take comfort in his warmth. "I know you want to fight with me for some reason, but I'm not letting you. Not tonight. You know that I love you and I will be by your side until the end of time."

He stares down at me, his features softening slightly.

"But I am also kind of disappointed in you right now," I go on.

His scowl deepens again. "Why?"

"Because I was so ready for you to fuck me in this alleyway," I say with a grin.

"Oh, sweetheart," he growls as he unbuckles his belt and unzips his trousers. "You are so getting fucked in this alleyway."

"Conor will be out here in five minutes," I giggle.

"Then you'd better come real quick," he says as he lifts me and wraps my legs around his waist. "Because I believe I owe you one."

"I think you're in credit where that's concerned, don't worry." I bite on my lip as he reaches between us and tugs my panties aside before pulling out his thick cock.

He presses his forehead against mine again and his warm breath dusts over my cheek. "Are you wet enough for this because I'm not going to be able to hold back, sweetheart?"

"What do you think?"

"Hmm. You're always wet," he laughs darkly before he sinks his cock into my pussy and my walls squeeze around him as I cling to his neck.

"God, Shane," I moan loudly and the sound echoes around the secluded alleyway.

"I got you, sweetheart," he growls against my ear and I

shiver making him lift his head and stare at me. "Fuck, you're cold?"

It's only now that I realize that the cold damp wall is at my back, but I had barely felt it until now.

"I guess," I whisper as another shiver ripples through me.

"Hold onto me," he says as he presses me closer to the wall, holding me up with the weight of his body as he starts to slip off his suit jacket. Then he slides it over one of my arms before grabbing me by my ass and lifting me away from the wall so that I can finish putting it on myself.

I smile contentedly as his residual body heat warms my cold skin.

"Better?" he asks.

"Much," I purr.

He winks at me before pressing my back flat against the wall again. Then he seals his lips against mine, sliding his warm tongue into my mouth and kissing me so hard that he steals all the breath from my body. At the same time, he nails me to the wall with hard, punishing thrusts.

I cling to him, pulling his hair and sinking my fingernails into his skin as I fight to take everything he can give me. Because that's the thing with me and him — it's never enough. No matter how hard he fucks me, or how much he gives me, I will always want more.

My inner walls contract around him as he drives harder and deeper, and the familiar warm waves of pleasure start to roll through my thighs and core.

I moan but he swallows the sounds as he refuses to let me up for air. I bear down, grinding myself on him even as he thrusts harder, desperate to take every millimeter of him.

He slides one hand down my body, over the curve of my hips and onto my ass, before he lifts my leg slightly higher so he can change his angle and deepen his thrust. When he drives

326

back inside me again my eyes roll back in my head and I swear I'm going to pass out if he doesn't let up soon.

He breaks our kiss and presses his forehead against mine as we both gasp for breath while he goes on fucking me like a demon. "You fucking own me," he growls. "You never get to walk away, you got that?"

"I know, Shane. I won't ever..."

He presses his lips against my ear and a shiver runs down my spine as his hot breath dances over my skin when he whispers. "Damn right you won't, because who owns you, sweetheart? Who. Owns. This. Sweet. Fucking. Pussy?" He punctuates each word with a thrust of his hips.

"You do," I whimper.

"Yeah I do."

"Y-yes," I gasp.

"No-one can fuck you as well as me and my brothers do and you know that no-one ever will. Because you're ours Jessie. Til death do us part, remember?"

"Shane," I pant, closing my eyes as my orgasm starts to ripple through my body making my muscles tighten and release.

"Good girl. Squeeze my cock while you come for me," he groans and it's my complete undoing.

"Jesus, Shane!" I moan as I coat him in a rush of slick heat and my climax shudders through my body.

"Jessie," he grinds out the word as he comes inside me with a final thrust.

His head is buried in my neck, his breath hot on my skin as the sound of the fire door opens behind us. Looking at it, I smile as my other three husbands walk out — all looking as delicious as chocolate dessert and as sexy as sin in their matching tuxedos.

"It's just your brothers," I whisper in Shane's ear.

"Don't give a fuck," he murmurs against my skin. "I'd fuck you in the middle of Times Square when the ball was dropping if it wouldn't get us arrested."

"I'm sure you could talk your way out of it," I say with a laugh.

"Hmm. I do happen to know the Chief of police," he chuckles as he lowers my legs to the ground and pulls out of me.

"You feeling better now, bro?" Mikey asks with a grin as he approaches us. Shane straightens my dress before he fixes his trousers but as soon as he's done he turns to his brothers.

"Yeah. I kind of got a little..." he winces, struggling to apologize because it's not in his nature, especially not where his brothers are concerned. "I'm sorry for taking it out on all of you."

"No worries, bro," Liam says with a shrug.

Conor walks up to his older brother and puts a reassuring arm around his shoulder. "That prick really got under your skin, huh?"

"I guess so," Shane replies.

Meanwhile Mikey wraps me in his arms and kisses the top of my head. "You handle him so well, Red," he whispers.

"I heard that," Shane says making Mikey laugh and the sound vibrates through his chest and into my body, making me smile.

"We thought we should head home," Liam says as he stands beside me and his twin.

"Really? It's not even midnight yet?" I reply.

"Yeah, but do you want to go back upstairs to the club?" Conor asks with a grin. "Or you want to just be with us?"

There is only one answer to that question. I love The Peacock Club, but right now all I want is right here.

Mikey arches an eyebrow at me. "We'd only be in that room anyway, and our bed at home is way bigger."

"True," I whisper as a blush creeps across my cheeks.

"The car is out front," Conor says with a wink before he pulls me from Mikey's arms and wraps me in a hug.

"Then let's go home," I say, pressing my face against his jacket and inhaling his familiar intoxicating scent.

FOUR

CONOR

J essie leans her head against my shoulder and I pull her close as we all walk to the waiting limo. I kiss the top of her head and the sweet smell of her makes my dick twitch to life. I should be fucking her in that private room in our club right now, but after our run in with the Boyles, and not knowing whether Shane would snap out of his bad mood, it seemed a better idea to head home.

She snakes an arm beneath my suit jacket, running her hand up my spine and my cock gets harder.

Yeah, I'm gonna fuck her in the limo.

Mikey opens the door for us as we reach it and she climbs in first. Shane hangs back a little, something still on his mind.

"You okay?" I ask him.

He runs a hand over his jaw. "Hmm."

"You don't sound all that convinced."

"You think she was right? Do we need to take a step back from all this?"

"Um, yeah," I laugh. "Not right now, but one day. That was always the plan anyway, right?"

"I guess somewhere along the way I forgot that. What if I don't know anything else though?"

I wrap my arm around his neck and kiss the top of his head. It's strange to be the one counseling him because it's usually the other way around, but he has changed so much since Jessie came into our lives, and even more so since we had kids. He doesn't close himself off from everyone and try to handle everything on his own any longer. And while we've always had an unbreakable bond, it has strengthened beyond measure these past few years. But him relinquishing any kind of control is still a struggle for him and I get that completely.

"What? You're Shane fucking Ryan. I have never ever seen you unable to do anything in my whole goddamn life."

He laughs at that.

"But you know we will keep doing this as long as we have to, right? If we can't all walk away clean then we never walk away," I assure him.

"Never?" he frowns at me.

"We're all in it together, bro. It's the way it's always been and that will never change. Just because Jessie worries about our kids doesn't mean she wants out. You gotta know that."

"I do," he says just as Mikey pops his head out of the door.

"Come on," he urges us to get into the car.

As soon as we're seated, I press the button to speak to our driver, Caleb. "Hey, buddy. Take the long route home, okay. And when we get home, park up in the basement and feel free to see yourself out. We'll take care of ourselves."

"Yes, boss," Caleb replies and then I release the button so that we have complete privacy again.

"The long way home?" Jessie asks with a pop of one eyebrow as she sits on Liam's lap.

"Yeah," I smile at her as I adjust my cock in my pants and

check my watch. It's a little before eleven. "Because I am fucking you at least once before next year, angel."

Her cheeks turn a deep pink that makes me want to throw her on the floor and fuck her like an animal.

"Me too, baby," Liam adds as he presses a soft kiss on her neck.

"Um, I am not being the only man in this car not to fuck my wife tonight," Mikey laughs.

"Well, Caleb ain't fucking her," I scowl at him and he laughs harder.

"I mean this part of the car," he waves his arms around the space for clarification.

"I guess I can wait until next year," Shane says with a sigh.

"Yeah, you already had two happy endings tonight," Liam says and both Mikey and I frown at him.

"Two?" I ask.

"Oh, yeah," Liam chuckles.

"Fuck yeah," Shane groans.

"Liam!" Jessie says as her blush deepens even further.

"I gotta tell them, baby," he says, brushing her hair back from her face.

"Tell us what?" Mikey demands.

"Jessie was sucking my cock when Liam disturbed us earlier so I could come deal with Declan Boyle for you," Shane answers instead.

"In public?" I ask. *Fucker*!

"It was in the private booth. Nobody could see," Jessie says.

"No wonder you were so pissed earlier. I'm sorry, bro," Mikey starts laughing again, holding onto his sides.

"Well, she had finished by the time Liam interrupted us."

"Not quite," Liam laughs. "I had to wait like twenty seconds for your soul to re-enter your body after Jessie sucked it out."

CHAPTER FOUR

That makes Mikey crack up and even Shane is laughing now.

"Liam!" Jessie says again but she is smiling as she looks around at the four of us. Fuck, she is so damn beautiful.

I hold out my hand to her while my brothers regain their composure and when she takes it, I pull her out of my brothers arms and into mine. "Let's get you naked, angel," I whisper in her ear and a shiver ripples through her body as I slip my hand beneath Shane's dinner jacket which she's still wearing, and start to slide down the zipper of her dress.

CHAPTER
FIVE

JESSIE

I shrug my arms out of Shane's jacket and Conor tugs my dress down over my body. When he reaches my ass, I lift up so that he can pull it all the way over my hips and down my legs. He places it on the seat beside him as I sit here in only my panties and heels.

"Are you boys all getting naked too?" I ask with a pop of one eyebrow.

"No," he states as he shakes his head.

"Why not?"

"Because if for some reason we get pulled over by the cops, four naked dudes in the back of a limo is going to draw a whole lot of attention, angel."

"But it's okay for me to be naked if we get pulled over by the cops?" I ask with a grin.

"No because you would be wearing my jacket before anyone even got near the door. Trust me," he growls possessively.

"And you're not naked, sweetheart," Shane says as he looks at my panties.

In response, Conor fists his hands in the expensive lace material and tears them in half. "She is now," he says with a grin as he wads the torn fabric in his palm and tosses it to Shane.

"You could have just taken them off," I say with a roll of my eyes.

"I just did. Now less of the eye rolling, angel," he growls as he lifts me, spinning me around until I'm straddling him. "Or I will spank your pretty ass instead of letting you come on my cock."

"Well that sounds kind of hot too," I whisper as he starts to unzip his fly.

"Maybe I'll spank you anyway," he growls. "But you're gonna ride me first."

He frees his stiff cock from his trousers and the crown is already glistening with precum. He wraps his hand around his shaft and squeezes hard, making me lick my lips as I think about how good he tastes. "Not now, angel," he groans. "I want inside your hot little pussy, so slide the fuck onto me."

I rest my hands on his shoulders and hover over him, lining up the thick head of his shaft at my entrance. A deep guttural groan vibrates through his body as I sink a little lower, edging the tip in just a little. Then as though he can't hold back any longer, he grabs hold of my hips and pulls me down onto him until I'm so full of him I gasp for breath.

"Fuck, your pussy feels so good," he hisses as his fingers dig into the soft flesh of my hips while he holds me still, allowing his huge cock to stretch and fill me.

"Conor," I groan his name as I grind down on him.

Shane is sitting beside us on the bench seat and he brushes a stray lock of hair back from my forehead. "Just so we're clear, when I say I'm happy to wait until next year, I mean like two minutes after midnight, okay?"

I smile at him before Conor grips my jaw in his strong hand

and turns my head back to him. "Don't look at him when I'm fucking you," he growls and I bite down on my lip.

"Sorry," I purr even though I'm not because I love bossy Conor so much.

He slides a hand up the inside of my thigh and rubs the pad of his thumb over my clit while he continues holding onto my hip with his other hand. He rolls me over his cock and I whimper and mewl as he hits the sweet spot deep inside me.

Then there are another pair of strong hands on my waist and a solid chest against my back as Liam joins us. He pulls my hair to one side, exposing the length of my neck before he peppers soft kisses over my delicate skin.

"You look so good when you're being fucked, baby," he whispers in my ear. Then his teeth graze my sensitive flesh as he starts to suckle softly while his hands glide over my ribs until he's cupping my breasts, squeezing them in his huge hands.

"Oh, God," I whimper as his and Conor's attentions have waves of pleasure rolling through my core and converging in one sweet spot between my thighs.

"Come on my cock, angel," Conor commands and like it's been conditioned to do, my body obeys.

My orgasm crashes over me and I tremble in their arms as my cells absorb every delicious aftershock of pleasure.

"Good girl," Liam growls in my ear and my pussy ripples around his brother's cock.

"Such a slut for praise, angel," Conor chuckles.

"You can't call your wife a slut," I protest feebly because I love every single word that comes out of these men's mouths.

Conor slaps my ass and I yelp. "Never said you were a slut," he says, his eyes narrowed.

"You kinda did, big guy," I grin at him.

He glares at me and the fire in his eyes ignites one low in my abdomen. "On your knees," he commands.

Liam shuffles back, allowing me some room to move and obey his older brother's order. Once I'm on my knees, I look up at Conor, fluttering my eyelashes as his eyes burn into my skin.

"Suck my cock," he growls. "See how good your pussy tastes on me."

My tongue darts out and I lick my lip, sucking in a breath before leaning down and wrapping my lips around his thick crown. I flick my tongue over the end and taste his precum, mixed with the taste of my own arousal, as well as Shane from earlier — and it makes heat flush my skin.

Conor weaves his fingers through my hair and I rest my hands on his waist to steady myself as he fucks my mouth.

As I'm focusing on sucking Conor, I hear the sound of Liam's zipper behind me and his groans of appreciation as he runs a hand over my ass. Then he's pulling my hips backward and spreading my thighs apart with his knees.

"Such a beautiful fucking pussy," he growls as he slides two thick fingers inside me causing me to groan around Conor's shaft as I surge forward.

A few seconds later, Liam replaces his fingers with his huge cock, driving into me in one swift movement and pushing me further onto his brother as I take the entire length of both of them at the same time.

"Good girl," Conor says as he rubs the pad of his thumb over my cheek, wiping away the tears as he hits the gag reflex at the back of my throat.

"Such a good fucking girl," Liam agrees as he rubs his hands over my ass before grabbing hold of my hips. Then he starts to fuck me slowly, angling himself so the crown of his cock sweeps over my G spot over and over again.

My thighs are trembling as I try to focus on bringing Conor to climax, but Liam is thrusting into me so deeply — with deliciously rhythmic rolls of his hips that make heat and pleasure coil around my insides – that it's hard to feel anything but my own pleasure.

Not to mention Conor's hands on me, guiding me further onto his dick as he grunts and growls in appreciation. I moan and mumble as he rocks deeper into my mouth until I take him even further, while he holds onto my head. My body goes lax — completely pliable as I let them take full control. I am literal putty in their hands, but this is exactly how I like it. I have never felt more free and safe and cherished as I am when I'm being dominated by these four incredible men.

"Fuck, angel," Conor groans as his grip on my hair tightens. He tugs at the roots as the muscles in his abs and thighs clench tightly. A few seconds later, he spurts his hot seed against the back of my throat and I mumble my gratitude as I swallow every single drop — sucking and licking his shaft until his muscles relax and his fingers slip from my hair.

He pulls his cock out of my mouth and I look up at him as he wipes my lips and chin with a sweep of his thumb. "You're fucking beautiful," he breathes out the words.

Then Liam leans over me, ghosting his lips over the shell of my ear. "You so fucking are," he whispers. "Hold onto Conor now, baby, while I fuck you properly."

Conor takes my hands in his, lacing his fingers through mine as I rest my cheek on his huge, powerful thigh while Liam grips my waist with his enormous hands, his fingers almost touching on my abdomen. Then he fucks me as hard as I have ever been fucked in my entire life, driving into me so deeply that my legs tremble as I squeeze him.

"Goddammit, Jessie!" he grunts as my walls ripple around his cock and I moan his name.

When my orgasm tears through my body like black powder a few seconds later, it seems to tip him over the edge and his fingers dig into my soft flesh as he holds me still while he pumps his cum into me.

Conor brushes his fingers over my cheek while Liam's hands rub over my back and ass as the last tremors vibrate through my body.

"You take our cocks so fucking well, baby," Liam groans as he pulls out of me, causing a rush of our cum to trickle out too. He catches it in his fingers and pushes it back inside me and that simple act makes my cheeks flush with heat.

"You mind using a little of that on her ass for me," Mikey asks with a dark laugh. "I don't think we brought any lube with us?"

"Hmm," Liam chuckles as he sweeps his fingers up my seam and slides a thick finger into my hole. I arch my back in pleasure, still wanting more.

"So needy, baby," Liam hisses as he works his finger deeper. "You ready for Mikey to fuck your ass now?"

"Uh-huh," I murmur, lost to the sensations that are overwhelming my body, until Liam withdraws his finger and I whimper.

"I'm right here, Red," Mikey growls as Liam moves and he slides effortlessly into his brother's place. "You ready for me?"

"Yes," I breathe.

He pushes his cock into my pussy first, coating it with cum before sliding back out and pressing the tip against my asshole. I push back against him, letting him know he doesn't have to take it easy.

He guides his length in slowly, letting me adjust to his size and once he's halfway in, he wraps my hair around his fist and pulls me upright, until the bare skin of my back is flush against his chest. His free hand slides to my hip and he starts to kiss my neck as he slides his cock deep inside me — filling me so thoroughly and exquisitely that I moan loudly, and his three brothers grunt and groan their approval.

Mikey laughs against my skin, keeping one hand in my hair as his other hand slides over my hip before he runs it over my body. Coasting over my breasts and my stomach, leaving a trail of heat in his wake before his fingers dip between my thighs.

"Mikey," I whimper as he slowly starts to circle my clit.

I rock my hips into his hand and he groans into my ear. "This pussy is so fucking sweet, Red. If you weren't full of Liam and Shane's cum, I'd make you ride my goddamn face while I make you scream."

His words vibrate through me, turning my bones to Jell-o. I writhe in his expert touch, but he holds me still while he goes on fucking my ass and rubbing my clit until wave upon wave of pleasure and heat is cascading through me.

"As soon as we get home we need to get you showered so we can all eat, angel," Conor growls and my eyes lock on his to find him staring at me like he's s starving man eyeing his next meal.

"I second that," Mikey growls as he drives harder and then sinks two of his huge fingers into my pussy while he grinds the heel of his palm over my clit.

"God, Mikey," I mewl as tiny specks of light cloud my vision.

"That's my girl, show my brothers how hard you come for me, Red," he whispers in my ear before he licks the length of my throat and I come apart in his arms.

Resting my head back on his shoulder, I close my eyes and pant for breath as he grinds out his release into me.

The sound of a champagne cork popping makes my head snap up and I look around to see Liam has just opened a bottle.

"It's midnight and we missed the countdown," Shane explains when he sees the look on my face.

"Oh no, did we?"

"I didn't miss nothing. Starting the new year balls deep in

my wife beats any countdown," Mikey chuckles and Shane rolls his eyes while Liam and Conor laugh.

With a kiss on my neck, Mikey pulls out of me and starts to fasten up his suit pants. Meanwhile, Conor takes his handkerchief from his pocket. He stares into my eyes before leaning down and gently wiping between my thighs from front to back.

"Thank you," I whisper.

"Any time, angel," he replies with a wink before he pulls me up to sit on his lap. "As soon as we get home, I'll help you get cleaned up properly."

"And then no more coming in Jessie's pussy for the rest of the night," Mikey suggests. "Cause I don't know about you all, but I gotta eat."

"How about no more coming in the pussy until our wife gives us an answer to the question we asked her on Christmas Day?" Liam offers as he hands out glasses of champagne to his brothers.

I frown at him. It's not like him to be the one to tease me, but I have kept them waiting on an answer. I was so shocked when they suggested that we start trying for another baby that I couldn't speak for a minute, and then by the time I could, we all got distracted because Ella took her first steps.

I've been thinking about it ever since, and they haven't pressed me on it, although I know they must all want to. It's not that I don't want more babies with them, I want lots more, but I didn't realize they would be ready again so soon.

"Hmm. See how long she holds out on us then?" Conor says with an arch of his eyebrow.

I smile at the four of them. "I can guarantee all of you would cave within a week."

"I'd cave within a goddamn hour," Shane says with a wink and then he holds out his hand to me. "Come here, sweetheart." I take his hand and shuffle onto his lap. "In fact, I can't even wait another minute," he growls as he runs his nose along my throat.

"I haven't had my champagne yet," I whisper.

"Conor will give you some of his," he says, setting his own glass down as he unzips his suit pants.

"Hmm," Conor agrees as he takes a huge mouthful. Then he leans over and seals his lips over mine, kissing me and passing the champagne from his mouth to my own. He goes on kissing me as Shane frees his cock and lifts me onto it, and a few seconds later I'm full of him and chasing my next orgasm.

CHAPTER

SIX

LIAM

The hot water runs down my back as I stare at her. Fuck me, she is too beautiful for words. After we said good-night to our babysitters, we all needed to take a shower, but Jessie and me are on baby duty tonight, so we went to check on the twins first. By the time we stared at them and wished them a very quiet happy new year my brothers were done, so now it's just me and her.

I take the shower head down from the fixture on the wall and she grins at me.

"What are you doing, Liam?" She bites on her lip.

"Well, we got to get you squeaky clean, Mrs. Ryan," I remind her as I push her back against the tiles. "Spread your legs wide for me."

She obeys me instantly and I bring the shower head between her thighs, angling the jets on her delicate pink pussy lips. Her eyelids flutter and her cheeks flush a little pink.

"Oh, you like that?" I arch an eyebrow at her.

"Yes," she whispers as she wraps her arms around my neck.

I flick the switch on the head to adjust the pressure as I direct it at her clit and she whimpers.

343

"You ever get yourself off like this, baby?" I ask, genuinely curious.

"Sometimes," she breathes. "But I rarely shower alone."

"Hmm," I nibble on the soft skin of her throat as she sinks her fingernails into the back of my neck and rocks her hips, chasing her orgasm. But if she's coming, then it's going to be on a part of me.

I shut off the water and toss the shower head onto the floor. She blinks at me as she keeps her back pressed against the wall. I run my hands over her wet body before I drop to my knees.

"Let's see how clean we got you, baby," I say as I hook her thigh over my shoulder to give me access to her hot pussy.

Her fingers thread through my hair as I pepper kisses over the top of her thighs and rub the tip of my nose over her clit.

"Please?" she moans softly and so I take her clit into my mouth, sucking off the excess water until all I can taste is her.

I sink two fingers inside her and groan against her skin when I feel how wet she is for me already. Then I finger fuck her as I feast on her sweet folds, sucking and licking and nibbling until she's grinding herself onto my face.

"Fuck!" I hiss because it's not enough. I need better access.

"Hold on, baby," I warn her as I lift her other thigh to hook it over my shoulder.

"Liam, I'm too heavy," she squeals but I've already lifted her and have her sitting on my shoulders before she's even finished speaking.

"I'm going to pretend you didn't just fucking say that, baby," I growl as I look up at her.

"Sorry," she whispers, catching her bottom lip between her teeth.

"You're lucky Conor or Shane didn't hear you, because you would so get an ass spanking for that."

"I did hear and she will be," Conor shouts from the doorway

and her walls squeeze around my fingers, reminding me how much she loves to be spanked.

"Maybe I'll have to join in then," I chuckle before I lick the length of her soaking wet slit.

"Fuck, Liam," she groans.

"You like that even better than the shower, baby?"

"Fuck, yes."

"Good girl," I say as I curl my fingers inside her and suck her throbbing little bud into my mouth.

She rewards me with a shuddering climax that explodes onto my fingers and tongue. I massage her inner walls with my fingers and nuzzle her skin as she rides out every last tremor. The only thing that gets my girl more worked up than a spanking is a little praise.

It's almost four am and Jessie is lying between Shane and me. Her head on my chest and his arm around her waist as he trails soft kisses over her back. We have been fucking her for hours and she's all but passed out now.

"The kids will be awake soon," Mikey says with a groan as he lays down beside me. "Who's on early morning duty?"

"Me and Jessie," Conor says with a laugh as he looks at her curled up on my chest.

"I'll get up with you," Shane says. "I think we fucked our wife into a coma again."

"You did not," she murmurs sleepily. "Almost though."

"I'll get up anyway, sweetheart," he replies softly.

"Thank you," she breathes.

We all lie in silence for a minute until she speaks again. "Tonight – last night — it was perfect. Thank you."

"Thank you, baby," I say, kissing the top of her head.

"It's only perfect because you make it so, angel," Conor replies with a yawn.

She sucks in a deep breath before she adds,"Oh, and also, I meant to say... yes."

"Yes, what?" Shane asks with a frown.

"Yes, we should have some more babies," she says with a soft smile as her eyes stay closed.

"You think she's dreaming?" Conor asks with a laugh.

"Don't give a fuck. We all heard it. Baby making is a go. I'm flushing those birth control pills as soon as I can feel my legs again," Mikey says, making all of us laugh.

"We might have more twins though, you know?" she yawns.

"That's okay. We'll still outnumber them," I tell her.

"Hmm," she mumbles as she drifts off to sleep.

So, we're having more kids. I mean I knew she'd agree but I wondered if she might need a little more time. I should have known she'd be ready when we are. She gives us everything we ever want and need.

I look across at my brothers and we've all got the same dopey ass grins on our faces.

The smile stays on my face as I close my eyes. This year is going to be our best yet.

ANOTHER RYAN CHRISTMAS

CHAPTER 1
MIKEY
8 MONTHS BEFORE CHRISTMAS

"Holy fuck, Red, are you trying to kill me?" My eyes rake hungrily over her delectable body, taking in every single delicious curve, which is currently encased in a skintight leather catsuit.

She sinks her teeth into her plump lower lip and runs her hands nervously over her stomach. "Is it too much? Too tight?"

I walk to her, reaching her in two giant strides before I slip my arms around her waist and grab her juicy ass, giving it a squeeze that makes her gasp. "It's perfect." I kiss her softly, pulling her close until our bodies are meshed together and my cock is twitching in my suit pants. She curls her fingers in my hair as I slide my tongue into her welcoming mouth and pin her to the wall. Then I pull back and leave her panting, looking over her beautiful body again. "But how the fuck do I get this off you, Jessie?"

She laughs softly. "There's a zipper right down the back, you deviant."

Before I change our date night plans and take her to bed instead of our club, I keep one arm around her waist and guide her to the elevator leading to the basement. "Says my horny as fuck wife who's currently wearing an outfit that she knew would have me hard before we even get to the car."

"You're always hard, Mikey Ryan," she says with a soft purr.

I dip my head and nip at her earlobe. "Around you, Red, fuck yeah I am. Who helped you to even get into that thing?"

She flutters her eyelashes at me. "Conor."

"Did he fuck you too?"

"Mikey!" she nudges me in the ribs.

"What? He can barely keep his hands off you when you're not dressed head to toe in skintight leather."

She laughs again and the sound makes me smile. I fucking love making her happy more than anything in this world. "Well, he didn't."

I squeeze her tighter. "Good, because I want to eat some pussy while we're at the club."

She bites down on her lip, her cheeks flushing pink. "Maybe I should have worn a dress?"

My cock throbs harder because I know exactly what's going through her mind. "You thinking I could have eaten you at our booth?"

"Yeah," she whispers, biting on her lip again.

I kiss the top of her head. "Well, you can suck my cock at the table and I'll return the favor when we get downstairs to our room."

As soon as I'm sitting on the back seat of the limo I pull her up onto my lap until she's straddling me. Running my hands up her thighs and my nose along her jaw, I inhale her sweet intoxicating scent.

Wrapping her arms around my neck, she rolls her hips, moaning softly as she presses her pussy against my hard cock. I sure hope this leather deal goes back on as easily as I'm about to tear it off. "You're so fucking sexy, Red."

She runs her hands down the lapels of my tuxedo jacket. "Ditto. You know how much I love you in this suit."

I flash her a wink as my fingers find the zipper at the nape of her neck. "I know."

She crushes her lips to mine, whimpering softly as I slide my tongue against hers and explore the sweet recesses of her mouth. I fist my free hand in her hair, holding her head in place while I taste her. I can't go more than a few minutes alone with her without an animal need to be inside her coursing through my veins.

She moans softly, just as needy for me as I am for her. I slide my hand between her thighs and palm her pussy, and now I'm the one wishing she'd worn a dress, because if she had my fingers would already be sinking into her wet cunt.

I snarl in frustration and she breaks our kiss. She rocks back, holding her hand to her mouth. Her face pales and my stomach twists into a knot. Something's not right. "Jessie? What's wrong?"

"Mikey," she whimpers and not in a sexy way. "I feel sick." Her eyes roll in her head.

I brush her hair back from her forehead, noting her cold, damp skin. "It's okay. I'm right here."

She shakes her head. "I'm too hot. It must be this suit." She reaches behind and starts pulling frantically at the zipper. "I need to get it off."

I take her trembling hands in mine, my brow furrowed in a frown. "Calm down, Red. I'll do it."

I pull down her zipper and she wriggles to get free as I work the leather over her arms. Perspiration beads over her skin. She groans softly.

I press a hand to her damp cheek. "You still feel sick?"

"Yeah," she whispers, her eyes brimming with tears. "I'm sorry I ruined our date night."

"You didn't," I assure her. "You want this all the way off?" I look down at the leather suit now bunched around her waist.

She nods. "Please."

Shifting her onto the seat, I take off her heels and then work the suit over her hips and thighs before pulling it all the way off her until she's left in only her black lace bra and panties. She rubs her hands over her arms and shivers.

I shrug off my jacket and wrap it around her, threading her arms through the sleeves before I pull her to sit on my lap. She presses her cheek against my chest and I band my arms tight around her, pressing a kiss on the top of her head and brushing her beautiful red hair back from her damp skin.

After a few minutes, she looks up at me, color back in her cheeks and her eyes green eyes sparkling.

I arch an eyebrow at her. I fucking knew it. "You feel better?"

"Yeah. You think it was that damn suit? Did I overheat or something?"

I laugh softly. "I don't think it was your sexy little outfit, Red. You can't think of another time when you were prone to sudden bouts of nausea?"

Her eyes widen and her mouth opens in surprise. "But we only just started trying again."

I tilt my head, taking in every detail of her beautiful face. She is perfect and I'm pretty sure she's about to make me a dad again. "You're full of cum pretty much twenty four hours a day, Red."

Her smile lights up her whole goddamn face. "We have no tests at home."

"Then we'll stop a drug store and get some." She glances down at herself, wearing only my jacket and her underwear. I cup her jaw in my tilt her head up so she's looking at me again. "Obviously *you* will stay in the car and I'll go get the tests."

She giggles. "Okay."

"Liam and Shane and Conor are going to lose their fucking minds when we get home six hours early, with you half naked and quite probably pregnant."

Her lip trembles. "What if I'm not though?"

I press a kiss on the tip of her nose. She is. I know it. "Then we'll all just spend all night fucking a baby into you anyway."

Her cheeks flush pink. I push my hand between her thighs and pull her panties aside, dragging the tip of my finger through her pussy lips, coating it in her wet heat.

"Always wet for me, Red." I slip a finger inside her tight pussy and her back arches in pleasure.

"Mikey, that feels so good," she whines.

I nip at her neck. "You want more?"

"Yes."

I want to fuck her but I don't want to be balls deep in her when we pull up at the drug store so I add a second finger and smile when her eyes roll back and her lips part in a perfect O. I sink deeper, rubbing over the sensitive spot deep inside her that has her walls rippling around my fingers, squeezing me like she'll never let me go.

"Fuck," she groans out the word.

I work her harder, desperate to feel her come. "That's my good girl. Come for me, Red. I want to suck you off my fingers."

She threads her fingers through my hair, riding my hand as I fuck her harder. When she comes a few moments later, she screams my name until it fills the car. I lean back against the seat and slip my fingers out of her tight channel. She pants for breath, cheeks flushed pink and her eyelids fluttering as she comes down from the high. I keep my gaze fixed on hers as I

SADIE KINCAID

place my fingers into my mouth and suck them clean, allowing her sweet taste to flood my senses.

Using my free hand, I tangle my fingers in her hair and bring her face closer to mine. "I'm fucking you as soon as I've been into the drug store, Red."

She smiles at me, her hand running down my chest toward the waistband of my suit pants. "Is that a promise?"

CHAPTER 2
SHANE

Movement catches my attention out of the corner of my eye as Liam tosses a stack of poker chips into the center of the table. I glance at the doorway and the sight of my wife in only her underwear and Mikey's tuxedo jacket makes my cock immediately jump to attention. I wasn't expecting them back for hours. "Jesus, sweetheart. I hope you didn't leave the apartment in that get up."

She laughs softly and shakes her head.

Conor checks his watch. "Not that I'm complaining, angel, but why are you back already? Is everything okay?"

"Where are your clothes, baby?" Liam adds.

Her beautiful cheeks turn red and she looks down at her attire, sinking her teeth into her plump bottom lip. "I got hot."

Conor flashes her a wicked grin. "You are fucking hot."

Something's wrong. I push back my chair. "Come here, sweetheart."

Nibbling on her juicy bottom lip she crosses the room and I pull her onto my lap before placing my hand on her forehead. She gives me a sweet, sexy smile. She doesn't feel hot although

355

my body temperature is sure on the rise from the way her perfect ass is nestled against my cock.

"Our girl also got a sudden and intense attack of nausea." Mikey holds up a white paper bag like the kind you get from the drug store. I can take a guess at what he has in there and it makes me suck in a breath. "The kind that passes after a few minutes," he adds with a knowing smirk.

"But you feel okay now?" I ask her, my eyes searching her face.

"Yeah. Perfectly fine now. And so Mikey thinks—"

"You're pregnant?" Liam doesn't let her finish her sentence.

Mikey grins. "We're about to find out." He thrusts the bag into Jessie's hand. "Go do the thing, Red."

Fuck, she's pregnant again. I swallow down the knot of emotion that clogs my throat while she glances between us nervously. I press my lips close to her ear, my breath ruffling her hair. "You want me to come with you, sweetheart?"

She shakes her head, aware that if I accompany her to the bathroom to watch her pee on a stick, there's every likelihood that my brothers will too. "But maybe you could all wait outside?"

Conor winks at her. "Like there would ever be anywhere else we'd be."

MIKEY PACES up and down the room chewing on his thumbnail and Conor leans against the wall beside the bathroom door, hands stuffed into his pockets a frown furrowing his brow. Meanwhile Liam and I sit on the edge of the bed, arms folded staring at the door while we wait for our wife. I can't help but think about when we were trying for a baby last time, and how devastated she'd be every month when her period arrived. We agreed to try again a few months ago but she only came off her birth control last month, and that was mostly my doing. The four of us want more kids so badly and I know we can be a lot, so I wanted to make sure she was ready. Not for the baby, because she's the best fucking mom in the world to our twins, but for the emotional toll the whole process might take.

And she is. Jessie Ryan is the strongest person I have ever known. Still, whatever the results are, we're all here for her. For each other.

The toilet flushes and Mikey stops pacing. Conor stares at the door now too. After the sound of running water, Jessie emerges from the bathroom, a nervous smile on her face as she holds the test between her fingers.

Conor cups her jaw in his hand. "How long, angel?"

"Two minutes," she replies.

"Fuck that. I'm checking now," Mikey says as he plucks the stick from her hand.

"Mikey!" she admonishes him before she goes to snatch it back but he dodges her and stares at the test. The giant goofy smile that lights up his face stops her from moving any further.

She claps a hand over her mouth.

Liam edges off the bed and moves closer to his twin. "Is it positive?"

Turning the white piece of plastic in his hands, he holds it up for us all to see. "Sure fucking is."

Jessie gasps and Conor wraps her in his arms. "You're sure, Mikey?" he asks with a frown.

"Yes I'm fucking sure. Two fucking lines. Pregnant!" he announces triumphantly.

"Yes, baby!" Liam fist pumps the air and then he wraps his arms around Jessie too, sandwiching her between him and Conor.

"I'm so fucking proud of you, angel," Conor says before

giving her a soft kiss on her head. She buries her face against his chest, her shoulders shaking like she's sobbing.

Mikey wraps his arms around the three of them. "You're fucking amazing, Red."

I swallow as I watch the four of them together—five if you include the new baby—and wonder how the fuck I ever got so lucky as to share the most incredible woman in the world with my brothers.

Jessie's head peeks out over Conor's bicep, happy tears streaming down her cheeks as she smiles at me. What the fuck am I doing still sitting here? My wife is about to make me a dad again. I jump off the bed and run over to them.

CHAPTER 3

LIAM

"This will be cold," Dr. Wilcox says as she squeezes some jelly onto Jessie's stomach. I squeeze her hand in mine and she smiles up at me, tears pricking at her eyes. This is her twelve week scan, the first time we'll get to see our new baby and I know she's as excited as fuck, but nervous as hell too. We all are.

She's been as sick as a dog though and Mikey, who is the font of all pregnancy knowledge, assures me that morning sickness, while bad for our girl, is a good sign that all is well with the baby.

"Let's see the jelly-bean, Doc," Mikey says as he stands on the opposite side of the bed, bouncing on his toes. Shane puts a reassuring hand on his shoulder and squeezes.

"Almost there," Dr. Wilcox says with a reassuring smile.

Jessie turns her head and stares at the monitor intently and a few seconds later a fuzzy image appears on the screen.

My beautiful wife sucks in a harsh breath. "Is everything okay?"

I squeeze her hand tighter, my eyes meeting Conor's as he sits directly opposite me, with her other hand in his.

Dr. Wilcox remains quiet, her eyes fixed on the screen as she runs the machine over Jessie's abdomen. It seems like we all hold our breath, frozen in anticipation.

"And there's the heartbeat," Dr. Wilcox says at last and I let out the air in my lungs while Jessie squeals with happiness. The doc turns up the sound and the sound of our baby's racing heart fills the small room.

"And there's only one this time?" Shane asks.

Dr. Wilcox laughs. "Just the one."

"One perfect baby," Jessie says softly.

Lifting her hand to my face, I kiss her knuckles. Another baby. I'm going to be a dad again. I can't fucking wait.

Dr. Wilcox shows us the baby's head and limbs as she takes plenty of pictures and when she's done, she hands me some tissues and leaves the room.

My brothers smother our wife with kisses and well-deserved praise while I wipe the jelly from her stomach. When I'm done I press a kiss on her abdomen. "Can't fucking wait to meet you, kid," I whisper before I fix Jessie's clothes in place for her.

She runs her fingers through my hair and when I look up she's smiling down at me looking like the most beautiful thing I've ever seen in my life. "Thank you."

I kiss her stomach again and wad the tissue into a ball. "No problem."

Mikey checks his watch. "We need to get back to our other tiny devils before Chester quits on us."

Conor gives him a nudge. "Don't call my children devils."

Mikey grins at our older brother. "They are though," he says, his voice filled with pride.

"Yeah, I know," I grin back. Our kids have hit the terrible twos—hard! But luckily for us, we outnumber them two to one.

"They're spirited," Jessie says trying to muster a scowl, even as the corners of her mouth twitch in a smile.

"Like their mother," Shane agrees before he kisses her forehead. "Chester can handle them. I told him we'd be out all afternoon."

Conor frowns. "You did?"

Our oldest brother shrugs, his eyes still trained firmly on our wife. "I thought we could go grab some food and celebrate."

Mikey's grin widens further. "*Celebrate*? You booked a hotel room, bro?"

"Not that kind of celebrating," Shane replies diverting his attention from our pregnant wife long enough to give Mikey a soft slap on the back of his head.

"Oh?" Jessie's bottom lip juts out a little and Shane's eyes immediately dart back to her.

"I thought you'd be needing something to eat. You usually get sick around this time of the day."

"Oh yeah," she groans and places a hand on her stomach. "And then it lasts for eight hours."

"Exactly, sweetheart."

Conor winks at her. "And carbs are the only thing that seem to help."

"I know." She sits up and jumps off the bed and rubs a hand over her gently rounded stomach. "I'm gonna get soooo fat with this one."

Shane gives her a soft swat on the ass. "Enough!"

She flutters her eyelashes at him and then glances at the door. "You know Dr. Wilcox won't come back in here, right?" she says with a devious chuckle. "We could celebrate before food?"

Shane wraps an arm around her waist. "If we start *celebrating* now, sweetheart, we won't fucking stop. So food and then we can all fuck you into a coma tonight once your nausea has passed."

Mikey arches an eyebrow at her. "And you're not mainlining bread rolls."

I put a hand over my mouth to stop the laugh that wants to bubble out. Conor shakes his head and Shane blows out a breath.

"Mikey Ryan, I do not mainline bread rolls," Jessie protests. But then her bottom lip trembles. "Do I?"

"Aw, Red." Mikey wraps her in his arms and kisses her forehead. "I was just playing with you, baby."

She sniffs, burying her head in his chest. "You can joke around but you'll be sorry when this giant Ryan baby makes my ass super fat."

Mikey burrows his face into her neck. "Just more to hold onto while I'm fucking it."

Conor rounds the bed, pulling Mikey from Jessie's arms and into his. "I love you, angel, but you make one more comment about getting fat, and I'll edge you for a fucking week."

Her cheeks flush pink as she stares up into his eyes. "Your brothers won't though."

"Yes we fucking will," Shane snaps.

She glances at me for support, but as much as I love making her come, I'm in full agreement. "I agree, baby. No more bullshit about getting fat. You will eat and do whatever you need to do to keep you and our baby healthy and safe. Okay?"

She rolls her eyes.

"And no more *joking* from you either, fuck-knuckle," Conor warns Mikey.

My twin winces. "My bad. I'm sorry, Red."

She nestles into his chest again. "It was kinda funny."

CHAPTER 4

LIAM

3 DAYS BEFORE CHRISTMAS

Shane leans back in his chair and places the large brown envelope I just picked up from the mail on his desk. "Can you pick my tux up from the dry cleaners on your way home from the park?"

I frown in confusion. We wore our tuxedos last month on a group date night with Jessie and they were all dry-cleaned after. "Yeah, but I only picked it up three weeks ago for you. You needed it cleaning again?"

He flashes me a wicked grin. "I tried it on last week. Then Jessie came into the bedroom and ..." He raises his eyebrows.

I grin back at him. "It got covered in her cum."

He runs a hand over his jaw, a wicked glint twinkling in his eyes. "And mine, kid."

I sigh loudly. "God, I fucking love her."

"Love who?" she asks as she strolls into the room, wearing one of my t-shirts and a pair of knee high socks.

"What the fuck have I told you about walking around like that, sweetheart?" Shane chides her good-naturedly. "You're going to give one of us a fucking heart attack from the rush of blood to our cocks one day, you do know that, right?"

Her cheeks flush bright pink and she giggles before perching herself on my lap. "Stop being so dramatic."

"It's true, baby. You look hotter than hellfire."

She tugs the t-shirt down over her swollen belly. "None of my clothes fit me anymore."

"I did offer to buy you some maternity clothes," Shane reminds her. "You know for next time too."

Her cheeks turn bright pink at his suggestion that she's going to be knocked up again soon enough—but it's true, we all want more kids, Jessie included.

I slide my hand up the inside of her thigh and she practically purrs with excitement and anticipation. "I think our wife enjoys wandering around the house barely dressed though."

"She always has." Shane rubs a hand over his stubble. "It's the knee high socks that I'm questioning though. They seem to be a new addition, sweetheart."

"My feet get cold," she whispers.

He narrows his dark eyes at her. "And it has nothing to do with the fact that they make us all harder than an iron bar, no?"

She giggles softly. "Sorry, Daddy."

Holy fucking fuckballs. Jessie Ryan has just tossed a lit match into a pool of gasoline. Shane's eyes blaze with fire and his voice drops at least two octaves. "I've warned you about calling me that, Jessie."

She chews on her lip, wiggling her perfect ass against my cock until I'm painfully hard. I dust my lips over her sweet-smelling throat. "Did you come in here looking for a good fucking, baby?"

"I came in here because I heard my husband saying he loved someone—a *her*," she moans as I trail my teeth over her skin.

Gliding my hand all the way up the inside of her thigh, I tug her panties aside and slip a finger into her wet pussy, making her gasp out loud. "I was talking about you, obviously."

Without a word, Shane gets up and closes his office door. When he's done, he walks to Jessie and me and his eyes drop to the spot between her thighs where I'm working my finger inside her. He grips her chin in his hand and tilts her head up to look at him. "What did you just call me, sweetheart?"

She flutters her eyelashes. "Daddy."

His lips twitch in a smirk. "You know I'm keeping a record of all of your brattiness, right?" He drops to his knees. "And as soon as the baby's born and you're healed ..." He slides his hand up her inner thigh and rubs his pointer finger over her clit. She tries to arch her back in pleasure but I hold her still. "I'm gonna take you to our cabin in the woods and punish your bratty." He slips a finger inside her to join mine. "Little." He pushes deeper. "Ass."

A rush of her arousal coats the two of us, dripping down our palms and onto our wrists. I press my lips against her temple as her body bucks and shudders. "You like the sound of that?"

"Fuck, yes," she moans.

"I think I'm gonna have to join you two on this trip, baby, because you're fucking drenched just from him talking about it."

Shane winks at me. "Be my guest, kid. I'll teach you how to spank her until she squirts." *Jesus fucking Christ, I'm gonna nut in my boxers just thinking about it.*

"Oh, fu-oh," she whimpers as the two of us go on finger fucking her.

I arch an eyebrow at my oldest brother. "You think we can make her squirt now?"

She shakes her head, but he looks down at her dripping pussy and grins. "I'll eat. You fuck her."

Fuck, yes! I tug my sweatpants down and free my aching cock. Wrapping my hand around the base of my shaft, I squeeze and white hot pleasure floods my core. Shane and I slide our fingers out of her and she lets out a frustrated sigh.

"You're gonna be filled with my cock soon, baby." I turn her on my lap so she's facing him, spreading her legs wide open.

"Jesus, fuck, your cunt is spectacular, sweetheart," Shane says with a low growl before he dips his head and starts feasting on her clit like he's a starving man at an all you can eat buffet.

"Shane," she whimpers, threading her fingers through his hair.

I lift her a little, lining my cock at her soaking entrance before pulling her down onto me. Her tight, wet pussy wraps snugly around my cock like she was made only for me. Slick heat coats my shaft, dripping onto my thighs as I sink balls deep into her. "Fuck, baby. You take me so fucking well."

"Oh, God, Liam," she whines, throwing her head back. I wrap a hand around her throat, holding her in place and sucking on her neck while Shane eats her cunt. I don't even have to move because she does all the work, her walls rippling and squeezing around my cock until we're both teetering on the edge of ecstasy.

"Not yet. Keep her there," Shane orders and I take hold of her hips and pull out of her a little.

"No. Please let me come," she whines.

I press a kiss on her cheek as her body trembles. "Soon, baby."

I look down between her thighs to see Shane teasing her relentlessly with his tongue. Tremors ripple through her entire body and I swear I'm going to have an aneurysm if I have to hold off from coming inside her for much longer.

"Look at me, sweetheart?" Shane commands and I release my grip on her throat enough that she can look down at him. He rubs the pad of his thumb over her clit now. "Who am I?"

She clamps her lips together and he presses harder, causing her pussy to spasm. "Who am I, sweetheart?"

"Daddy," she breathes out the word.

He grins widely. "That's my good fucking girl." Then he gives me a knowing nod before his tongue joins his thumb on her swollen sensitive bud of flesh.

I drive all the way into her again and relief and euphoria flood my body. Her walls flutter around me as tremors ripple through her.

"That's it, baby, let go for us," I growl in her ear and she does. Soaking me and Shane as she comes hard and fast, covering us in her sweet juices.

CHAPTER 5
JESSIE

2 days before Christmas

"The team outdid themselves with the decorations this year," I say glancing around our packed club. It's the annual Christmas Eve, Eve masked ball and the theme this year is angels and demons.

"Holy shit! Is that ...?" Mikey asks, his hand around my waist tightening.

Shane's jaw clenches and his eyes narrow. I follow his and Mikey's gaze to the woman approaching us. She's tall and willowy with long dark hair and a tiny waist. Her hips sway seductively in her floor length red gown when she walks. I look down at my own gown, green with a thigh high split. I was a little worried that it clings to every inch of my heavily pregnant body, but from the looks on their faces when I came out of our bedroom wearing it earlier, my husbands most definitely approve.

Whoever this woman is, she's absolutely stunning. And

she's smiling as she looks in our direction, but her focus isn't on us, it's a few feet away. I follow her line of sight to see who that perfect smile is aimed at and when I realize who she's so happy to see, my stomach twists in a knot.

"Conor," she says when she reaches him. I can't hear her over the noise of the club but I can read her lips. I bet she purrs the word seductively too, like even her voice is hot.

My entire body tenses and Mikey gives me a reassuring squeeze.

Conor smiles and even though it seems forced and not one of his genuine smiles that he reserves for the people he loves, I feel a surge of jealousy running through me. I watch as the beautiful woman with the impossibly long legs, one of which I can see through the thigh high split in her gown, runs a hand down the lapel of his black tuxedo jacket.

Rage prickles beneath my eyelids. "Did she just ...?"

Shane laughs darkly and laces his fingers through mine. "Calm down, firecracker. Let me introduce you to Conor's ex-fiancée."

Conor's what now? How did I not know about her? What the ...? I open and close my mouth but before any logical words can come out, Shane clasps my hand tightly in his and leads me a few feet across the room to Conor and the mystery woman, who's now standing so close to him, there's barely a sliver of light between them. An unfamiliar feeling of intense anger bubbles beneath my skin. She leans forward and brushes her full red lips over his cheek and that simmering rage boils over like an overfilled crock pot.

"What the hell do you think you're doing?" I shriek like a crazy woman, making both her and Conor turn sharply. Her mouth hangs open in shock but Conor has one eyebrow quirked in amusement.

He slips an arm around my waist and pulls me to his side. "Diana, I'd like you to meet my wife."

Her eyes drop down to my swollen belly and the hint of a sneer curls her lip before she smiles again. "Your wife?"

"Yes. His *wife!*" I say with a possessive snarl.

She laughs, throwing her head back a little and showing off the diamond choker on her slender neck. "I never thought I'd see the day you'd commit yourself to any woman, Conor Ryan," she says with a seductive purr that makes my blood boil.

I inch forward, a possessive growl rumbling in my throat. "And what exactly is that supposed to mean?"

Diana blinks at me, her face a mask of shock at the venom in my tone. I'm kind of shocked myself to be honest. I have no idea what's come over me, but I'm all in now. Full on crazy jealous wife mode has been activated and I have no idea how to switch it off.

Conor glances down at me, and damn that bastard is almost grinning, like he thinks this is funny. A scowl furrows my brow and that makes the corners of his mouth curl up into a full on smile. "You think it's funny that she's hitting on you right in front of your pregnant wife?" I snap.

His shoulders shake a little like he's suppressing a snigger and I ball my hands into fists. All it would take is me stamping my foot and I'd be having a full on toddler tantrum in the middle of our club but I can't stop it. "Conor!"

His eyes twinkle with amusement and before I can protest any further, he scoops me into his arms. "Excuse us, would you?" he says before he starts walking through the crowd.

"Where are you taking me?" I insist as he strides so purposefully through the crowd that people move out of his way like the parting of the red sea.

"To put you in a time out, angel," he says with a soft laugh.

"I can't believe you—"

He cuts off the rest of my rant with a soft kiss and he goes on kissing me until we reach the manager's office, which is thankfully empty. He breaks our kiss only to kick the door closed and sets me on the edge of the desk, his eyes still dancing with unrestrained amusement. He brushes a curl back from my face. "What the hell was that, angel?"

I fold my arms over my chest. "You mean your ex-fiancée throwing herself at you out there?"

He laughs again, pinching the bridge of his nose. "My what?"

"Your ex-fiancée!"

He frowns. "She's not my ... Who told you that?"

"Shane." I pout.

"Asshole." He shakes his head, planting his hands on the desk either side of my hips and pushing himself between my thighs. He smells so good. My heart rate spikes. "She was never that. It was a misunderstanding."

I suck in a breath through my nose, the intense anger I felt a few moments ago already reduced down to a mere simmer again now that he's so close to me. "You misunderstandingly proposed to her?"

He sighs deeply. "It was almost Christmas. I saw this cute ring at a market that I thought she might like. It wasn't a diamond. It was *not* an engagement ring. I've never proposed to anyone in my life but you."

He cups my jaw in his hand, titling my head until I'm staring into his dark eyes. "I have never wanted to marry anyone except you." He presses a soft kiss on my lips and rubs a hand over my stomach. "Never wanted kids with anyone but you." He kisses the tip of my nose. "Never wanted to fuck anyone quite so much as I fuck you," his voice comes in a deep growl now and the atmosphere in the room changes in a heartbeat.

I wrap my arms around his neck. "I have no idea what made me act like that out there. I'm sorry."

He brushes his lips over my cheek, his warm breath on my skin making me shiver. "Don't apologize, angel. Seeing you all possessive over me was fucking hot."

"It was?" I giggle despite my embarrassment.

"Yeah. I love how feral you got for a minute. Like you were about to rip her throat out for touching me."

My cheeks flush pink and I wince. "I almost did. I don't know what came over me. The pregnancy hormones, maybe?"

He laughs again, wrapping me in his arms. "Whatever it was it made my cock leak, angel. But just so you know," he trails his lips and teeth over my neck, "*you* are the only woman who exists in my world, Jessie. *You* are the only woman I see in any room. The only woman I want and the only one I'll ever need."

Grabbing my legs , he wraps them around his waist and grinds his cock against me, creating a delicious friction against my clit that makes me moan. He grabs my chin again, his thumb brushing over my bottom lip before he pulls, opening my mouth for him. His eyes crinkle as he smiles. "So fucking needy for me."

I don't get a chance to respond before he seals his lips over mine, taking my breath away with a fierce kiss full of fire and dominance that leaves me in no doubt at all that he meant every word he just said. Not that I've ever doubted his love for me, but I'm hormonal and feeling bloated and I guess that made me a little crazy.

Conor pushes me back, his warm hands skating up my thighs and beneath my dress. He breaks our kiss, dragging his lips over my jaw. "You need me to remind me how fucking hard you make me, angel?"

I fist my hands in the lapels of his jacket, pulling him closer and grinding myself against him. "Yes."

He swipes two fingers over the wet spot on my panties. "I love how horny being pregnant makes you."

I tip my head back, allowing him access to my neck and he takes full advantage, running his tongue from my jaw to the base of my throat. He bites me gently before sweeping his tongue over the mark he's left. I whimper, rocking my hips to chase more friction.

The door opens.

"I fucking knew it," Shane says with a deep throaty laugh as he walks into the room, closely followed by Liam and Mikey.

Mikey rolls his eyes. "We got a room downstairs for this, you know?"

"I know." Conor gives my forehead a final kiss and then steps back, leaving me wanting. "But I had to deal with our wife before she lost it on Diana." He turns and glares at Shane. "My ex-fiancée?"

Shane laughs harder as he crosses the room, taking my hand, he helps me off the desk. "It was worth it to see Jessie react like that."

I try to scowl at him but I can't quite manage it. "Wasn't funny."

He presses his lips to my ear through my hair. "It so was."

My lips twitch in a smirk. "I'll make you pay for that, devil."

A low growl rumbles in his throat that makes a shiver run the length of my spine. "I'd like to see you fucking try, sweetheart."

CHAPTER 6
CONOR

I look at the huge two way mirror at the far side of the room and shake my head. "This isn't the room I booked," I say with a snarl to Shane.

He holds up his hands in surrender, a smirk on his face. "I had nothing to do with this, Con. I swear."

"The other one was taken," Jessie says with a sweet smile. "And you did agree that we might do this one day."

Shane places a hand on my shoulder. "And what better way to show your crazy ex, who if I recall correctly, called you ..." He cups his jaw and looks at the ceiling like he's deep in thought. Then his dark eyes twinkle with mischief as he drops his gaze back to my face. "A *heartless psychopath incapable of loving anyone but himself,* just how wrong she was when you show her how much you adore our wife."

Jessie lets out a tiny squeal of excitement before clapping her hand over her mouth. *Well fucking played, Shane!*

I scrub a hand over my beard as both Jessie's and Shane's eyes burn into my skin. Holy fuck! My girl really wants this, and I can't deny how much seeing the jealousy that Diana sparked in her earlier makes me hard as fucking iron.

The sound of the door opening snatches all of our attention as Mikey walks into the room. Closing it firmly behind him, he leans against the wall, arms folded and a devilish grin on his face like he knows what's about to happen. He wants this as much as they do. "Exactly who is in that fucking room watching?" I bark.

Mikey's grin widens. "Diana and her friend. A couple of our regulars, Javier and Enzo, but they're discreet and they're more likely to be looking at you and Shane than at our girl. And two women who use this place a lot but whose names I don't know. The ones with the tiny dog."

"That will be Sapphire and Britt. They're some of our most loyal customers and they're good people," Liam says, drawing my attention to him. He's sitting on the leather wingback chair in the corner of the room. "Although they will *definitely* be paying more attention to our girl than to any of you," he adds with a chuckle. Like me, he's not really into the public fucking thing either, but for different reasons.

I yank off my tie. "You okay with this?"

"All good with me, bro," he says with a soft smile.

My attention is drawn back to Jessie, who's biting on her beautiful full bottom lip and staring at me like I'm the man with all the answers. Trailing my fingertips over her cheekbone, I cup her jaw and tilt her head back and the softest, sexiest little moan that falls from her lips makes my hard cock throb to be inside her.

"You want me to fuck you in front of my ex-girlfriend, angel?" Her perfect tits shudder as she gasps in a harsh breath. I slide my hand to her throat and wrap it around the base, squeezing gently. "You want me to prove to her that I belong to you? Shall I show her how hard you make me come? How I'll fucking fall apart for you?"

Her tongue darts out, licking her lower lip. "I want her to

see *you* making *me* come. I want her to know that you own me. I'm yours, Conor," she whispers, wrapping her arms around my neck.

Holy fuck! How the hell do I resist that?

I glance over her shoulder at Shane. "She keeps her dress on at all times while those curtains are open. Nobody sees her body but us."

A soft gasp falls from Jessie's lips and she practically vibrates with excitement as she obviously realizes this is happening.

Shane nods his agreement. "If that's what you want."

I look up at the ceiling, barely able to believe that I'm even contemplating this. But I would do anything for this woman in my arms. Even fuck her in front of strangers it seems.

I brush my lips over the sweet smelling skin of her neck, allowing her scent to flood my senses. She soothes me in a way that no-one has ever been able to before. My fucking everything. If this is what she wants then I'll give it to her. "Are you sure, angel?" I give her, or maybe me, one final chance to back out.

She places one hand on my cheek and I stare into her bright blue eyes. "Yes. But it's okay if you don't want to. We can close the curtains and I can just pretend they're watching."

My chest tightens with dark, possessive need. "No," I growl. "Let them watch me take what's mine." I seal my mouth over hers, kissing her so hard that my head spins as I guide her toward the bed.

Shane is already ahead of me and is lying on the bed by the time Jessie and I reach it. I break our and cast an anxious glance at the window. I need to get out of my own head and forget they're there.

"Take off her panties, Con," Shane says, his voice deep and husky.

I kiss her again and she moans into my mouth. Crouching to the floor, I slip my hands beneath her dress and find her panties. She looks down at me, eyes burning with desire as I slowly pull her underwear down her legs, unable to resist dragging a finger through her soaking folds as I do. The scent of her arousal is thick in the air. My cock throbs. And now I'm right where I need to be. Now there's only me, her and my brothers.

After I've taken her panties off I toss them to Liam, who holds them to his face before stuffing them into his jacket pocket with a wicked grin.

"Come here, sweetheart," Shane's deep commanding growl makes Jessie shiver.

She bites on her lip and keeps her eyes on me, as though making sure I'm still okay with this. I wink at her. "You heard him, angel."

With my permission given, she turns to him, allowing him to take her hand before he helps her to straddle him. He pulls up her beautiful gown until it's bunched at the top of her thighs.

Shane rests one hand on her hip while he frees his cock with the other. "You're getting so fucked, Mrs. Ryan."

"I sure hope so," she replies with a soft giggle.

Mikey lies on the bed beside Shane, hands behind his head as he watches her intently—waiting his turn.

Shane grips her waist, his eyes almost rolling back in his head as he shifts his hips. I know from experience how good her wet pussy feels on his cock right now. "Slide onto me, sweetheart. I need to be inside you right now."

Jessie grabs his shaft and guides him into her and the sight of her sinking down onto him has my mouth watering and my dick leaking in my boxers.

"Holy fuck!" Shane grunts.

CHAPTER 7
SHANE

My eyes roll back in my fucking head as my wife's pussy squeezes me like a vise. I tighten my grip on her hips but I allow her to remain in control. She's heavily pregnant and I'm constantly aware of the need to be careful with her, because I could easily fuck this woman into oblivion any single time I'm inside her—and she'd let me too.

"Your cunt is fucking perfect, sweetheart," I grind out the words as she takes me all the way into her silky wet heat.

"Y-your cock is too," she moans, planting her hands on my chest and rocking forward.

The thought that we have an audience behind that two way mirror makes me harder than ever for her and I clamp my jaw shut and try to picture the least sexy thing I can think of.

"Fuck, Shane," she murmurs as she coats me in a rush of slick heat and I realize how futile that plan is. All I can ever think of is her. She consumes me. Every-fucking-thing I do and everything I am is for her. And now the scent of her sweet cum is filling this room and I want to throw her down on this bed, spread her wide open and feast on her dripping cunt before I fuck her. But I can't. This is about me and Conor taking her together in front of an audience. About giving our girl what she's been craving since the very first time we came to this club. And afterward, I'll fuck her with Mikey while they all watch too, and our girl will come harder than she ever has in her life.

I still Jessie's hips, before she rides both me and her to a finish before Conor gets anywhere near her. "Hold on, sweetheart." She sinks her teeth into her plump bottom lip and whines. "Such a needy little slut for our cocks," I say quietly and her cheeks flush with heat.

Conor climbs onto the bed behind her, pulling her hair to one side, he drags his teeth over the side of her throat. "So fucking needy, angel." She shivers and her pussy pulses around my cock. "Look at you waiting her for me to fuck you with my brother in front of a room full of strangers."

She drops her head back and her pouty lips open on a moan.

Looking over her shoulder at me, Conor flashes me a wicked grin. "You want my cock in your ass while Shane fucks your sweet pussy?"

"Y-yes," she whimpers as her walls squeeze my dick tighter.

"You look fucking beautiful with them, baby," Liam says from his spot on the wingback chair where he watches her intently. He's always watching her. We all are.

Mikey sits up and gives her a brief kiss full of tongue that makes her tremble. "Fucking incredible, Red."

"Oh, fuck!" she moans so fucking loudly that Mikey and Liam grunt their approval and I figure Conor is currently edging his way into her tight ass.

He lifts her dress a little, careful not to expose her to the people watching outside of this room. "So fucking tight, angel, but so fucking ready for me too, aren't you?"

She rocks forward. "Yes!"

"Hold her still, Shane," Conor growls and I grip her more firmly, my fingertips digging into her soft flesh.

Jessie's chest heaves with the effort of her panting, her perfect round tits straining against her gown. I tighten my grip on her, stopping myself from tearing her beautiful gown from her body so that I can see her hard nipples. I want to bite and lick and suck them. But I will soon. As soon as the five of us are alone. Conor presses his lips to her ear. "That's my good girl, I'm almost there."

I feel him sinking deeper inside her, his cock fitting snugly in her ass as mine goes on getting milked by her greedy cunt.

I let out a breath. "Jesus, fuck, sweetheart!"

"Is our girl fucking you, Shane?" Mikey asks with a devious chuckle.

"Uh-huh," is all I can manage to say as she squeezes and releases over and over again. Jessie trails her hands down my chest and my eyes fucking roll again. "Stop that, sweetheart," I growl.

"I c-can't," she whimpers. "You both feel so good."

"Are you all the way in, Con?" I snarl at my younger brother because if I have to hold off from fucking my wife a second longer I will fucking implode.

Conor thrusts forward, a deep sigh falling from his lips as he does. "I am now."

"Fuck me," Jessie whines.

"We're about to, sweetheart." I rock my hips upward and drive into her so hard I'm sure her teeth rattle in her head, but I can't hold back any longer. And fuck me, but my girl groans my fucking name and bears down on me like she's desperate for more.

"You love being fucked in front of strangers, angel?" Conor asks as he ruts into her from behind.

"Y-yeah."

"You like people seeing us lose control for you?" he growls. She nods her head, her pussy fluttering around my dick and her breathing growing faster and heavier with every thrust of our hips. "Like showing everyone how you fucking own us?"

"Yes!" Tears leak from the corners of her eyes and she becomes almost boneless as her body goes limp between ours. We hold her upright, railing into her with an urgent need to claim her—every inch of her body, every breath, every-fucking-thing she has.

"And who owns you, sweetheart?" I growl.

Her head drops back, resting on Conor's shoulder as her orgasm begins to ripple through her incredible body.

"Who, Jessie?" I bark.

"Y- you do," she screams the words so loud that I'm sure the entire club must have heard her and the thought that they have makes my balls draw up with hot pulsing need. I drive into her harder and my head spins with the force of the climax her tight cunt pulls from my body.

Conor bands his arms around her, holding her in place while he fucks her through her

climax, chasing his own while she comes apart around us both. Her eyes shutter closed, her mouth hangs open and tears run down her cheeks and I have never in my life seen anything so fucking perfect as her.

CHAPTER 8
MIKEY

I can't sleep. Memories of fucking my wife in front of those people in that room earlier has my cock harder than an iron bar. If she wasn't almost nine months pregnant and needed her sleep, I'd wake her up and eat her sweet cunt before burying myself inside it again.

I brush a thick strand of her red hair behind her ear. Even if I woke her up now, she'd let me do whatever the fuck I want to her. A quick kiss on her neck and a hand in her panties and she's putty in my goddamn hands and I fucking love it. I love her. I love the life she's given us.

Jessie shifts onto her back, rubbing a hand beneath her bump.

"You okay, Red?" I whisper.

"Yeah. More cramps," she says through clenched teeth.

Shit! Did we fuck her too hard earlier? No. So, is this ...? I push up onto my elbow and rub my free hand over her stomach. "Contractions?"

Shane stirs beside me. "What?" he mumbles sleepily.

Jessie sucks in a harsh breath before answering my question. "I dunno."

"Tell me what I can do, Red."

She shuffles into a seating position before drawing in another deep breath. "I ... fuck, it hurts."

"What is it, sweetheart?" Shane asks, wide awake now and voice full of concern.

She screws her face up like she's in intense pain and it makes me feel fucking useless that I can't do anything about it. A moment later, her features relax again. "Contractions, I think. But we have three weeks left."

"Us Ryans are impatient fuckers though, angel," Conor growls as he pushes himself up to sit beside her.

Liam sits bolt upright blinking in the dim room. "Is the baby coming?"

"Maybe. I dunno," Jessie whispers.

Conor places his hand on her stomach next to mine. "Poor kid's gonna have his birthday on Christmas Day."

"I'll try and hold out until Boxing day," Jessie says with a soft laugh before she gasps loudly, her hand flying to her lower stomach again.

"Fuck! Is that cum from earlier or did you water just break, angel?"

Liam switches on the lamp and sure enough there is a huge wet patch spreading across the covers beneath Jessie.

"M-my water," she pants.

"Call the doc," Shane orders and Conor jumps out of bed and grabs his cell phone.

I brush Jessie's hair back from her face. "Our boy's gonna be here soon, Red."

"Are you gonna be able to handle it this time?" she grits out the words and I'm reminded of when she gave birth to the twins. Liam and I couldn't stand to see her in pain so we let Conor and Shane hold her hand while she pushed our beautiful children into the world. Not this fucking time.

I kiss her forehead. "Yeah, Red. I'll be right there with you every step of the way. I promise."

"Me too, baby," Liam assures her.

I wrap my arm around her and she leans her head on my shoulder. Shane gives me a knowing smile, like he's proud of me for stepping up and suddenly tears are pricking at my eyes. How the fuck did I ever get so lucky to have a family like this one?

Jessie doubles over. "Holy fuck!"

A knot of anxiety settles in my throat. I feel so fucking useless.

Shane puts a hand on my shoulder and offers me a reassuring squeeze. "You got this, son."

I lace my fingers through my incredible wife's and she squeezes my hand in a death grip. Like she's never ever gonna let me go. The feeling is mutual, Red.

Fuck yeah, I got this.

THE FINAL EPILOGUE
(FOR NOW)

Jessie
New Years Eve

"You want me to take him?" I sit down on the sofa next to Shane as he nestles baby Cian in the crook of his arm.

He shakes his head, lifting his free arm and allowing me to snuggle next to him before he wraps it around me. Pulling me close he drops a sweet kiss on the top of my head. "I got him." He squeezes me tighter. "And you."

I brush my cheek against his soft cotton t-shirt and yawn.

"Why don't you go to bed and try to get some sleep, sweetheart?" he suggests.

"No," I grumble, wrapping an arm around his waist and burrowing my face deeper into his chest. "I like it right here. And Finn and Ella will be awake soon."

"I like you right here too, but we can handle the kids if you need a few hours sleep."

"I know," I whisper. "But I'm good with you as my pillow."

A soft laugh rumbles through him making Cian wriggle a little and let out the cutest baby whimper I think I ever heard.

"I love you," I say with a soft sigh. "Comfiest pillow I've ever owned."

He brushes my hair behind my ear. "And you do own me, Hacker. You know that, don't you?"

My chest fills with warm fuzzy feelings and tears prick at my eyes. "Yeah."

"Thank you for everything, sweetheart. I mean it." His voice is thick with emotion and I look up into his beautiful green eyes.

"There wouldn't be any of it without you. I would be nothing without you and your brothers."

His eyes narrow. "*You* would be everything, no matter what, Jessie Ryan. Never forget that, sweetheart. You are the most extraordinary woman I've ever known."

"But I'll never have to be because we're together forever."

He winks at me and insides contract. "Of course we are, sweetheart. Written in the stars, remember?"

The sound of squealing laughter in the hallway snatches both of our attention.

"The tiny terrors are awake," Shane says with a chuckle.

I arch an eyebrow. "You mean Liam and Mikey?"

That makes him laugh harder. I sit up as Ella comes charging into the room, closely followed by Finn, Conor, Liam and Mikey. Ella makes her way straight to Shane and me, fascinated by her baby brother from the second she met him.

"Is he sleeping, Daddy?" she asks sweetly.

He smiles at our daughter. "Yes, princess. At last," he adds with a weary sigh, no doubt recalling how many times Cian woke for a feed last night.

She wrinkles her cute button nose. "Can I kiss him?"

"Of course. But be gentle."

She rolls her eyes. "I know."

Shane glances at me. "She is so like you," he whispers.

"Mommy. Cookies for breakfast," Finn says as he clambers up onto my lap.

I brush my fingers through his thick auburn curls. "No, baby."

He pushes his bottom lip out and pouts. Liam sits on the sofa beside us and plucks Finn from my lap and hoists him over his shoulder, making him giggle. "No cookies. But Da will make you some pancakes if you're a good boy."

Mikey nods his agreement and flops down on the sofa next to his twin while Conor leans down and gives me a kiss on the forehead. He looks at our youngest, still sleeping soundly despite the noise in the room now. "How was he last night?"

I rub my tired eyes. "He woke four or five times, I think."

"Six," Shane corrects me.

Conor frowns. "You need to start expressing so we can all do some feeds, angel."

I nod. I've been too tired to express but he's right. We turned my old room into Cian's nursery and every night one of them stays in there with me to help me, or to keep an eye on Cian if I nod off while feeding him. But it would be easier if we could move his crib into our room and each take turns. "I'll start today. Promise."

He brushes my hair back from my face. "Why don't you go get some sleep while he's sleeping?"

"I'm good here. With all of you," I tell him too.

He rolls his eyes but then he scoops me up into his arms. "Conor," I give a quiet squeak of protest, thinking he's about to force me to go to bed, but instead he sits down in the empty space until I'm curled up on his lap and we're all squished together on the huge sofa.

Ella puts her hands on her hips. "Where am I going to sit, Mommy?"

"Right here, my little princess," Mikey replies, patting his thigh.

She giggles and runs to him, scampering onto his lap before squishing his cheeks together and kissing his nose.

"Cartoons," Finn demands.

"I'm kinda comfy here, so I say let them watch some TV," Conor says with a shrug and a few moments later we're all snuggled together watching cartoons.

Liam laces his fingers through mine. "This sofa is where it all began, baby," he says quietly but loud enough for his brothers to hear.

I smile at him, remembering that night all those years ago when he first kissed me. And then he and Mikey ... My cheeks flush with heat at the memory.

Shane glances sideways at us. "Yeah, when we walked in on the three of you ..."

"Ballooning," Mikey finishes his sentence with a chuckle.

Conor nips my shoulder blade gently. "And you looked so fucking hot," he growls in my ear.

"Sure did," Mikey says with a sigh. "By the way when can we get back to that?"

"Mikey!" Conor chides him, making me laugh.

"I'm just asking. No pressure, Red," Mikey says, reaching over and giving my thigh a reassuring squeeze.

I burrow my face into the crook of Conor's shoulder and close my eyes. "I know. And it's okay. I want to get back to it too."

"Has that dog always had an Australian accent?" Shane asks, changing the conversation abruptly.

Liam laughs. "Um, yeah."

"Never noticed," Shane mutters.

"I prefer the cartoon with the pigs," Mikey says.

I close my eyes and listen to the sound of my four husbands

discussing their preferred kids cartoons as well as Finn and Ella giggling softly. Maybe I can get an hour of sleep before Cian wakes for another feed.

I feel a soft kiss on my head and warm hands resting on my thighs as sleep finally takes me, and I dream of more babies and a life full of love with the four most incredible men in the universe.

The End ...

ALSO BY SADIE KINCAID

Sadie's latest series, Chicago Ruthless is available for preorder now. Following the lives of the notoriously ruthless Moretti siblings - this series will take you on a rollercoaster of emotions. Packed with angst, action and plenty of steam — preorder yours today

Dante

Joey

Lorenzo

If you haven't read full New York the series yet, you can find them on Amazon and Kindle Unlimited

Ryan Rule

Ryan Redemption

Ryan Retribution

Ryan Reign

Ryan Renewed

New York Ruthless short stories can be found here

A Ryan Reckoning

A Ryan Rewind

A Ryan Restraint

A Ryan Halloween

A Ryan Christmas

A Ryan New Year

Want to know more about The Ryan Brothers' buddies, Alejandro and Alana, and Jackson and Lucia? Find out all about them in Sadie's internationally bestselling LA Ruthless series. Available on Amazon and FREE in Kindle Unlimited.

Fierce King

Fierce Queen

Fierce Betrayal

Fierce Obsession

If you'd like to read about London's hottest couple. Gabriel and Samantha, then check out Sadie's London Ruthless series on Amazon. FREE in Kindle Unlimited.

Dark Angel

Fallen Angel

Dark/ Fallen Angel Duet

If you enjoy super spicy short stories, Sadie also writes the Bound series feat Mack and Jenna, Books 1, 2, 3 and 4 are available now.

Bound and Tamed

Bound and Shared

Bound and Dominated

Bound and Deceived

ABOUT THE AUTHOR

Sadie Kincaid is a steamy romance author who loves to read and write about hot alpha males and strong, feisty females.

Sadie loves to connect with readers so why not get in touch via social media?

Join Sadie's reader group for the latest news, book recommendations and plenty of fun. Sadie's ladies and Sizzling Alphas

Sign up to Sadie's mailing list for exclusive news about future releases, giveaways and content <u>here</u>

Made in the USA
Monee, IL
16 August 2024

63989902R00236